The MIDWIFE of HOPE RIVER

The MIDWIFE *of* HOPE RIVER

patricia harman

DOUBLEDAY LARGE PRINT HOME LIBRARY EDITION

WILLIAM MORROW
An Imprint of HarperCollins*Publishers*

This Large Print Edition, prepared especially for Doubleday Large Print Home Library, contains the complete, unabridged text of the original Publisher's Edition.

To the brave and beautiful midwives around the globe, who deliver 80 percent of the babies into their loving hands

P.S.™ is a trademark of HarperCollins Publishers.

THE MIDWIFE OF HOPE RIVER. Copyright © 2012 by Patricia Harman. All rights reserved. Printed in the United States of America. No part of this book may be used or reproduced in any manner whatsoever without written permission except in the case of brief quotations embodied in critical articles and reviews. For information address HarperCollins Publishers, 10 East 53rd Street, New York, NY 10022.

ISBN 978-1-62090-469-5

Printed in the United States of America

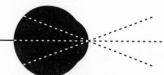

This Large Print Book carries the Seal of Approval of N.A.V.H.

Acknowledgments

I'd like to thank first my husband, Tom Harman, MD, and my family for their support for my writing, as well as my staff at Partners in Women's Health Care, who put up with my changes in schedule for book-related matters.

I'd also like to thank my editor, Lucia Macro, and her great team for helping me give birth to this book, as well as my agent, Barbara Braun, and her staff for all their assistance.

In addition, I can't fail to mention my appreciation for my fellow writers, mid-wives, friends, and muses (you know who you are) for the early reading of the manuscript.

And finally, readers, dear readers, one more round of thanks, this time for your e-mails of encouragement. Like Patience, we must listen to the great heart that beats for us all.

Most of my life I've felt I was dreaming. Now and then I wake up, sometimes for months, sometimes for minutes. I'm a character in a play, and I can't tell if I'm making it up or if a great puppeteer is making me dance.

—From the private diary of
Patience Murphy, Midwife
Wild Rose Road,
Liberty, West Virginia, U.S.A.
1929–1930

Autumn

1

Stillbirth

"How long do you think my baby's been dead?" Katherine turns toward me, and I can tell she's still crying.

"Five days, maybe less," I answer my patient. "I heard the heartbeat when I checked you last Friday, and you said the baby moved during church. Shut your eyes now. Try. You need to rest."

I place my new leather-bound journal on the maple table, lean my head back, and gaze across the dark room. Fire crackles in the blue-tiled fireplace, flickers on the armoire, the canopy of the birth bed, and the wallpapered walls. A watery image in the dressing table mirror catches my eye. It's me, a small woman with long auburn hair, a straight nose, and a round chin, pretty enough but not beautiful.

I'm sitting at the bedside of Mrs. Katherine MacIntosh, the wife of William, owner of the MacIntosh Consolidated Mines. Yesterday was Black Tuesday, that's what they're calling it. Wall Street fell, and then I had to tell the MacIntoshes that their unborn baby was dead. The crash, a faraway earthquake, rumbled even here in Appalachia, and I'm thankful I don't keep my money in the bank; not that I have any.

As I desperately searched for signs of life in Katherine's womb, moving my wooden fetoscope over her round belly, up and down and then across, a line of customers fought to get their money out of the First Mountain Federal in Liberty. The queue of men snaked down Chestnut and around the corner to Fayette, though any fool who strolled along Main and saw the closed shops should have known what was coming. When the coal mines begin to shut down in Union County, everything else does.

"Hold me, Patience. I'm so cold." Katherine reaches for my hand and pulls me toward the bed.

Mary Proudfoot, the MacIntoshes' cook, and her grown daughter, Bitsy, are asleep in their room by the kitchen, curled around each other like kittens. William MacIntosh snores in his bedroom down the hall. This room is not chilly. It's Katherine's heart that is cold, knotted up like a chunk of ice thrown up on the banks of the Hope River. It doesn't seem proper for a midwife to sleep with her patient, but if I rest a few hours, what harm can it do? I'll need my strength to get us all through this.

I breathe out a long sigh, carefully place my wire-rimmed glasses with the journal, kick off my slippers, move over to the bed, and fold myself around Katherine, giving her comfort where there is no comfort, remembering Pittsburgh when, in the winter, I used to sleep with Mrs. Kelly and Nora.

* * *

I'd like to tell this mother about my own stillborn baby, the one I carried when I was sixteen, the very same baby whose father died before he was born, but I can't add to her burdens.

I pull the covers over Katherine's shoulder and put my arms around her as she sobs in her sleep. The loss of this child is all the sadder because her first son, not yet two, a little blond boy just learning to talk, died of pneumonia last winter.

Her contractions are mild and come every ten minutes.

Dream

At 6:30 A.M., as light crawls under the heavy drapes illuminating the rose carvings on the tall maple armoire and the pattern on the red-flowered carpet, Katherine sits straight up in bed, her hand on her belly.

"I felt it," she says. I rub sleep from my swollen eyes, thinking she dreams.

I'd listened for the sound of the infant's heartbeat with my wooden horned fetoscope for a full hour yesterday as the room got quieter and Katherine's eyes rounder. There was nothing to hear but the rumbling of the woman's bowels. No *tick-tick-tick* of a baby's heartbeat. No baby kicks, either. I'd even called for Dr. Blum—tall, thin, hair thinning on top—and he listened for another thirty minutes . . . still nothing. Katherine screamed when I first told her the baby was dead, and when the physician nodded agreement, patted her hand, and took her husband out of the room, she screamed again.

The sound of that wail goes right to your heart. I'd only heard it once before, at Manny McConnell's delivery in Pittsburgh, when Mrs. Kelly, the midwife, told her the twins had expired, but you never forget. Even if you were outside on a warm summer evening and heard it through an open window, you would know what I mean.

Downstairs, on William MacIntosh's new RCA console, we could hear the faint voice of a newscaster describing what was happening to the stock market. Then, before I had time to discuss the case with Dr. Blum, he was called away to attend a sick child and left the stillbirth to me. I was the midwife, and she'd signed up to deliver at home instead of in his small private hospital. He must have thought I'd know what to do.

Katherine is still kneading her white belly like bread dough, pushing it back and forth. "I felt it," she says. "I felt something!"

I stretch and sit up. "It was probably just a gas bubble or maybe a labor pain. Do you need to go to the bathroom?"

In addition to electric lights, the MacIntoshes have an indoor latrine and running water. In town this is not unusual, but in most of rural West Virginia both electricity and plumbing are still rare.

"I felt it. I did. I know I did."

"Katherine . . ." I straighten my rumpled flowered shift, embarrassed at the impropriety of sleeping with a patient, and put on my glasses. "Let's go to the toilet. I'll listen for a heartbeat again after you've relieved yourself, but don't get your hopes up. Your baby's spirit has gone back to Heaven." I talk like this, as if I'm a believer, but in truth I haven't been to church, except for funerals and weddings, since my husband, Ruben, died on Blair Mountain along with 150 other union men. This was back in the fall of '21, a bad time.

"I *think* I felt it . . . *something* woke me." She's no longer sure.

In the MacIntoshes' water closet, I study the apparatus. The high porcelain potty has a round polished oak seat, more like a piece of furniture than a commode. When Katherine finishes, she pulls the brass chain and water rushes in to rinse out the contents.

Stepping out of the small green mosaic-tiled room, my patient turns. "I have to go some more!" She's a tall woman, taller than I, with the face of a film star and a rumpled short blond bob like Jean Harlow. The pregnant woman lifts her white embroidered nightdress and plunks down on the seat again.

I let out my air, glance at the rumpled

covers, and decide to straighten the bed. While I'm fluffing the feather pillows, I hear a low grunt. "Uhhhhhg!"

"No, you don't, Katherine!" I know that sound well. I jump over the needle-point footstool, trip on the edge of the red-flowered carpet, and skid across the shiny wood floors in my sock feet. It's the grunt of imminent birth.

Nothing's ready! Katherine showed no signs that she was in hard labor or any labor at all. Maybe that's how it is with stillbirths; the woman's body desperately wants to get rid of the baby. I wouldn't know. In the births I've attended before, the infants were alive, at least for a while.

I have packets of needles with suture in case Katherine tears, I have clean cloth pads, I have sterilized scissors, I have oil to help the vagina stretch, but everything's wrapped in my satchel downstairs, where I left it by the front door.

"Bitsy!" I call. "Bitsy! Mary! Help!" A door downstairs flies open, and bare feet pound up the stairs. "Somebody bring Mrs. Kelly's bag." The feet pound back down again. I don't know why I said "Mrs. Kelly's bag." Mrs. Kelly, my mentor, my unofficial guardian, my friend, died a year after we moved to West Virginia, and I'm alone again.

"Mr. MacIntosh!" Ordinarily I don't have fathers in the room when women give birth—they can't take the intensity—but I need someone fast.

The husband arrives in his white-and-blue-striped pajamas, rubbing his eyes. He's a big man with short sandy hair and a mustache, a handsome guy with the build of an ex-athlete gone to seed. Mary and Bitsy, still in their night-clothes, their eyes white and wide in their brown faces, their dark braids flying, crowd in behind him.

"William, bring clean sheets, towels, anything."

I'm dragging Katherine back to bed when her water bag breaks. She understands now that it's not a bowel movement but a dead baby coming.

Katherine growls again and squats on the floor. She's unconcerned about the expensive red carpet, aware only of the terrible pressure, the need to push.

I put my hands under her bottom and am startled to feel a head right there, as round and hard and warm as a living baby's head.

I'd read, in Mrs. Kelly's worn text *The Principles and Practice of Obstetrics* by Joseph DeLee, that stillborn babies, when held in the womb for more than a week, start to decompose, and I had expected to feel something starting to get squishy.

"No, you don't, Katherine! Up on the bed." I twist her around and guide her backward. Bitsy lowers her down and gets clean towels underneath her. Mr. MacIntosh still leans against the rose-covered wallpaper, his face so white it would make the sun blind.

There's no time to pull on the special-order rubber gloves I just purchased from Stenger's Pharmacy, so I place my bare hands like a crown around the head. Katherine grips the sheets, wide-eyed and frightened, staring up at the chandelier. I motion to Bitsy to lift the woman's head.

"Look in my eyes, Katherine. Look at me! With the next pain I want you to pant. The head is right here. You don't have to push. Your womb will do the pushing. If you pop the head out, you'll tear." Out of the corner of my eye, I catch sight of the father as he swoons and slides down the flowered wall, but we let him lie there.

"Okay, Mary, be ready with a towel to wrap the baby." I'm not worried about keeping the dead infant warm; I'm thinking that the child may be deformed or the skin already peeling.

The head, with dark hair, turns and emerges between my hands, first the brow, then the chubby cheeks, then the chin. "Pant, Katherine, pant!"

There's a cord around the neck, but it's loose. Once, twice, I loop it over.

"Now the shoulders. Just a gentle push." I give the wet, lifeless infant to Mary, the cook, whose hands shake so hard I fear she might drop it. "Hold steady now. Hold tight."

The limp baby boy, gray blue as Lake Michigan, is placed in the towel, and I drape the tail end over the body. At a glance, he looks perfect and the cord wasn't too tight. I wonder why he died.

Maybe a heart defect, I've heard that can happen. Or a missing kidney.

The cook, a six-foot-tall, big-bosomed colored woman, hasn't moved. Her arms, outstretched, like the limbs of a maple, still hold the corpse. What do you do with a dead baby? Take it to the kitchen? Put it into the new white cradle? I had never thought of this.

While I wait for signs that the afterbirth is separating, I motion Mary over and lift up a corner of the towel again. The dead baby's eyes are glazed and wide open.

Then the ribs move, just a tremble like an old lady's hand. *Holy cow!* If I hadn't been staring I wouldn't have seen it, a sucking-in action.

"Give me that baby!" I grab the wet infant, almost dropping him on the bed, then, without hesitation, kneel as though I'm praying, put my mouth to his tiny blue lips, and breathe for him three times the way I saw Mrs. Kelly do once. Three tiny puffs.

As the air fills his lungs, Katherine's son coughs weakly and lets out a mew.

He turns from blue-gray to pink, starting in his face and trunk and then out to his hands. Katherine rolls slowly on her side. "My baby," she whispers. "My baby. My baby!" She's sitting up now, reaching out, crying over and over "My baby. My baby!" And the baby is crying for his mother too. I lay him on her lap so she can see his little face.

"Praise Jesus!" sings Mary, her hands clutched to her chest, holding her joyous heart in.

Bitsy, who's sharp as a briar and half the size of her towering mother, has the good sense to cover the crying newborn with another dry towel and rub him all over. I finish cutting the cord and deliver the afterbirth, all the time staring at the Madonna and Child. William MacIntosh, who has missed the whole event, wakes up from his faint and crawls across the carpet toward the bed.

"Mother of God! It's alive?" he asks, turning to Bitsy, unwilling, I imagine, to trust the blunt-headed midwife who had told him his baby would be dead.

* * *

I recall Katherine's proclamation that she had felt the baby kick a few minutes before. I'm new at this, but it wasn't just me. Dr. Blum, the family physician, confirmed the absence of a heartbeat. Now I wonder . . . had the unborn child been lying in Katherine's womb with his limbs curled up in a way that we couldn't hear his heart with my wooden fetoscope or even the physician's new metal one? Even in the best of positions it's hard to hear that faint sound. Had the cord been pinched, causing the fetal heart to slow so that I confused it with the mother's pulse?

I feel like a fool and maybe a dangerous one. What makes me think I can be a midwife with only a few years' apprenticeship and no Mrs. Kelly to guide me? On the other hand, the baby's alive . . .

I show Bitsy how to gently massage Katherine's womb every ten minutes so that it stays rock hard. She's a quick study and repeats everything I say. Then I show her how to inspect the placenta for any missing pieces and how to weigh the baby in the old-fashioned hanging scale that Mrs. Kelly left me.

Finally I sit back in one of the satin chairs and observe the new family. The mother is already breastfeeding. When I pull up the fringed window shade, the sunlight bursts into the room.

This child will be stronger than any of us.

October 30, 1929. New moon high in the daytime sky.

Seven-pound live-born male, thought to be dead. Name: William MacIntosh the second. Son of William MacIntosh the first and Katherine Ann MacIntosh. Active labor, five minutes. Pushing, one minute. Blood loss minimal. No birth canal tears. I had to breathe for the baby three puffs. Also present, Mary and Bitsy Proudfoot, the MacIntosh servants, and the father, although he fell down in a faint.

2

Home

To be a midwife was never my goal. As a girl, I imagined myself an explorer in the Amazon or maybe an around-the-world traveler and journalist like Nellie Bly, yet here I am, a thirty-six-year-old widow, wanted by the law in two states, living alone in the mountains of West Virginia, too old and too obstinate for courting.

I drag my bicycle up on the porch steps, exhausted from little sleep, and watch as Mr. MacIntosh turns his Olds around, thankful that he offered me a ride home. It's one of those crisp, clear, cloudless days of autumn, with little boats of white clouds sailing across the blue sky, and my two brown-and-white beagles tumble from under the house whining and jumping up on my legs. "Hi, Sasha! Down, Emma! Miss me?"

The female, Emma, is named for the radical anarchist Emma Goldman and the male for her lover, Alexander "Sasha" Berkman. Those monikers were as familiar to me as Santa Claus and Jesus Christ a few years ago. That was back when I worked with the unions in Pittsburgh. Now here I hide, lost to that world.

I press my forehead on my periwinkle blue door, so glad to be home but dreading the emptiness. When Mrs. Kelly and I moved to this farm at the base of Hope Mountain, her grandmother's home place, a little over two years ago, we thought of coating the weathered clapboards white, but after paying two hundred dollars for the adjoining ten acres, we couldn't afford it and decided to paint just the door. I found the gallon of periwinkle marked down at Mullin's Hardware in Liberty.

As I enter the house, I reach down to ruffle Emma's fur, then stop to admire my parlor. Though it's small and nowhere as elegant as the MacIntoshes', I like the space better and it pleases me that everything in the room is handmade or cast off. It was from my mother that I got the desire to make things pretty, from my grandmother my sense of thrift.

There's the secondhand davenport Mrs. Feder gave us for helping with the birth of her daughter-in-law's twins. I've covered it with a blue-and-white quilt that I made myself in the flying goose pattern. There's a pine table I pulled out of the cellar and sanded till it looks almost new. There are shelves of worn chestnut barn boards for books and a potbellied stove in the corner. (The cookstove and the heater stove, an oak rocker, two iron bedsteads with feather mattresses, and the bicycle were all that we found when we moved here.)

Other than that, there's just the ornate black-and-gold mantel clock that

Mrs. Kelly brought on the train from Pittsburgh and the piano, a used dark upright I bought for thirty dollars when the Mt. Zion Church purchased its organ. That was back when I could get work now and then and still had some cash. Now the jobs have dried up, and, let's face it, there's not much money in delivering babies.

Whether a birth is long or short, I'm always done in when I get home. I step out of my shoes, flop down on the sofa, and glance at the painting on the white-washed pine wall above me.

My baby's father painted that oil portrait when I was sixteen. Lawrence was a student at the Art Institute of Chicago then. In the picture, a girl stands on a pier overlooking Lake Michigan with a strand of long loose auburn hair across her face. Her head is thrown back and she's laughing. That girl was me, Elizabeth Snyder. I adopted my alias, Patience Murphy, when we left on the run from Pittsburgh, and the name fits now, has a nice ring. Patience Murphy. Patience the midwife . . .

* * *

Lawrence, my first husband—I call him my husband, though he died before we could marry—was a scene designer when I was a chorus girl at the Majestic Theatre. I had lied to get the job, told everyone I was eighteen, and got chosen out of a queue of girls because of my voice. The House of Mercy Orphanage was probably glad to be rid of me. One less mouth to feed.

I throw some wood on the coals in the heater stove, fill the teakettle with water from the bucket, and pull the rocker up to the fire. Light fills the room through the two tall front windows.

Why didn't my baby live? Katherine's lived.

I think I know the answer, have read about it in DeLee's heavy text. My afterbirth, or placenta, as Dr. DeLee refers to it, separated too early, an obstetrical emergency, and they didn't do cesarean operations routinely then, certainly not on an orphan like me. I experienced two deaths in two weeks: Lawrence's in the train wreck and then the baby's. I still don't know how I made it, didn't crumble into dust. Somehow I went on, as we all have to go on; stuffed my grief in my pocket like a chunk of black coal and stumbled forward. I carry it still, but over the years the lump has grown smaller, harder, like a diamond.

The girl from so long ago stares out across the inland sea. Birth and death, so intertwined. Love, birth, death, my trilogy.

There's a distant moo from the barn. *My animals!* I had stayed for breakfast at the MacIntoshes' . . . sausages, biscuits, and home-canned peaches with maple syrup, a real celebration breakfast, Big Mary called it. We three ate in the kitchen, Bitsy, Mary, and I, after we helped Katherine clean up and dress in a dark blue silk robe so that she and Mr. MacIntosh could enjoy breakfast together.

Now it's past noon, the chickens haven't been fed, and poor Moonlight's udders must be bursting! The cat, Buster, is okay because I leave a bowl of milk on the stoop and he can find field mice and chipmunks. My beagles can hunt, but the critters confined to the barn this time of year are helpless. I grab a clean metal bucket from the pantry, step into the high black rubber boots I keep on the enclosed back porch, and curse myself for my forget-fulness.

When I pull open the double barn doors, the animals' cries assault me. The chickens are squawking, and poor Moonlight moans in pain. I throw the fowl their grain and toss hay into the cow's stall, then sit down on my three-legged stool and beg her forgiveness.

"I'm so sorry, girl," I apologize. "I was at the MacIntosh house in town all night. I still can't believe it! I was *sure* their baby was dead. I listened so long for a heartbeat . . . I even had Dr. Blum check. Katherine told me that for over two days there'd been no movement.

"Now I feel foolish, and by tomorrow every woman in Union County will know I'm inept. Even though Dr. Blum was there to confirm the stillbirth, I'm the one they'll blame."

As I rhythmically express the milk from the tense udders, I look around this warm space, the sunlight coming through the cracks high above me, the rough golden walls and the hand-hewn oak beams. There's the smell of hay and sweet manure. Moonlight looks around, sympathy in her brown eyes. She accepts me just as I am, energetic or tired, inept or confident, in love with life or walled off in pain.

3

Summons

On the way back to the house, with my bucket of milk and six eggs in my pockets, I laugh as the wind sweeps the red and yellow leaves off the maples and oaks and scatters them across the blue sky. There was a time, after Mrs. Kelly died, that I didn't notice such things, just kept my head down, plodding along, careful not to step in the puddles of my own tears.

It happened our second spring here, a sudden massive heart attack, Dr. Blum called it. One afternoon, coming in from the garden, I found my dear

Sophie slumped on the sofa. On some dark nights, she's sitting there still.

I ate little, lost weight, stopped washing my long hair. There was no more singing as I worked or dancing in the field on a sunny day. I'd come to a similar black place not long before, after Ruben died at Blair Mountain, but experiencing loss is not something you get used to. The more death one experiences, the more painful it is. For almost a year, I hovered on the edge of my own dark grave; then one afternoon I raised my head, sniffed the air, and recognized the changing light. It was spring again.

"Grief takes about a year," Mrs. Kelly once told a young mother who had lost her son. "You have to get through each holiday, each new season. You will cry at Christmas and New Year's and Mother's Day and Thanksgiving. You will suffer with the first daffodil, the first falling red leaves, the first snow . . . Each occasion, each new season will rip your heart out; then, when there's nothing left, you'll get better." She was right, and she knew from experience.

Sophie, like me, had suffered great loss: her sister from typhoid fever when she was little, her mother from stomach cancer, and, worst of all, her young husband and daughter in that big flood in Pennsylvania, the one in 1911 where a thousand people died when the pulp mill dam broke and flooded the whole town. My teacher, protector, and friend had lost everything, home and family, all in one day, and had been found, more dead than alive, a mile down the river, hanging on to a tree limb. For a while, she told me, she wished she *had* died. I know the feeling.

In the kitchen, I wash my hands again, wipe my glasses, then tenderly clean the brown eggs and gently place them in a woven basket. I strain the milk though cheesecloth and pour it in a clean gallon jar. Through the small window over the sink, the green hills tumble toward the valley where the Hope River twists, fuller now than in summer.

I am just getting ready to pour boiling water from the top of the woodstove into the washtub to rinse out some necessaries when I spy a small figure moving up the hill, a solitary fellow who leans forward on his burro as if in a hurry. He's leading a second animal. At the first mailbox, the Johnsons', a half mile away, he stops and looks at the name, then stops again at the second, the Maddocks', and moves on up the mountain. I have a sinking feeling he is coming for me.

Carefully, I haul the jar of milk out to my springhouse, where cold water collects in a rock basin and stays cool all summer, and when I come back, I see a tall black man tying his two animals to a tree. He's wearing a gray fedora and a gray canvas jacket that's torn at the sleeve, maybe a miner looking for help. The companies used to have their own physicians, but most of them are gone now, the best of them anyway. Sanitation and health conditions are so poor in the mining camps that Dr. Blum refuses to go into them.

The man tips his dusty felt hat. "I'm Thomas Proudfoot, Mary Proudfoot's son. Izzie Cabrini, one of the miners at King Coal, asked me to fetch you. His woman's in trouble." I know what the word "trouble" means.

"How long's she been paining?"

"A day, maybe two."

These cases worry me. I don't know the Cabrinis and have never been to the King Hollow Coal Camp. I don't know if the missus is too early or too late or what the situation is.

"Has she had babies before? Won't the coal camp foreman drive her to the hospital in Torrington?"

Thomas shakes his head no.

"Doesn't King Coal have a doctor?"

Thomas looks me right in the eye and shakes his head no again. I see by his look that he's an intelligent man who believes this is wrong but knows enough to keep his mouth shut.

Coal Camp

It's three miles on rocky dirt roads to King Coal, and we move right along, although burros are not much for hurrying. Three vehicles overtake us, and we have to get down into the ditch while they pass: a Pontiac roadster, a Ford Model T, and a John Deere tractor, moving just a little faster than we are.

I think of the Frontier Midwives in Hyden, Kentucky. I've been told the nurses ride horses into the hollows and over the mountains to attend the laboring mothers. Maybe I should get a horse! I brighten at the thought, but at once my hope dims. Money would be the problem. I don't have more than a few dollars, and Mr. MacIntosh didn't offer me anything except a ride home. Maybe they're still in shock that their dead baby lives.

I cringe again, thinking of my mistake and how it will look to the community. Maybe people will just chalk it up as a miracle! *The baby was dead, but it came back to life!* Maybe they'll say that I performed the miracle. Not likely.

At last we arrive at the mining village. The King Coal camp is a ramshackle community set up along King Lick. Though the camp has been here only five years, the water in the creek is already brown and the rocks have turned yellow from the mine's acid runoff.

Coal camps that are unionized have a one-room schoolhouse, basic cabins for the miners and their families, a clinic, and a store, but this camp, from the looks of it, is a makeshift affair, no unions, no benefits, nothing. The houses are little more than shacks.

Passing us, a ragged line of men wearing metal hats with lights on the front turn to stare. Their faces are so covered with coal dust, their eyes are the only thing alive, and you can't tell by looking who's Scotch Irish, who's Negro, who's an Italian brought in by the coal barons to work the black gold. Five years ago, 20 percent of the miners were black, former sharecroppers who found better work and better money by leaving the South. Now, with the closing of the mines, the numbers are way down. Trailing along behind the men are two little boys not more than ten, also wearing miner's hats.

When we lived in Pittsburgh, Mrs. Kelly, Nora, and I fought alongside the International Workers of the World, the

Wobblies, for the Child Labor Amendment of 1919, but the Supreme Court shot it down. Somehow the judges believed the federal government didn't have a right to regulate the industrialists and it would be just fine for young children to work in sweatshops or miles underground.

Trotting hurriedly through the village on the burro, I make note of the lack of outhouses. There's not one privy anywhere, and when it rains the human waste seeps into the ground and runs downhill to the communal well. Despite the chill in the autumn air, children play barefoot in the yellow-brown creek. A rail-thin woman wearing a thin blue-and-white-flowered feed-sack dress walks out on her stoop and throws the water in her dishpan across her yard.

At last Thomas halts in front of a sloping black tar-papered shack where a girl of about eight watches the road through the dusty four-pane window. The youngster's face brightens, and she announces my arrival to whoever's in the room. From the looks of the place, this is another birth for which I won't be paid, and it's not because they lost their money in the stock market, either.

The dark man helps me off my burro, hands me my satchel, and prepares to leave. "Thanks for escorting me, Mr. Proudfoot."

There's just the flicker of a smile. "Ma'am," he responds, tipping his hat. That's all he says; then he's gone.

Delfina

Stumbling up the rickety steps with my birth satchel, I wish Thomas Proudfoot had at least stayed to introduce me. Inside, who knows what I'll find? But before I can knock, the door flies open.

"She's doin' poorly," a nervous man says. His little mustache quivers, and his large brown eyes with long lashes illuminate his worried face.

I take in the room. Newspapers cover the interior walls to keep out the wind. There are two big beds, a worn sofa, a rocker, and a cradle. In one corner, a crude kitchen counter has been put together with shelves of weathered boards. The iron cookstove, a wooden table with six unmatched chairs, and the one lightbulb that hangs on a long cord from the ceiling—that's all there is.

I'm surprised to see that the family *has* electricity, but remind myself that all coal camps do. The mines need electric power to bring mechanical shuttles up on tracks. It used to be donkeys that brought the coal out; before that, men were used as pack animals, and before that, children and females because they were small.

A woman lies moaning under a tattered brown quilt in one of the rumpled beds. Three little boys dressed in rags sit at the table, hiding their faces, but the girl, still perched on the windowsill, looks right at me. Nobody smiles. Nobody says hello. I've entered a Charles Dickens world.

I skip the introductions. They know who I am. "How long has she been having pains, Mr. Cabrini?" When she hears my voice, the woman on the bed looks up, and I see that she's about my age, maybe younger. Her curly brown hair is matted on one side, and her face is flushed and sweaty.

"Since last night." The man has a strong Italian accent, and I wonder if his wife and children speak any English at all.

"Is she leaking fluid?" Cabrini shrugs that he doesn't know.

"Is your water trickling out?" I direct my question to the woman louder than I need to. Why do we always increase the volume when we think someone can't understand?

"Her under-bloomers is wet," the girl tells me. Obviously, the daughter speaks a little English.

Four children. The patient may have delivered several more that died at birth or a few months later. Infant mortality is high in the mountains. If a mother has ten children and she's impoverished, without good sanitation, two, at least, will die. Even in the best of conditions, like those of Katherine MacIntosh, the chance of stillbirth or death within the first year of life is one in ten.

I turn to the girl. "What's your mother's name?"

"Mama."

"Delfina," the man corrects.

"Delfina." I sit down next to my patient and place a hand on her shoulder. "Delfina, my name is Patience Murphy. I'm the midwife." I dropped my married name, Gordesky, after Blair Mountain, and I say "midwife" with reservation following my blunder at Katherine's delivery.

"I know you're weary and have been in labor for a long time, but could you roll on your back, please, so I can check you?" Her pains, by the change in her breathing, are mild and about every five minutes; she hasn't had a strong one since I entered the room. This is not a good sign. We want robust contractions to get the baby out, and if the womb is exhausted, it won't clamp down afterward and the mother will bleed.

I turn to the mister. "We'll need boiled water. Have the boys bring a bucket from the well. Send them outside while I figure out what's going on. Your daughter can stay. I might need her.

"Can you roll on your back after the next pain?" I ask the mother again.

The girl says something in Italian, and her mother rolls slowly, dragging her belly along with her hands, then plopping it down. I note the dried blood on the inside of her legs when she pulls up her shift.

The first thing I do is listen to the fetal heart rate with my wooden horned fetoscope. I do so with dread, afraid of another stillbirth, but finally find the *tick-tick-tick* high on the abdomen, higher than I'd expected.

By Mrs. Kelly's gold pocket watch, which I wear just as she did, on a ribbon around my neck, the infant's heartbeat is regular, about 140 beats a minute, and I'm grateful that Delfina's skin is still cool—no fever yet.

The next thing I check for is the presenting part. I run my hands over Delfina's abdomen, searching for the baby's head. Finally I think I find it, a hard bulge the size of a small acorn squash on the right side, almost out of the pelvis. Too high.

A couple of explanations come to me: This mother has had more than five children, and her abdominal muscles and womb are so flaccid that even a full-term baby could float around in there any way it likes. Or, and this is potentially more serious, something is blocking the opening, a large fibroid tumor or, even worse, the afterbirth, stuck low in the womb.

The safest thing to do would be to leave at once for Liberty and get help, but that option isn't open. We have no transport except Thomas Proudfoot's burros. And even if the camp boss would drive us, on these steep, winding country roads it would take over an hour to get to the big hospital in Torrington. Finally there's the issue of money. It's clear that Mr. Cabrini doesn't have any. Dr. Blum, in Liberty, has told me before that he can only afford to take paying patients, and God knows what the hospital in Torrington costs.

I open my case and pull out the new rubber gloves I didn't have time to use at Katherine's birth. They're still clean, sterilized with bleach, and wrapped in roasted newspaper. The only way to find out what's going on is to do an internal examination, but that's risky, and also against the law.

The West Virginia Midwifery Statute of 1925 bans midwives from doing internal exams. We are also "expressly forbidden to assist labor by any artificial, forcible or mechanical means, or administer, advise, prescribe, or employ any dangerous or poisonous drugs." The local medical societies jealously guard their right to prescribe and treat. In addition, the law requires that we must be "of good moral character." I smile to myself. That leaves me out.

Knowing I'm violating the rules, I adjust my glasses and pull on the gloves. I'm already wanted for far worse crimes. What can they do to me for a vaginal exam? The mother stares with big eyes.

"Delfina, I need you to open your legs so I can feel what's keeping the baby from coming." The husband turns away and steps out on the porch, aware that this is female business. He leaves the white-haired girl as an interpreter, and she creeps up on the bed.

"What's your name?" I ask the dirty-faced urchin.

"Antonia."

"Antonia, can you tell your mama that I need her to lift her bottom so I can put down a clean pad and to open her legs again so I can wash her and feel where the baby's head is? Tell her I will be very gentle. It won't hurt."

As the girl explains this in Italian, the woman does what I say and lets her knees fall apart. With the new brown soap I got at Stenger's when I purchased the gloves, I carefully wipe her bottom, then pour some over my fingers. If the afterbirth is attached too low and I poke a hole in it, Delfina will bleed to death. Then I will lose both mother *and* baby.

The first thing I come to is . . . *nothing.* No foot, head, or butt poking through the opening of the cervix. No cervix, either. The patient is fully dilated. Gently I palpate the lower wall of the womb for a hard gristly growth or soft squishy afterbirth but find none. This is good news, but then what's keeping the baby from coming?

A cord. It could be a short cord wrapped tightly around the infant's neck, another potential disaster. If the woman pushes vigorously, the cord will make a noose and choke the baby or, even worse, pull the afterbirth away from the womb. I take my fingers out and stare at the wall, where a carved wooden crucifix hangs over the bed.

I gave up on the church a long time ago, and I'm not even privately religious. In fact, I'll admit it: since Lawrence, my first love, perished in the train wreck and then years later Ruben, my true love and husband, was killed during the battle of Blair Mountain, my faith in God, like a tallow candle, has sputtered and gone out.

Still, looking at the carving, I silently ask Jesus and myself what to do.

"As far as I can see, we have to give it a try," I mentally converse with him. "If I do nothing, the baby will eventually die, then the mother will become in-fected, and she will die too. If I do *something,* there's a chance; the baby and mother *might* live . . ."

The man on the cross seems to nod in agreement.

"Antonia, get your father."

Clouds have come over and the room is getting dark, but when Izzie returns with the water and reaches up to turn a knob above the hanging bulb, the newspaper-covered walls burst into harsh light.

"Mr. Cabrini, the safest thing to do is get your wife to the doctor in Liberty or the bigger hospital in Torrington, but I don't think that's possible without putting Delfina and the baby in more danger. I've checked inside her, and there's nothing in the way. The infant is alive, but the head is too high. I think we can get the baby out in a few minutes if you'll help us and maybe a few other women from the camp."

Izzie shakes his head no. "The women won't come. I've already asked them. They don't like dagoes. They think we take their men's jobs."

I frown. When I was working with the Wobblies in Pittsburgh, I'd thought that all workers would stick together, but I am naive; people have told me this. With the gradual failure of the economy, there has been less need for steel and even less for coal, and the unions have all but disbanded. To cut costs, the mine owners bring in cheap labor, immigrants from the North and blacks from the South. Local men live in fear for their jobs, and their women try to protect them.

"Okay . . ." I think for a minute. "Then I'll need you and the oldest boy to help. Tell him he won't have to look." The man throws his hands into the air and spits out a few words in Italian. It's clear he doesn't like this. The girl argues back in their native tongue, and he slams out the homemade oak door.

At last, reluctantly, Mr. Cabrini and his son of about nine return and we're ready. While he was gone, I straightened the bed, propped up the limp patient, and laid out my oil, sterilized scissors, sterilized string to tie off the cord, clean rags, and a pan of warm sterilized water.

"Mother." I address the woman through her daughter, reminding the patient, by the appellation "Mother," what her suffering is about. "The baby's head is too high and the cord may be wrapped around his or her neck, so we won't have much time." I wait for the translation.

"Your children will help you sit up, and I want you to pull back on your knees and push as hard as you can. Push with all your might. Your husband will use his hand on your abdomen to guide the head down." I take Izzie's hand and show him how to palm the baby's head through his wife's flesh.

"I'll have my fingers inside to feel if it's coming. If there's a cord, I'll try to push it aside." This all sounds so complicated, but Antonia, using her hands to illustrate, translates quickly. "Once the head is in the pelvis, I'll want you to squat, but don't stop pushing for anything, don't let the head slip back." Delfina nods that she understands, and I see by the light in her deep brown eyes that despite her exhaustion, she has plenty of grit.

When we're ready, I look up at Jesus and make the sign of the cross the way I've seen Mrs. Kelly and the Catholic women do, and the whole family follows. The minute I feel Delfina's womb get hard, I nod and we get into position. Izzie cups the fetal head, and the round orb begins to slide down. The mother pulls back her legs and strains forward. The children, Antonio with her eyes wide and the older boy with his eyes scrunched shut, support their mother from the back.

At first I feel nothing—no cord, no limb protruding, then just the tip of something hard. "Yes!" I shout. "It's the head. It's coming!" What I lack in expertise I make up for in enthusiasm. This is where my two years on the stage at the Majestic come in.

Delfina takes a deep breath and strains down again. We don't wait for another pain; I'm afraid that if she stops, the head will slip back. The children push their mother up a little higher each time, and Izzie, with the wisdom of a gentle man, keeps the head steady. He knows he can't shove this baby out, though no doubt he would like to. With each maternal effort, I feel the skull lower until it fills the floppy cervix and then comes through. I could check the baby's heartbeat, but that would take time, and besides, what would I do if the heart rate dropped? No! We keep on.

"It's coming!" I shout.

Izzie hollers something in Italian that I think must mean "Push!"

"Okay, this is it! Children, help your mother to squat." I get down to show them. "Izzie, you keep the baby's head low, don't let it work back."

The woman is straining for real now. The urge is spontaneous, and the whole head is crowning. I reach behind me with one hand, dip my gloved fingers in the oil I use to counteract tears, and swipe it around the woman's opening. Usually I would slow things down at this point, but a birth canal tear is the least of my worries.

"Yi, yi, yi!" Delfina is yipping. I don't know Italian, but her meaning is clear. Her opening burns like a ring of fire.

Then the head is out . . . silence.

Everyone stares, even the boy. There's nothing stranger than the sight of a woman with a baby's head sticking out of her, one life emerging from another.

I lean lower, feel for the cord around the neck, and am surprised when I find none. The newborn is already scrunching up its face, a good sign. I wipe its mouth with a clean piece of rag. "Last push!" The baby spins three times as a cord at least three feet long unwraps around his chest and a little boy falls into my lap.

Now we are all laughing. Laughing and crying. Language doesn't mean anything in the presence of true joy. My eyes meet Izzie's, and I see how much he loves his wife and new baby and these dirty kids. Delfina's head falls back into his arms.

Praise Jesus, the words come to me as I look up at the crucifix.

October 30, 1929. New moon setting over the mountain.

Live-born male, 6 pounds, 4 ounces. Name, Enzo Cabrini.

Seventh or eighth child of Izzie and Delfina Cabrini. Presentation, cross lying, cord around the body three times. Active labor, two days. Pushed five minutes with father holding the head down. No tears. Blood loss one cup. Mrs. Cabrini knew to put the baby right to the breast. Also present two young children, who helped the mother squat. No payment again. The women in the camp wouldn't help us.

4

Midwife

It's been one week since Mrs. Cabrini and Mrs. MacIntosh delivered.

I remove the blue ribbon from the last used page of my journal. The day I went to check on them, both mothers were doing well and seemed to have plenty of milk. Bitsy and Mary will wait on Katherine for her two-week lying-in period. Delfina is already up cooking and cleaning.

A few years after Ruben's death and the disaster at Blair Mountain, when the fog around my heart finally lifted, I began to assist Mrs. Kelly with births along the south shore of the river in Pittsburgh. I couldn't go back to Westinghouse, not after what happened. Sophie took me with her at night, more to shake me from my grief and self-absorption than because she needed me. I attended another fifteen births here in West Virginia before she died, that made thirty-five, but I'm still a novice, and after the last two births, I'm beginning to wonder if I should be attending mothers at all.

I didn't refer to myself as a midwife at first. That changed when Dr. Blum gave my name to the state health department and I was required to register. I'd met Blum only that one time, when Sally Feder had her twins. Mrs. Kelly had never needed him again. At first I was flattered that he remembered me. Later I realized that it wasn't because he thought I was so great; he just wanted someone to take care of the poor so he wouldn't have to. That came after Sophie's heart attack. Now I'm the only midwife between Delmont and Oneida, except for an elderly black woman, Mrs. Potts, but I've never met her.

It's easy to be a licensed midwife in West Virginia, no exam or anything. All I had to do when the home health nurse, Becky Myers, sputtered up Wild Rose Road in her Model T was demonstrate that my house was clean and I could read and write. Then I signed some papers saying that I understood the regulations, and that was it.

Mrs. Rebecca Myers sat on my worn sofa in her pale blue nurse's uniform with the crisp white collar and dark blue sailor tie and showed me how to fill out the birth certificate. I watched her, wondering where this very precise woman with the midwestern accent, obviously university-trained, came from. She wasn't a local, that was for sure.

The public health nurse asked to see my birth kit. I offered her tea and had a few books on my shelves and paintings on the walls, so she must have thought I was a decent person. That's the other requirement I mentioned before: you must be of good moral character . . .

Becky is my friend now, and I know

a little bit more about her. She's a widow like me, and she's not from the Midwest. I had the accent wrong. It's Vermont, but she worked at Walter Reed during the war, then came to West Virginia to work in the mining camps during the typhoid epidemic of 1918. The Presbyterian Women's Mission asked her to stay, and now she's employed by the state Department of Health in Charleston.

It hadn't been easy, she told me. This was on her second visit, and we were sitting out on the porch. Local doctors had objected to her presence at first, thinking she was practicing medicine. If you ask me, she probably knew more than they did, but she'd never say it. "You have to understand how to work within the system," she warned. "Don't overstep your bounds."

Becky's the one who told me about the Frontier Nursing Service in Hyden, Kentucky, and encouraged me to keep records of my births in this diary. Before that, I just wrote the date and baby's name in the family's Bible like Mrs. Kelly did.

Mrs. Myers asked why I didn't go to the nursing service in Kentucky for more formal training. She's a registered nurse with a degree from some fancy college up north, Yale, I think, and that's where she heard about the school for midwives. She forgets that I'm not a nurse and have no money for travel or tuition. Anyway, who would take care of mothers like Delfina while I was gone? Not Dr. Blum. He charges twenty-five dollars if he comes to your home, thirty dollars if you go to his hospital. Twenty-five dollars would buy shoes for the whole Cabrini family for two years.

I pull my rocking chair over to the front window to admire my journal in better light. It's a beautiful book and quite too expensive. When I saw the bouquet of tulips embossed on the brown leather cover, I had to have it.

Inside, in the top corner of each lined page is a small colored print of a poppy or rose, a toad or snail, some living thing. There's a lock and a key that I keep on the cord with Mrs. Kelly's gold watch. My life has been difficult, and the delicacy of the empty pages is what charmed me, like a friend I could talk to, some gentle, sensible woman . . .

Mr. Stenger, the balding pharmacist with one lazy eye, gave the journal to me in trade, as well as twenty dollars, for taking care of his seventy-three-year-old mother, Cora, when her foot went bad from sugar several months ago.

I stayed in her home in Delmont, bathing her, cleansing the open sores, using my comfrey and goldenseal poultices and some of the medicated powders from the pharmacy. More than anything, I cooked, did her household chores, and kept her foot elevated so it could heal.

That was before I inherited my cow from the Johnsons and had to be home every evening. When the bank foreclosed on their farm at the bottom of Wild Rose Road, they couldn't take the cow with them to Wheeling. Besides, I'd delivered their son and they wanted to repay me.

I inherited this house and land too, from Mrs. Kelly, after she passed.

Turned out she'd made an appointment to prepare her will with Mr. Linkous, the lawyer in Delmont, just three weeks before her demise. I found that out later from Mr. Johnson, who'd driven her into town in his truck. It made me wonder if she'd known she was dying . . . but she never let on. Dr. Blum explained that some vessels in Sophie's heart had burst from hard farming work, that women weren't meant for it, but I knew better. Her heart broke when her lover, Nora, left us. After that it was just a slow bleed.

I throw another log into the woodstove. Outside, a few snowflakes float down, gentle reminders that winter is coming. Somehow I must find money to buy wood. Coal would be nice, but it's far too expensive. The bare trees shiver in the gray light and only a few groves of pines splash green higher up on the mountains. You can see the Hope River clearly now, but not the rocks and the rapids.

Treasured Child

Sometimes I get confused. Most of my life I've felt I was dreaming. Now and then I wake up, sometimes for months, sometimes for minutes. I'm a character in a play, and I can't tell if I'm making it up or if a great puppeteer is making me dance.

I've played too many roles in too short a time; had too many names, lived in too many places. It helps me to go back to the beginning.

I was born Elizabeth Snyder on October 19, 1893, in Deerfield, a small town north of Chicago and a few miles inland from Lake Michigan. My mother was a teacher, the daughter of a prominent farmer who died before I was born, and we lived with my grandmother in a two-story white Victorian on Third Street.

My father was a seafaring man, a first mate on a lake freighter hauling wood and iron from Wisconsin to Ohio. His parents died in the yellow fever ep-

idemic of 1878 in New Orleans, so I
never knew them.

As a little girl, I attended the Congre-
gational Church, where Mama played
organ and Papa sang in the choir when
his ship was in port. I was an avid
reader and devoured every book I could
find, as well as the *Chicago Tribune*
that Papa brought from the city. I played
the piano, loved to sing and dance, and
fished with my pa in a canoe on the
Des Plaines River, a treasured only
child, but that didn't last.

In the winter of 1902, my beloved
grandma passed away from a lung condition and we buried her in the hard,
cold ground. Not three years later, more
tragedy followed. My father's ship, the
Appomattox, on its last run from Mil-
waukee, foundered in a November fog.
The freighter, the longest wooden ship
on the Great Lakes, carrying a load of
iron ore from Lake Superior, grounded
on a sandbar in the mist. Papa was the
only crew member who died, swept
overboard by a ten-foot wave.

When the representative from the
shipping company brought the news,

Mama looked at me and said, "At any minute your life can change. Remember this. Between one breath and another, the song can stop and everything can be different."

Later I wondered, in my childish mind, if in actuality Papa had just jumped into a lifeboat and rowed away, faking his death to escape his debts. His body was never recovered.

In our first months of grief, things went from bad to worse. Mama was shocked to learn, from her solicitor, that we were destitute. The money my grandmother had left us was gone, gambled away by my father in high-stakes card games out on his freighter. Because of his debts, the Trust Company of Illinois foreclosed on our home and we moved to a rooming house in Deerfield. Those were hard times. It was Christmas, and I was twelve.

Fortunately, Mother was able to retain her teaching position, but our quarters were cramped and her pay was minimal. We sold our furniture, the piano, everything but our clothes, the family Bible, her hymnal, and a few favorite books. In the evenings, Mama did washing for the traveling men. I was taken out of school and sent to work with Mrs. Gross, the seamstress, on Westgate.

Only two years later, Mama developed a cough and came down with consumption just like her mother. She was spitting up blood when she died. I was shipped to Chicago to stay with the widowed sister of our solicitor, Mrs. Ayers, and worked as a laundress in her small inn, washing and ironing the linens and cleaning the rooms until Mrs. Ayers found a new husband and shipped me off to St. Mary's House of Mercy, an orphans' asylum for the destitute. Mrs. Ayers cried a little when I left, but I wasn't her responsibility. Not even kin. I understood that.

5

Mastitis

The weather has turned warm again, blue sky dotted with innocent white clouds, the smell of leaves rotting, a last shower of gold from the big oak out front, but there's something wrong with Moonlight. When I went out to milk her last night, one of her teats was as tight and red as a German sausage. I suspect the problem is an infection brought on by an injury or, more likely, from my not milking her on time, letting her bag get too tight and full, but I don't know much about cattle.

Consumed with guilt, I've been going

out with hot water and rags to wrap around her udders every few hours. She seems to like the warm compresses but hates it when I try to milk her. Still, it's the only thing I know to do. A breast infection hurts like the holy devil. I should know; I had mastitis a few times myself when I was a wet nurse.

First, to get the milk flowing, I pull on the teats that aren't quite so tender. It's what I tell my mothers when they have a red, tender breast: "Nurse on the good side first, rest, drink fluids, apply warm compresses. Keep the breasts empty, and leave the nipples open to the air." Good food also helps and sometimes cabbage leaves, but I can't figure out how to tie cabbage leaves on the cow's udders, so I skip that part. Meanwhile, I lay my head against the side of my beautiful black-and-white bovine, and my eyes fill with tears. *I am so sorry, Moonlight.*

This morning, finding my cow with her head hanging low, I get up my nerve, hike down the road to the neighboring farm, and ask Mr. Maddock what I should do. Maddock is a stern-faced old bugger who always wears a black felt hat and never waves when I pass, despite the fact that I've lived here two years. I was hoping he might be out in his fields mending fence or cutting brush, but I have to go up to the house.

"She's stopped eating and doesn't even look up when I come in the barn," I tell him through the screen door. Maddock doesn't invite me in, though a stiff wind is blowing and I have to keep brushing my hair from my face. "She just looks at me with big eyes and moans. I'm milking her six times a day, even getting up at night and using warm compresses. Can you think of anything else I could do?"

Maddock owns four or five Holsteins; I've seen them in his field. He pulls on his coarse black wool jacket, steps out on the porch, and yanks down his broad-brimmed headpiece. "You could ask the new vet; maybe he'd have some salve." He scratches his chin through his gray-speckled beard. "He doesn't live far. You can walk around Salt Lick

Road to his farm on Titus Hollow or just hike over the top of Hope Ridge on the old Indian trail that goes through the woods. His place backs up to yours on the other side. Either way, you'd be there in an hour."

Behind the weathered man, in the parlor, sitting by a kerosene lamp on a table, Mrs. Maddock, a pale woman with her silver-and-gold hair twisted up in a bun, sits knitting. She doesn't get up or come to the door. I catch her eye and smile. She doesn't smile back. There are books on shelves behind her and a display of framed needlework on the walls. Ordinarily, women in Appalachia would invite you in, but Mrs. Maddock, who looks, from her books and artwork, like an interesting person, must not approve of me, a woman without a man living alone just up the road. She turns her head and goes back to her knitting.

House Call

The hike over Hope Ridge, through a thick forest of stunted spruce growing out of flat sheets of granite, takes longer than I'd expected. Just when I decide that maybe I'm lost, I smell coal smoke and see, through the trees, a stone house with a white barn down in the hollow. The two-story dwelling, situated in a long narrow valley, appears to have been built a hundred years ago. Three horses graze in the pasture.

It's a picture-book place but so quiet that it occurs to me, for the first time, that I don't know the veterinarian by sight or even his name, and the closer I get, the more I begin to fear that this trip may be wasted. He could be out on a call or, now that I think of it, probably has an office in Liberty or Delmont.

A pileated woodpecker laughs from the top of a bare sycamore and I can hear a vehicle winding along Salt Lick, a pickup, maybe the mail carrier. As I work my way down the hill through the stubby yellow grass and outcroppings of rock, I sight a man dressed in coveralls, next to the barn, wearing black rubber boots and hammering on a piece of metal. *Clang. Clang. Clang.* He has a strong back; a tall fellow, maybe six feet, his light brown hair receding. Around forty, I think; I'd expected the vet to be someone much older.

A rock about the size of a cottontail rabbit catches under my foot and begins to roll downhill straight toward him. "Look out!" I yell.

He steps aside and watches as it lands near his feet. "Where'd you come from?"

"I'm sorry, I should have called out. My name is Patience Murphy." I've been using this name since Mrs. Kelly and I came to Union County, and by now it rolls off my tongue like honey.

"I'm the midwife from over Hope Mountain." I'm not sure why I tell him I'm *the midwife.* Maybe I feel it gives me some kind of legitimacy. "I have a cow with a red swollen teat, and Mr. Maddock, my neighbor, told me you might help."

"A house call is five dollars. You could

have used the telephone and saved yourself some trouble." He looks me over, head to toe, and I'm suddenly aware of the sight I must be. Usually when I go into town or make a social call, I spruce up, wear a dress and hose (if I have any), but today I'd come in my work boots, the trousers I wore when I worked at Westinghouse, and a heavy men's red-and-black-plaid jacket that Mrs. Kelly and I bought secondhand, before we exiled ourselves to these outer lands.

That's how I think of it, as though I've been banished from civilization, all because of what happened in Logan County at Blair Mountain. Some would say I should forget it. The feds can't still be looking for me after all this time.

I pull my long, straight hair away from my face and continue my plea for help. "I was hoping you could just give me some advice. I've been milking Moonlight every six hours the last few days and using warm compresses, but one of her teats is swollen and painful and now she's not eating. If you have any salve, I could work in trade."

One corner of the man's mouth turns up, and he raises his eyebrows as if he thinks my work wouldn't be worth much.

"Dr. Hester!" A woman, wearing a flowered apron, leans out the back door. "Phone call."

The vet lays down his hammer and strolls toward the house. "Wait," he commands.

I take a deep breath and let it out slowly, looking around. I'm not sure what I expected, but some kind of neighborly welcome would have been nice. Maybe I should have come by the road and dressed like a woman. I find an empty bucket and turn it over for a seat, wishing I'd just stayed at home.

While I kill time, I survey my surroundings. The open door of the barn reveals an old tractor, and the smell of hay and manure drifts through the yard. Parked in the drive is a newer-model black Ford covered with dust and mud. The woman watches me out the kitchen window; his wife, I suppose. I nod, and she ducks back from the glass.

When Hester returns, approaching

from the side, I jump up. He walks softly with a little limp, like maybe he has a sore knee.

"Let's go." He's carrying a small bag and a wooden box and has a canvas jacket thrown over his shoulder.

I frown. "I can walk home."

He's already hurrying toward the vehicle. "I'm not taking you home. We're going to Clover Bottom to deliver a foal." I hear by his clipped accent that he's not from Appalachia. No drawl or nasal twang like many of the natives.

"Clover Bottom? That's over eight miles."

"Afterward I'll see what I can do for your cow."

"But I don't have the five dollars . . ."

"If I need you for an assistant, this can be your payback. Do you have small hands?" I stare down at my work-roughened mitts. They're narrow with long fingers, not especially dainty but good for the work I do. I observe his wide hands in leather driving gloves.

"They're smaller than yours. But what if you don't need me?"

"Then you've wasted your afternoon

and you'll still owe me for the home visit."

I climb into the Ford. What else was I planning for the afternoon, anyway? Not much. I have a few hours before Moonlight needs milking. Maybe this excursion will be interesting. As strange as it sounds, I've never seen anything born but humans. Not even kittens.

"So where were you trained?" Hester asks, making an effort to be civil as we bump over Salt Lick, where the creek runs clean and clear over the rocks.

"Pittsburgh," I lie, knowing he means at what *midwifery school.* It isn't a complete fib. I *did* apprentice a little with Mrs. Kelly when we lived there. "For two years," I add, hoping that will be the end of it.

"I went to University of Pennsylvania."

La-di-da! I say to myself. But I ask in an interested voice, "What made you want to be a vet?"

I expect him to answer, "I like animals" or "My father was a vet."

We hit a big pothole and jolt up in the air. "I volunteered for the Great War early in 1917, fresh off the farm, only in my twenties, and was assigned to be a driver and take care of the livestock. It was hell for the horses. They stumbled through mud and rain to bring us supplies, food, water, and ammunition. I watched them die of exhaustion, broken bones, bloody wounds, and tetanus. There was nothing we could do. They should never have been there. Modern weapons made them sitting ducks. Eight million died in combat . . . Eight million beautiful horses. Most people don't know that." He has a strong jaw with a big nose, a manly face but not overly handsome. He flashes me a look out of gray eyes, yellow around the middle. Then he lets out his air and drums on the steering wheel.

"Seeing them suffer was almost worse than seeing men die. At least the soldiers, whether they volunteered or were drafted, knew why they were sacrificing. The horses had no idea, and it was sheer terror for them. They gave up their lives for a cause but never knew what the cause was. In the end, I forgot the cause too. Maybe war is always that way."

He says all this as the terrible sights and sounds roll like a picture show in the back of his mind and I watch the side of his face as he talks. If he served in the military in 1917–1918, he'd be about my age. I'm just beginning to warm up to him when he changes the subject.

"So you're the midwife that thought the MacIntosh infant was stillborn." One corner of his mouth twitches up like he thinks this is funny.

My breath is knocked out of me. "Yes."

How dare he ask such a question? It's easy to make judgments when you aren't in the birthing room. He wasn't the one who knelt by Katherine's bed and frantically searched over her abdomen with the fetoscope for that quiet *tick-tick.* He wasn't the one who'd had to call tall, silent Dr. Blum and ask for a second opinion. He wasn't the one who had choked back her own tears as she told the parents that their long-awaited baby was dead.

Hester glances over, waiting for a response, but my jaw is clamped shut and we drive the rest of the way in silence, across the stone bridge over Hope River, down Main and through town.

Liberty is a small settlement of some two thousand souls that looks like a village that comes with a wind-up train set. Main Street is populated with two-story shops and a water tower next to the wooden train station. There's a bank on one corner, a pharmacy, and a courthouse. There's the engine and coal cars waiting on the tracks that runs along the Hope River. No stoplights, just a stop sign at the corner of Chestnut and Main. It takes about five minutes to traverse the whole town.

Out into the country again, following Route 92 and the B&O Railroad tracks, Hester breaks the quiet. "Did I say something wrong?"

I pull my gold timepiece out from under my wool jacket and flip it open. "It's already three. I'm a little worried about Moonlight."

"I'll get you home well before dark."

"No, I mean Moonlight, my cow." I'm still not looking at him. "That's her name. I've been trying to keep her udders empty by milking at least every four hours."

"I'll drive you," the vet says again, and I don't know if that means he'll get me home in time, or he doesn't think it matters. It matters to me . . . and to Moonlight.

6

Foal

At the bottom of a hill a few miles the other side of Clover Bottom, we make a right turn at the small yellow train depot, cross the tracks, and follow a streambed into a hollow. The road ends at a large barn with peeling red paint. Inside I can hear a mare whinny and snort, whinny and snort. The vet winces. It's the same way I feel when I arrive at a pregnant woman's home and hear her scream.

Mr. Hester jumps out of the car and heads for the open barn door. "Bring my bag and the birth box, will you?" he yells back. "In the trunk." As the able assistant, I find the black leather satchel he stowed in the backseat and the wooden box with a hinged lid in the trunk, then trip along after him. In the dim barn, a dappled gray mare lies in the straw, her eyes wide with terror, and I instantly want to comfort her, tell her it will be all right.

Hester shakes hands with a farmer whose thick red hair sticks up as though he's been on an all-night bender, then kneels at the horse's side and says something to the animal that I can't hear. The farmer hands me a bucket of warm soapy water and a clean white feed sack. "You the new helper?" he asks. "Ain't seen a woman veterinarian before."

"Thanks," I say, taking the vessel, remembering that I'm dressed for the part in my heavy plaid jacket and pants. If I'm playing the vet assistant I better act like one, so I find a place out of the way, set the bucket down, and open the birth box to see what's in it. Behind me the horse screams again and stands up. Something's hanging out of her birth canal, a leg maybe, covered with membrane.

"How long has she been this way?" Hester asks.

"Four hours. She won't settle. It's her first. I tried to help her, but she kicked me away." He holds out his arm, pushes up his flannel shirtsleeve, and shows us a large purple bruise.

Hester hangs up his coat and takes off his upper clothing down to his wool undervest, then motions for me to bring over the bucket. "You better scrub too. There's supposed to be two feet." That's all he says, as if I know what this means.

When's he's done washing thoroughly, he slathers his arms and hands with soap again and waits. I set the bucket down, take off my jacket, roll up the sleeves of my work shirt, start washing like he did, and wonder what I've gotten myself into.

The mare is lying down again, groaning and straining, but nothing's coming out. "We're going to have to go in for the other leg," the vet explains. "Let me get her to stand. Then I want you to pull down on the limb that's dangling while I reach in." I nod and do what he tells me. For ten minutes he fools around while the mare strains, and I see that with each contraction his brow beads with sweat as if he's in pain. Sometimes a muscle in his face twitches, but other than that there's no way to tell. Finally he withdraws. "I can't get it. Will you try? Your arm and hand are smaller." He spreads his fingers, which would play an octave and a half on the piano: big, powerful mitts, good for many things but not for mucking around in an animal's vagina, not even a horse's.

"What should I do?" I whisper. We both face away from the farmer, who stands respectfully back by the barn doors. "Go in like I did and see if you can find the other hoof. I can just touch it. If you can get in a little farther, you should be able to hook your fingers around and bring it down."

I soap up again, this time past my elbow, and slowly wiggle my way inside, doing as he says. Between contractions I wait and it does hurt a little, but not badly. There's no point trying to go farther while the mare bears down.

I'm surprised when I find the second foot where he says and smile; then, following his instructions, I carefully manipulate it toward the opening.

At last both legs hang out. Hester takes them in his big hands and pulls, while the mare pushes. There's no whinnying now. She's all business, feeling her efforts accomplishing something. I've seen this before with my own patients. A mother who appears exhausted from an obstructed labor will revive and find strength when a malpresentation is resolved.

I stand next to the vet, my arms at my sides, amazed that with steady traction the legs emerge and then the head with the membrane still covering it. Suddenly, without warning, the whole mass swivels and plops out on me, my glasses fall off, and I collapse into the straw. The mare lies down too, her hard labor over, and looks behind her at the baby horse in my lap. She sniffs her offspring, who lifts his head with the amniotic sac still covering it.

Without asking I begin to peel the membrane off the little face, then look up at Mr. Hester for approval. He nods okay and hands me a towel to work with. The colt opens his eyes and I blow on him, the same way I blow on a baby if it doesn't breathe right away. The breath of life, I call it, and the little horse gasps from the cold air the same as a newborn human baby does.

Hester is already finished washing up and is inspecting the farmer's arm. "It's a nasty one," he says of the bruise. I feel around in the hay for my specs, squirm out from under the seventy-pound chunk of new life, and give the little one and his mama some time to get to know each other. How like a human mother she is! Nuzzling her newborn, eyes shining with love, sniffing it, licking it.

"Nice colt," I say to the men as I wash my hands. There's nothing to be done about my wet trousers.

"It's a *filly,*" the vet corrects. I snap my mouth shut, feeling foolish, and go out to the car.

Milk Stone

Twenty minutes later, motoring toward home over the stone bridge that crosses the wide and rocky Hope River, I'm still embarrassed about my mistake in calling the filly a colt but also elated from the experience of witnessing new life. It doesn't matter if it's a horse or a human, I decide, it's still amazing. If I believed, I'd call it God's miracle.

"Thank you for taking me with you," I say humbly. "I've never seen anything born before, except a human. Are they always that way? Or was that an especially hard delivery?"

"No, it wasn't especially hard. *I've* never seen a human born. Seen all kinds of animals . . . but . . ." He changes the subject. "Every now and then I need an assistant for the hard deliveries. I'm the only vet in the county now, and my practice is new. Some of the farmers are helpful, and some I wish would just go back in the house. Mr. Hicks was okay, not as nervous as some.

"Horses are like people, all different.

Each will react to foaling in her own way. Mares that haven't foaled before can foal late; then you worry about the size. Also, mares that are nervous struggle more and impede the process." He's lecturing now, almost as if I'm a student.

"Just like women in labor," I comment. "Turn here." I direct him down Raccoon Lick to Wild Rose Road.

As we pull into the yard, the vet looks around. "I haven't been up here before."

I take out my timepiece; it's been four and a half hours since Moonlight was milked. "The barn is in back, but we better wash up."

"Sorry the water's cold," I murmur. We're in the kitchen, and I ladle almost cool water from the hot-water reservoir on the side of the cookstove. There are only coals left, and the house is growing chilly. "When the fire's going, the water's nice and warm."

Mr. Hester shrugs and turns to stare through the doorway into my living room. He takes in the piano, the books, the framed paintings on the wall. I realize that he's the first male to stand in this house since the men from the church brought the piano two years ago.

In the barn he's all business, goes right to Moonlight.

"See what I mean? It's a breast infection, isn't it?" I comment. Then correct myself. "A teat infection, I mean."

Hester doesn't answer. He takes a thermometer out of his box and sticks it into my cow's rectum. Moonlight barely reacts, just looks back once, her head hanging low. Gently he washes the whole udder with soap and water, then squeezes some kind of salve on his hands and palpates the red, swollen teat. The cow moans and he sees how it hurts her, but he keeps on with his examination.

I hand over the milk bucket, and he wraps his index finger and thumb around the red, swollen teat, then squeezes down with the other three fingers, careful not to force the milk uphill into the bag. I wince when blood squirts into the bucket.

The vet stops and examines the sick teat again. "The straw looks clean. Are you routinely washing your hands with soap and water before you milk?"

"Yes." What I want to say is "What do you take me for, a dummy?" but I bite my tongue. No need to be disagreeable.

The vet gently compresses the bloody teat, up and down, side to side, searching for something. First one side, then the other. I watch his hands, wondering what he's looking for.

"I think she has an obstruction, not simple mastitis. It might be a milk stone."

He reaches into his satchel, selects a small metal box with sterilized instruments, pulls out a scalpel, and before I can say *no* makes a slit down the side of Moonlight's sore teat. This time she almost kicks him, but he's ready for her and ducks away. When she settles, he takes a long pair of curved tweezers and pulls out a white object about the size of a pea. He hands the instrument back, then gets out suture and gauze and begins to blot the oozing red as he sews up the incision in my poor cow's teat.

"That's a milk stone, probably what caused the infection in the first place," he says as he works. "I could feel it in there. I'm surprised you didn't."

I tighten my mouth. "I've never heard of a milk stone. I wouldn't have known to look for one."

"That's why you call a vet," he says, and I feel my face flush.

"I did call a vet."

"Keep your shirt on. Just next time get me sooner."

"Not everyone has the money to call a veterinarian for the least little thing. Not everyone has a phone." That shuts him up.

He stops for a second and stares at me. "Hemostat." He picks up the instrument he just used and holds it out for me to see. "Needle driver." He picks up another one. "Forceps." He shows me the rest. "Retractor. Scissors. Scalpel . . . Do you do any stitching in your line of work?"

I'm surprised at his interest. "Some, not often. I'm good at getting babies out without tears, and I've never had to do an episiotomy. I know how, though."

"Here." He hands me a needle holder and a curved needle. "You can have these. I have several. Old Doc Collins, from Liberty, gave them to me when I bought his practice. They might help if you have a deep laceration. I'll show you how to use them someday." He stands and stretches his back, looking around. "Don't forget, you owe me one more trip as an assistant."

I stare down at the shiny silver needle holder. "Thank you," I mumble, then jerk up. "What do you mean one more trip? I thought I'd paid for Moonlight's visit by helping you with the foal. I did my job and more, bouncing around in your dusty old car."

(Actually, I'd enjoyed myself. I don't get to see a baby horse born every day, even if I did get covered with amniotic fluid and slime. Still, he irritates me.)

"Yeah, but I had to do surgery on your cow's teat, and surgery costs more. It might even be *two* more trips."

Again the one corner of his mouth twitches. *Is he joking?* I can't tell.

"Well, you'd have to come around Hope Ridge to get me, and sometimes I'm away at a birth . . . it would be hit and miss, and remember, I don't have a phone."

"Yeah, you told me that. Don't you need one in your line of work?"

"You're not getting the picture. I'd love one. It would help a lot, but the co-op electric and phone lines haven't come out Raccoon Lick yet. None of my neighbors care about a telephone or electricity, and I couldn't afford to pay extra to get the poles and line set just for me. I'm not a rich veterinarian. I don't think there *are* rich midwives."

"Not many rich vets either," he says. The dig doesn't faze him. "I guess neither of us do it for money." We walk back toward the house and I let him into the kitchen so he can wash again. Against my better judgment I ask if he would like tea. It seems only neighborly, but I'm relieved when he says he has to get going. I'm not used to company, and when you're as old and cranky as I am, you don't miss it.

"Thank you for helping with the foal," he responds, reaching out his hand. I shake it like he's a banker or lawyer. I'm surprised that it's so warm and folds over mine like a quilt on a snowy day. I've never felt a hand so warm, except Mrs. Kelly's.

"Thank you too," I mumble, not looking at him. "Is it okay to still milk Moonlight, with the stitches and all?"

"Yeah, but use Bag Balm to make your hands slip." He looks around the kitchen to see if I have any, and I point out the distinctive bright green can with the image of red clover and a cow on the lid. "You can take the stitches out in two weeks when she's healed. Keep her bag empty. I'd continue to milk her every four hours. How much does she give, anyway?"

"Not that much. Two or three quarts a day. How much do you get from your cows?"

"Three gallons a milking." My eyebrows shoot up. "If you had her bred," he continues, "and freshened, you could get that much too, but you'd have to let her go dry so she'd ovulate. I have a bull; no charge, if you're interested. You'd want to do it right away. As soon as the mastitis is over."

I let that sink in. "How long is a cow's gestation?"

"About nine months, same as a human's. Let me know." Hester shrugs back into his coat, which he'd laid on the seat of the wooden rocker, and glances around the parlor once more. His eyes rest on the picture of me overlooking Lake Michigan, with the west wind blowing my hair.

"Better bring in some wood. It's going to be cold tonight." He pulls on his old brown fedora and goes into the dark.

Outside, a crescent moon sits in the branches of the naked oak tree. I pull on my jacket and stand for a minute looking up at the clear star-filled sky. Under the porch there's only enough coal to fill a milk bucket, and the stack of split oak is almost gone.

7

Big Mary

Today the sun shines, a strong wind blows in from the west, and I have no excuse for not making my visit to the MacIntoshes'. I'm embarrassed to ask them for payment outright. Mrs. Kelly always told me that delivering babies was an act of charity, something a person did for love, but that was before the economy collapsed, and back in those days almost everyone gave us *something*—a few dollars, a side of ham or maybe a chicken. I'm hoping that William MacIntosh will get the hint when I return, because I badly need cash for fuel, wood and coal.

As I pedal down Wild Rose Road, then along Raccoon Lick and the three more miles into Liberty, I make note of the last of the wildflowers. Only a few goldenrods still droop in the ditch with the six-foot-high purple ironweed lording it over them. A long V of geese flies low overhead, and I stop in the road to admire them.

Each spring and fall they pass near here, doing what their species has done for aeons, making our human struggles seem petty and small. They don't know about wars or stock market crashes or union struggles. The geese give me hope, fill up my heart.

I step down hard on the bike's pedals and push on, but the wind blows in strong gusts, and twice I waver and almost fall off. A horse would be nice, I think, but there's no way I could afford one, and a vehicle like Mr. Hester's is unthinkable.

The whole way into Liberty no one passes, except one big truck from MacIntosh Consolidated that almost runs

me off the road. When I finally arrive at
the three-story brick house, I stop to
catch my breath and straighten my hair.
Holly bushes with red berries grow
along the drive, with a few last red roses
up the porch rails. I park my bike to the
side and knock on the back door like a
delivery boy. I know this isn't right. I
should enter through the front, as Dr.
Blum would do. A midwife is a professional, isn't she?

"Well, come on in," Mary Proudfoot,
the big coffee-colored cook, greets me,
a white scarf tied behind her head, covering her neatly braided hair. "Bye Bye
Blackbird" by Gene Austin is floating
out of the radio in the dining room.
*Pack up all my care and woe, here I
go, singing low. Bye bye blackbird."* I
grin when she pulls me close to her
bosom, a soft pillow. I'm underendowed
myself.

"Miss Patience," Bitsy greets me
without enthusiasm, looking down and
away as she carries a load of laundry
through the kitchen and out to the side
yard.

"Sorry I've not been back sooner . . ."

I trail off. "Is Mrs. MacIntosh doing all right?"

"Oh, she's right as rain, honey. Bitsy and I know about newborns. The missus is upstairs nursing . . . Speaking of Bitsy, she'd make a good midwife assistant, don't you think? Didn't she do right good at the delivery?" The cook pours me a cup of black coffee without even asking and pulls out two wooden kitchen chairs, indicating I should sit.

I'm taken aback by her comment about her daughter, but Mary allows the thought to sit on the back burner and rambles on.

"It's the mister I'm worried about. Talk about your care and woes." She leans forward, glancing first at the door to the dining room. "He's wearing his tail to a frazzle! Says he's lost all he's worth, except this house and the coal mines. Everyone in town is holding on by a thread. No one can believe it's happening. The banks are tied in knots, and all because of that President Herbert Hoover. Worthless!

"I don't even think the mister told Miss Katherine that Bitsy has to move out. They can't afford her. Mr. MacIntosh says they don't need a maid, the missus and I can manage. I told him Bitsy would work just for keep, no cash pay, but he says no. She'd still require food. Things are that tight.

"I asked him what she's supposed to do . . . The few people that used to have servants in Liberty are letting theirs go too. I'm just glad I've been here so long and Katherine has the new baby. They can't let me go; I practically raised William, used to work for his parents. If he put me out they'd turn over in their graves."

She stands and stirs a fragrant chicken broth on the stove. "The mister told me not to bother Katherine about Bitsy! He doesn't want his wife upset. Might lose her milk, he says, but I don't know what Bitsy's supposed to do . . . where she can go . . ." There are tears in her brown eyes, not falling yet, just resting in a pool below her lower lid. "Our closest kin are in North Carolina."

Outside the tall twelve-pane kitchen window, I study Bitsy as she struggles with the wet sheets in the wind. She's a small woman, about my size, half as big as her mother, but she seems tough, like the little blueberry bushes that grow on the granite rocks at the top of the ridge.

"Mary, I'd help you if I could, but I'm broke too."

"Thomas was at your house. He says it looks like you have extra rooms. I've studied it out. Bitsy could learn to help you with the deliveries and on the farm. She'd work for room and board. No salary. My daughter is thrifty and smart. She'd be company for you out there in the sticks. You'd like her."

I can't believe this conversation is happening. Sometimes it would be nice to have another person around. Mrs. Kelly and I lived quite comfortably together in our little white house before she had her heart attack, but Bitsy and I together, a black and a white? I don't really care what people think, but I can't afford to bring attention to myself. I've just met Bitsy, and I've never known a white woman to live with a colored before, unless she was a servant.

"She has one week to move out of here."

"You know, Mary, I don't have electricity or gas or a telephone or a car. It would be a tougher life than Bitsy is used to. Has she ever lived in the country?"

"Sure. We stayed with my pa near Fancy Gap in the mountains of North Carolina when she was a girl. That was before we moved to West Virginia so my husband could work in the mines. Mr. Proudfoot, Bitsy's pa, was killed in the Switchback Mine explosion along with sixty other men. By that time my daddy had passed on and lost his farm, and there was no place for us in Fancy Gap. The children and I moved north with the MacIntosh family when they opened their new mines in Union County." She says all this without a trace of self-pity.

"Bitsy knows how to kill and dress deer. She can fish. She could clean and do laundry for you so that you'd have more time. My daughter graduated from the colored high school in Delmont. She can read, even big books, and she's as hard as cowhide if she needs to be." The cook is as relentless as a Fuller brush salesman.

"Is that the baby crying?" I grab my satchel and make a hasty escape up the back stairs. At the landing, I slow and give the prospect some thought. Bitsy's moving in with me could be a gift or could mean the demise of my peaceful hermitage. I picture the two of us curled at the opposite ends of the sofa, reading in the evenings, as Mrs. Kelly and I once did. Would Bitsy squirm? Would she talk too much or sing under her breath? Does she snore or click her teeth when she eats? Would I have enough food? Those are the little things that concern me.

I let out my air, wondering how the community would feel about us. I couldn't call her my servant, and I couldn't stand someone waiting on me. It riles me even to think of it!

Crescent Moon

"Katherine? It's Patience," I call softly from the upstairs hall. "I came to check on you and the baby." The bedroom door is half open, and I see the woman pull her shift over her breast and stand up. "I'm sorry it's taken so long to get back," I apologize. "Mary says you're both doing fine." I note that the baby is asleep in his cradle, nursing his little tongue.

"Oh, Patience. I've missed you." Katherine plunks down on the edge of the bed, and by her action, I see that her bottom doesn't hurt anymore, but things are not as hunky-dory as Mary implied.

"Are you okay?"

Dried milk is caked on the woman's lavender chemise, her hair is uncombed, and her pale face, without makeup, looks lined and tired.

"Yes . . . oh, I guess so . . . no, not really. I just feel so rotten about Bitsy."

That takes me aback. "I thought you didn't know about that—about her having to leave and Mr. MacIntosh's financial problems."

"I know more than he thinks! William treats me like a child. I can hear the news on the radio, for heaven's sake. I can put two and two together.

"The day the baby came I was so distraught I didn't realize what they meant by Black Tuesday, but since then there's been a string of men in and out of the house, bankers, creditors, investors, people like that. I hear their raised voices. I hear their fear.

"Then Martha Stenger came over to see the baby, the pharmacist's wife, with her six wild children. I thought they'd never leave. The kids were squirming all over, and the two littlest boys got in a fight!" She rolls her eyes.

Here I see a sly smile, and I remember why I like Katherine. Despite her sweet face and gentle feminine demeanor, there's a little piss in her vinegar.

"I know what you mean. They're a rowdy brood, bright but so noisy."

"Martha Stenger told me that Mary Proudfoot has been asking everyone in town if they'll hire Bitsy. I was so angry when I found out William fired her! I would have confronted him if it wouldn't have meant a big fight. He has so many other worries. Has to make payroll for his miners this week. I just feel so bad. I don't have any money for *you* either, after all you did."

I'd felt this might happen, yet still I'm disappointed. The MacIntosh family could at least offer *something*. I try to let Katherine off easy. "That's okay. I know you'll get to it when your finances are better." (She should know about my finances! A flimsy two-dollar bill is all that stands between the poorhouse and me.)

I change the subject. "Mary told me about Bitsy just now in the kitchen. She asked if I would take her in, maybe train her to be my birth assistant, but I don't have any extra money and don't really need help."

"Oh, would you, Patience? *Could* you? I'd feel so much better if she was with you." Katherine stands, rocks the cradle with her foot, then floats to the window.

Why are some women so graceful? Is it learned from their mother or something they're born with? I compare myself to my patient. Today I wore my second-best dress, the dark blue one with the little white dots with a white apron over it. One strand of my long hair has caught on my glasses, and I smooth it back.

Even in the wrinkled, breast-milk-stained gown, Katherine looks like a queen, moves like a dancer. She holds the heavy curtain to one side and stares out the window to where the tops of the trees whip in the wind.

"Did you see the snowball bushes? Mr. MacIntosh planted them last year. The roses too." (She calls her husband "Mr.," as many of the older women do.) "He started the roses when we first moved here."

"They're beautiful," I confirm. Then she turns to face me.

"Look, Patience . . . times are going to get worse. You need to be realistic. A girl to work on the farm would be helpful. We'll all have to put in vegetable gardens and do things we aren't used to."

I smile to myself. Having a garden won't be that different for me. I learned how to cultivate from Mrs. Kelly and from trial and error. Though Katherine has a point; I may have to enlarge the plot and preserve more food.

"Also, it doesn't look right you living alone. People talk. And it's not safe. What if something happened to you?"

"Nothing's going to happen. I've lived alone for more than a year. Anyway, what do you mean, talk about me?"

"William heard them at the Oneida Inn when he had his Elks meeting." The Oneida Inn, twenty miles away, is a restaurant and hotel that's far too rich for me, and there's a speakeasy in the back. Not that I've ever been there.

"What do they say? What *could* they say? I live a good, clean life."

"People just talk. They wonder about you. A single woman living all by herself on the side of a mountain. You must admit it's unusual. If Bitsy lived with you, it would seem more proper."

"You don't think it would cause more

gossip? A black and a white woman living together?"

"Well, she'd be your servant, right? Your maid."

My maid! I've been a maid myself in the past, a milkmaid with the Chicago Lying-in Dispensary. I've never had hired help, never had the money, and anyway, having someone wait on me makes my skin crawl.

"There's something else." Katherine continues her pitch. "Bitsy could bring you some business."

I frown, not sure what she means.

"Black babies," Katherine whispers, her hand to her mouth as if this is hush-hush.

"What?"

"The Negro expectant mothers would start coming to you if Bitsy was your helper. The only midwife they've got now is Mrs. Potts, but she's over eighty and is slow getting around. Bitsy would bring you clients, and you'll need them now that Dr. Blum has dropped his fees and put a sign in his window, 'New patients welcome.'"

That surprises me. He's always

seemed so expensive. "What's his fee now?"

"Twenty dollars for the delivery and a two-night stay at his hospital. Fifteen dollars if he comes to your home, but that's only for people in town or the rich farmers. He won't go out to the coal camps."

That's almost the same fee I charge! Not that I get it.

Katherine turns and strolls to her vanity, sits on her padded chair, and combs her short blond bob with her silver brush. Then she picks up the carved silver mirror with a little handle and stares back at me. "If you will take Bitsy, I'll give you this." She pulls a gold-and-pearl brooch out of her jewelry box and holds it out, dangling in her thin hand.

I stare at the offering, a gleaming crescent moon with a pearl the size of an eyetooth. You can tell it's real gold.

"I couldn't. That's ten times too much. I'll just wait until you and William get on your feet."

"Patience, it could be years . . . Mary's daughter is like family. This will

be for my beautiful baby and a beginning of a new life for Bitsy. You can
teach her to be a midwife." She stands
and drops the heavy brooch in my lap.

"Won't Mr. MacIntosh object? If he
needs the money, he could sell this."

"It's not his. My mother gave it to me.
Anyway, he hardly notices what I wear
for jewelry, or even my clothes. He
probably doesn't know I own it."

I shake my head and pointedly lay
the ornate crescent moon with the pearl
at the tip on the bedside table. It must
be eighteen carats, though my experience with jewelry is limited.

"I need to examine the baby." I
change the subject. "He's beautiful. I'm
sorry I put you and William through the
pain of thinking he was dead. I'm still
not sure why I couldn't find the heartbeat, and then you said you didn't feel
him move."

Katherine sits beside me on the bed
and smooths the dark brown satin quilt.
"You gave me comfort in the night. You
gave me my son." Her face is flushed,
and there are tears in her eyes.

Our happiness for this one live baby

drowns out my other worries, my lack of cash to survive the winter, my fears that I am over my head in calling my-self a midwife. I don't even notice when Katherine drops the golden brooch into my apron pocket.

8

Bitsy

First hard frost last night, and all the remaining tomatoes are ruined. I thought if I left them on the bushes, they might redden up, and I was mad at myself all day until Charles Travers came for me and I was called to another delivery. This one made up for the near tragedy at the MacIntoshes' and the strangeness of Delfina's birth in the coal camp. It reminds me that most of the time Mother Nature knows best.

November 15, 1929. Almost full moon and the first hard frost.

Uncomplicated delivery of Ruth Ann Travers, firstborn of Charles and Abigail Travers of Liberty. Six pounds, 9 ounces. One small tear that didn't require stitching. I bicycled home singing because I was paid five dollars! Others present were Abigail's mom, a mother of seven. She was a great help to me.

Mrs. Kelly's ornate parlor clock chimes five as I rest my leather journal across my chest. It's extravagant, I know, and the fire will burn out faster, but I've left the door of the heater stove open to enjoy the flames in the late-afternoon light. The coals shimmer like rubies. I allege that I don't know much about jewelry, and that's true, with the exception of Mrs. Vanderhoff's ruby. *The ruby . . . the ruby ring.*

Under the sound of the wind, I catch another sound, the clatter of wagon wheels coming up Wild Rose Road. When I jump off the sofa to look out the window, I see in the gloom a cart piled with split wood pulled by two burros, which are also laden with bulging gunnysacks. A small dark woman balances on top of the logs with a bicycle tied on beside her. Mr. Cabrini is driving, and Thomas Proudfoot, Mary's son, walks by his side. They pull up to the porch and tie their animals. The woman climbs down. She has a worn cardboard suitcase and two firearms, a rifle, and a shotgun. It's Bitsy.

Before I left the MacIntoshes' a few days ago, I returned to the kitchen and conferred again with Mary. I tried to be honest, tried to explain. "It's not the color thing. You know it's not. It's just I'm not used to people waiting on me, and truly I have so little money. I know I look better off than I am, with a house and a small farm to my name, but that's only because I inherited the land from the older midwife, Mrs. Kelly, and the cottage is so tiny, really, I've no need for a maid. Right now I have only a few dollars to my name and not enough coal or wood for the winter."

Mary, looking worn, stared out the window at the last of the black-eyed Susans along the back fence. Her chin rested in one hand, the other hand smoothed the tablecloth.

"So," I continued, "I'm uncomfortable, but I guess we could try it—"

The big lady jumped up, knocking over her chair. "Praise Jesus! You were my last hope."

"—on a trial basis. We'll see how it goes. See how we get along. At least it will solve the problem for a while."

Now Bitsy is here, climbing off the top of a load of firewood, and my privacy's gone. I lock my journal with its little key, tuck it under the sofa cushion, and open the door.

For a week, Bitsy and I tiptoe around each other, careful not to offend. At six A.M. I wake to hear her shaking the grate, taking out ashes, tossing in the kindling and split oak that Mr. Cabrini and Thomas brought: not only two cords of wood but gunnysacks full of small chunks of coal, spilled by the railway cars, that the Cabrini children had picked up along the tracks.

The pile of black gold and the stack of oak and hickory are my pay for delivering Mrs. Cabrini's baby. If you don't count the golden crescent moon that Katherine dropped in my apron pocket before I left, it's the best payment I've received in a long time.

By the time I rise and dress in an old sweater and trousers, the downstairs is warm and fragrant with the sweet smell of bread toasting on the top of the cast-iron cookstove. Bitsy and I eat together in the kitchen (there's nowhere else to eat), though I suppose she and Mary dined separately from the MacIntoshes. We comment on the weather and discuss the chores for the day. There's no milk or cream with our meal. Moonlight has dried up and is at Mr. Hester's, consorting with his bull.

"Do you want some more toast?" Bitsy asks me.

"No, I'm fine."

We don't talk about anything personal. The habit of hiding my past is so much a part of me, I wouldn't know where to start. We just tread the surface of the backwaters, never diving into the stream.

I could ask Bitsy if she has a sweetheart. Does he live in town? Does she miss him? I could ask what her favorite food is or what books she likes to read, but I just eat my bread with blackberry jam and hot tea. Then Bitsy gets up and clears the table.

At first I insisted she let me take my turn at cooking breakfast and washing up, but the young woman always rises before I do. I had to draw the line when she got out the washtub and washboard and started to launder my underclothes!

Yesterday, at breakfast, a deer and her fawn crossed the yard just outside the picket fence that circles the house.

"Bitsy," I hiss. "Look!"

The small woman leans over my chair. "Should I get my rifle?"

My head goes up sharply. "No! Not the mother with her baby!"

"Most female deer will have babies this time of year." She looks at me as if I don't know anything. "They give birth in the spring, and by fall the young ones are following them around. If you want to eat meat this winter, as soon as it stays below freezing, I've got to hunt. The fawn is old enough to survive."

It's the first time Bitsy has argued with me. Usually it's "Yes, ma'am." "No, ma'am." "Whatever you say, Miss Patience." It gets on my nerves.

9

Ice Storm

All night it sleets, and toward dawn the house gets cold. I toddle down the stairs in my long red flannel nightgown to build up the fire and find Bitsy already standing there.

"Ice," she says, pointing at the window. She's wearing the faded pink chenille bathrobe that Katherine gave her before she left town.

I shove a few logs into the firebox.

"Here, let me do that."

"No, Bitsy. I managed to keep warm before you came. I'm not helpless." She turns away hurt, and I regret my sharp words, but I stir up the coals with the wrought-iron poker. Then we both move toward the window.

Outside, when the clouds part, you can see by moonlight that every branch and twig is covered with ice. The limbs are so heavy they droop to the ground, and as we watch a branch breaks and shatters like crystal. We look at each other with big eyes.

Then the clouds close in again and everything's black, like the curtain dropped at the end of a picture show. In the silence that follows, there's a new sound, the crunch of footsteps in the distance, coming up Wild Rose Road.

"You hear that?" I ask, hoping I'm imagining it.

The footfalls don't frighten me. It's the thought of someone being in labor on a night like this that makes my stomach turn. I do a quick review of the women who've already arranged for my services. Minnie Boggs is not due until Christmas. I shut my eyes and hope it's not her. She's only fourteen and the baby would be five weeks early. Then there's Clara Wetsel, but she's had four kids and shouldn't deliver until mid-January. She'd be so early that her husband would know to go to Dr. Blum, no matter what his wife said.

"Can you see anyone?" I wonder. "It's darker than a coal mine. Wait . . . a man on a horse."

"He's leading another horse." That's Bitsy.

"We'd better get dressed. Light a lantern."

Minutes later, Bitsy and I, each holding a kerosene lamp, stand in the doorway watching as Thomas ties two burros to the closest maple tree. The Proudfoot brother and sister give each other fierce hugs, and I see now how much Bitsy misses her family. Not having any relations myself, I hadn't thought much about it. She misses her mother, with whom she's lived her whole life. She misses her brother. She most likely misses the fellowship of the Liberty A.M.E. Church.

"They need you in Hazel Patch" Thomas finally says by way of a greeting. There's no "Howdy" or big smile.

What now? I don't know anyone in Hazel Patch, an isolated village of about a hundred souls where mostly blacks live. Becky Myers, the home health nurse, told me their story, how they had migrated up from the southern part of the state to work the Baylor Mine near Delmont, then stayed on after the cave-in when seventeen men were killed. That was in '21, before Mrs. Kelly and I got here. Most of those who weren't killed won't go back underground again and now make out a living as subsistence farmers.

"What do those people want with Miss Patience?" Bitsy demands protectively. "It's after midnight and a terrible ice storm. Those people got no call for us. Anyway, they have Mrs. Potts to help them." She emphasizes *those people* a second time as if they are *country* and we are too good for them. Hazel Patch is also way on the other side of Spruce Knob.

"Come in, Thomas. Is someone in labor?"

The tall man, an oak like his mother, Mary, steps up onto the porch and ducks though the door. Cold radiates off his green mackinaw, and flakes of ice shed on the floor.

"It's bad, Miss Patience. There's a baby coming, or trying to come, but the arm's coming first. It's Cassie Washington. This is her fourth child, maybe fifth. I think one died. Mrs. Potts has been trying for three hours, and the aunties say the baby's arm is turning blue. You got to come help."

"We can take Raccoon Lick to Hope Ridge," I offer, "and cut past the Harpers' through the woods, until we hit the south fork of Horse Shoe Run. It will take an hour if we hurry."

"If you're going, I might as well come," Bitsy grumbles, but I smile, glad on this dark night to have her company. She can boil water, get the extra people out of the bedroom, and deal with Mrs. Potts, who may or may not be happy to see me.

As soon as I step out, I slip on the porch. I had forgotten about the ice.

"Damn!" I land hard on my butt.

Bitsy starts to giggle, but Thomas

punches her lightly on the forearm and pulls me up.

"You be careful now, Miss Patience," he says. His hand is bare and warm, with coal dust forever under his fingernails, and I wonder if he has any mittens. Then I notice that Bitsy's hands are bare too. The night is just a little below freezing, but I'm wearing a blue tam, gloves, and scarf that I knit myself.

"Are we going to be able to make it?" I ask Thomas. "Can the burros' hooves cut through this ice?"

Thomas grunts. "Reckon. The old gals did okay on the way here. The ice is melting a little now. We have to try." I imagine the birth scene, a woman thrashing around with a baby's arm presenting. She's crying and trying to push, but nothing happens.

Thomas helps me mount the larger of the animals and puts Bitsy behind me; then we ride bareback and I adjust the younger woman's hands so they're under my arms where they can stay warm.

* * *

Twenty minutes later we're at the cross-roads of Wild Rose and Raccoon Lick. When the moon comes out again, I see the damaged trees. Limbs dangle like broken arms everywhere. Down the slope the Hope River roars, an invisible lion. Three times we stop while Thomas gets off his burro to drag a large branch off the road.

Another mile and we're trekking up the Harpers' long tree-lined drive. The *crunch, crunch, crunch* of the burros' hooves sounds like broken glass under their feet, and I estimate that the flakes of ice are two inches deep. At the Harpers', dogs bark, but no lights come on.

Just past the hulking shadow of their big barn, we cut into the woods and follow the south branch of Horse Shoe Run. Here in the dense spruce and hardwood forest, branches are crashing down everywhere. I look up and realize the danger we're in.

Bitsy holds on tighter. All I can see is Thomas's shadow in front of me. Thank goodness the last wolf in West Virginia was eradicated and the bears are hibernating. I *think* they're hibernating.

They wouldn't be out on a night like this, would they?

At last we see lights and in another few minutes the village of Hazel Patch, a collection of a dozen or so houses and small farms associated with a little white chapel. Thomas quickens his pace, and though I'm dreading what we're about to walk in on, I hurry my mount to catch up with him.

What was I thinking when I pulled on my boots? How can I help an experienced midwife like Mrs. Potts, someone who's probably been delivering babies for fifty years, while I got my certificate only two years ago just by signing my name? And the family . . . I don't even know them. I'd rather be home in my cozy warm bed.

We pass the little church, a small clapboard affair with a wooden steeple, and then follow Thomas down a private road bordered on either side by a neat split-rail fence. At the end is a two-story log house with light pouring out of every window. A woman howls into the night, a wild sound. Bitsy and I shiver. The woman stops for a few minutes and then starts up again.

Mrs. Potts

Sensing my apprehension, Bitsy gives me a squeeze and slides off our mount. Though she hadn't wanted me to come, she grabs my birth satchel without hesitation and accompanies Thomas up to the door. I follow carefully, determined not to make my grand entrance by falling on my butt again.

Thomas knocks twice while we stomp the ice off, but he doesn't wait for an answer. He opens the door and lets us into a large living room with oak book-shelves against the log walls, an organ, and a fawn velvet sofa. It's the kind of room I imagine a judge or a physician would have had in the pioneer days, only there wouldn't have been electric lights. Hazel Patch is located right on the main road, close to the power lines. The way Bitsy referred to the Hazel Patch folk as "those people," I thought we were coming to a hardscrabble place more like the mining camp.

Across from the door is a bright yellow kitchen with a pale green enameled high-backed gas stove. Two dark-skinned women and a shorter coffee-colored lady are laying out food. The three, all wearing flowered house-dresses and aprons of various shades, turn to greet us.

"Mrs. Potts?" Thomas calls, removing his hat.

The stooped brown midwife, dressed all in black, with a neat white apron, a white lace collar, and a white bandanna, comes down the hall. She walks as though her joints need oil, but her face is nearly unlined. From another room, the patient in labor wails like a trapped animal.

I'm surprised when the elderly lady passes Thomas and Bitsy and wraps her arms around me. "Honey," she says, "I'm Grace Potts. I'm so sorry to bring you out on a night like this, but I didn't know who else to call and we have a *sitiation* here." She says *situation* in a funny way, like a lot of older Appalachians do. "Dr. Blum won't come to Hazel Patch or allow coloreds to come to his clinic, or we would have already gone. You'll see what I mean in a minute."

"Thomas says the arm is coming out first. Can you feel the head at all?"

Grace Potts holds out both her worn hands, gnarled with arthritis, each knuckle of each finger distorted, the tops ebony and lined with veins twisted and crossed like a road map but the palms as pink and smooth as mine. "It's way up there. I was hoping you could—"

We are interrupted by cries from the bedroom, and I hurry that way with Bitsy right behind me. "Will she let me check her?" I'm all business now, and whatever trepidations I had are gone. There's a job to be done, a puzzle to be solved. I can at least try. Thomas turns toward the kitchen, where the trio of cooks fusses around him, proffering coffee and coffee cake.

"She'd let the vet check her if it would rid her of this pain," Mrs. Potts observes. I wonder if she means Hester or she's just making a general observation. Maybe someone should call him. He did pretty well with the horse.

In the bedroom we discover the patient, a dead ringer for the cabaret singer Josephine Baker. She's on her hands and knees wearing a white nightshirt, and she looks at us with big tear-filled brown eyes.

Bitsy, who already sorted through my satchel a few days ago, opens the bag and hands me my sterilized rubber gloves while I sit on the side of the bed and place my hand on the woman's calf. I'm impressed with my new assistant, who doesn't hesitate but gets out her own new gloves too, the ones Mrs. MacIntosh bought her at Stenger's Pharmacy before she left Liberty.

Mrs. Potts makes the introductions. "Cassie," she says, "this is another midwife, Patience Murphy, and her assistant, Bitsy. She's going to check you inside, real gentle, and see how we can get this child out."

I wonder if the older midwife realizes that according to the midwifery statute of West Virginia we are now breaking the law, but I have to admit she's clever, the way she says "*how* we can get this child out," not "*if* we can get this child out." She also legitimizes Bitsy by calling her my assistant, not my helper or maid. I'm surprised to hear that she even knows my last name.

"Here, honey, roll over so Miss Patience can feel."

Cassie moans but does what we ask of her. I indicate that Bitsy should pour oil on my gloved fingers, and when I lift up the patient's gown, I am stunned.

Arm Presentation

Though I wouldn't have come all this way through an ice storm if I hadn't been prepared for the complication, the sight of an infant's arm sticking out of a woman's vagina is something you don't want to see. I meet Bitsy's brown eyes and note that she shows no shock, a good trait for a midwife. (You never want to alarm a patient.) You'd think she sees this all the time.

"Can you open your legs a little wider, Cassie?" I ask. "Squeeze Bitsy's fingers, and if you feel like yelling, try panting like a dog . . . pant, pant, pant . . . don't push. I'm going to grease my fingers and go all the way in and find the baby's head. Heart rate?" I turn to the older midwife for confirmation that this baby still lives.

Mrs. Potts pulls a metal stethoscope, a fancy one like Dr. Blum's, out of her deep apron pocket. "There was a heartbeat a few minutes ago." She listens intently and then nods. "Right lively," she tells me.

"Good. Ready, Cassie?"

Cassie screws up her face and nods, but her eyes are on Mrs. Potts. Bitsy pours some more olive oil on my glove and, following the limb up to the shoulder, I use my other hand, on the mother's abdomen, to find the head. It's a tight fit, but if I could get the arm back inside, I might be able to get the head down into the pelvis. I remove my fingers and think how to do this.

"Don't push, Cassie. Don't let her push, Bitsy. I'm going to go all the way in and try to reinsert the arm, then bring down the head." I don't mention that the one time I tried something similar was with a horse and I was bringing a hoof out, not putting it in.

"Mrs. Potts, can we get her bottom up in the air? I need her buttocks to be higher than her chest, upside down almost. Some pillows?"

Despite her apparent fragility, the old lady has quite a voice, and she whips into action. "Samantha, Mildred, Emma!" she calls as if with a bullhorn. "We need every pillow from the bedrooms upstairs, and I mean now."

I have no idea which of the three ladies lives in this well-appointed log home, but within two minutes the room fills with feather pillows. I wince, seeing the lace-trimmed pillow slips. They won't look so nice with blood on them. "Bitsy, get rid of those nice covers. Can we get some towels too?"

My helpers assist me to build a pile of pillows about two feet high, which we cover with towels. I then have Emma and Mildred lift Cassie's bottom up on the cushioned platform. It sinks down, of course, but I've still achieved my objective. As the patient's buttocks go up, the baby recedes and only the wrist and hand stick out. When we see the fingers move, everyone cheers and the mother smiles for the first time.

"Mrs. Potts," I address the elderly midwife, "I'm going to flex the arm at the elbow and push the hand in. Then I'm going to push up on the shoulder. When I tell you, can you guide the head down? Maybe one of these ladies can help if you get tired."

The old lady rolls up her sleeves. "Here, Mildred." She takes one of the tall woman's hands and places it under her own arthritic fingers exactly where I want it. This birth is becoming a real community event.

"Everyone ready? Cassie, don't push! Don't push until we get the head in the birth canal and get rid of the pillows. Mrs. Potts will tell you when it's time. Once you begin to push, don't stop for anything."

I think of the cord, the possibility that it's wrapped around the baby's neck. Except for the arm hanging out, this is so much like Delfina Cabrini's birth at the King Coal camp. The woman called Samantha begins to sing in a low voice, *"Joshua fit the battle of Jericho, Jericho, Jericho."* A fighting song!

"Joshua fit the battle of Jericho and the walls came tumbling down." The other ladies join in, even Bitsy, everyone but Mrs. Potts and me. I'm way too busy worming my way up the birth canal.

This time, because of the tilt, the shoulder is much higher and I'm almost up to my elbow when I begin to nudge it to the left with two fingers. Mrs. Potts senses what I'm doing and begins, at the same time, to slowly guide the head down on the right. It helps that the patient has had several babies; I have room to work in.

Cassie is getting more and more uncomfortable, and Bitsy tells her to pant. The laboring woman's eyes are so big I think they might pop, but she doesn't cry out. She just pants like Bitsy instructs her and I wonder how my new assistant knows how to do this; she's only seen one birth, Katherine MacIntosh's.

By the placement of Mrs. Potts's and Mildred's hands, I can tell that the head's coming down nearer and nearer to the brim of the pelvis. To make room, I slowly slip my hand out, and the head follows easily into the space.

"Okay, push now, honey," Grace Potts commands. "Push with all your heart!"

The aunties whip the pillows away and help the mother sit up in bed just as the head with long black curls crowns at the opening.

"Sweet Jesus! I'm gonna faint," the shorter of the trio exclaims and feels for a chair as the baby shoots out, dragging an afterbirth that looks like a two-pound calf liver. The cord is only eight inches long! Quick as a wink Mrs. Potts ties it off and hands the baby to Mildred, who wraps the tiny crying girl in a clean towel.

"Praise Jesus!" "Thank the Lord!" everyone exclaims.

Another healthy baby. If I believed in God, I would bow down . . .

Hemorrhage

The blood that follows within minutes is the real emergency—as if an arm presenting weren't bad enough. I start massaging the womb, talking to it as if it could hear. "No, you don't. You stop bleeding! Stop it right now!"

"Get your fist back in there," Mrs. Potts orders. I know what she means, but I've never done it before. It's called, by DeLee, bimanual compression. There's a picture of the procedure in my obstetrics textbook. "Use your other hand on the outside. Fold the floppy uterus over your fist and hold on tight." The older midwife spits out her instructions as she fumbles behind her for a small brown bottle on the dresser. "Drink this," Mrs. Potts commands. Bitsy holds the flask to Cassie's lips.

Potts is in total control now and the blood is slowing, so I try to remove my hand.

"Not yet," she directs.

I go back in and hold on when I see the hemorrhage start up again.

"Vinegar," Potts demands, and the shortest of the three ladies trots to the kitchen, returning with a small ceramic jug. The midwife pours the pungent liquid over one of my sterilized rags and hands it to me.

"Clean her uterus out. There must be clots. The vinegar will help stop the hemorrhage while the blue cohosh and shepherd's purse tincture that we gave her takes effect. Any time a woman has pain with no progress, be ready for this. If the bleeding doesn't stop pretty quick, we'll try ice."

At the sight of so much blood, the three musketeers, Mildred, Samantha, and Emma, have backed out the door with the baby. Bitsy takes Cassie's hand, softly singing *"Joshua fit the battle of Jericho . . . Jericho . . ."* into her ear to keep her calm.

"Ice?"

"Ice in the uterus will cause the blood to contract." I think she means blood vessels, but I don't ask. I've read about surgeons using ice to stop a hemorrhage during a cesarean section, but it always seemed to me it would cause such shock that a woman would die of chill instead of blood loss.

Mrs. Potts takes Cassie's wrist while she stares at her gold wristwatch, the kind nurses have, and her lips move as she counts the patient's pulse. "You are such a good girl, Cassie. We'll have you fixed up in a minute.

"Go, ahead, bring the rag out and all the thickened blood you can find," the elderly lady instructs me. When I do what she says, I find myself holding a handful of clots the size of chicken gizzards. Mrs. Potts then takes over and from the outside squeezes the uterus like she's wringing out a dishrag. More clots plop out, and I wipe them up.

"All right, then!" the old midwife calls. She takes a big breath and kisses her patient on the top of her head. "You can stop rubbing now. Bitsy, check every few minutes and make sure the womb stays firm." My assistant—I think of her that way already—knows what to do from Katherine's birth. Tears are streaming down both sides of Cassie's face. "Let's give the mama her baby and get it on the teat. That will help them both feel better."

Still shaking as I wash up at the kitchen sink, I take a big breath. Bitsy cleans up the bedroom, and Mrs. Potts dresses the infant's cord. Outside, the sky lifts the pink hem of its nightdress along the eastern edge.

"Here, honey." Mildred, who turns out to be the baby's granny and the mistress of the house, hands me one of her clean housedresses to wear over my top. She points down the hall. "You can change in my bedroom."

"Mr. Miller! Reverend Miller! All clear!" She calls out the back door to her husband and the menfolk hiding in the barn. "Come on in. Food's on the table!"

By the time I've tidied up, the three cooks are harmonizing in the kitchen. *"There's a rainbow 'round my shoulder and a sky of blue above."* A catchy Al Jolson song. The older midwife pads down the hall, smiling, and shocks me when she does a little boogie at the kitchen door. In the parlor she sits down to reorganize her birth kit, so Bitsy and I sit down beside her.

"I try to keep everything fresh," she tells us, giving instructions as if she's talking to herself. "You never know when you might be called again . . . not that I go out as often as I used to." Her little brown eyes sparkle at Bitsy, then at me, and I wonder which of us she's training. "Do you need some of my bleeding medicine? I have an extra bottle." She holds a glass vessel out and I take it, grateful for the gift.

"What's in it, again? Is it something I could make myself, or is it private?" In the Appalachian Mountains cooks jealously guard their recipes for black velvet cake, potato salad, fried chicken, and sticky buns. It might be the same with medicinal tonics.

"Don't be foolish. If it could help save a mother's life, of course I'd want you to have it." She proceeds to write down, on a torn piece of wrapping paper, the herbs she uses and how to prepare them as Mildred pokes her head into the hall.

"Come on, Auntie Potts! You're first

to eat and then Patience." I smile at their thoughtfulness and am a little surprised when I enter the kitchen. In this household, at least after the hard work of birthing, the women eat first. Three black men stand back, leaning against the wall or the counter, eyeing the food. There's Thomas, our escort; Darwin Washington, the father of the new baby; and an older gentleman I take to be the reverend. Then there's the women bustling around, a sea of black and brown faces, with mine as white as the full moon in October. I note that no children are present and decide that in this tight-knit community, there would be plenty of willing attendants down the road.

As if she lives here, Bitsy steps up to the table and begins to serve collards and mashed potatoes, along with meat sandwiches on homemade white bread. Mildred takes a breakfast tray into the bedroom for Cassie and Darwin.

"They give her a name yet?" Thomas asks when Mrs. Miller returns.

"Couldn't be more fitting." The grandma laughs, glancing out the window toward the crystalline trees. "An old-timey West Virginia name." Everyone stops chewing and waits. "Icey."

"Good-bye." "God bless." "Thank you so much, girls!" We are standing on the porch staring out at the glitter that covers every twig and branch. The holly bush by the Millers' front door is sheathed in ice. Even the power lines that come up the drive droop low and are hung with icicles. Reverend Miller, the grandfather of the infant, stands and stares across the yard. "We don't have much," he says, shaking hands with me, "but what we have is yours. Please call on us for anything."

I cannot help comparing this joyful scene with the Cabrinis' isolation in the coal camp or the MacIntoshes' seclusion in their brick mansion. The feeling in this happy home gives rise to thoughts of my time in Pittsburgh with the suffragettes, radicals, and union organizers of both colors, and a shadow passes over me. Gone are those days, and they can never come back. I must stay here, on the edge of the world . . .

When the sun rises over the mountain, we are blinded by light. *"Morning has broken,"* I sing the old song. *"Like the first morning . . . Blackbirds have spoken . . . like the first bird."*

November 28, 1929. Quarter moon waning.

Arm presentation delivered with Mrs. Potts, colored midwife of Hazel Patch. Female infant. Icey Washington. Second baby of Cassie and Darwin Washington. I had to go inside and push the arm back and out of the way while Mrs. Potts held the head down. No vaginal tears. After the birth, the arm was very swollen and blue but seemed to bend without making the baby cry. I was proud of myself for figuring out what to do, but then there was heavy bleeding. Mrs. Potts showed me how to do womb compression, which I had read about, and she gave me her recipe for an herbal tincture. Weight

6 pounds, 15 ounces. Present, Mrs. Potts, Bitsy, who was a great help, and all the Miller women and the other ladies, whose full names missed me.

Afterward I explained everything to Bitsy, just like Mrs. Kelly once taught me. How you have to watch women who've had more than five babies for malpresentation and hemorrhage. Their womb is so stretched that a baby can flop around any old which way in there and it doesn't clamp down well afterward. Bitsy paid attention as if someone's life might depend upon that knowledge . . . which it someday might.

Payment, one fine ham and a sunrise.

Winter

10

Solitude

"I don't think I should go!" Bitsy worries as I step out of my high boots after feeding Moonlight. She has just taken a bath in the washtub in the middle of the kitchen, and her body, wrapped up in a sheet, steams when the cold air hits the room.

"Of course you should! The arrangement's been made, and the MacIntoshes are counting on you. Besides, you'll have time to spend with your mother. I'm sure she misses you. Katherine and the baby too." I take my chair and reach for my plate of corn bread and baked beans, salted with the last of the Millers' ham.

"But I worry about you all alone way out here, Miss Patience."

This really irks me. *"Miss Bitsy,"* I spit out, "I've told you before to drop the 'Miss Patience.' You're not my servant. Anyway, I got along last winter alone and I can do it again for a few weeks this year. You'll go and have a good time while Mr. MacIntosh pays you."

This part I wonder about, since he's never had the money to pay *me*.

"He promised he'd give you five dollars for helping Mary over the holidays," I continue my argument. "Five bucks would go a long way this winter. Maybe you can even bring home some more coal and tea. Maybe some sugar and flour. That's cash money, and you know we need it."

"But it's *Christmas*. You shouldn't be alone."

"Really, it doesn't bother me. I don't believe in all that." I know this hurts Bitsy. We've talked religion a few times, how I grew up Presbyterian but lost my faith a long time ago. She grew up in the A.M.E. church, African Methodist Episcopalian, and hates to hear me talking like a sinner.

The discussion is cut short by the sound of an automobile laboring through the mud on Wild Rose Road, and Bitsy runs upstairs to get ready. Mr. MacIntosh is here, right on time, and after he wipes his feet, he takes a seat on the edge of the sofa. He takes a deep breath and looks around curiously.

"How are Katherine and the baby?" I ask to fill the silence.

"Good. Great." He strokes his sandy mustache. Must have been a real looker when he was young, as handsome as Katherine is beautiful, but worry now alters his face. "Her mother and sisters are coming up on the train from Baltimore for the holidays. Bitsy will be a big help." Despite their new poverty, the MacIntoshes will put on a big show for their relatives. Upstairs Bitsy clumps around, packing her few belongings.

"Radio out of Wheeling says a massive storm's coming," William says, changing the subject. "Big snow from the southwest. They're always the worst, the ones from the south. You better get some more wood in." It's the second time recently that some fellow has felt the need to advise me about basic survival.

I glance toward the window. The shadows of low gray clouds skim over the mountains. He could be right, but the ground's still bare and the sun shines intermittently. In five minutes, Bitsy is dressed in a full-length navy coat, a hand-me-down from Katherine MacIntosh, and standing on the porch with tears in her eyes. I hold out her Christmas present, a pair of green mittens that I knit for her, and she hugs me so tight I lose my breath. It's the first physical sign of affection she has shown, and I find myself grinning. Except by a few of my mothers, I don't get hugged often.

"Really, Bitsy, I'll be okay."

Then the sound of the auto fades as it takes the bend on Raccoon Lick and I'm alone. Still no snow, but the air is colder and the pale dove sky has turned slate. "Alone," I say out loud as I smile, then tidy the kitchen, bring in more wood, and get out my yarn to begin knitting a pair of brown mittens for Thomas.

While I work, I keep an eye on the clouds.

December 18, 1929. Rising moon, half full.

Called to another birth, not four hours after Bitsy left with William MacIntosh.

Female infant, Dora, 6 pounds, 9 ounces, born to Minnie Boggs, only 14 years old. She surprised me by delivering quickly. Labor eight hours. I only made it for the last hour. Small tear, no repair. Blood loss minimal.

Minnie wanted to get up and bathe right away, but I said no. Not for one week. Her granny and mother agreed with me, but I doubt she will do what I say. Her husband, Calvin Boggs, ten years her senior at 24, has no control over her either. I found myself missing Bitsy. She would

have been a comfort going out after dark, but she's at the Ma- cIntoshes' helping Big Mary with Christmas.

Mercy

I pull up a chair, balance my cup of peppermint tea on the windowpane, and stare out at the gray day. Spend- ing a few hours with fourteen-year-old Minnie reminds me of my year at the House of Mercy in Chicago. Gray. That was the color of everything, or that's how I remember it. Gray walls. Gray uniforms. Gray gruel for breakfast. Gray sheets.

The girls in my dormitory were a mixed lot and, despite their poverty, were nearly as spunky as Minnie. Most were children of immigrants, Polish, Italian, Russian, Irish, new to the coun- try and struggling with English. When their parents died of consumption, cholera, or an industrial accident and they had no family in this new land, there was nowhere else for them to go.

Some were thieves, pickpockets, or child streetwalkers. Some were disabled, defective, and unwanted. A few still had one parent who visited.

Those were the saddest. Their widowed mother or father, working twelve hours a day in a sweatshop or tannery, still couldn't afford to keep them at home, like the redheaded sisters from Ireland, nine and seven, who cried when their mother came on Sunday and then cried again when she left.

I'd been doted on, growing up in Deerfield, so I nearly drowned at first in that sea of despair, but I quickly learned to swim and those two years in the House of Mercy changed my life. Living with the poor, the lonely, and the discarded embroidered them into my heart.

To survive I made myself useful and ingratiated myself with the nuns by singing the youngest girls to sleep and reading to the older ones. I sang hymns: "Rock of Ages," "Will the Circle Be Unbroken?," "Come to the Savior Now." I sang popular tunes: "After the Ball Was

Over," "Ta-ra-ra Boom-de-ay" . . . anything I could think of.

None of the girls had been to school. The sisters gave me a worn copy of *The Fairy Tales of Hans Christian Andersen,* and I read to them at bedtime and on rainy days: "Thumbelina," "The Little Mermaid," "The Emperor's New Clothes." Even the girls who didn't understand English were soothed by my voice. "The Princess and the Pea" was their favorite.

By day I was a laundress, like my mother had been, in the institution's basement. We used newspapers to bundle the sheets, and one morning, at the bottom of page 10 in the *Chicago Tribune,* just under an advertisement for SEARS MODERN HOMES, ARRIVES BY TRAIN, WITH INSTRUCTIONS AND ALL MATERIALS, was an announcement of tryouts for the chorus line at the Majestic Theatre.

I was well spoken, could sing, and wasn't unpleasant to look at, so, determined to audition, I waited until dark, then slipped out the side door with my few belongings and the sisters' worn copy of Hans Christian Andersen. It was the first thing I ever pinched but sadly not the last. Under the cover of darkness, I arrived at Mrs. Ayers's boardinghouse, the last place I'd lived after my mother's demise.

"Child!" she exclaimed. "What's happened?" She was wearing a rose silk dressing gown with her hair loose, flowing down her back like black rain. I'd never seen her that way before. Having a man had changed her.

"I know I'm not your responsibility," I began, "but I beg of you this one kind favor." I'd read a line like that in the sisters' storybook. "Lend me your best dress for three hours tomorrow." She took me in with open arms, making sure I understood that it was only for the night, and put me to bed in my old room.

In the morning, Mrs. Ayers, now Mrs. Swartz, pulled a cream ruffled tea dress with lace panels on the sleeves out of a round-topped wooden trunk. It was the dress she had married Mr. Swartz in. We took in the waist with basting thread and her new husband, a kind soul, hired a horse-drawn cab to take me to the Majestic at three.

When the driver left me off on Monroe, I pinched my cheeks to give them more color, stared up at the ornate Art Deco–inspired hotel, the tallest building in Chicago, and tried to pretend I was used to such places. I told the man with the tooth missing who stood out in front that I was there for the audition, then found myself a seat in the third row.

A heavily made-up redhead in a low-cut green satin gown was on stage belting out "Sweet Adeline," and I was glad to have a chance to look around. The colors of the theater were rich and dramatic, with dark gleaming wood, red plush velvet, and silver accents. Box seats rose to the ceiling. I was so enchanted that I didn't hear the gentleman with the clipboard call my name.

"Elizabeth? Elizabeth Snyder!" That was before I took on my alias.

"Oh, me, sir!" (No one I knew ever called me Elizabeth. I'd always been

"Lizbeth" to my family. That's my heart's name.)

"Sheet music?"

I felt silly. "I don't have any. I'm doing my mother's favorite song, 'Oh Promise Me.' The man with the missing tooth rolled his eyes but perked up when I sang without accompaniment, in my clear alto, *"Oh, promise me that some-day you and I will take our love together to some sky."*

I never went back to the House of Mercy, not even to visit, and I felt bad about that, about not saying good-bye to the girls, especially the little ones, but I'd left without permission, stolen their storybook, and lied about my age to get the job at the Majestic. If I returned, they might try to keep me.

11

The Majestic

It was at the Majestic in '09 that I met my first love, Lawrence Clayton, an artist, scene designer, and student at the Art Institute of Chicago. During rehearsals, I'd stare at his hands as he painted the canvas sets, watch his delicate strokes. Eventually he asked to walk me home. We took the long way.

Soon it was a regular arrangement. We'd stroll along the boardwalk and throw bread to the pigeons in Washington Park. It didn't matter what we did, we were so happy just being together.

I guess I was reckless, but that's the way of young lovers, isn't it? I missed one period and then another few. Since I'd never been regular, I wasn't concerned; in fact, I didn't know I was pregnant until Cassandra, my roommate, another chorus girl, asked me when I'd last had my monthly.

It seems strange now that I couldn't tell I was carrying, never even thought of it, but my mother had died before my first flow and no one had ever discussed the birds and the bees with me.

When I finally told Lawrence about my pregnancy, he was thrilled but apprehensive. His mother, an Episcopal minister's daughter, and his father, a professor of history at the University of Iowa, were sure to disapprove. The money for his education came from a small stipend his grandmother had left him, and he depended on his parents for his room and board, but he had little cash. That's why he worked part-time as a scene designer.

Finally we could wait no longer. We wanted to marry, and he had to inform his family. (It was easier for me. I had no one to explain things to, no one to judge me.) My beloved was on his way home to ask for their blessing when he was killed in that train wreck at Western Springs. I read about it in the *Tribune* over soft-boiled eggs and rye toast. The front-page article listed the sixteen dead, *Lawrence Frederick Clayton* near the top. I traced his name with one finger and then collapsed like a tree cut off at the base. Lawrence was gone, his mouth that had kissed me, his hands that had touched me, his mind that had loved me.

It was shock that brought on my labor, I'm sure of it, and then the bleeding and the terrible pain. The baby was too early; not that it would have mattered, even a full-term infant couldn't have survived that kind of blood loss.

The professor and his grief-stricken wife never learned about me or their son's child. If the baby had lived, maybe I would have searched for them, but when the blood poured out of my womb, erupted like a flash flood on the Des Plaines River, I knew all was lost.

Milkmaid

"I *can't* bring your baby to you, because your baby is dead."

I wake in the little house on Wild Rose Road with tears wetting my pillow. That's what the matron at Chicago Lying-in Dispensary told me. That's what she said. *"I can't bring your baby to you, because your baby is dead."* The chatter of the other women in the small hospital ward turned off like a spigot.

"Dead?" I feel myself shoot down a long dark cold tunnel. This was the baby I'd made with Lawrence, my lover who had died not one week before.

"Smelling salts!" the nurse yells.

When I come out of my faint, a cool cloth mats down my long hair and the nurse leans over me. *Is she telling the truth?* All I can remember is blood running out of me and the night ride in the horse-drawn ambulance down the brick streets.

But why would she lie? If she wants

a baby, infants born out of wedlock are a dime a dozen. I should know. I had lived in the House of Mercy, just one of the scores of foundling and orphan asylums in Chicago.

The nurse scrapes a chair across the wooden floor and sits down beside me, but she isn't interested in easing my grief. She's a hawk eyeing her prey. I am just sixteen.

"Elizabeth, if you'll join the staff as a wet nurse," she puts on the pressure, "you won't have to go to an orphanage or back on the streets. You'll be given a bed in the room with the other wet nurses, and you'll have plenty of food. We only take healthy and well-spoken young women. It's a respectable pro- fession . . . *and,*" she threatens, "if you don't get the milk out, your breasts will crack and fester."

My eyes fill. I had planned to breast- feed, as my poor deceased mother did and all sensible women do, but I have no baby to suckle, and let's face it, no home or livelihood either. My friends from the Majestic don't know where I am or what's happened to me. After Lawrence died, I never went back to the theater . . . just couldn't walk in there all pregnant and weeping.

Now here I am alone with milk dripping down my front and an offer of good food and shelter. It seems the easiest way. I put my hands on my breasts, already as hard as doorknobs. I thought there were no tears left, but the well of sorrow never runs dry.

There were three of us then, Wilma, Nola, and I. Wilma was twenty and had been a wet nurse the longest. When her milk dried up, to get more, she went out and got pregnant again, *on purpose.* After the birth, Dr. Shane took her unwanted baby home to his wife, who couldn't have one.

The other wet nurse—she came after me—was Nola. The nurses found her on the steps of the hospital, shivering in the cold, breast milk frozen on her thin cloak, and the matron took her in eagerly. She'd delivered at home with a midwife, but her pa had taken her

baby because Nola was only thirteen.
Then he'd sold it.

When we weren't needed for suck-
ling, the three of us were assigned to
housekeeping; none of the dirty jobs
like emptying bedpans, just dusting
and mopping, and we weren't allowed
in the rooms when patients had fevers
either. That's why we called each other
milk*maids,* because of our cleaning duties.

I wasn't bitter. We laughed when we
said it: *Milkmaid* . . . "Milkmaid" sounded
nicer than "wet nurse."

12

Advent

Tick-tock, tick-tock . . . with Bitsy gone, my only company is my dogs, Emma and Sasha; my calico cat, Buster; and Mrs. Kelly's ornate black-and-gold mantel clock. Still no change in the weather, but on a trip to the barn the air smells like snow, a clean winter smell.

When Mrs. Kelly and I first moved here, I felt I'd been dropped into a foreign land, Greenland or maybe Madagascar; everything was so strange. I'd been cut adrift. And I was scared too. For the past twenty years I'd lived in the city. I was scared of snakes and bears and skunks. Scared of hoot owls and night noises. Scared of the dark and the huge sky, so lonely without humans around. It wasn't so strange for Sophie; she'd grown up in Torrington, just forty miles away, had gone to nursing school there before moving to Pittsburgh, and had spent summers on the farm with her grandparents.

It was hard at first to get used to no indoor plumbing, electricity, or access to a telephone, but over the last few years I've adapted. The lack of machine noises soothes me. The yellow kerosene lamplight is restful. Even the outhouse isn't so bad. It gets you outside, and there's always something to see. Today four mallards came in from the north and landed in the yard. I ran inside to get cornmeal, but when I came back they were gone, heading south.

Around ten, just before bed when I go outside to be sure the barn is secure, I notice that a wind has come up, but still no snow. I lift my head, scanning the sky, as my father, the sailor, would do. Clouds scuttle past the moon, moving fast, blotting out stars. Later, when I get up to use the porcelain potty that I keep, on cold nights, behind the bedroom door, I stop at the window. A few lazy flakes float down like torn paper. "There's the big storm MacIntosh warned me about!" I think.

The next time I stir, it's morning and my bedroom is filled with a strange white light. Outside, every bush and tree, every limb and twig is laced with snow, a fairy wonderland. I throw on my robe and run downstairs to build up the fire. There's eight inches of powder on the fence rail, and the flakes are still falling.

"Snow for Christmas! Sasha and Emma!" I exclaim, dancing around and rousing them into a frenzy. I dress quickly, pull on my boots, and go out to feed Moonlight, then take the dogs for a walk up the back hill to cut a small pine tree. I even fall backward in the snow, creating snow angels.

Last Christmas I didn't have a tree, didn't celebrate at all. Mrs. Kelly was dead. Ruben was dead. Nothing to celebrate, really. It was bitter cold, and the frozen ground was as bleak as my soul.

Now back in the house, I prop my small pine in a bucket of spring water and craft paper chains from colorful ads in the *Ladies' Home Journal*s I found in the attic. For icicles, I cut foot-long pieces of thick white yarn, and, since I don't have a star, I attach one of Mrs. Kelly's wooden angels at the top. My project takes most of the day.

"Don't you think the tree looks nice?" I ask Emma and Sasha as they sprawl on the braided rug next to the heater stove. They tilt their heads back, considering; then Emma stands up and licks my hand. Buster, my calico, snoozing on the back of the davenport, is unimpressed.

Last winter, I cried all the time, cried because I missed Mrs. Kelly and Ruben, cried for Lawrence and my mother and father and all the others long gone to me. The tears could have filled a washtub. Even the pregnant women stopped coming around, not that I was in any shape to help them.

The rest of the season was a long hibernation, but in spring I woke up. Sally Feder, who'd given birth to twins with Mrs. Kelly when we first moved here, was pregnant again and asked me to help her. Sally was a big, calm woman with nice hips and utter sureness in her body, so I picked up my bruised heart, stuffed it back into my chest, and went back to work as a midwife.

Calamity

William MacIntosh was right. For three days it snows, a real blizzard, and the only time I step outside is to milk Moonlight. Then at noon today the sun comes out and, like the Count of Monte Cristo, I'm released from the dungeon, given back my life.

"Let's go sledding, dogs!" I dress hurriedly, pull on my boots, coat, scarf, and mittens. In the barn I find a sheet of old corrugated tin and struggle through two feet of powder up the back hill.

"Hi-ho, world!" I shout. "I'm raised from the dead!" I shout some more. "Hi-ho. Hi-ho!" There's an echo, and I'm just happy to hear a human voice, even if it is my own. "Hi-hooohhhh! Hi-hooohhhh!" Over and over again. The dogs leap up on me and then wallow in the deep white.

The first trip down the slope is awfully slow as I pack the run.

The next jaunt is better.

The third ride is really fun. I stand grinning at the top of the rise, panting from the exertion, my cheeks flushed, my nose running, my knit tam half off.

The fourth excursion is slick as slime.

On the fifth trip I rip my left calf open on the corner of the rusted metal.

"Damn!" I say to the dogs, not yet aware of what's happened, thinking at first that I've only torn my thick wool trousers. Then the blood comes and finally the pain.

"Damn! Damn! Damn!" I curse some more, and the swearing seems to help.

"Oh, Emma, look what I've done!"

Emma bounds over and licks my hand, then noses the blood, but I shoo her away. The barn is an eighth of a mile away, and beyond that is the house. Already I'm chilling and my damp clothes begin to freeze. If I could find a stick for a crutch it would help, but I'm out in a field without trees or bushes. I try first to move my knee, and though the pain brings tears to my eyes and I swear like a sailor, it still bends.

For the next hour I scoot, hobble, and limp toward the house. The dogs follow, and when I look back, they are licking at a trail of red in the pure white snow.

" 'Twas the night before Christmas and all through the house" . . . blood and tears. The gash on my leg is as long as my thumb, with a flap of skin a quarter inch deep. A tight pressure bandage, made from a dish towel, stops the bleeding, and I consider sewing myself back together with the suture from my birth kit. But my satchel is upstairs and anyway, I don't have the courage to stick a needle though my own flesh.

Since the sides of the wound come together, I pour a little soap and water into the tear, rinse it out, place a goldenseal compress across it to help prevent infection, and tie on a new bandage, hoping it will heal. Eventually I make myself a splint and hobble into the pantry to find some Bayer Aspirin. The bottle says to take two, but I take three, hoping it won't kill me.

It is never fun to spend Christmas alone, despite what I told Bitsy, even if you're a nonbeliever. Last year, the holiday passed in a fog. This year I have a tree, but with my injury I'm in no mood to celebrate.

I light the kerosene lamps, build up the fire, and, after I hobble out to feed the cow and chickens, lie back on the couch. The little pine in the corner looks so forlorn, all decked out like a streetwalker with nowhere to go. Emma and Sasha stare at me with big eyes. "Okay, guys, we can at least sing." My mother's old hymnal is in on the bookshelf with her Bible, just within reach.

"Any requests for your favorite carol?" I ask Emma. Sasha raises his eyebrows, but neither makes a comment. "Okay, then, we'll sing them all."

"O, come, all ye faithful," I begin, *"joyful and triumphant."* I'm not very joyful; in fact, I almost choke on my tears, remembering times my family stood around the piano, my mother playing and my father singing in his bright baritone with his head thrown back. *"O, come ye, o, come ye to Bethle-hem!"* He wasn't a gambler yet or much of a drinker. That came later.

Then there was the year with Lawrence when we strolled along the Lake Michigan docks on Christmas Eve caroling to anyone who would listen. *"Come and behold Him, born the king of angels . . ."*

Even in Pittsburgh, in the good years, when Mrs. Kelly and Nora and I lived together and half our friends were Jewish or agnostics, we sang the old carols, celebrating not so much the birth of Jesus as our collective hope for light in a dark world.

"It's a pagan festival!" Ruben would

laugh, but he knew all the words and sang louder than the lapsed Christians.

I swipe my tears with the back of my hand and determinedly sing on. *"The first Noel the angels did say was to certain poor shepherds in fields where they lay."* I sing louder and louder, banishing the memories, one song after another banishing the ghosts of Christmas past. *"It came upon a midnight clear."*

The dogs howl with me, both of them now standing next to the sofa, their snouts pointing up like wolves. *"Whooooo! Whoooo!"* I wail with them, egging them on. Buster escapes up the stairs, his hair standing on end. *"O, come, all ye faithful!"*

I'm singing so loud, I don't hear the sound of a car whining up the hill. I don't hear the footfalls in the snowy path to the house. I don't hear the first soft knock on the door.

13

Visitor

I'm in the middle of *"Star of wonder, star of night"* when the beagles start growling and run for the door. Someone knocks again, louder. My face goes hot and my stomach cold.

I have nothing on but my long johns with one leg rolled up above my knee, my camisole, and Nora's old red silk kimono. On my feet are wool socks with holes in the toes. I can't imagine who would make a social call on Christmas Eve. Maybe it's the traditional stranger you read about and I must let him in and give him dinner or it will be bad luck all next year. Realistically, I know it must be about some woman in labor.

"Who's there?" I wrap my kimono closer and pull my long underwear down over my cut.

"It's Daniel Hester. I saw your lights."

The vet? Possibly he's passing this way after tending a sick horse, but the intersection with Raccoon Lick and Wild Rose is a half mile away. I crack the door and find him standing on the porch with a bottle of booze swinging in his hand, totally illegal.

"Where'd you get that?" I ask, indicating the glass container with a nod. "You could get arrested for violating Prohibition." He's wearing a dark brown trench coat with his brown felt hat pulled low on his head and already smells like booze, but his stance is steady, and without asking he steps out of his rubber boots and walks in. "The music sounds great. You have a nice voice, and the beagles do too!" He smiles at his little joke and flashes his strong white teeth. ("All the better to eat you with, little Red Riding Hood," comes to me.)

"Were you really making a sick call on Christmas Eve?"

"No, just lonely," he says without embarrassment, looking round the room.

"What about your wife?"

"My wife?"

"The lady at the window . . . in your kitchen."

"Nah, no wife. She's my part-time housekeeper."

"So you thought *I* might want some company?"

Hester ignores my question. "I like your Christmas tree. Reminds me of when I was a kid. We made those colored paper chains in my one-room schoolhouse in upper New York State. Got colder than hell up there. Sometimes forty below. Coldest I've seen, since I moved south, is thirty below. What happened to your leg?"

I look down at my lower limb and notice the blood seeping through my long johns. Not a pretty sight.

"What happened?" he asks again.

"Cut it on some corrugated metal this afternoon. It's okay." I don't mention the sledding. "I can get around. All

I need to do is get to the barn and back."

"Can I look?"

I feel like saying "Do you have to?" On the other hand, he *is* almost a doctor, and this is like getting a free house call.

"I guess . . . Will you make me pay with more veterinarian assistant jobs?" I think this is funny, but the vet is all business, leading me back to the sofa, sitting me down, picking up my ankle, gently removing my crude bandage.

When he gets down to the laceration, we both wince. It's an evil-looking wound, and the edges that I thought had come together are now peeling apart.

"I need to do something about this," Hester says as he stands up and puts his coat on. "My bag is in the Ford."

I contemplate arguing, but he's out the door.

When he returns, he goes into the kitchen, washes his hands, and sits down in the rocker. He reaches into his black doctor bag and pulls out one of his curved needles with suture, a glass syringe, and a vial of clear liquid.

"Is that numbing medicine?" I asked hopefully. If it isn't, I'd better find something to bite on, like in the old cowboy movies when the Doc gives Tom Mix a stick to grip between his teeth.

The vet looks at me. "You don't think I'd stitch you without topical anesthesia, do you?"

I shrug, thinking, Yeah, maybe; you didn't numb Moonlight!

Twenty minutes later, my cut is cleansed, dusted with some kind of antiseptic powder, stitched back together with black thread that makes my leg look like one of Frankenstein's limbs, and bandaged with a clean white surgical dressing.

The vet gives me a packet of the white powder from his bag. "In three days, remove the gauze and start dusting your wound with this on a daily basis. It might help prevent infection. You have to be very careful in the barn. Don't get the wound dirty. You could get tetanus or lose your leg."

Is he kidding? The man has his back turned while putting his needle holder back in its case. Tetanus! I roll my eyes.

"You ever have a rum toddy? Holiday cheer?" Hester holds up his booze bottle.

My leg is throbbing, and I think that the alcohol might do me some good, but I remember what Katherine MacIntosh said about rumors. Did Mr. and Mrs. Maddock hear the vet's car come up the road?

I throw caution to the wind. "Okay."

The vet steps back on the porch and brings in a bottle of fresh milk. "A Christmas present," he says with a laugh. "If you didn't answer the door, I was going to leave it on the steps . . . Where's the sugar?"

I try to stand.

"Keep your leg up. I'll find it."

Through the kitchen door I watch him pour the milk into a pot and stir the coals in the cookstove. "What are your dogs' names?" he calls over his shoulder.

"Emma and Sasha."

"Like Emma Goldman? The anarchist?"

"Yes. How did you know that?"

"My grandmother was a Russian immigrant. Sasha was Emma's name for her lover, Alexander Berkman, wasn't it? My gram told me the story of the riot at Homestead in '92. How Sasha Berkman tried to assassinate Frick, Carnegie's henchman, *the dastardly opponent of the workers.*" He says this in a mocking tone, and I wonder whether he mocks himself for knowing this history, his grandmother for her tales, or the union men who struck Carnegie Steel and battled the private security guards in hand-to-hand combat. If he is mocking the unions, it pisses me off. The struggles of workers and labor unions have been dear to me for the last fifteen years.

A few minutes later he returns with two steaming mugs and his bottle of rum, which he sets on the floor near the sofa. I'm surprised and a little alarmed when he plunks down next to me, careful not to jiggle my leg.

"You know, the neighbors may have

seen you coming up the road. You can't stay long."

Hester grins. "I cut my headlights."

That makes me smile. "What made you so sure I'd let you in?"

He shrugs and looks away. "I wasn't sure. Thought I'd give it a try."

The warm milk and rum go down easy. It's the only alcohol I've had since the blackberry wine Mrs. Kelly made when we first moved here as grieving widows—but this is much stronger. One cup, I think, and this fellow will be on his way.

He swallows the sweet liquid, nods with appreciation, and goes back to his story. "My maternal grandmother was Russian and my grandfather Polish. When they first came to the United States, neither could speak English. They took classes at the settlement house in New York City. That's how they met.

"My grandparents on the other side were German farmers, here since the 1700s. I told you we had a farm in upper New York State? My parents met at

Cornell." He recounts all this as though I'd asked him for his pedigree.

Despite myself, I'm interested. "Did they both graduate from Cornell?"

"My father took a degree in agriculture, my mother in teaching. That was in the 1880s."

"My mother was a teacher too."

The vet picks up his bottle, reaches over, and, before I can say anything, pours another dollop into my mug, then pours a larger one into his own and knocks it back. Both the dogs stand with adoration at his knee, and he ruffles their fur. Even Buster has crept back downstairs. They must know he's an animal lover.

"Want to sing some more?" he asks, moving over to the piano. I could have guessed that with such hands he'd know how to play.

"I guess." I'm already feeling the effect of the rum.

For an hour we sing while the horse doctor bangs out the tunes. *"Angels from the realms of glory, wing your flight o'er all the earth . . ."*

"Good King Wenceslas looked out on the feast of Stephen . . ."

At first I just recline on the sofa like a good patient, but later I hobble over and sit on the end of the piano bench so I can see the words in the vesper book. We are careful not to touch, not even our shoulders. The man smells faintly of pine and fresh mowed hay. We have another drink.

"Okay, one more carol and you better go. Do you know this one?" I laugh. We are old friends now, thumbing through the hymnbook, singing in harmony.

" 'I Heard the Bells on Christmas Day.' It's one of my favorites. Longfellow wrote the words during the Civil War when he heard that his son had been wounded."

It's so nice to talk to someone who would appreciate that bit of trivia or even know who Longfellow was. I have two other acquaintances in Union County who would be familiar with the New England poet: the pharmacist's wife, Mrs. Stenger, and my nurse friend, Becky Myers, both college-educated women, but I haven't seen either of them for months, not since my trip to town in November. Katherine MacIntosh reads books too, but only romances. Bitsy reads well, but so far just my medical textbook. She won't put it down.

"I don't remember this one. Go through it once."

I sing the first verse while he plays the piano.

I heard the bells on Christmas Day
Their old familiar carols play
And wild and sweet
The words repeat
Of peace on Earth, goodwill toward
men.

Hester catches the tune and joins in on the second verse. It isn't until the third that his voice breaks.

And in despair I bowed my head.
There is no peace on Earth, I said.
For hate is strong
And mocks the song

Of peace on Earth, goodwill toward men.

He stops there with tears in his eyes and when he stands, he almost knocks the kerosene lamp over. The man sways and holds on to the piano, then plunks back down on the bench.

"I don't know what's gotten into me." He tries his half smile. "Those words, 'For hate is strong and mocks the song of peace on Earth'—for a minute I was back in the trenches with bullets flying over my head. I did things I'm not proud of, killed other men just to survive. They weren't *my* enemies; they were someone else's enemies.

"There was this one guy, a big German blond, he shot down my horse. This was at the Battle of Saint-Mihiel in 1918. I could have taken him prisoner, but I was so blind with rage, I bayoneted him three times. Blinded by fury . . . I think of it sometimes. He was a mother's son. There was no reason for it." He shuts his eyes tight and swings his head as if to banish the vision. "I'd better go." With one hand on the piano he lurches to his feet again.

"You'd better not!" I catch him in my arms to keep him from falling over. For a second we stare at each other, but it's only a blink.

"You're right. I'm in no shape to drive. Drink doesn't usually get to me." We both turn to the empty bottle of rum.

"You can sleep on the sofa. Just wrap up in the quilt." He flops down without argument.

What else am I going to do? I can't send him out on the snowy roads in this condition. He'd end up in a ditch.

"Here's a pillow." I hand him the green quilted one from the back of the rocker and notice I'm none too steady myself. It would amuse me if it weren't for the worry that my reputation could be ruined; a midwife is supposed to be of *good moral character.*

By the time I let the dogs out and get them back in, build up the fire, and blow out the lamp, Hester is snoring quietly. I dim the kerosene light and sit down in the rocker. *"Silent night, holy night,"* I sing softly, remembering what he told me about the bloody battles of the last Great War. *"Sleep in heavenly peace."*

In the morning when I limp down-stairs with a headache, the veterinarian is gone.

14

The Vanderhoffs

I'm surprised to say that I'm counting the days until Bitsy returns. Only a few months ago, when Mary asked me to give her daughter shelter, I had reservations. Only a few weeks ago, I almost packed her suitcase and shooed her out the door. Now Christmas has come and gone and New Year's Eve too, which I spent watching the snow fly like sparks through the light from the lantern on the porch. I'm not sure why I put the Coleman lamp out there and turned it up high. Was it a signal to the vet that I might want company?

Whatever it meant, he didn't come . . . and I ate my black-eyed peas and home-canned collard greens alone.

Alone, I think. I was alone when I worked at the Vanderhoffs' home too, though a different kind of alone. Alone surrounded by people.

After working at the Chicago Lying-in Dispensary as a milkmaid for more than a year, I was hired by the mother and father of one of our premature babies to return with them, as a private wet nurse, to their Lake Forest home. It seemed, at the time, like a good plan. The pay was better, I'd have my own room, and they promised to keep me as a baby nurse and nanny when my milk ran out.

Unfortunately, my life in the three-story brick home on Colonial Avenue wasn't as pleasant as I'd expected. The rest of the house staff, the cook and the upstairs maid, resented me. Every three hours I breastfed the baby, as Dr. Shane from Lying-in had ordered, and kept the nursery and my adjoining sitting room tidy, but other than that I had no duties at all. When I offered to help in the kitchen, the cook turned away and Beatrice Vanderhoff, the baby's mother, shooed me upstairs.

Breastfeeding the infant around the clock meant there was never a day off. What's more, the couple's first child had died of smallpox and the parents refused to let me take Baby Gerald out in the pram. Augustus Vanderhoff, a lawyer with a firm in downtown Chicago, a heavy man with a handlebar mustache and an annoying tic that made him look like he was winking, had an expansive library next to the parlor, and I was allowed to read his books. Other than that, until the weather warmed up, there was nothing to do.

For five months, I lived there, lonely and bored, before I grew daring enough to explore the house. One Sunday afternoon, when the maid and the cook were on their half-day and Mr. and Mrs. Vanderhoff had gone to a charity tea for Hull House, I took off my shoes and tiptoed upstairs to the third floor.

The first room I entered was an empty round turret with windows that looked out in every direction. I thought of asking if I could have it for my sitting area, but it was much too far from the nursery. The other three bedrooms were for guests, nothing much there but empty armoires, soft beds, and velvet-backed chairs.

Back on the second floor, I ended my investigation by peeking into my employers' bedchamber, which was dominated by a huge maple four-poster bed. I'd never seen such a bed, and I crept in and lay down on it, smoothing the deep rose coverlet under my hands. Little Gerald was still sleeping in his wicker bassinet down the hall, so I continued to poke around. It was the first time I'd had fun for almost a year.

Pushing open the door to the walk-in closet, I ran my fingers through a row of my mistress's gowns. Some of the dresses I'd never seen her wear, like the blue satin floor-length one with ruffles and the deep purple velvet with leg-of-mutton sleeves. The far end held the master's clothing, only four suits, all black, a few white shirts, and a mourning coat.

Returning to the main room, I sat down at the vanity. The smell of my mistress's perfume, Lily of the Valley, in a frosted glass atomizer, intrigued me, and I gave it a spray. In the mirror, a young woman, pale from no sunlight, her hair wound up tight in a chignon, her gold wire-rimmed spectacles perched on her nose, stared back. Momentarily, I was ashamed to see myself snooping . . . but only a little.

Careful not to disturb things too much, I lift the lid to the embossed silver jewelry box and one by one hold the lady's necklaces up, imagining I'm a rich debutante getting ready for a party. There's one ornament I particularly fancy, an emerald pendant on a thin silver chain. On the lower shelf of the velvet-lined box, I discover a gold ring with a solitary ruby. I slip it on and admire my hand. Then the kitchen doorbell rings.

Red alert! I jerk up, almost tipping over my stool, and look around wildly to see if there's any evidence of my trespassing. When I try to slip the ring back into the box, it's stuck on my finger.

The back doorbell rings again. I lick and pull, lick and pull, but the ring won't come off! It's probably only a deliveryman at the back door, but if I don't answer soon he'll wake the baby. All the way down the back stairs, I keep licking and twisting the ring on my finger, and just as I skid across the kitchen floor it slips off and I stuff it under my chemise. It wouldn't look right for a lowly wet nurse to be seen with a huge red ruby twinkling on her hand!

I'm surprised to discover, when I unlatch the back door, that the person ringing isn't a delivery boy. It's Mr. Vanderhoff.

Betrayal

I should have known right away that something was off, but I'm innocent that way, always have been.

"Hey, thanks, kid. Took you long enough. You the only one home?" Mr. Vanderhoff slurs. He smells like he's been swimming in gin. This was before the Eighteenth Amendment, and alcohol was still legal. "I lost my key." I stand back against the kitchen table. He's never called me anything but Miss Murphy before. "Mrs. Vanderhoff home yet?"

"No. No one's here but little Gerald and me. I thought you might be the coal man."

For some reason Augustus Vanderhoff thinks this is funny. "Coal man! Give me a hand here, honey. I'm feeling kind of weak." I offer him my arm as men do with ladies on the street. Not weak, I think. More like drunk.

"Upstairs," he commands as we careen through the kitchen. Twice he almost falls, and he throws his meaty arm around my waist for support. Besides the stench of booze, there's the sickly odor of cigars and aftershave.

"I just have to get to my bedroom," he mumbles.

The bedroom! I hope he's too inebriated to notice if anything's been disturbed. I can't even remember if I closed the door. If he passes out, I think I can put the ring back.

The master suite door is still open when we stumble around the corner, but Mr. Vanderhoff is too drunk to notice. He circles around, takes me in his arms as if to dance, and begins to warble a ragtime. That doesn't work. He can't get his feet to do the two-step, and he falls over onto the big bed, taking me with him. I jump up quickly and straighten my skirt.

"My shoes, kid." The big man is lying on his back with his hands under his head.

Where does he come up with the "kid" appellation, anyway? I'm not a child, and I'm not a floozy he picked up at the saloon. He sticks his legs out over the side of the bed.

I step reluctantly forward and undo the laces of his high-top ankle boots while he pulls off his shirt collar and unbuttons his vest. As I yank off the second shoe and drop it onto the floor, his legs circle my waist and he pulls me toward him, laughing.

"Mr. Vanderhoff!" I shout into his face. His oiled mustache has a smell of its own, a sweet sickly cedar smell. "You don't know what you're doing!"

He yanks me down on him. "I know all right."

I can feel his enlarged organ against my belly, and I'm sick to my stomach with fear. This man isn't playing around, and he's stronger than you'd think for his state of intoxication.

"Let me see those boobies little Gerald gets to play with."

"Mr. Vanderhoff!" I shout again as he rips the buttons from my navy blue work blouse and gropes for my chemise. My milk is already leaking, and he squeezes my breast and licks his thick fingers. We struggle silently. What would a cry for help get me? There's no one home. No one to hear. I bring my elbow down on his nose, and that makes him bellow.

"You damn tart. Who do you think you are?" Then he gets rough, grips me tighter with his legs while his hands keep ripping at my shirtfront. My arms are now pinned, so I use my only weapon. I spit in his face.

This time there's no expletive, but his eyes darken. I can tell he doesn't care about intercourse, doesn't care about the cost to his reputation or his family, he intends to hurt me. He pulls up my skirt and rips down my bloomers, but instinctively I go for his man parts.

It wasn't like I thought to do it. My brain stopped when he first grabbed my breast, but my knee slams into his testicles.

"You bitch!" he growls, the fight suddenly out of him. While he rolls back and forth with his legs drawn up, I pull up my bloomers and run down the hall. Sobbing, I grab the crying baby, who was awakened by the commotion, and lock the door so there's no easy way for Mr. Vanderhoff to get in unless he crashes through panels like a rutting bull, and if he tries that, little Gerald will have to be my protector. Mr. Vanderhoff is a father, for God's sake, not crazy enough to attack me in front of his son. I don't *think* he is, anyway. Just in case, I take the baby with me into my small clothes closet and brace my feet against the door.

There are no words to my tears as I open my torn navy top for the baby. No need to unbutton. No buttons left. They popped off on the satin bed cover. As I pull out my breast, the ruby rings plops out of my chemise and falls into my lap.

"Rock-a-bye baby, in the treetop," I sing softly to quiet the baby, *"when the wind blows, the cradle will rock."* Tears run down my face. I'm still afraid that Mr. Vanderhoff will find me, drag me out of the closet, and force himself into me.

It isn't as if I'm a virgin. I was with Lawrence. I gave birth to his baby. If I don't struggle too much, the rape itself might not be too physically painful, but there would still be injury, a wound that starts in the vagina and goes straight to the heart.

I slip the gem back onto my little finger. Now what? I can't get back into the bedroom to return it, and I can't stay in this home any longer. Seeing Mr. Vanderhoff every day at breakfast and dinner . . . I couldn't eat, couldn't sleep. My fate is sealed. I must leave tonight.

But what about the baby? I wipe my wet face. My little baby . . .

Not *my* baby, I remind myself, swallowing hard. Not my baby at all, though he feels like mine and I'm the one who nurses him and cares for him . . . but no matter. Gerald is theirs, the cold Mrs. Vanderhoff and the randy Mr. Vanderhoff. *Gerald is theirs.* I look down at the chubby-cheeked five-month-old. He lets go of my nipple, milk dribbling down his chin, and gives me a grin that would melt Antarctica. For a moment I think of kidnapping him, but that would be folly. I'd be hunted down and imprisoned for life.

At dusk, hours later, my head resting on my rolled-up wool cloak, I wake, still lying with the baby on the floor of the closet, and hear voices, then the *clip-clip-clip* of Mrs. Vanderhoff's hard high-heeled shoes coming down the hall. The door to her bedroom squeaks, and I freeze. Will she see on the bed the buttons that popped off my blouse? Should I try to tell her about Mr. Vanderhoff's behavior? Would she believe me? What if she notices that the ruby ring is gone?

"What the hell do you mean, leaving me at the tea?" she starts out on her husband in a high, insistent voice. "Even Mrs. Palmer could see you were soused, and she's half blind. I've never been so embarrassed . . ." Mr. Vanderhoff mumbles apologies. She yells some more.

I wait, but no one comes to my room. No one calls me to supper. No one asks for the baby.

At midnight, by the twelve chimes of the downstairs grandfather clock, I creep out of the closet, put the baby into his bassinet, and pack my few belongings. Then, in the still hours, while the rest of them sleep, I nurse baby Gerald one last time, wetting his golden hair with my tears, tuck him in, and slip down the back stairs with my old satchel.

Rain drips from the eaves as I stand on the back porch. I have forty dollars in my pocketbook, money I saved from my weekly stipend, the ruby ring sewn into the hem of my cloak, and nowhere to go nor a friend in the world.

15

The Midwife

"What's wrong, honey? You in some kind of trouble?" whispers Colleen, the yellow-haired waitress at the café across from the train station in Pittsburgh. I know her name from the stitching on her white uniform dress.

Tired and scared, I took the first train out of Chicago, not caring where it went, sure that the coppers were after me. Up until that day, I'd never been more than fifty miles from Deerfield.

Next thing I know, I'm getting out of a cab in front of Mrs. Kelly's house in Homestead. Colleen told me there was a midwife, a lady who delivered babies all over town, who might know of a job for a wet nurse. My milk is already leaking, and I tried to express it twice in the lavatory.

Embarrassed by my wrinkled attire and my sad, limp hair, I knock on her door.

"Yes?" It's a tall, dark-haired woman with an aquiline nose, dressed in a flapper outfit and smoking a cigarette; not what I'd expected.

"I'm Lizbeth Snyder , a wet nurse from Kansas City, looking for work." (Afraid of the coppers, I'd come up with the idea of Kansas just five minutes before.) "Colleen, the waitress at the café near Union Station, told me a midwife, Mrs. Kelly, lives here and could maybe help me find work."

"Sophie! Get down here. There's a girl with breast milk all over her front!"

The flapper turned out to be Nora. She talked like that, kind of brassy, but she'd grown up in Shadyside, in a Victorian mansion, and could speak properly when she wanted to.

Mrs. Kelly trotted down the stairs, a

big woman with graying black hair pinned up in a bun. None of the trendy flapper girl clothes for her. She wasn't fat and she wasn't skinny, just a tree you could lean on.

"Well, dear me! Come in."

Sitting in Sophie Kelly and Nora Waters's apartment over the bread shop, having tea, I was at once comforted. Nora brought me one of her clean white long-sleeved work blouses, and Sophie lent me her brush. I couldn't tell them why I'd landed in Pittsburgh, and they had sense enough not to ask.

The midwife insisted that we go right away to see a lady who had just delivered twins and might need a girl like me. She lived a few miles away with her husband and two other children in one of those big homes near Friendship. Sophie was like that; if there was a problem, she went straight at it like a bull toward a red wool shirt.

As luck would have it, there was no work for a milkmaid with the family in Friendship or anywhere else, but Mrs.

Kelly, a hospital-trained nurse turned midwife, admired my grit, or maybe just took pity on me, and offered me their back bedroom upstairs. There was only a cot, a chifforobe, and a small table, nothing much, but with the two women, I felt really safe for the first time in days.

This was 1913, just about Christmas. Mrs. Kelly bound my breasts with comfrey leaves until my milk dried up, and Nora found me a job on the line where she worked at Westinghouse. The United States was gearing up for the Great War, over many objections, and Pittsburgh was booming. I didn't care if the factory made munitions or who got killed with them. I had friends and a home. I was happy.

Nora and Sophie

It was months before I figured out that Sophie and Nora were lovers. I caught them kissing in the kitchen, and I don't mean a smooch on the cheek either. Nora's blue eyes shimmered, and she had her hand down Mrs. Kelly's blouse.

Not that I minded; I'd known other les-
bians when I worked at the Majestic.

When you've been a milkmaid for
other people's babies; lived in other
people's homes; lied about your age;
stolen jewelry; run away with nothing
but your cloak, your favorite painting,
and your mother's old Bible and hymnal, you accept that people survive and
find happiness however they can.

At first, I always called Mrs. Kelly "Mrs.
Kelly" instead of "Sophie" because she
was old enough to be my mother,
though forty-four doesn't seem old
now. I called Nora "Nora" because she
was thirty-four, more like a girl, though
now that I'm thirty-six, I don't feel at all
girlish.

In the fall, the three of us moved to a
little row house near Kenny's Park, the
one they later turned into Kennywood,
the place with merry-go-round rides
and an arcade. The two-story white
clapboard had a huge living room with
a bay window. There was a larger
kitchen and a trolley stop one block
away. We took the streetcar to work or

into the city when we wanted to go to a rally, a free concert, or a baseball game at Forbes Field. It cost only a nickel either way and with Nora and I each making seven dollars a week, we could afford the extravagance.

After work and on weekends, Nora distributed birth control information on the downtown Pittsburgh streets, and sometimes I went with her. At night Nora and I would go to the Crawford Grill in the Hill District, where we heard Duke Ellington and some of the local jazz musicians, like Erroll Garner and Billy Strayhorn. And then there were the gardens and the zoo at Highland Park. Mrs. Kelly liked that.

Those were the days when on Friday nights we'd have friends, both men and women, over for Irish stew and home-made bread. We'd read out loud the poems of Walt Whitman, passages by Tolstoy and polemics from the International Workers Association. Once Emma Goldman stopped by and several times Mother Jones, the union organizer, did too.

Mother's given name was Mary Harris Jones, and she'd been a dressmaker before her four children died of yellow fever and she joined with the United Mine Workers. Most people don't know that. She carried her sadness like I carry mine, under her heart. If you'd asked how she dealt with it, for a moment she wouldn't have known what you meant. Then she might pull the dried knot of pain out and stare at it like a foreign thing until she remembered . . .

Mother Jones brought John L. Lewis with her. This was before he was president of the UMW, but I didn't like him. He watched me from under his thick black eyebrows and smelled like Mr. Vanderhoff. Daisy Lampkin, our black suffragette friend, introduced us to W. E. B. Du Bois when he was in Pittsburgh on NAACP business. Daisy was a real firecracker. I'd never seen a woman with so much energy and passion for justice.

As the night wore on, we'd drink homemade wine that Nora made and sing Joe Hill's songs, "The Tramp,"

"There Is Power in a Union," and my favorite, "The Rebel Girl."

"That's the Rebel Girl, that's the Rebel Girl, to the working class she's a precious pearl. She brings courage, pride and joy to the fighting Rebel Boy." Ruben came with Mother Jones one time too, but we didn't even say hello.

On cold nights, when the temperature outside was below zero and the coal heater stove couldn't keep up, the three of us slept together in Mrs. Kelly's big bed, Nora, Sophie, and I. We'd snuggle under the feather quilt in our long flannel nightgowns and call ourselves the three bears. Nora was the papa, though she dressed the most womanly, Mrs. Kelly the mama, and I was Baby Bear. We'd laugh so hard, Mrs. Kelly would have to run to the potty to pee.

16

Dreams

Lately, I've been bothered by dreams, and I suspect Mr. Hester's presence in the house has affected me.

First I dream of Lawrence.

We're walking along the boardwalk in Chicago on a warm fall day. He's a tall, slim man with the yellow hair of a Swede and light blue eyes. I'm sixteen, and when his baby kicks, I grab his hand to show him, then step up on a park bench and leap on his back. Laughing, Lawrence runs around the park, holding my legs, my arms outstretched like a seagull. "I'm flying!" I yell.

My face is wet when I wake. It's been so long since I was young and in love. A pounding on the door downstairs jerks me out of my tears.

December 29, 1929. Dark moon, dark night for travel.

Unexpected summons to the home of Mrs. Clara Wetsel of Liberty. She was in labor with her fourth baby and having heavy bleeding. Her husband and she didn't want to call on Dr. Blum because they're still beholden to him for forty-five dollars after her husband, J.K., lost his arm at the sawmill.

Clara gave birth one hour after I got there, and I gave her some pennyroyal tea, which caused her to cramp, and massaged her uterus until the clots came out and the bleeding stopped. (Reminder to myself for next spring! Grow more pennyroyal, as it's useful for many things, including getting fleas

**off the dogs.) I was paid a loaf
of bread and a bushel of potatoes. Got back into bed and
dropped into sleep as if I'd never
been disturbed.**

Ruben

The second dream is of my late husband.

The Polish Club is crowded with
steelworkers and radicals. There's a
smell of tobacco and beer. Ruben sits
at the end of a long table, surrounded
by friends.

Ruben's a big man, over six four, with
a large jaw and a flat nose like a prize-
fighter, but his brown eyes snap with
intelligence and good humor. His stories are funnier and his laugh louder
and more infectious than anyone else's.
Even if he weren't wearing a red shirt
open at the throat, he'd be hard not to
notice.

He winks at me and the pink rushes
into my cheeks. When I get up to buy
a glass of cold cider, he meets me at

the bar, spins me around, and gives me a kiss.

Waking to the cold room, I can still taste his mouth, feel his familiar skin, one day from a shave, and his curly wild hair. I run my hand across the bed, reaching for him. He always took the left-hand side.

My socialist husband didn't start out to be a union organizer. He wasn't ever a miner or a factory worker, which embarrassed him if it ever came up. He was a college graduate from the University of Pennsylvania (the same school Mr. Hester went to, now that I think of it) and a writer for the *Pittsburgh Press.* In December of 1907, as a green reporter, he was sent to get a story about the Monongah mine explosion in West Virginia, fifty miles southwest of Pittsburgh.

"I spent a week there," he tells me on our first date over coffee and crullers at the German café near the Point. "And it changed my life, talking to the widows and the priests watching the bodies being brought out of the mine.

"The corpses were carried on stretchers by the dozens and taken to the morgue, where a steady stream of people filed past day after day. Three hundred and sixty-two boys and men, dead, burned, mangled, leaving two hundred fifty widows and over a thousand children without support. Three hundred and sixty." The big man has tears in his eyes. "When relatives or friends recognized a miner the wails would rip the gray sky open . . .

"There was one guy, the coroner, Mr. Amos, who had been on duty since the first man was found. I don't know how he did it, day in and day out, looking at all those bodies, cataloging them, wading through the deep sorrow.

"Outside the mine openings and in front of the morgue, masses of mostly women stood in the rain shivering, braving the cold to get a chance, one last time, to see the face of their dead. Most spoke Italian, but you could be deaf and dumb and still understand, just from the tear-stained faces.

"I talked to one rescue worker, a mining engineer they sent over from Torrington State College. He let it drop that it was so dangerous down under that even the trained rescuers had been pulled out for three days. Fire belched from one of the holes, and you could smell burning flesh, but there was no way to get to the victims. They were probably all dead anyway . . ."

Ruben stops to chew his lip, looking away. It's a strange conversation for a first date. Ragtime tinkles on the player piano.

"A mine inspector I'd met at the Monongah tipped me off about the Darr Mine in Westmoreland County, twenty miles east of Pittsburgh. Said there was a ventilation problem there and that, as usual, the foreman from the Pittsburgh Coal Company told him they'd get to work on it.

"Not two weeks later, I was up at the Darr, doing a piece on unsafe mining practices, when *it* blew up. I was right there, heard the explosion myself that time, felt the earth shake, saw the women and children trying to dig their fathers, brothers, and sons out with their bare hands. I joined them, scratching the earth until it was clear that another two hundred thirty-nine miners were dead. No one survived but the few men at the opening . . ." He stops his story and looks straight at me.

"This is crazy," he chides himself, wiping his face. "Let's dance."

Someone put a polka roll in the player piano. My napkin fell to the floor as Ruben pulled me up. He was a big man but light on his feet. We danced to escape the sound of the explosions, the mothers crying, the dead miners' bodies piling up at the morgue. Everyone was clapping as we whirled around the room. Half the time, my feet missed the floor.

I'd been with a few other men before Ruben: Lawrence, of course, and Michael the glassblower and Peter from the Brotherhood of Russian Workers. We were all anarchists or socialists then, or leaning that way. That first night with Ruben, we celebrated Henry Ford's announcement that he was giving all his employees an eight-hour workday. My love felt bad he couldn't take me home to his all-men boardinghouse near the steel mills, so I took him home with me. Nora and Mrs. Kelly were already asleep, but they wouldn't care.

Oh, Ruben . . . heart of my heart. I am so sorry.

17

Runaway

All day it rains, turning the snow to mush, and I do nothing but reread the first three chapters of DeLee's *Obstetrics* and wonder when Bitsy will return. I am beginning to wonder *if* she will return. I expected her right after New Year's, and it's already the fourth. If she doesn't come back, I will be sad. I've gotten used to her.

It's well after dark when, lying on the sofa, I close my eyes for a moment and have *another* dream! This one is about the veterinarian. An indignity! What's he doing inside my head?

In the dream it's summer. Hester and I are lying in the loft of a dark barn. Not my barn, another larger one, with light that comes in through the cracks in the rough-cut oak boards. Our bodies, still clothed, are pressed together. Nothing else happens, but when I wake, my heart's pounding and I try to remember what his body felt like.

A few minutes later, I hear the drone of a motor coming up Wild Rose Road and then banging at the door. As usual, the first thing I think of is the law, like that night the feds came looking for Ruben and we hid him in the attic, or the other time, after he died, when they came looking for me. Turned out they just had some questions about the IWW at Westinghouse, but Mrs. Kelly and I were so scared we didn't go out for three days, and not long after, we left the city for good.

I grab my red kimono and hurry to the window. A dark coupe is parked at the fence. The pounding starts up again.

"Miss Patience! Don't be afraid. It's Bitsy and Miss Katherine."

"Oh, Bitsy! You *did* scare me!"

I open the door, to find Bitsy assisting Mrs. MacIntosh up the steps. When I help her out of her long cream coat with a fur collar, Katherine turns away.

"Where's Mr. MacIntosh?" I ask. "Where's the baby?"

"He wouldn't let me have him." The mother looks up. Her eyes are both black, there's a bruise on her cheek, and her face is red from crying.

"Did William do this?"

"He didn't mean to. He was drinking and got angry because I wouldn't come to his room and play cards with him."

"Cards?" This seems an exaggerated response, though I know men have put women under the ground for less.

"Not just cards. He meant something else." She flops herself into the rocker, and as I put more wood into the heater stove, I notice her arm. Big bruises, with finger marks, circle both wrists.

"Oh, Katherine! Can you move your hand?" The woman waves a little. You can see that it hurts; her wrists are probably sprained but not broken. I place the green patchwork pillow on her lap and rest her forearm over it, then busy myself making hot water for valerian tea, a nerve relaxant that seems warranted for all of us. I also make up some warm comfrey compresses. There must be more bruises hidden under her clothes. She looks like the loser in a prizefight with Jack Dempsey.

Bitsy is stomping the snow off her boots. On the floor by the door sits one of Katherine's monogrammed linen pillowcases, stuffed, I assume with a few clothes and toiletries. I bring in the tea and help Katherine lie down on the sofa. Bitsy covers her with the flying goose quilt and props her head up on the pillow.

Questions buzz through my head like yellow jackets when you kick up a nest, but it seems wrong to ask for the blow-by-blow details. Katherine will tell me tomorrow—if she can talk about it.

"We stole the car," Bitsy announces. "Mama stood in the bedroom door and blocked Mr. MacIntosh's way, but we had to leave the baby. He wouldn't let go of him." I can picture Mary Proudfoot facing the mister down. She's as tall as he is and thirty pounds heavier. I don't worry about little Willie; as soon as his father passes out, Mary will get her hands on him and feed him cow's milk or cereal.

"He'll be awful pissed," Bitsy continues, "when he finds his precious Oldsmobile is gone. Probably call the sheriff."

"We'll worry about that in the morning." I glance out the window to see if anyone's coming. "Who drove?"

"I did." That's Bitsy. "Miss Katherine showed me what to do. We took it real slow. That's why we got here so late." I look at Bitsy with new respect; her fearlessness amazes me. It took me a year to learn how to drive; Ruben taught me. That was back when he had an auto, on loan from the union.

Katherine MacIntosh hasn't uttered a word since she told me about refusing to "play cards." "Is there anything you need, Katherine? Do you want to wash up? We can help you."

"My chest," she says. "I'm so uncomfortable. The baby still nurses every few hours."

Cripes! I've been so concerned about the woman's bruises, I hadn't even thought about her breast milk. I reach over and touch Katherine's cheek, wipe the tears off her face. "Can I check? If you're engorged, we have to get the milk out or you'll get an infection. Here, sit up."

I pull her yellow cashmere sweater up to her chin, undo her brassiere, and find that her breasts are as hard as baseballs.

"Bitsy, get a shallow bowl and more warm compresses. Do you think you can express the milk, Katherine? Or do you need our help? We have to get it out somehow, and we don't have a baby to help us."

The beaten woman shakes her head and lifts her sprained wrists, opening and closing her fingers with difficulty to show that she can barely move them.

"Well, Bitsy and I will have to do it, then. Is it okay?" Katherine shrugs and I help her lean forward so her breasts hang down. We surround them with warm compresses; then I teach Bitsy how to grasp the nipple between thumb and fingertip and squeeze down. Milk drips into the bowl and mixes with Katherine's tears.

Some people would say that this is too strange, to be milking another woman like a cow, but I am a midwife, a former wet nurse. I'm used to touching women's bodies and have taught many mothers to breastfeed. For Bitsy, granted, it must be odd, but she's always interested in learning new things and midwifery may be her calling.

When we're done, we put the bowl of breast milk in the kitchen and cover it with a pie pan; then I carry it out to the springhouse. I'm not sure what we're saving it for, but human milk, since my days as a milkmaid, has always seems like liquid gold to me.

"You can sleep in my bed, if you want, Miss Katherine," Bitsy tells our exhausted guest. "I'll change the sheets real quick." She puts the dogs out to pee and banks the fire.

Katherine declines, maybe because she wouldn't want to sleep in a colored person's bed but more likely because it would hurt too much to get up the stairs. Regardless, we tuck her back under the quilt.

It's a bad night. Twice I get up to put wood on the fire and look out the window, apprehensive about what the next day will bring. I open my diary and write by candlelight. Will Mr. MacIntosh really send the sheriff after Katherine and arrest her and Bitsy for stealing his car? Or will he be too ashamed about assaulting his wife to get the law involved? Next door in her bedroom, Bitsy grinds her teeth in her sleep, something she does when she's upset. My friend is probably worried too. She's the driver of a stolen car—a Negro driver of a stolen car.

I toss and turn, wake, and fall asleep again, studying the problem of what I should do. We need to get the mother and baby back together, but is it safe? I have no doubt that William's as thick as thieves with the constable and all the lawyers in town. And what will the repercussions for Mary and Bitsy be?

William could claim that Katherine went hysterical on him and he had to fight her off, was only defending himself and the baby. The only witnesses would be the two black females, who are not likely to be listened to. I don't know what the wife-beating statutes in West Virginia are, but in some states it's considered a husband's right to keep his woman in line with a whack or beating.

In the deepest part of the night an idea takes shape, and first thing in the morning, I take Bitsy aside and explain my intentions: "I am going to go around the mountain by road to the vet's and call the MacIntoshes'. If Mary answers, I'll ask if it's safe to bring Katherine home.

"If William answers . . . I don't know what I'll do; see if he's concerned about Katherine or is still in a rage. If he's drunk or angry . . . well, my strategy hasn't gone that far. I'm just hoping things have calmed down and we can bring Katherine home to the baby."

"After we return the Olds to Liberty how will *we* get home?" Bitsy wonders aloud.

"Good point. Maybe Mr. MacIntosh will be so ashamed he'll drive us. Or maybe I could ask Mr. Stenger, the pharmacist. Or maybe we'll walk . . . It's only fifteen miles."

Bitsy gives me a deadpan look. She's doubtful about hiking home in the cold, and I don't blame her.

"You want me to drive you to the vet's?" she offers.

"No, I can drive. My late husband taught me." I realize I've never talked to Bitsy about Ruben. "Anyway, someone has to stay with Katherine. If William MacIntosh shows up, turn the dogs on him and keep the door locked. I'll be back as quick as I can."

The ride around Hope Mountain turns out to be harrowing. On the slick part, coming down the hill past Maddock's, I skid into a ditch but am able to gun my way out. The mud is thawing and the snow is slush, which actually makes the conditions worse. How Bitsy and Katherine made it home in the dark is hard to imagine.

As I approach the vet's drive, I begin to wonder what I'll do if he's not home. As usual, that hadn't occurred to me. He could be out on a visit or in his office in town. I'm relieved when I see his Ford in the drive.

I bump over his wooden bridge and park next to it. Both cars now show the weather. William MacIntosh's pride and joy, the once shiny black Oldsmobile, is covered in grime. I notice that Hester's vehicle has chains on the tires, probably a good idea.

I slam the Olds's door, and before I can think what I'm going to say, Daniel Hester sticks his head out the kitchen door. He's wearing a flowered apron and wiping his hands on a dish towel.

"What are *you* doing here?" he asks by way of a greeting. It's the first time we've seen each other since Christmas Eve. He nods at the vehicle. "Your car?" He knows it's not; he's just being funny.

I tilt my chin. "No. It's my friend Katherine's. I wonder if I could use your phone? I need to call the MacIntosh residence in town. It's sort of an emergency." I don't want him to think I came for a visit.

Hester shrugs. "Sure."

At the stone threshold of the back door, I stomp my feet and walk into a bright kitchen that's seen better days. Dirty dishes are piled on every surface. The vet points out a wooden telephone box on the wall, but my glasses have steamed and it takes me a minute before I can see.

"Where's your housekeeper?" I ask, indicating the condition of the room.

"She left me. Her husband got work down near Beckley. King Coal closed last week and MacIntosh Number Three, near Delmont, too. It's just as well. I couldn't afford her anymore. When money's tight, people only call a vet if they're desperate."

He takes down the black receiver and cranks the phone for me, unembarrassed about the feminine apron. The brass bells on the front seem especially loud, but it's been a while since I've used a telephone.

"Susie," the vet says, speaking louder than normal into the metal horn on the front of the oak box. He motions me forward. "Yeah, this is Dan Hester out on Salt Lick. . . . I'm fine. . . . How are you? Can you give me the MacIntosh residence in Liberty? That's—" He snaps his fingers, and I hand him the slip of paper that Bitsy gave me. "That's 247."

I take a deep breath. The phone rings once, twice, then three times. Finally there's a click, and a low female voice comes on. He hands me the receiver.

"MacIntosh residence."

"Mary, is that you?"

"Yes?"

"It's Patience."

"Where are you, girl? Are Bitsy and Miss Katherine with you? They took outta here so fast last night, I didn't get a chance to ask where they were headed. Is the missus okay?"

"She's pretty busted up." I look over at Hester to see if he's listening. I know that he is, despite his concentration on the soap bubbles in the sink.

"Is it safe to bring her home?"

"Lordy, child, I hope so. I've never seen the mister like this before. He threw all the whiskey out of the house and has been crying all morning. I gave him a talking to and told him he didn't deserve that nice wife and baby and he'd be lucky if Miss Katherine didn't go back to her mother in Baltimore. Then he blubbered some more. I've seen him push Katherine around before, but this was the worst. He has one foot in a hell of his own making."

"We were worried he might call the cops about the car."

"Nah, he wouldn't do that. Wouldn't want to lose face by admitting his family has troubles. Tries to keep up a front, you know, though everyone in Union County understands MacIntosh Consolidated is finished."

She changes the topic. "I been feeding baby Willie cereal and canned milk, but he's getting mighty fussy. When can you get here?"

"Well, I have to talk to Katherine, but

I imagine we can be there by noon. I just don't know how we'll get home. Would William take us?"

"Hon, I don't know. His head hangs so low. We'll figure out something."

Hester taps me on the shoulder and points to his chest. Then he picks up his car keys and shakes them, meaning he'll bring us.

"Okay, will you tie dishrags to the front and back doors if it's safe for us to come in? See you in a little while."

I stare at the box, then turn to the vet; it's been a few years since I used a phone. "Is that all?" Hester puts the earpiece back in its holder, then sets a cup of coffee on the table in a white mug, the kind they have in the Mountain Top Diner.

"Cream?"

"I can only stay a minute."

He streams the white liquid from a quart mason jar, then clinks it back into his electric fridge. Mary Proudfoot has a similar Frigidaire at the MacIntoshes', and she told me it costs almost as much as a Model T! In Pittsburgh we used an icebox, but there's no iceman this far out in the country.

"I guess you heard." I tilt my head sideways at the phone.

"Hard not to. Domestic quarrel?"

"Worse. It got physical."

The veterinarian shakes his head, and I slurp my coffee down in a hurry.

"I'm going into my office in an hour; I'll drive you home from town at four P.M."

I'm standing, pulling on my jacket, and I lay my hand on his arm without thinking. "Thanks."

I hadn't meant to do that. I'm so used to touching women, I'd forgotten he wasn't a patient or hardly even a friend.

William

The ride into town goes smoothly once we get to the main road, though I'm a little rusty and stall the Olds twice. Bitsy offered to drive, but between the two of us, I'm more experienced. She sits up front to offer advice.

The car's cozy, and when I ask about

it, Katherine tells me, from the back, that the warmth is transferred somehow from the engine. Something new every day! It's the first heated vehicle I've traveled in. That's her only comment. The rest of the time, she just stares out the window like a woman without hope, and it saddens me.

I recall another time a battered woman came to our house. This was when we still lived in Pittsburgh. In the middle of the night, Kay Dorsey pounded on our door. "Let me in. Please!" she was screaming. It would have been about this time of year, still winter, and she had her baby wrapped up in a shawl and bruises all over her face. Nora took her in a cab to the Women's Hospital, but Kay never got a divorce. Father O'Malley wouldn't allow it. Nora was madder than hell.

And another time she was madder than hell . . .

"I can't live like this," Queen Nora announced one afternoon in mid-December.

She's decorating the Christmas tree that we bought for fifty cents at the corner lot and has already eaten half a rum cake. "Always hiding, keeping low. It's been years and Lizbeth is still wearing black, for Christ's sake, and it's Christmas." Sophie's lover was throwing tinsel at the tree as if it were chicken feed—and she hated chickens.

"How long is this going to go on? There were thirteen thousand battling the coal company troops at Blair Mountain. How does she know anyone even saw what happened?

"There's just no fun here anymore, no parties or salons, always lying low! I can't live like this, I tell you." She stands glaring at the room, the gaslights illuminating the shiny tinsel, and Mrs. Kelly's face, white as snow. "I tell you, I can't live this way! It won't do. It's no good. All the life is sucked out of me!"

Looking back, I think maybe she just wanted to leave and was searching for an excuse. Two weeks later, Nora left with the novelist Jacqueline Lyons for San Francisco, and that was the end of her. On Christmas Eve, Mrs. Kelly didn't even go to Mass. I watched the midwife's brave heart collapse like a hot-air balloon losing air. Now we were both widows.

Nora was right. How do I know anyone even saw? But I might as well say it: I killed my husband during the battle at Blair Mountain while trying to get two goons off him. It was an accident, but that one misplaced blow shattered something essential in me: reason . . . hope . . . sensibility.

Still I go on, too much of a coward to do anything else. There was a time I thought of suicide, wanted not to feel the terrible grief and guilt anymore, but there's a difference in wanting to be dead and doing it. Besides, now there are Moonlight and Buster, Sasha and Emma to think about . . . and Bitsy. I might as well admit it. She'd take my death personally, as if it were her fault.

The dark sky echoes my mood. Twice we pass deer on the way into town and I point them out. It isn't until we enter Liberty that I reach for Katherine in the backseat, squeeze her knee, and slow down.

As we pass the courthouse, we are surprised to discover a score of miners walking back and forth in a picket line. Their faces are clean, but they wear their hard hats with lamps on the front and hold placards and signs.

"Is it a strike?" Bitsy asks.

"I don't think so. Strikes are usually at the work site. It's some kind of demonstration. What do the signs say?" I'm gripping the wheel, nervous to be driving in town.

Bitsy reads the rough handmade inscriptions out loud as we pass: WE DEMAND FOOD AND CLOTHING FOR UNEMPLOYED MINERS' CHILDREN. FREE FOOD FOR OUT OF OUT-OF-WORK-MINERS.

"But *who* are they picketing? Is there anyone at the courthouse that can help? The County Health Office? The churches?" I ask out loud.

"William is really going to love this!" Katherine mutters. "Most of those men are from his mines. They were at the house last week begging for help, but he maintained it wasn't his responsibility. The truth is, he's broke."

We're surprised when, as we roll forward, Thomas Proudfoot steps out of the crowd. He's the only colored man in the group, and he flashes us a big smile, raising his sign higher. FEED THE CHILDREN!

"Damnation!" Bitsy lowers her head. "Ma's gonna be *pissed*."

"Why?" I ask. "What's so wrong? He's standing in solidarity with his fellow miners. Mr. Wetsel told me, when I helped his wife have her baby, that the owners shut off the electricity in the closed mining camps and shut the company stores. The workers have no money and no scrip to get food or kerosene. They're stranded in an isolated area where there's no other employment. Why shouldn't those that still have jobs stand with those that don't?"

"He's a *black* man," Bitsy mutters, slashing her eyes at me. "That's different."

As we pull up at the MacIntosh home, I'm relieved to see white dishcloths hanging from both doors. We go in through the kitchen and find William sitting at the table, his head bent and his hands running through his hair. Katherine scoots silently past him, takes the crying baby out of Mary's arms, and goes upstairs. Bitsy follows with the monogrammed pillowcase.

I plunk down across from Mr. MacIntosh. "We have to talk." The man flinches, meets my eyes, and then looks down again.

"William, I know things have been rough on you," I say, trying the sympathetic approach, though I don't feel a bit sympathetic. "The economy is hard on everyone." I make as though I haven't heard about his bankruptcy. Mary is standing around the corner in the pantry, pretending to tidy the shelves.

"William, look at me." The unshaven man lifts his head, and I see that his eyes are red from crying. "This can never happen again. If you touch a hair on Katherine's head, I'll call the cops. Lay one finger on her, and I'll do it. I probably should this time."

"I'll die before I do it again," William

finally whispers. I have to lean into his yesterday-whiskey breath, his voice is so low.

"You better bathe, shave, brush your teeth, and go say those words to Katherine. I'm not leaving until she feels safe." The man shuffles toward the stairs, and I let out my air.

Sometimes I surprise myself. When I entered the room, I had no idea what I'd say and was actually hoping I wouldn't see him.

"You done good, girl," Mary whispers, and I grin and raise my eyebrows.

"Hey, wait a minute, William." I yell up the stairs, now feeling powerful. "Come back a second. You still owe Bitsy five dollars for her work over the holidays!" The man looks around like he's waking from sleep and edges back down the steps.

"God, I forgot. Do we have any money in the cookie jar, Mary? I'm out of cash." Mary rolls her eyes where he can't see her and lifts the honeybee on the top of the beehive ceramic cookie jar.

She takes out a small handful of coins and one bill and spreads them on the table. "One buck, twenty-eight cents."

Not enough, but I'm not letting him off. "Bitsy was here for three weeks, so you can pay her the rest in food. Mary, can you fix us a sack of flour and beans, whatever you think is worth about five dollars if we shopped at Bittman's Grocery Store?"

"Good idea," William agrees. "I don't want to go to the bank just now." He reaches out his hand so I can shake it and I notice his ring, gold with a ruby. I have a ruby too, though he wouldn't know it. That's the way of the rich; they lament about the state of the economy and their businesses and go on with their life in the same regal manner. There's a difference in the wealthy lamenting about being poor and being really poor. If you're rich, you can go bankrupt and still wear a ruby.

"Thank you, Patience," MacIntosh says, looking right at me. "Thank you for all you've done."

"You are welcome," I answer formally, but then harden. "You better thank Katherine for bearing your child and coming back to you." He nods and turns to go upstairs. "And thank Mary too, for feeding baby Willie while Katherine was gone."

The cook smiles, shakes her head, and gets out a sack of flour.

Bitsy is in awe when I hand her the money. She lays it on the table and counts it again, then hefts the sack of goods Mary has stowed away for us. It must weigh thirty pounds. My friend's so excited to get paid and I'm so relieved that the scene at the MacIntoshes' didn't turn ugly that we're in a celebratory mood.

"Let's go shopping," I suggest. "We have one hour before the vet leaves. You said you need stockings."

"Miss Katherine has to do our shopping," Bitsy says in a low voice. "There's no dry goods store for black folks in Liberty. We can go in Bittman's Grocery for food, if we're shopping for our employer, and there's Friedman's in Torrington or the Sears catalogue, but no one but Stenger's Pharmacy caters to coloreds, and they don't sell cloth-ing."

That feels like a splash of cold water in the face, and I realize how little I know about my housemate's life. I don't know where she and Mary shop for personal things or get their hair trimmed. I don't know if there's a colored dress-maker or what they do when they're sick.

This is West Virginia, part of the Union in the Civil War, not Alabama or Mississippi, but Bitsy and I still can't stop for an ice cream together in the summer—"No coloreds allowed"—or go to a picture show together—"Whites on the ground floor and Negroes in the balcony"—or get a sandwich at the Mountain Top Diner.

I give up the shopping spree and settle for purchasing a two-gallon can of ker-osene at the Texaco station. Two blocks down as we stroll toward the vet's, I link Bitsy's arm in mine, the way I would with Mrs. Kelly, Nora, or Daisy Lampkin in Pittsburgh. Bitsy stiffens, looks around to see who's coming, and tries to pull her arm out, but I hold on tighter, daring anyone to say anything.

I do it on purpose. We're only forty miles south of the Pennsylvania state line, for God's sake. One hundred miles from Pittsburgh, where I did the Charleston with colored men in the jazz clubs and where, since 1887, it's been illegal to deny any person of color service in a restaurant, hotel, or streetcar.

When we round the corner of the courthouse, the demonstrators are gone and I think maybe we'll stop off at my friend Becky's women's clinic downstairs, but two men in heavy ankle-length overcoats stride down the sidewalk. Bitsy pulls harder and yanks her arm out.

Their black shoes are shiny, not country shoes, and their eyes take us in. They must be from Pittsburgh or Charleston. Maybe cops? Maybe feds? Bitsy turns to watch the outsiders get into their long gunmetal vehicle but I look away. Above us, Sheriff Hardman, a rail-thin man of about fifty with a notable scar straight across his chin, leans on a pillar at the top of the steps. He tips his hat but doesn't smile. On the second floor, in the county jail, a prisoner leers down through the bars.

"Come on," I insist. "We don't want to miss Hester."

18

Twilight Sleep

As we bump out of Liberty in Hester's Ford, I note the stone house with the green-shingled roof where Prudy Ott and Mayor Ott live. She's due in a month. Becky Myers has been seeing Prudy at her clinic to check on the growth of the baby. Since I haven't heard otherwise, I assume she's okay.

Prudy makes me uneasy. The birth of her only daughter four years ago, at Boone Memorial in Torrington, was a disaster. She's told me the story twice, and it's clear that she's terrified.

"I was assaulted by nurses and doctors," she announced the first time we met. Those were her exact words, not overcome or treated badly—*assaulted.* I think she meant raped.

"Mr. Ott wanted me to have the best of care, so we went all the way to Torrington for my first baby, where I could have an obstetrician and twilight sleep. For two days I was in labor, in a ward with five other patients, and all that time I was delirious, in and out of a dream. My husband slept in the waiting room. He had no idea what was going on.

"I would wake and hear the women scream as one by one they delivered. I must not have had enough medicine or maybe it didn't take, but unlike most of the mothers I talk to who had twilight sleep, I remember everything. The sounds ripped right through me, and I was strapped down in a high bed with bars so I couldn't get away. One patient untied herself and crashed to the floor. The doctor yelled at the nurses, blamed them for not watching her closer.

"Finally they took me to the delivery room. By that time I was screaming like the rest of them." Her hands shook and she put down her cup of tea. "They strapped me down, though I begged them not to. The harder they tried to control me, the more I struggled. Finally one of the nurses slapped me across the face.

" 'If you want us to help you, you better cooperate!' she yelled. 'You're worse than a child!' That shut me up. Once my wrists were tied to those boards on the delivery table, I felt like Jesus on the cross.

"Finally the specialist came in. He had a trainee, a younger intern eager to learn. Before the gas mask was forced over my face, I saw the two doctors playing with the forceps and I knew what was coming."

Prudy let out a long sigh, shaking her shoulders. "When I came out of it, back in the maternity ward, I couldn't believe the pain I was in. My whole bottom was on fire. I called the nurse to look at me, and she laughed.

"'What did you think it would feel like after pushing out an eight-pound girl?' she asked in a superior way. I hurt so badly, I couldn't hold my baby.

"Finally on the fourth day after the birth, an older nurse took time to do an examination. I could tell by her face that something was wrong. I was so swollen *down below* that some of the stitches had pulled out and it was already too late to replace them.

"A month later, I went to Dr. Blum here in town and he said I must have had a reaction to the iodine in the soap they wash women with. He shook his head when he saw the gaping wound. It was a year before I could have relations—you know, the married kind.

"Now my husband doesn't understand why I want to have this one at home. He can't fathom why I don't want to go to the hospital. I would rather die!"

What was I going to say? I promised that when she went into labor, I'd be there.

February 15, 1930. Rainbow ring around the moon.

Stanley Elton Lee, 7-pound, 3-ounce male, born to Clara and Curly Lee of Hickory Hollow, just outside of Liberty. Our first colored family, with the exception of Cassie out at Hazel Patch. Mr. Lee was so kind, he even brought us blankets to keep us warm on the way into town. We got stuck in a drift, but Bitsy and I got out and pushed Mr. Lee's car, and we made it to the house just as Clara's water broke.

The baby came twenty minutes later. Five-hour labor. Fourth baby. First son. I saw their little girls peeking through the curtain they use for a bedroom door, but they were so cute, I didn't care. Very little bleeding. Bitsy was helpful in cleaning the baby and getting everything ready. Present, Mr. Lee, Bitsy and I, and the girls.

Paid $3.00 and a gallon of home-made sorghum, which will be very handy on corn bread.

Prudy

Late February, and snow is still on the ground. It's been a rough winter. The snow at one point was up to our windowsills. Now, in only a month, the apple trees should be blooming. Hard to imagine.

Today, Bitsy and I, at her insistence, went around the outside of the house and knocked off the icicles, some reaching five feet long. I actually enjoyed it, cheered when each big one crashed.

"The weight of the ice could bring down the gutters," Bitsy explained "And if ice builds back up under your shingles, it will ruin your roof."

That was all news to me. I didn't do *any* home maintenance last year. I've never owned a house before, but Bitsy has lived in town with the MacIntoshes all her life and she knows these things.

In many practical ways she's so much more knowledgeable than I am. She even went to school five years longer than I did, though I consider myself just as educated.

Around noon, as small flakes of snow like cold ash begin to fall, an unfamiliar vehicle whines up Wild Rose Road. At first, from a distance, as it slips and slides through the slush, I think it might be Katherine, on the run again, and my heart grows cold, but as the vehicle rumbles closer I make out a Ford, not an Olds.

The auto stops by our mailbox, and a stranger, dressed in a dark trench coat with double buttons, gets out. He stands at the gate, stares at the house, and tilts his gray homburg. The walk isn't shoveled because we get so little company in the winter; what would be the point?

For a minute I think it's the lawmen we saw on the steps of the courthouse. I remember the months after Blair Mountain, when nine hundred miners were indicted for murder, conspiracy to commit murder, and treason against the state of West Virginia. Those were the days when we laid low, and Nora grew bitter. Though it's been almost eight years, I still fear they'll find me.

"Hallo!" the man calls out. "Is this the midwife's house?" Bitsy and I are dressed in trousers, tall rubber boots, and knit watch caps so there's no way he can tell we are women.

"It's me. Patience. I'm the midwife. Come up to the house." I can't imagine who the guest might be, so we scurry inside to make the place presentable. A tax collector? A preacher come to save my soul? Certainly not a salesman, not in this weather! The stranger stops on the porch to stomp the old snow off his feet and knocks softly. He speaks before he gets into the parlor.

"I'm J. B. Ott, Prudy's husband. She said I should come for you. The pains are mounting. I'm new to this. Last time she had a baby, she went to Boone Hospital in Torrington."

I look over at the Stenger's Pharmacy calendar hanging on the nail in the kitchen and see that I've circled March

16 as Mrs. Ott's birth time. She's two weeks early if this is for real, but it's still okay. "Did you leave her alone? Is anyone with her?"

"She's got two lady friends there and the home health nurse. I told her I'd be back as quick as I could." He nervously rocks back and forth on his feet, anxious to get going.

"Is she leaking water?"

"She didn't say."

"How often are the pains?"

Mr. Ott looks puzzled. "I don't really know. Not close yet."

Bitsy is already getting the birth satchel. I run upstairs, pull on a dress, and tell her to change too. Then we bundle up and head for the auto.

"Your girl coming?" Mr. Ott asks as he cranks up the engine.

"She isn't my *girl*," I start to say but bite my tongue. No use getting hostile. "Bitsy is my birth assistant. She comes to all my deliveries."

The ride into town is uneventful; no traffic, no other autos. As we cross the bridge over the Hope, I note that the ice is breaking up. Below us, huge chunks pile up, then fall apart and race each other around rocks that stick up like teeth.

Fruit Flies

The Otts' two-story brick home, with white trim like a gingerbread house, looks inside about how I remember it. White doilies are draped over everything: the arms of the chairs, the back of the sofa, and all the shiny mahogany tables. Though I know the couple has a four-year-old daughter, I don't see a sign of a child or a toy anywhere, and I imagine she's been sent away to her grandmother's.

Upstairs I hear arguing, and I don't wait for an invitation. I take the stairs in the front hall two at a time.

"Hi," I say pleasantly to Prudy and the other women huddled with her in the master bedroom. Mrs. Wade, who attended one of the births I did with Mrs. Kelly, fancies herself useful but only gets in the way. Priscilla Blum, the town doctor's wife, tells us she's Mrs.

Ott's best friend. I'm surprised to see Becky sitting in a rocking chair in the corner, twisting her handkerchief. I smile, but her face is creased with worry and she doesn't smile back.

"I tell you, you'd be better off resting! This baby won't come till after midnight!" exhorts the Wade woman. She looks at me, expecting support, but I'm mum, wanting first to get the lay of the land. Mrs. Wade rolls her eyes.

"How are you doing?" I ask Prudy. She is wearing a blue chenille bathrobe, and her shoulder-length dark hair is disheveled and stringy.

"Oh, not good. Not good at all, Patience. I don't know what to do! There's never a break! When I lie down, my back hurts. When I stand up, the pains come closer . . . Oh, what should I do? Help me!"

I shake my head. It's going to be a long day.

All afternoon, the female companions hover like fruit flies. I get Prudy to lie down for an abdominal examination, but before I can see how firm her belly gets or determine the baby's position, she screams and they help her get up. If I suggest she try rocking in the rocking chair, Mrs. Wade and Mrs. Blum want her to lie down on her side. If I show her how to bounce up and down to shake the baby into the best position, they want her to kneel and pray. The heartbeat, from my brief check, is steady, and the contractions are every six minutes.

Becky doesn't get very involved, and I'm not sure what her role is, maybe just moral support, since she saw Prudy at her clinic. I'm sure she's wondering how she got roped into this. Bitsy too, stays out of the way, sitting in the corner by the fireplace, keeping a low profile, reading her book, *Up from Slavery,* one of my favorites. Now and then we catch each other's eyes without expression. We both know that the scene is out of control, but we don't know what to do about it.

I'm Charles Lindbergh, flying through the dark without instruments. Prudy's response to the pains is so exaggerated, she could be close to delivery or two days away. Now that I think of it, I don't even know for sure if the baby's head is down.

Finally I decide I'd better do a vaginal exam. I'll be outside the law again, and I glance at Becky, knowing she's aware of the midwifery statute, but the information I can get by doing it is essential.

"Prudy, I need to do a better examination. If you lie on the bed for a minute and bring down your bloomers, I can tell you, by feeling inside, how your labor's coming." She finally agrees, and pulling on my gloves I find the baby's head low in the pelvis, but she's only half dilated. As soon as I'm finished, she pops off the bed and begins to wail again.

"That was horrible! I can't stand it on my back. I keep seeing myself spread-eagle, strapped on the delivery table, the shiny metal forceps in the doctor's hands!"

As the shadows in the room slip across the floor and evening draws near, the situation only gets worse. Prudy's whining turns into a high-pitched cry, the sound of a dog with its tail in the door. It makes your toes curl. "I can't do this! I can't. I won't! Make it stop, Patience!" The two support ladies keep wiping her brow, their faces gray with worry. Becky has tears in her eyes.

"I think we need to take her to the hospital," Mrs. Blum, the physician's wife, pronounces, her face pale, her bright green eyes brimming with tears. Mrs. Wade nods her agreement.

I'm surprised when Becky jumps up and concurs with them. "I agree," she asserts. "There must be something wrong. Disproportion or dystocia." Fear in the room goes up like a bottle rocket, and I wish the nurse wouldn't use such big words. I know what she means, but no one else does. Basically she's concluding that the baby won't fit and this labor is a waste and a dangerous one.

"I don't think it's stuck," I counter. "From what I can tell, the back is anterior and the baby's not very big."

"No! I'm not going. I'd rather die!" Prudy screams as her water bag breaks.

Where's Mrs. Kelly when I need her?

Where's Mrs. Potts with her calm presence?

Water Birth

Observing the puddle of clear fluid on the floor illuminates a way . . .

"Mrs. Wade, Mrs. Blum, the labor is almost over, and it's time for Prudy to take a birth bath. She needs to get ready for the delivery." The two women raise their eyebrows. They've never heard of a *birth bath* before! Becky frowns; she hasn't heard of a birth bath either. Come to think of it, neither have I.

"You two go across the hall and get the tub ready. Make the water comfortable but not too hot, then go down to the kitchen and help Becky boil more water and sterilize the linen in the oven."

Bitsy puts her book down with a thump and gives me a look. She knows that taking a bath is not part of the usual process; she also knows that the pads in our satchel have been sterilized and wrapped in newspaper for days.

She did it herself. I give her a half smile, hoping she'll understand that this is just a ploy to get the patient calmed down and these meddlesome insects out of my hair.

The water closet in the Otts' home is nicer than the MacIntoshes'. There's a green-tiled floor, with lighter green tiles halfway up the wall, an indoor toilet, a sink, and a very shiny white bathtub with claw feet. When I helped Prudy to the lavatory earlier and admired the tub, she explained that it was her husband's gift to her when they married five years ago. "It even has a gas water heater," she told me.

Now Prudy's in the tub, warm liquid up to her chest, and I kneel at the side, pouring water over her back. "Is your pain less, Prudy? I haven't heard you cry for a while."

"Yes. It must be the warm water. Here comes another one!" She throws her head back and commands me, "Pour faster! Pour more!" I'm rinsing her with a copper dipper as fast as I

can, and this time there's no screaming, only a low "Muhhhhhhh!"

Her moan makes me think of Moonlight. I've completely forgotten my pregnant cow, and she needs to be fed and
watered. I know only one person I can
ask for help, and my obligations to him
are growing.

"Bitsy," I call. She's still in the bedroom, still lying low, and for the first
time I realize why. Her presence here is
awkward with the society women of
Liberty. Only a few months ago, she
served them tea in the MacIntoshes'
parlor.

"Can you sit with Prudy? Just pour
water over her back and shoulders
when she has a pain. She'll tell you
what she wants."

I trot downstairs, and when I enter
the kitchen, all heads go up. Becky, at
the sink, half turns. Mr. Ott is there too,
and he drags himself from deep between the pages of the *Torrington
Times,* a pack of Lucky Strikes on the
table and a lighted cigarette in the corner of his mouth.

"Prudy's fine. Bitsy's staying with her.

The bath is relaxing her. Do you have a phone?" I spit this all out in a hurry because I want to get back to my patient.

"Well, I never," I hear Mrs. Wade whisper. "Taking a bath in labor, and that nigger girl with her!"

I steam at the comment but again bite my tongue. No use getting in a fight. It wouldn't change their minds anyway. Black and white miners and their families have worked together for decades, but these upper-class women probably never had a Negro friend—or a Negro servant, either, in many cases. Most West Virginia families don't use nannies or maids. At most, they might have a cook and a hired hand, usually someone off of a farm and most likely white.

Mr. Ott scrapes his chair back and walks me to the telephone in the front hall.

"I have to get someone to take care of my livestock." I say this as if I have a whole herd, when really it's only Moonlight and the chicks. Taking hold of the crank, I twist it three times the way I saw Hester do. A woman's voice answers.

"Is this Susie?" I take a guess at the name and apparently get it right. "This is Patience Murphy, the midwife. I'm at Mr. Ott's home. I need to speak to Daniel Hester, the veterinarian on Salt Lick. I don't know the number. Can you connect me?"

"One moment." There's a buzzing in the background and then four short rings. The vet finally answers.

"Hester here. Large and Small Animals." This makes me smile.

"Murphy here. Large and Small Women." I can't help it. It's funny.

"Patience?" I like it that he uses my first name.

"Sorry. Just a little joke. Listen, Bitsy and I are in Liberty with a patient in labor. The woman, Mrs. Ott, the mayor's wife, is going to have a baby tonight, and—well, I hate to do this, but you're the only one I know to ask. Could you go over and feed and water Moonlight? Since she's with child, I don't want her to have to go hungry all night."

"With *child*?"

"You know what I mean. I'll repay you whatever you want." I rephrase this. "I mean, I'll go with you to an emergency call or whatever . . ."

"Yeah, I can do that. You want me to feed the chickens too?"

"Would you?"

An ear-splitting roar comes from upstairs.

"Patience!" Bitsy hollers. All heads go up, and Mrs. Wade and Mrs. Blum collide in the doorway.

"Stay!" I hiss at them as I drop the phone on its cord and take the stairs two at a time.

"Prudy! Don't push! Tell her to *blow*, Bitsy!"

In the bathroom, I grab the woman's chin. "Prudy, don't push! We have to get you back in bed!"

Prudy whips her head back and forth to say no, her wet hair flying, spraying us with water like one of my beagles just out of the creek. She grabs the side of the tub and bears down again. I hold her chin tighter. "Listen to me,

Prudy! Blow like this. *Whoo, whoo.* Bitsy, my satchel!"

When the contraction is over, I explain to the mother, as well as her friends, now standing at the lavatory door, what's happening. "That was an urge to push. You never felt it before because in the hospital you had twilight sleep and then gas as the doctor pulled the baby out. We need to get you out of the tub and back—"

Before I can finish, Prudy growls again and instinctively pulls her legs back. This is not the prim woman who has lace doilies layered over every surface in the house. Bitsy runs for my gloves, and I struggle into them.

I know that there's no way we can get the patient out of the tub, down the hall, and into bed in time. This is her second baby. The train has left the station and is heading downhill, so I just lean over the tub's side reach into the warm water, put my hands around the infant's head, and hold on. Within less than a minute, the baby is born. I lift him up out of the warm water, cord still attached, and he cries as soon as he hits the cold air. "Towel?" I request casually, as if this happens all the time. I look up and see Becky, beaming and holding out a clean cloth, all the pain and worry of the last few hours now wiped from her face.

"My baby. My baby," Prudy insists, her arms stretched out. What harm can it do? I give the sobbing woman her still wet infant.

"Keep all of him under the warm water, except his little face." Becky takes back the towel and gasps at the idea of submerging the baby, but the infant stops screaming and opens one eye to take in his world.

Bitsy hands me the scissors, and I trim the cord. When I turn to drop the scissors into the sink, I'm surprised to see Mr. Ott in the doorway too, wiping his eyes, gazing at Prudy and their new son. "I love you," he mouths as his wife looks up. Their eyes fall into each other's and the rest of us fade, like the blurred images on the edge of an old family photo. "I love you," he says again, louder.

February 25, 1930. Dark sliver of a moon.

Birth of Harrison Ott, 7 pounds, 12 ounces, second child of Mrs. Prudy Ott and J. B. Ott of Liberty. An eight-hour labor with very frightened mother. Prudy's last baby was born in Boone Memorial Hospital with twilight sleep, gas, and forceps. This baby was born in the bathtub! The water seemed to relax the mother. Baby did fine. I talked about this with Bitsy later. When you think about it, the baby has been in the water all along. It probably felt comfy to him.

No complications. No vaginal tears. As tense as Prudy was for the labor, she sat there in the warm water and nursed the baby in front of us all.

Present were myself, Bitsy, Becky Myers, and two of the mother's lady friends, who got in my hair, Mrs. Wade and Mrs.

Blum, the doctor's wife. I hope they don't come to many more deliveries! The father saw everything from the door to the lavatory! Paid $10, which is pretty good for these times and made us feel rich.

Spring

19

Thaw

A week of heavy rain, and patches of green appear. New icicles melt as soon as they form, and shoots of purple and yellow crocus push up through the earth.

Yesterday, just after Bitsy went hunting for turkey down on the flats near the Hope River, I saw, through the kitchen window, something move.

It's Mr. Maddock working on the road again, I figure, but as I stare, the open cart with two burros passes the Maddocks' mailbox and continues to travel fast up the hill. Emma starts barking, and Sasha chimes in. The cart pulls to a halt, and the driver jumps down and ties his animals to the picket fence.

"Mrs. Potts says come quick." It's Reverend Miller, the pastor of the Hazel Patch Baptist Chapel. At the gate he ties his animals to the picket fence. "The melting snow has caused a flood in the Wildcat Mine. Twelve miners are trapped. They fear a cave-in."

The poor man is panting. "There's going to be injured, and there's no doc to be found. She wants you now." I don't think to argue but step into my tall rubber boots, grab my birth satchel, scratch a note to Bitsy, and jump onto the cart. The reverend turns the topless carriage around and slaps the mules into action before I sit down.

"I had to bring the wagon. There's no way an auto could make it through this muck," he offers. Other than that he doesn't say much, and we take Salt Lick Road around the mountain, slipping and sliding in the mud and slush. At the bridge we meet Daniel Hester coming home from town and pull over so he can pass. I wave him down. The vet's not a doctor, but he did a good job stitching my leg.

"Wait!" I yell to Reverend Miller.

"Mr. Hester," I call, standing up in the cart. "There's trouble at the Wildcat Mine. A flood. Men are trapped. They fear a cave-in, maybe injuries. Can you come?"

"He won't make it in that auto," the pastor advises under his breath. "That's why I didn't bring my hack. Roads are too rutted. Tell him to get in with us."

"Did you hear? The pastor says the roads are no good. Your Model T won't make it."

"Give me room to turn around!" Hester shouts back without hesitation. "I'll get as close to Wildcat as I can. If I go ahead and get stuck in the mud, you can pick me up. If I make it to the camp, we'll have another vehicle to drive the men to the hospital." The preacher complies, backing into Hester's drive.

Thirty minutes later, we pull up the hill into a mining camp much like the first one I visited, only, if possible, more dilapidated. A crowd presses around the gaping mouth of the mine while a disaster siren blasts over and over. The fear is so thick you can taste it.

"Oh, God!" a gray-haired woman screams. "Oh, God, my son's in there." She falls to the ground, then rises and tries to fight through the throng. Two other women pull her back. "Let me go! I have to find him!" The two holding the distraught mother are Mildred Miller and Emma, the Hazel Patch ladies who made the feast after Cassie's birth.

I'm surprised to see Thomas here too, with Izzie Cabrini at his side, consulting with a huddle of black and white men, all wearing miner's hats. In a disaster, color and nationality don't seem to matter.

The vet had mentioned that King Coal had folded, so the two must now be working at Wildcat. Mr. Hester, who made it through the muck and arrived well before we did, stands at the edge of the pack, listening.

On an empty wooden dynamite box near a pile of dirty snow, I find Grace Potts, sitting with her hands folded in prayer, and I step into her circle of calm.

Thankfully, someone shuts off the disaster siren and my heart slows its pace. One of the Italian women gives the thin lady a shawl.

"Oh, honey," the old midwife greets me, "I'm so glad you're here . . . and that fellow . . . what's his name? They told me he's an animal man, some kind of doctor. Thank the Lord. Thomas Proudfoot, that little Eye-talian fellow, and Byrd Bowlin, one of the young men who attends our chapel, are going down now. There's a low place where the water has collected about three thousand feet back and a thousand feet under. The walls there are starting to slide. One timber already crashed down on a man. The miners on this side of the water scratched their way through and brought him out, poor fellow. He was half buried under the mud."

She indicates a sobbing wife and daughter kneeling over a corpse covered with a rough wool blanket. I leap up to go to them, but Mrs. Potts pulls me back. "Not now, honey." Two other very tall women stand crying nearby, leaning into each other like trees.

"Not now," she repeats her counsel. "Give them some time." I know she's right. Though I yearn to hold them, take some of their sorrow into my body, it's not my place.

Hester wanders over, frowning and rubbing his chin. "They're rigging up ropes and cables to tie to the last solid post, then a few of the miners are going down. They plan to swim through the water on the other side of the slip, see if they can get to those trapped. It's dangerous as hell." He looks back at the three as they head into the hole. Thomas is in the lead, tied to Cabrini, who's tied to the young miner Mrs. Potts mentioned, a tall narrow black man about twenty-five.

"I don't know anything about mining codes, but this place is a mess," the vet rants as he paces back and forth. "Notice the leaning timbers. That can't be regulation!"

I stand and take his hand. Hester looks surprised but doesn't let go. My heart is so full of fear for the families. If I were a believer, I'd kneel down and pray.

Resurrection

Inch by inch, the sun crosses the sky. It lights the windows of the miner's shacks and then ducks down over the mountains in the west. There's the drip, drip, drip of melting snow. This morning, I welcomed that sound of spring; now I hate it because it means more water flooding into the mine.

Delfina Cabrini, with her baby tied around her under her wrap, brings Mrs. Potts and me two blue-speckled tin cups of coffee. Hester wanders over to talk to Sheriff Hardman, who's just arrived with a posse from town. I duck my head when I notice the two city slickers from the courthouse. Are they some kind of feds investigating moonshiners or marshals looking for me? It's been years since the riot at Blair Mountain, but I feel sure my mug's displayed on a yellowing wanted poster somewhere. When you've been a radical, lived with radicals, marched in the streets, and spent time in jail, you are, forevermore, wary of coppers.

* * *

Dark pours into the hollow, and lanterns appear. I find another empty dynamite box and drag it over next to Mrs. Potts, all the while keeping my back to the lawmen. So many times I have waited like this, stiff with worry outside a mine, waiting for Ruben while he confronted the bosses. I could always tell, by watching, when he was angry. He'd stuff his hands deep in his pockets to keep his big fists from flying into someone's face.

"Amazing Grace, how sweet the sound," the old lady begins in a deep contralto, *"that saved a wretch like me. I once was lost, but now am found, was blind but now I see."* Mildred, Emma, and a few of the other Hazel Patch ladies join in and then three white ladies and then the vet and me. It's funny how music can soothe, can heal, can give us courage, especially singing together.

"Through many dangers, toils and snares we have already come. 'Twas Grace that brought us safe thus far . . . and Grace will lead us home."

* * *

There's movement at the opening of the mine, then a rending cry from the waiting assembly. Hester grabs his bag, grips my arm, and leads me forward, but the new victim, carried by Izzie Cabrini like a rag doll over his shoulder, has no use for our medical services. He's a broken man, his face gray and covered in mud and his eyes wide open. I look away, and the vet steps forward to check his pulse with his stethoscope. He shakes his head to confirm that it's hopeless . . . and Izzie moves on. The immobile victim is the second man crushed under the slide.

Now the crowd surges forward. More miners are coming out, five of them, staggering, limping, shuffling, crying. I search for Thomas. Maybe his dark face doesn't show in the gloom—and then I catch sight of him hobbling forward, supporting another injured coal miner, whose left arm dangles from his shoulder. From nowhere a small brown body shoots forward. It's Bitsy, who jumps up on her brother, shouting "Praise God!"

Where did she come from? How did

she get here? Last I knew, she was heading down Wild Rose Road toward the banks of the Hope River, carrying her shotgun, planning to shoot a wild turkey for dinner. She must have come home, seen my note, heard the distant wailing siren, and, fearing for Thomas, run through the woods and over the ridge all by herself.

Hester motions me forward. "Patience! Over here." The women of the camp have made pallets on the ground, and he is kneeling over a man with a gash on his head. "You clean the wound and bandage it. There's a lot of mud. Wash it thoroughly. I'll check this fellow, it looks like he may have a broken arm."

No one asks who we are or if we are a qualified physician and nurse. They're just glad to have us. Bitsy trots over with my birth satchel and gets out the yellow antiseptic soap and clean rags. Mrs. Potts brings over a vial of echinacea tincture and a fifth of whiskey. I'm shocked when she boldly pulls the booze from under her shawl.

"Had it since my husband passed

away in '19, before the Prohibition," she explains. The injured man reaches for the bottle. "No, you don't." She blocks him. "It's for cleansing your wounds, and it's gonna burn some." She drips the liquid over the four-inch gash in his forehead. "Now bandage him good, and he'll stop bleeding."

"Patience!" It's Hester calling again. Bitsy finishes the dressing, then collects our gear, and we move where we're needed.

"His arm isn't broken, just dislocated," the vet explains. "I'm going to try to put it back in place. Save him the expensive hospital admission and the painful trip to Torrington over the muddy rutted roads. What I want you to do is hold his right shoulder down. You may need to kneel on it."

The injured man looks at me, his face white with pain.

"What's your name?" I ask him.

"Farley Tuggs."

"It will be okay," I comfort him. "Mr. Hester's very good at this." In reality, I have no clue what we're doing.

I fix my glasses behind my ears, put

the man's arm against his side, and, with both my knees against his shoulder, pin him down, like the vet said. Bitsy, without anyone asking, cradles his head, protecting it and at the same time keeping the poor fellow from thrashing around. Mrs. Potts shows up and this time gives the man a slug of whiskey for the current pain and the greater pain he has coming.

"Ready?" Hester asks. The miner shuts his eyes.

I watch as the veterinarian first folds the victim's forearm in and across his abdomen, then rotates his arm and shoulder out. Slowly, steadily, he rotates the limb back and forth. Tears make white rivulets down the sides of the patient's coal-blackened face, but he doesn't make a sound, just bites his lower lip till it bleeds. When the dislocated shoulder pops back into its joint, Farley screams. Then "That wasn't so bad! Thanks, Doc." The relief is instant. He sits up smiling. It reminds me of a woman after she's just given birth. "That wasn't so bad!" It's the fear of the pain more than the pain that gets to you.

"Can you fellows make him a sling?" Hester asks two men in the crowd around us. "I need you to stabilize his whole left side." Then he stands up and goes on to the next miner, who is sitting on the ground holding his leg. A woman with tears streaming down her face, who I imagine is the guy's wife, hovers over him and has already brought a pan of warm water out of their shack. The leg is not broken, just cut down to the bone, and Hester sews it up in layers as I watch.

In an hour, the crisis is over. Two miners are dead, but the rest have survived and, if they aren't too banged up, will go back to work as soon as the water subsides and the walls are shored up. They have families to feed and are paid by the ton. There's no camp medical care. No disability benefits. No life insurance for the dead miners' families. I look around for someone in charge. If there's a foreman, I can't tell. Thomas and the miners seemed to have organized everything.

For twenty years, the United Mine Workers fought for mine safety, higher pay for hazardous work, and cash compensation rather than scrip at the company store. They won victory after victory, but there was a price: union men were injured in riots, sometimes killed.

As steel production dropped after the boom, the need for coal went down too. Union membership dwindled. Mine owners returned to the practice of treating miners like chattel, and now here we sit on the wet earth, tending the nonunionized miners of Wildcat Mine.

Few here remember the massacre at Matewan in 1920, when miners defended their family and homes. Few remember the Battle of Blair Mountain, a year and a half later, when thirteen thousand miners fought in open warfare for their rights.

Bitsy decides to stay overnight with Thomas in his two-room cabin, and just as Hester gets ready to leave, Becky shows up in an ambulance that's covered in mud. It's been stuck in the slick clay down near the bridge all this time. We stand in the dark, telling her what happened, and I can see that she's

glad she missed the whole catastrophe.

As I turn to leave, Mrs. Potts stops
me. "Thank you for coming, young lady.
The Lord was watching over us today.
It could have been much worse. And
thank you too, young man." I can hear
Hester thinking, *Young man?* But to an
old woman, the two of us must seem
like spring chickens.

20

Pay Back

I run cold water into the sink and fill the teakettle, still shaking from the sights of chaos and death at the mine. Outside Hester's kitchen window snow drifts down again, not sticking yet but filling the air. The kitchen door bangs as Hester rattles in with two metal buckets of fresh milk that he strains into three-gallon jars. He sees me staring.

"Want some?"

"I can't really afford to pay for it." Hester shrugs and fills a quart jar for me with the warm white liquid.

The shrill ring of the vet's phone startles us both. "Hester here," he answers. "What's the trouble? How long? Okay, I'll be there as soon as I can. It may take an hour." He looks at me sideways. "Want to pay back some more of what you owe the practice?" I like the way he says "the practice" . . . not him personally, but the practice.

"Tonight? I guess."

I'd accepted a ride back from the Wildcat Mine and didn't mind waiting while he milked his cow, but now, exhausted and filthy, I just want to get home. On the other hand, how can I refuse? I'm obligated; he's done us so many favors. "I'll need to change first. What's up?"

"Mr. Dresher, a German farmer on the other side of Clover Bottom, has a bitch in labor, Hilda. She's been nesting all day, fooling around with the bedding in her basket, licking herself. The owner was going to leave her till morning, but for the last hour she's been panting hard. He's embarrassed, but he loves that dog like it's one of the family. He's also a *big* farmer with a lot of stock and is one of my best clients. Duty calls."

The drive around Salt Lick and then up Wild Rose is uneventful. It's still muddy, but we manage to stay on the road. When we get to my house, I jump out of the Model T. "It will take a few minutes. Are you sure you need me for this?"

"I'll feed your dogs and chickens and give Moonlight fresh water and hay. It's nice that she's pregnant; we don't have to milk her." The vet hops out too and slams his side door. By his speed, I take it he thinks the dog is in trouble and that I'll be useful somehow . . . or maybe he just wants company. Either way, I'm in no position to quibble.

In less than ten minutes, I've put on clean slacks and an old green jersey, washed my arms and face, and we're back in the car bumping down Salt Lick, this time toward town. As we drive through the empty streets of Liberty, I notice that the city lawmen's shiny gun-metal auto, still parked in front of the courthouse, has Virginia plates.

On the other side of Delmont we pick

up 92, a dirt road but less rutted. A mile past the little B&O train stop at Clover Bottom, we make a hard right, cross a wooden bridge, and pull up in a spacious farmyard. An electric porch light comes on, and a man with an expansive belly and black suspenders steps out of the two-story white house. If he's surprised to see a woman with Hester, he doesn't say anything.

"Hey, you old son of a gun," he greets the vet warmly. "In here." The farmer leads us though a front hall into a well-appointed living room where a four-foot-high wooden console radio dominates the room. Gene Austin is crooning "Carolina Moon" out of the speakers. It's the largest radio I've ever seen, bigger than the one at the MacIntosh home, with a built-in sound chamber over the assembly and carved wooden legs. By this luxury alone, I understand that Mr. Dresher, even in these difficult times, must be doing quite well.

"Oh, honey!" His tiny wife, wearing a pink-checked housedress, greets me and takes my coat as if I was someone important. "We're so glad you could come." Maybe she thinks I'm Daniel Hester's sister. Or maybe his wife.

I'd expected Hilda might be a large German shepherd, a golden retriever, or a valuable black-and-white sheep-dog, but instead I see a cute mongrel with short legs and a fluffy white coat waddling toward us. Her sides heave at the rate of about 120 heartbeats a minute. I'm not sure what's normal for dogs, but this doesn't look right. The pitiful little animal stumbles and gives the vet's hand a lick. Hester sits on a footstool and palpates her abdomen, then nods for me to come over. I sit down on the carpet next to him.

"Feel her. She's bulging with pups, as round as a basketball. And look, see the fluid trickling out?" I run my hands along her sides. Her tail droops sadly between her little legs, and her big brown eyes stare at me hopefully. *Sorry, pup, I'm a midwife for women and have no idea how to help you.*

"What do you think?" the farmer asks, bending over and touching his pooch on the head.

Hester grunts. "Something must be

blocking the way. I'll examine her first. Can you get me some hot water, soap, and a stack of towels? I want to put her up on something."

He carries the little dog into the kitchen. I layer two towels onto the oil-cloth-covered table, then, hoping to look useful, open the vet's bag, dig around in it, and pour some of the antiseptic soap I find inside into the wash-bowl. Hester carefully cleanses his hands, takes the dog's temperature, then sticks out his finger for more soap and reaches inside her. Hilda doesn't even look back; she's that miserable.

"It's a big one," he says as he pulls out. "And it's still alive . . . You feel." He pours the antiseptic soap on my finger, and I copy his action. It is nothing like doing a vaginal examination on a woman. For one thing, the doggie's vagina is extremely tiny, and for another, whatever is presenting is all bumps and lumps. I have no idea what I'm feeling and wonder how he can be sure that the pup is alive when I feel its mouth open and a little tongue sweep by.

"It licked me!" I whisper.

"Can you get a grip on anything? Your fingers are smaller than mine."

I frown. "What would I grip?"

"Just give it a shot," he whispers with his back turned to the Dreshers, who stand respectfully back at the kitchen door. "I don't want to use forceps. If I fail, I'll have to take her back to the office for a cesarean section. She's in such bad shape she might not make it."

I take a deep breath and mull things over. "If we could lift her front legs up, support her somehow, that might bring the presenting part lower. Once or twice I've had women squat for a birth." Mr. and Mrs. Dresher stare at us hopefully. They probably think we do this together all the time.

The vet looks skeptical but does what I ask, supports the small animal under her forelegs and lifts her head and trunk up eight inches.

"A little more?" He goes up another four inches until Hilda is standing like a poodle in the circus. The unborn puppy's snout comes down an inch, and it licks the tip of my finger again. That gives me an idea. I reach a little farther, turn my hand over, get the tip of my index finger into the animal's mouth, and pull down on the jaw. Mrs. Kelly did something like this back in Pittsburgh when an Irish woman, Jennie O'Hare, had a baby in a face presentation. You have to be very gentle.

I smile and look up at Hester and then across at the worried Dreshers. "It's moving!"

Hilda feels it too, and a little strength returns to her pushing. I know she can't understand me, but I can't help myself and I get excited. "Push, Mama. Push with all your heart!"

Mrs. Dresher comes over and joins in the cheerleading, pulls up a chair, puts her chin in her hand, and concentrates all her energy toward the little pooch. "Push, honey. You can do it!"

Hester shakes his head and grins that crooked smile, but soon we can see the tip of a black snout at the opening. I don't let go, just keep up with my gentle traction until the widest part of a good-sized head appears at the opening and the water gushes out. Then the vet tips the mother dog on her side to catch her breath.

The first large puppy lies very still, and I want to jump in and blow on it, but the vet elbows me out of the way and brings the newborn around to Hilda's head, where she licks it until it squirms and finally breathes.

After the first pup, the rest of the births are easy, with four more dogs born in their sacs slipping out one after the other.

When we are all done and Hilda is stable and resting, Mr. Hester and I take turns washing up in the indoor bathroom and Mrs. Dresher sets out tea and coffee cake in the living room. Companionably, we observe the brown-and-white newborns, now in a basket near the hearth with their mother, whining and squirming for the best place to nurse while George Olsen belts out "A Precious Little Thing Called Love" on the radio: *"What's the one thing makes me say Heaven's just across the way. It's a precious little thing called love."* Animals, I reflect, are not much different from humans when it comes to birth and the feelings they have for their new-borns. The little white dog's eyes are moist with love.

Back in the Model T, Daniel Hester and I drive in silence. As we pass through Liberty, I notice the copper's car is now in front of Mrs. Barnett's Boarding House. *Have the lawmen moved here permanently?* At last Hester's auto slugs up Wild Rose Road. It's been a long day.

"I appreciate your coming with me," he says formally. It's the first time we've spoken since we left the Dreshers'. "It's always a pleasure having your company." Briefly, I imagine we're returning from a charity ball at the Oneida Inn.

"I'm beat, but I enjoyed it. It's interesting . . ." We pull up in front of my house. "Do you want to come in?"

"For another rum toddy?" He gives me that grin, and I can see his white teeth in the very dark car.

"Out of luck there, no rum," I tease.

"Then I better be going." He reaches over and pats my arm, and I can feel his warmth through my jacket.

"Drive safely," I say and jump from the car.

"You know me." He guns his motor and turns around, skidding like a race-car driver in the mud.

The hounds bark wildly out back, but I stand on the porch watching until his little amber taillights wink out at the bend.

21

Five Crows

Bitsy hasn't come home since the cave-in. The first night, after the Wildcat disaster, she slept at Thomas's. Now it's Sunday and she must have stayed for church and maybe a potluck afterward. Who can blame her? I know she misses her family.

So many times she's asked me to come to church with her, but my faith in God is as thin as the cheesecloth we used to use to strain milk. Though the Hazel Patch flock are black, it's not a matter of color; it's that they are true believers and I'd feel out of place.

Yesterday five crows landed in a row on a branch of the bare oak just outside the kitchen window. I sat drinking peppermint tea and stared at them as they stared at me. It was strange because crows don't usually come right up to the house. I felt that they had brought me a message, only I was too deaf to hear it.

Another day passes, and still Bitsy's not home. It's been three days and it's a free world, but I miss her footsteps and even her clanging around with the iron poker in the stove at six A.M. Just as I'm preparing for bed, the dogs begin to growl and someone knocks on the door. I haven't heard an engine, so whoever it is must have come with a horse or a cart. Resentfully, I pull on my clothes, clump down the stairs, and light a kerosene lamp.

"Miss Patience," a woman's voice calls. She pounds on the door again, and when I swing it open, she almost falls in. "I'm Ruth Klopfenstein. Sorry to wake you, but we live on the other side of Hope Ridge on Bucks Run and my sister-in-law, Molly, is in labor." The young woman, in her early twenties, dressed all in black with a black scarf and gold wire-rimmed glasses like mine, is a wholesome farm girl with sandy hair that shines in the kerosene lamplight.

"Granny says something's wrong and I should get you. We've been driving around for the last hour. Missed your road the first time."

"Is this her first baby? How long has she been in labor?" I ask the two questions almost as one. If this is a second or third child, she may have already given birth.

"It's her first. She started paining yesterday. My granny's not a midwife, but she brought all of us into the world, my brothers and sisters and my four cousins. This is the first time she's been stumped."

Great, I think. Wait until you have trouble, then call the midwife! On the other hand, how can I not go? A life is at stake, maybe two. I grab my birth satchel and trot out to the road, wishing Bitsy were home to share this night's adventure. It's true, I've become dependent on her.

In the mud-spattered buggy, I'm surprised to find an old man. Again the black clothes and the wire-rimmed glasses, this time with a floppy-brimmed black hat. Ruth doesn't introduce me, so I hop in and we ride the rest of the way in silence.

It takes fifty minutes to travel through the muck around Raccoon Lick, past the vet's house, and then another half a mile up Bucks Run until we turn off. This is a hollow I've never seen before, never even heard of. There are four log homes along the swollen creek. A narrow meadow follows the run back toward the mountain. Lights are on in each dwelling, and I imagine that they are all Klopfensteins. We stop at the first building, a sturdy two-story log house with a long front porch. I don't wait for an invitation but hop out of the wagon and head for the door, already opening.

"Hi. I'm Patience Murphy, the midwife." I still feel that calling myself "the midwife" is a little overstated, like I'm playing a part in a novel. My experience is so limited compared to Mrs. Kelly's and Mrs. Potts's.

"I'm Mrs. Klopfenstein, Molly's mum." A worried woman, her worn face pale in the kerosene lamplight, grips my hand, adjusts her specs, and guides me into the front bedroom. I take in the occupants. The laboring woman is young and looks so much like Ruth, same round face with golden hair, that they could be twins, only her yellow mane is matted and sweaty. She's doesn't even open her eyes when her mother introduces me.

"Child, here's the midwife," she announces, then takes her seat. Ruth sits down too. There are five of them on five hard-backed chairs arranged alongside the bed, and they are all dressed in black with the same round eyeglasses. This must be a family with very bad eyesight. Five black crows.

I turn to the oldest woman, the one who appears to be the grandmother, a wisp of a thing, with white hair in a bun. She's skinny and flat-chested but has brown arms that could still lift a bale of hay. "Ruth told me you planned to deliver your great-grandbaby, but there seems to be a problem. Something's not right?"

The old woman pinches her mouth, stands up, and leads me toward the kitchen. In the long narrow room with a fireplace at the end, there's a table covered with oilcloth, a sink with a metal hand pump, and a cast-iron cookstove against the wall.

"The baby's not coming. It's as simple as that. Little Molly went into labor two days ago and seemed to be making some progress. All night she pained, and then around dawn she just petered out. I washed my hands and had a feel about suppertime. The head was there and she was about half open, but since her water broke everything's stopped. The baby's still alive, I know that much; we seen it move."

I take a deep breath and try to look competent. "So have you considered going to the hospital in Torrington? The doctors there could do an operation . . ." Grandma vigorously shakes her head and looks as if I've just asked whether she'd consider taking a tour of Hell.

"Have you tried any herbs?" The old woman shrugs. "Okay, I'll do what I can, but if the baby's too big, I can't change that. Let me study the situation. When did her water break?"

"Last night at the strike of twelve."

I calculate back. That's twenty hours gone already, and Mrs. Kelly always said never to let the sun set twice on a woman in labor.

Molly

Back in the bedroom, I find the patient still lying on her side with a wet towel between her legs. At first I think she's sleeping, but when I touch her on her shoulder her blue eyes flick open.

"Molly, I'm Patience Murphy, the midwife. Your granny says you've been in labor a long time and the pains seem to be spacing out and getting weaker. I'm going to try to figure out what's wrong. Can you turn on your back?"

The girl has spent all her energy but with assistance rolls over. Next I lay my hand on her abdomen and wait for a contraction. I wait and wait, but if she's having them they're too weak to feel. The uterus has all but given out.

While the other five women watch, their pale blue eyes following me behind the round glasses, I move my wooden stethoscope back and forth until finally I find the baby's heartbeat just below the belly button, right where it should be. I raise my hand and count out the beats to demonstrate the rate and then pull on my sterilized gloves.

"Here come my fingers," I warn as I slide them into the young woman's opening, aware that once again I am violating the law.

The first thing I find is the head, just like Grandma described, only it's not flexed; I can feel the baby's soft spot right in the middle. DeLee calls this the military position; the head is held like a soldier's at attention instead of flexed.

"Has Molly been out of bed much?" I ask the five crows, stalling for time.

"Not since her water broke," they answer in chorus.

"Not at all?"

"Not since she started leaking," they answer again. That's twenty hours!

"Once the waters come, we never let the woman out of bed," says Granny. "You don't want the cord to suffocate." I've heard this before, the idea that the cord will get trapped or prolapsed, but if the head of a full-term baby is deep in the pelvis, that's highly unlikely. There's no reason to immobilize a woman when moving around can ease the pain, make the pains stronger, and help the baby get into the most favorable position.

"Is she drinking?"

"We've tried to get her to suck on a rag dipped in sugar water, but she just turns her head." That's Granny again.

No wonder the mother has lost her contractions. It takes as much energy to give birth as it does to load a wagon with split wood, so this woman's running on empty. I smile to myself, actually happy now to have something to work on—the basics, fluids and sustenance—but I have to move fast. Too much time has been lost.

"Molly, I think your bladder is full. That could keep the baby from coming. When did you last go pee?" Molly looks at her mother, waiting for her mother to answer.

"We just put a cloth between her legs so she won't have to get up. It's been a few hours, but there hasn't been much."

I wince. This isn't good. "Okay, bring me the chamber pot. We have to have her get up. The bladder isn't disposed to empty when a person is lying down."

The five crows gape at me in disbelief.

"The potty? The chamber pot!" I repeat.

The crows fold their arms across their black chests like Supreme Court judges who've come to a verdict—and not a good one. Finally, the younger woman, Ruth, rises slowly, leaves the room and returns with a white enamel pot on a wire handle, the kind they sell at Mullin's Hardware for two bits. She sets it down next to the bed and without a word goes back to her chair.

"Okay, ladies." I lay it out. "I'm going to need your help to get Molly up, then we need to get some broth in her. Chicken soup would be good or ginger tea with raspberry leaf, ginseng, and honey to give her strength. Do you have any?" Mrs. Klopfenstein nods.

"Molly, give me a hand with your sister. The rest of you go whistle up some grub." As soon I say it, I regret my choice of words. I sound like a foreman at a lumber camp. Nevertheless, the women rise and head for the kitchen.

Alone with Molly, Ruth and I struggle her up, sit her on the pot, and change the linens.

"Were you able to go?" I ask the patient as I fluff up her pillows.

"A little." They're her first words. "I'm having a pain, though. Not like last night but a small one." I reach over and touch her belly. She's right; her uterus is trying to contract. After she's back in bed, Grandma feeds her the broth and ginger tea with sugar while I try to figure out what to do next. I consider getting out my black cohosh tincture, but Mrs. Kelly always warned that it could cause dangerously strong contractions and should be used only as a last resort.

Male Energy

An idea comes to me. "Okay, I know you are *so* tired, Molly, but it's time to walk." Molly doesn't budge, and the five ladies-in-waiting, who've drifted back to their chairs, stare at one another, probably wondering why they ever called in this crazy midwife. I try the positive approach, though I'm making this up as I go along.

"Molly, your baby's head is deep in the pelvis, but it's not flexed, so there's no way it can come out." The girl turns toward me slowly. "If we get you moving, the baby will shift and the contractions may come back. If you just lie here, you'll be pregnant forever." I don't say what I really mean: And you'll eventually get a fever and the baby will die . . . and you will die with it.

"Come on, Ruth, you can help. Come

on, Mrs. Klopfenstein! Each of you stand on a side." The older woman shakes her head but does what I tell her. "Now, up you go, Molly. Where's Molly's husband?"

"Next door with the menfolk. This ain't their place," declares Grandma.

"Well, I know men aren't usually included, but I think in situations like this the baby's father needs to come see his wife and give her some encouragement." No one moves. "Which house is he in, anyway? I'll get him." That does the trick. The stiff crow in the middle, who I now notice is pregnant and has one withered leg, limps out the door.

"Hairbrush?" I ask Mrs. Klopfenstein, adjusting my glasses, which are half falling off. "Hair ribbon? Warm facecloth." All the ladies, in similar eyewear, now bustle around, getting my meaning: we must make Molly presentable.

Mrs. Kelly once told me that brushing a laboring woman's hair brings her mind and spirit back to her body and I do this part myself, combing the tangles out of the golden strands and braiding them in two plaits. When we're done, we put on her spectacles so she can see, and her blue eyes seem to focus.

The front door swings open, and a reluctant young man wearing the regulation family gold specs, black pants, a white shirt, and black suspenders follows the woman into the bedroom. He looks so much like Molly and Ruth, it crosses my mind that he could be their cousin.

"This is Levi," the sister announces.

I take his arm and lead him forward. "Molly," he says. "You all right, wife?"

"Here, Levi," I order. "You must walk with her. Things are slow, but she's doing fine. These ladies are tired. We need to rest. Call us if anything happens." Before anyone can protest, I hustle the shocked crows out of the room.

"What's this about?" Grandma challenges. "Birth is a female thing."

"It's okay," I reassure her, as if I know what I'm talking about. "Sometimes when a woman is very tired, the male vigor can energize the womb." Bitsy would laugh. "Male vigor!" "Energize the womb!" Where is Bitsy, when I need her, anyway?

"Can you make us some tea?" I ask the aunt as I consult Mrs. Kelly's pocket watch hanging around my neck. My plan is, I'll give them ten minutes and then I'll peek in.

The ladies begin to bustle around again. Not only tea but also biscuits and homemade blackberry jam appear on the table. In the bedroom there are voices, and I think I hear singing. Could there be singing? We all look up, and I raise my hand to indicate that everyone else should stay seated while I creep back down the hall. In the bedroom, in the lamplight, Levi holds Molly in his arms and sways back and forth . . . back and forth.

"*Oh, Shenandoah, I long to hear you. Away, you rolling river,*" he sings into Molly's ear. Her face has such peace as she rests on his shoulder . . . then her eyes come wide open.

"Mmmmmm," she moans, somewhere between pleasure and pain.

"*Oh, Shenandoah, I long to hear you. Away, I'm bound away, 'cross the wide*

Missouri," Levi continues. Molly stops her moan and returns to her trance again, but two minutes later she moans again and then again . . . it's as though they are singing a duet, him the words and melody, her the bass.

"Help, something's coming!" It's Molly.

Levi leaps back as if he's just stepped into a nest full of rattlers. "Midwife!" he yells.

"I'm right here."

Grandma bustles in and begins to prepare the birth bed. "Set her down. Set her down!" she orders as if expecting the baby to fall out.

"Not yet," I counter. "Levi! Back to work. Keep singing. Molly, don't push yet. You can lean on the baby, but don't push, it can't be time." I squat down on the floor, pulling my rubber gloves on. The young woman gaps a little on the outside, but there's nothing to be seen.

Levi stares straight up at the ceiling, afraid to look but still crooning, *"Away, I'm bound away, 'cross the wide Missouri."*

Within minutes the moans turn to

growls and a round bald infant's head appears at the opening. "Okay, she can lie down now," I command. "The head's right here." Everyone is happier when we get Molly back in bed, but I barely have time to get my birth stuff out.

"Oh, no!" the young woman cries. "It's coming! It's coming!" And it is.

"Okay, Molly. This is it. Push like your life depends on it. Push like your baby's life depends on it. I'll hold your bottom so you won't tear." Everyone joins in with encouragement, including Levi, who has slipped from the room and collapsed in the hall.

"Push, Molly. Push hard! You can do it!" he yells, and I catch sight of his long legs and his farmer's boots sticking out past the door.

"*PUSH!*" he roars, louder than any of us—and Molly does.

In two more woody hard contractions, a baby boy is born, screaming and pink, and I lay him in his mother's arms.

"Praise the Lord!" hollers Grandma, picking up Molly's glasses and gently adjusting them behind the ears.

"My baby. My baby. Oh, Levi, our baby!" Molly cries as she kisses the infant.

The other women fall on their knees and begin to pray. I'm kneeling too, checking the womb for the final contractions, watching for the afterbirth.

Levi creeps into the room, keeping his eyes averted, and kneels with us. "Great God," he prays aloud. "Thank you for your bounty and for this gift which you have bestowed upon us." There is more, but I don't get it.

Light lifts me as I deliver the afterbirth. Light lifts us all.

March 7, 1930. Quarter moon rising.

Wyse Klopfenstein, male child of Molly and Levi Klopfenstein of Bucks Run, born at 7 pounds, 2 ounces. Head presented in the military position. The young patient had pained for two days to the point of exhaustion. She hadn't been out of bed for almost twenty-four hours, and I

see now that what we do or don't do for the mother influences the course of labor. Immobilizing the woman in bed, not letting her eat or get up to pee, slowed down everything, and then the uterus got tired.

Whether it was getting her up to the commode, feeding her broth with ginseng and raspberry tea, or calling her husband into the birthing room, we'll never know, but within an hour, Molly pushed four times and the baby came out. No tears. No hemorrhage. I found myself on my knees praying "thank you" with the others of the sect, who I later learned are a variation of Old Order Amish.

22

Gift Horse

Today is St. Patrick's Day, which was a big time for us when we lived in Chicago. The celebration was important for Mrs. Kelly too, and I became used to her parties with Irish soda bread and Irish stew and even a little Irish whiskey. I kidded Bitsy at breakfast for not wearing green, but she didn't get it. It's been good to have her around again. With the exception of the three days with Thomas, she hasn't been off the farm at all, unless it's to church on Sunday. I hate to say that I'm jealous of her relationship with Thomas and the Hazel

Patch community, but it's a little true. It's unseemly and makes me feel small.

Nevertheless, it's spring, and that's something to be thrilled about. The apple tree is blooming, a warm wind comes up through the valley, and there will be a full moon tonight. Though it's really too early to plant, the kitchen garden has been turned over and we are raring to go. As soon as the breakfast dishes are done, we head out to the side yard, which is fenced with barbed wire to keep the deer out. Bitsy carries the yellow *Old Farmer's Almanac* that her mother, Big Mary, lent us, and I carry the hoes and rakes. Mary also shared with us the seeds saved from her garden last year.

This will be my third garden, and though I don't care much for the relentless physical work or getting muddy and sweaty, I still marvel at the miracle of placing seeds in the ground and watching them sprout. My companion has been helping Mary grow vegetables since she was little, so it's not quite as thrilling for her.

We bend low, sowing our early crops:

peas, collards, carrots, and beets. Bitsy shows me a few tricks about seeding evenly. After the danger of frost is over, we'll put in corn and beans, tomatoes, squash, and potatoes. When I stand to straighten my aching back, I'm startled to notice a Model T creeping up Wild Rose Road. The auto appears to have a horse tied to the back. It's Daniel Hester. As we walk out to greet him, I tuck my loose hair back and wipe my face on the back of my sleeve.

"Little early to start a garden, isn't it?" he observes after he parks and gets out.

Bitsy jumps in with her chin tilted up. "Not according to the almanac. It's a full moon tonight and going to be an early spring. We won't get another frost. *The Old Farmer's Almanac* uses science to make their predictions." I'm surprised that she's treating the vet as an equal. So often with whites she eats the humble pie, never disagreeing. "Yes, sir, and yes, ma'am," and all that.

Hester looks skeptical but cuts short the discussion when his horse starts to flop down in the road. He runs to the back of his Ford and grabs the rope. "No, you don't, Star. On your feet! She tries to do that," he explains, "whenever I stop."

I meander over and touch the big animal's nose, but she whinnies and turns away. She's a beautiful horse, brown with a blaze on her forehead. "Is something wrong with her?"

"She's Mrs. Dresher's horse; the farmer with the dog that had puppies. She has founder, a disease of the hooves. The other name is laminitis." He waits to see if I know what that means, but I shrug. "Causes the hooves to become deformed, very painful and hard to cure. The old man wanted me to put her down this morning, but I couldn't do it. I asked if I could have her instead. See if I could bring her back to health."

Hester bends down and picks up one of Star's front hooves. I've never seen the bottom of a horse's foot before, and I'm almost sick when I see the blood and what looks like bone sticking through. As a midwife, most things don't bother me, but this gives me shivers.

"Yuck." I wrinkle my face. "How did this happen?" Bitsy is silent, leaning over my shoulder.

"Well, we aren't sure. Star had lameness last year, but I wasn't called in. Since money is so tight, most of the farmers, even the well-to-do ones, don't call me unless they think the situation's critical. After a week the limp went away. Then, a few days ago, she got into the cattle's grain.

"I guess that was it. An overrich diet can cause the horse's gut to release toxins that go into the bloodstream and eventually settle in the hoof, resulting in an abscess. The same thing can happen after a retained placenta, but this animal hasn't been bred for years . . . Cushing's disease can cause it too, but that's more chronic than acute." I'm mildly interested, but Bitsy has gone back to the garden. "The point is, the condition is severely painful and usually a death sentence, but I thought of you."

"Me?"

"Yeah. If you and Bitsy have the time, I think we can turn this around and then you'd have a good horse. You need one, don't you?"

I watch as the mare staggers back and forth on her front hooves, rolling her eyes in pain. I know nothing about horses, and I doubt that Bitsy does either.

"What would we have to do?"

"Well, first off, I'd show you how to bandage her feet; then you'd have to change the dressings. You'd also have to take her down to the creek three times a day to let her stand in cold water. I'd have to keep trimming the bare hooves while the new hoof material grew in. You'd have to keep a very clean stall and give her feed that's low in carbohydrates. Hay would be okay and maybe a little grass, but not grain. Your pasture would be okay. It doesn't look too rich."

I glance over at the ten acres of green, with yellow and white wildflowers that surround the barn. Looks pretty rich to me, but I'm no farmer.

"What's the worst that could happen?" Hester questions. "She could die. Or, if she gets well, it will take around two months and she's yours. She's a good mare . . . or was a good mare. Only fifteen. She could still even foal."

I run my hands along her sides, like I know what I'm feeling for. She doesn't look bad. Her back doesn't sway. Really, I'm just feeling her life force. Mr. Hester admits that this foot disorder might be fatal. Do I want to care for an animal that I will get fond of . . . and then watch her die? I make a snap decision, throw caution to the wind.

"Okay, we'll do it. Bitsy," I declare, "we have a horse. It's very sick, but Mr. Hester thinks we can cure her. What do you say?"

"Whatever you say, Miss Patience." *Cut the subservience, Bitsy,* I flash with my eyes. Maybe I should have consulted with her first. It's as though I've broken a rule and she's putting me back in my place. Funny how that "Miss Patience," in this setting where we live as equals, lets me know that something is wrong.

"Great. I'll come by to trim the bare hooves twice a week," the vet promises, missing the whole interchange. "And we won't use horseshoes anymore, *ever.*" We lead Star into the barn and clean up a stall, and the vet shows us how to wrap the feet.

When he leaves and Bitsy is back in the house starting supper, I stand in the barn alone, taking in our new animal. She turns to me, her brown eyes wet with what I think of as tears. "It will be okay, sweetie," I say, like she's one of my patients.

We have a horse!

March 20, 1930. No moon, overcast sky, fog so thick you could eat it with a spoon.

Eula May Mayle, female infant born to Carl and Ruby Mayle, Upper Raccoon Creek. 6 pounds, 4 ounces. Third baby. No problems. Bitsy and I barely made it to the house. Ruby laughed that she was waiting on us but couldn't wait much longer! Carl

told her she had to hold on because he wasn't catching no damn baby! Present were just Bitsy and I and the couple. We were paid one live chicken and a hand-knit blanket that will be very useful next winter.

Twyla

The first rush of spring has come and gone, and now there's more rain. A month ago we were confined by snow. Now it's red clay and mud.

Yesterday was Easter, and when Thomas came with a cart, Bitsy pleaded with me to go to the chapel at Hazel Patch, but I begged off, saying I wasn't in the mood, and stayed at home to work in the garden . . . A few hours later, I was surprised to see Thomas and Bitsy returning from church early, the cart laboring back up Wild Rose Road.

"Mrs. Potts wasn't at church, but she sent word with a neighbor that she wants us to come into Liberty for a delivery," Bitsy announces. I wrinkle my nose. It's not that I don't want to help the older midwife, but I feel as though I'm being dragged into another emergency. It's a beautiful spring day, and I have farm chores to do.

"What's up?" I ask, knowing I won't refuse.

"It's Twyla, Nancy Savage's daughter," Thomas puts in. "Nancy is Judge Hudson's cook, and her daughter, Twyla, is the Hudsons' upstairs maid. The kid is having labor pains. She's only fourteen, has been crying since yesterday, and refuses to go to the hospital. Hudson's wife is so upset, she fainted, and the judge stormed out. Mrs. Potts has been sitting with her all night, and the judge told her he didn't want any damn nigger girl wailing in his house when he got back."

You can tell by the way Thomas tightens his jaw that he's really angry. "Mrs. Potts wants Bitsy to come too. She says Bitsy may be able to calm the girl down."

"Who's the father? Is there a father?"

"Nobody's saying, but we think he's Judge Hudson's son, Marvin, a student at Princeton. He was home this summer. It would be the right time."

I blow through my mouth. I can't refuse Mrs. Potts, but a fourteen-year-old girl may not be big enough to birth a good-sized baby and I don't even know the family.

An hour later we're clip-clopping across the bridge into Liberty with the Hope River spilling over her banks below. Two bufflehead ducks, with their black-and-white feathers and overlarge teal-and-purple heads swirl in the backwater. Bitsy is still wearing her go-to-church clothes and I'm looking presentable enough, I think. My dress is a ten-year-old blue chemise, and hers a yellow flowered affair she inherited from Katherine MacIntosh. We have aprons for the birth in our satchel.

Poor Thomas, he's hardly said a word. Everyone must call on him for everything. Tonight he has to work the night-owl shift at the mine, and I wonder how we'll get home.

* * *

We enter quietly through the back door of the Hudsons' white colonial. A wraparound porch with swings and ferns in pots and wicker furniture graces the front. Before we get into the kitchen, I hear a scream, and for some reason, it crosses my mind that the way the girl got pregnant might not have been consensual. The judge's son would be eighteen or twenty, a fully grown man; she's only fourteen, little more than a child.

Mrs. Hudson, with gray-streaked brown hair done up in a bun, sits at the long maple table with a cold compress on her head. She doesn't get up. The cook, Nancy Savage, a thin coffee-colored woman in a white uniform, welcomes us in. Upstairs the wailing starts up again.

Thomas takes his hat off and bows with his head to the judge's wife. "Mrs. Hudson." He nods to the colored woman of about his mom's age. "Miss Nancy, this is Patience Murphy, the midwife from over Hope Ridge, and her assistant, my sister, Bitsy."

"Bless you!" The cook stands and directs her comment to both of us. "I hope you can get that girl to settle down. She's going to tear herself up or lose that baby if she don't behave."

"Yes, thank you so much for coming," Mrs. Hudson murmurs, glancing from under the comfort rag on her brow. "Nancy, take their things and show them up the back stairs. I just hope you can do something. The child has already run my husband off, and if this keeps up, I'll have to leave too."

The wailing starts once more. By the sound of it, the pains are about every four minutes. Mrs. Kelly always told me to let laboring women find their own way. "It's their journey," she said. "You can't lay the road for them." I take a deep breath. Maybe she's right, but screaming has never seemed helpful to me, and despite my chosen name, I'm not as patient as she was.

Upstairs, Nancy nervously pushes the guest bedroom door open.

"Twyla," she whispers, "the other midwives have come." A pillow flies across the room and hits me in the face. It doesn't hurt, just offends me a little. "Now, Twyla, don't be that way! These nice ladies are going to help you get your baby." The girl's mother retreats and slips down the stairs, understandably at her wit's end.

"I don't want no baby!" Twyla shouts after her. So that's the trouble. It's hard to suffer the pains of childbirth if you don't welcome the infant.

"Hi, Twyla," I try. The girl turns her back and starts wailing again. She's a slip of a thing, probably not five feet tall, with wild curly hair and very light, almost golden, eyes, strange in a brown face. Mrs. Potts sits in the corner in a rocking chair, her hands empty in her lap. She's clearly had enough of this, but a midwife can't give up, can't leave her patient until the baby's out and the mother and infant are stable.

"Whooooooooooooooooooooo!" Twyla shrieks. Bitsy surprises me by dropping the satchel, going right up to the patient, and putting her hand over the young woman's mouth. She pats Twyla's lower face so her wail sounds like a barn owl. "Whoooo. Whoooo. Whooooo. Whoooooooo." The girl slaps Bitsy's palm away. "Who are you?"

"I'm the midwife's assistant, and I'm here to get you under control," Bitsy states firmly. Mrs. Potts and I stare at each other, shocked at such boldness.

"Yeah? Have you ever had a baby? I feel like my whole damn body is being ripped apart!" The profanity doesn't bother me, I've heard far worse on the union picket lines, but Mrs. Potts cringes.

Bitsy doesn't miss a beat. "Well, I've never had no damn baby, but I know enough not to struggle with the contractions. They always win. You're just making a mess of this. Your baby would have come a long time ago if you weren't fighting it. And you are scaring him, don't you know. When you scream, you scare the baby. They can hear everything." I smile, thinking how well Bitsy puts this. *You scare the baby.* I'll use that line myself with my next out-of-control patient.

Another pain hits before the older midwife and I can consult about the baby's position. Twyla starts her yell, but Bitsy, undeterred, lays her hand over the girl's mouth again and this time pats so fast that the *Whooooooooooo* comes like an Indian war whoop. Twyla laughs. She's met her match. Bitsy wipes the girl's face with a cool cloth, and that's the end of the screaming.

"Thank you for coming, dear. I'm getting too old for this," Mrs. Potts confides in a whisper. "I don't mind when a woman is serious about her job, but this girl struggles and there's no father. You heard?"

"Thomas told us."

The old lady shakes her head. "We've been doing this all night. I checked her one time, four hours ago. She was only halfway dilated, but the head was real low. Maybe you can check her now. See what you think. If she's not progressing, we're going to have to get her to the hospital, no matter how she kicks and screams. We can't let anything happen."

I approach the patient for the first time. "Twyla," I say softly, not wanting to upset her again or be hit with another pillow. "I'm Patience. Mrs. Potts and I think you might be getting close to delivering. I'd like to check you after your next contraction to see if the baby's getting lower."

I don't offer the alternative: And if it's not coming, we are going to have to struggle you into an auto against your will and drag you to the hospital in Torrington, fifty miles away, where you'll be strapped down, given gas, and have the baby cut out. (Dr. Blum could probably do it, but he doesn't take coloreds.) The Hudsons are a respected family in the mountains and would pay for a cesarean section, even in hard times.

I remember the story Mrs. Kelly told me, that the first successful cesarean section in the United States was, in fact, performed in Mason County, West Virginia, back in the late 1700s. According to her, a physician performed the operation on his wife, who was in obstructed labor. The doctor, a Mr. Bennett, accomplished the surgery with only laudanum for anesthesia. Amazingly, both mother and infant survived.

Bitsy persuades Twyla to lie still and

open her legs while I wait with my sterilized rubber gloves on. When the next contraction ends, I kneel at the bedside. Mrs. Potts is right. The head *is* very low, and I'm pleased to discover that there's only a ring of cervix left. "You're almost there!"

"I thought so," crows Bitsy. "She's so cranky! I knew she must be close."

Mrs. Potts smiles and wearily begins to get out her birth gear. She turns to my assistant. "Would you like to deliver the baby, honey?"

I raise my eyebrows, surprised and a little miffed. I don't want to contradict Mrs. Potts, but I don't think Bitsy's ready . . . On the other hand, Bitsy doesn't seem nervous.

"Ugggh!" Twyla moans. "I got to go pooh!" I reach for the flowered ceramic chamber pot and have the patient squat over it. I know the girl feels the head moving down, not a lump of stool, but what harm can it do if she thinks it's a bowel movement? Everyone turns away while Twyla squats, her long white nightgown covering the receptacle.

"Do you want me to call your mother

and Mrs. Hudson? It won't be long now," I say over my shoulder as we lay out the sterilized scissors, string, and towels. Other than my olive oil, that's all we need. The old lady plunks back down in her rocker.

"No," the girl says firmly and then grunts again. Her eyes are big now, and I think she knows she is pushing out more than a large stool. "I just want there to be us."

Ten more contractions and "Eeeeee-eee. It burns bad." Twyla stands and puts her hand on her vagina. "It's the head!" she exclaims and for the first time smiles.

When Bitsy and I lean down to look, the infant is almost crowning and a shock of thick black hair hangs out an inch.

"You're right, Twyla." This is Bitsy taking charge, saying exactly what I would say as we lay the patient down. "The baby is coming, and I'm going to need your cooperation while I ease the head out.

"Push and blow. That's how to do it.

Push a little . . . blow a little." She sits on a stool at the edge of the bed, between the girl's legs. "Push a little. Blow a little." Twyla does what Bitsy tells her, and slowly the head crowns—so slowly I don't know how the girl stands it. Then I see an ear and then the whole head. I wipe its face with a clean cloth, wipe its mouth out too. Then my able apprentice, without any instruction from me or Mrs. Potts, presses the head down to deliver the top shoulder, lifts up to deliver the bottom, and a wet infant tumbles into her lap, already screaming.

My friend holds the very brown baby boy out to the young mother, but Twyla lifts her hands in protest. "No! It's so slimy!" Some mothers, I've observed, like to have their wet newborn against their chest, and others are afraid of the mucus. Mrs. Potts whips one of the towels open, wraps the baby in it, and places it back on the girl's chest. With one finger Twyla tentatively touches the squirming thing, transfixed, amazed that something alive came out of her body.

"Everything okay up here?" Nancy Savage calls from the hall.

The door cracks open, and Mrs. Hudson peeks in with Nancy behind her. "It's so quiet, but . . . we thought we heard a baby cry."

Twyla smiles. "See, Ma? I did it. I really did it!"

April 21, 1930. Sliver moon in a purple sky at dusk, the trees silhouetted in black.

Mathew Hudson Savage, healthy male infant, was born at 6:15 yesterday evening to Twyla Savage. Twyla is 14 years old and was out of control when we got there, yelling like a wild woman! Spontaneous vaginal delivery performed by Bitsy, with no difficulty. Seven pounds, 4 ounces. Mrs. Potts also present. Father unknown. No tears. Minimal bleeding. Bitsy's first delivery. Twyla refused to breastfeed, and there was no convincing her.

23

Warning

Since Thomas has already gone back to his job at the Wildcat, I leave Bitsy at the bedside and walk to the vet's office to see if we can catch a ride home. Before leaving, I check the mother and baby one last time. Mrs. Hudson is ready with a warm nippled bottle, the kind you can get in the Sears, Roebuck catalogue. I hate to see it, but one thing I've learned is that if a mother really doesn't want to breastfeed, it won't help to pressure her. She won't be successful, and everyone will be miserable, including the baby.

Crossing Main, I spy my friend Becky Myers coming out of Gold's Dry Goods with Priscilla Blum, the doctor's wife. Becky's short black hair, in a new bob, blows in the April wind, and her wide-spaced brown eyes sparkle. Mrs. Blum wears a long lavender scarf that trails in the breeze. They both look so fresh that for a moment I'm jealous. Becky's my friend, but I've never lived in their world of store-bought clothes and styled hair.

"Hey, Becky!" I call out, swallowing my resentment and waiting until the doctor's wife turns off on Second Street. "I was just thinking of visiting. You have time for company?" Her house is a block away, around the corner on Sycamore. "I'll just stay a few minutes and tell you about Twyla Savage's birth. Then I have to find a ride home."

I put my arm through hers, companionably, the same way I do with Bitsy, but without any self-consciousness or feeling I'm defying an unwritten law. "It's a beautiful infant. His hair must be two inches long. Can you make a home visit later this week?" I babble on, still elated about the good birth.

"I hope Twyla will be okay," Becky thinks out loud. "At one point she declared she didn't want the baby. What she really wants is to go back to school."

I frown. "Can't her mother take care of the baby while she goes to class?"

"Her mother has to work for the Hudsons, and word is, Judge Hudson is looking for a family to adopt it. A *black* family."

We take the steps up to her neat porch with two high-back rattan chairs and enter her white-tiled kitchen. As Becky makes tea I stare out the window and wonder who that black family might be. Twyla was so proud of herself in the end. I'd hate to see the baby taken away.

Becky changes the subject. "You know, Patience, there's something I've wanted to talk with you about since Bitsy Proudfoot moved in with you."

This puts me on alert, and I pause with the teacup halfway to my mouth. "What?"

"You know the Klan is reorganizing in Union County, don't you?"

I draw back as if slapped. "The Ku Klux Klan?" Why do I ask? Everyone knows there's only one Klan, the hooded white supremacist Klan that asserts its power by intimidation and violence. The anti-Catholic, anti-Jewish, anti-Communist, anti-Negro-who-doesn't-stay-in-his-place Klan.

"I heard they were on the way out the last few years—down from four million to a few hundred thousand left in the Deep South."

"The South *and* the Appalachian Mountains. Wherever people are poor and oppressed, the Klansmen look for someone to bully. That's what's happening around here, and I just don't want that person to be you."

"You think I'm a target?" I'm in shock. "I thought I was keeping a low profile, way out in the country . . ."

"Be real, Patience. You are *not* low profile. Everyone knows who you are. Times are hard. Men are looking for ways to take out their frustration, and you're involved with a group of uppity

Negroes . . . There's been talk. You live with a Negro woman . . . For God's sake, you walk around with her arm in arm. I'd watch it, if I were you."

"Like who? Who's uppity? Thomas and Bitsy?"

"Thomas and Bitsy . . . and the Reverend Miller and all those folks at his church. Mrs. Potts is accepted because of her skills. She's delivered a lot of babies, black and white, in Union County, but people say the pastor preaches equality and white people don't like it."

"Well," I go on. "I'm not responsible for what people say in the pulpit or anywhere else. Anyway, I agree with the preacher."

Becky and I have never before discussed politics, and she has no idea how important the issue of equality is to me. "Some people may think Negroes are inferior, but you and I know it isn't true," I lecture. "The Proudfoots and the Millers are as smart and able as any of us, maybe more. Anyway, if we want to see the world change, we have to change it, and I'll put my arm through Bitsy's whenever I want!"

"Let's just let it drop," my friend mutters and puts her cup in the sink. "I wish I hadn't brought it up. I was only trying—" The phone on her kitchen wall rings three times. "Hello," she answers. "Okay, I'll inform her." You can tell by the way she's going to *inform* me that she's mad. "That was Bitsy. She's over at Mr. Hester's, and he's going to give you a ride home."

"Becky, I'm sorry. I didn't mean to get into an argument. I just have a hard time believing that in 1930 the Klan could be a problem. West Virginia fought with the North in the Civil War, for heaven's sake . . . this isn't Mississippi or Georgia. Anyway, why shouldn't all people be proud and free regardless of color?"

Becky shakes her head and sits down, staring out the window at the daffodils along the walk. She doesn't even give me a good-bye hug. I lean over her chair and give her a half hug anyway.

"You're too innocent, Patience. You need to face reality. Not everyone is as nice as you."

Nice as me! If she only knew.

The ride home with the vet and Bitsy is a quiet one. We each rest in our own thoughts as we chug along in the Model T. I keep wondering what Becky means by "uppity." I'm shocked at her attitude, an educated woman. Though maybe I shouldn't be. Someone like me, who lives in my own little world, I don't really know how the MacIntoshes, the Hudsons, and the Blums think.

It was at the Westinghouse walkout in 1916 that I first saw black and white workers, men and women too, demonstrating together. Before that, the employers used to pit us against one another. If whites struck for better working conditions or shorter hours, blacks were used as strikebreakers. If men in the all-male AFL struck for higher wages, the bosses would hire more women. But at the Westinghouse munitions plant, six thousand workers, including three hundred women and a few dozen Negroes, walked out together.

In the second row of the all-female Dish Pan Drum Corps, just in front of the band, Nora and I linked arms, proud and happy, with the Rosenberg sisters and Daisy, our colored suffragette friend, singing at the top of our lungs, *"Solidarity forever! Solidarity forever! Solidarity forever! For the union makes us strong."* The five of us were thrown into the slammer that day when the coppers said to disband, but we were out in seventy-two hours. Daisy Lampkin got out in a day. Her husband was a rich restaurateur.

Despite my intention not to let Becky's warning about the KKK bother me, my stomach grows cold and I wonder what she isn't saying. I would like to go back and ask her. Who's talking about me, anyway? What are they saying?

Threat

Mr. Hester comes only once a week now to check on Star. Most of the time he goes straight to the barn, doesn't stop at the house, but yesterday he had good news.

"Star's really healing well," he told me as he washed his hands at our kitchen sink. "Her hooves can bear more weight. You still taking her down to the creek three times a day? You could try riding her if you want to."

"She seems to like the creek," I reply. "Likes to stand in the water, and I enjoy my time there too. It feels like I'm doing a chore while I lie on my back and look at the clouds." I pour him a cup of sassafras tea and pull out a chair. "The sound of the water soothes me, reminds me of my childhood on the banks of the Des Plaines River."

The vet nods as if he understands but returns quickly to the horse, where he's no doubt more comfortable. "Just start riding her in the pasture, and eventually take her down to the Hope."

"I've never been on a horse before. If Bitsy has, we'll do it tonight . . . but can I pose a question?" The vet shrugs, alert to the change in my voice.

"This is awkward, but have you heard

any rumors about the Ku Klux Klan in Union County?" Hester blows across his cup, doesn't say anything at first, just takes a sip of the tea, so I go on. "I feel funny asking . . . I don't know why, it's just that Bitsy and I never talk about anything to do with race. In some ways I don't know her world at all. We live as if it doesn't matter, and it doesn't to me, but Rebecca Myers, the health nurse in town, told me last week that they're reorganizing the Klan in West Virginia. Is there anything to it?" Hester stares out the window and shrugs.

"Maybe. I was invited to a Rotary Club meeting at the Oneida Inn last month. Went with Dresher, Star's previous owner. He's a big supporter of my practice, and he thought I should make local contacts, but I don't think I'll go again.

"There was a lot of bitter talk about the folks at Hazel Patch, how they're forming an agricultural collective, buying things in bulk from the Farmers Co-op in Torrington, even arranging to have feed for their cattle shipped down the Mon River on the steamboat from

Pittsburgh. The locals don't like it, especially the merchants." He shrugs.

"Mostly it was just men complaining. Businesses are hurting; everyone feels threatened. Another big mine closed, the Minute Man west of Liberty. William MacIntosh is part owner of that one too."

I ask him straight out, "But do you think the Klan presents any danger to me, to Bitsy and me? Becky says she's heard talk. Is this for real or just men spouting off?"

"Nah. Just talk." He sets his cup on the counter. "It'll blow over. Anyway, what are you going to do about it?"

That stops me. What could I do about it? Kick Bitsy out? Pretend she's my servant and make her shuffle and bow? Go to Sheriff Hardman? He's probably one of them. Call the editor of the newspaper and have them exposed? He might be one too.

24

Magda

Running my fingers over the embossed tulips on the cover of my leather-bound diary, I breathe a long sigh. It's Mother's Day, and I'm sad. I'm always sad on Mother's Day. It just gets to me.

All across the land, families are at Mama's having fried chicken and dumplings, or, if they can't afford a chicken, they're digging into a good pot of beans. Children will bring their mothers bunches of wildflowers—pink and white phlox from the roadside, yellow iris from the edges of streams, bluebells from the forest floor—but I have neither children to thank me nor a mother to go home to.

Bitsy has taken her bicycle into Liberty to spend the day with Big Mary and Thomas. Even Daniel Hester found another vet in Delmont to cover his practice and has taken the train to see his mother near Buffalo.

We didn't have Mother's Day when I lived in the white house in Deerfield. It became a national holiday later, started in 1910 by a woman from Grafton, West Virginia, I hear, not seventy miles from Liberty.

I wish we *had* celebrated Mother's Day; then I could have taken my mother flowers and thanked her for all the times she'd tucked me in or ironed my bed on a cold winter's night or sewed my dresses or read me stories, but she's gone now, gone many years.

I had Mrs. Kelly too, a second mother, who took me in when I was homeless and alone, taught me all I know about delivering babies and living on the land. I stayed with her thirteen years, as long as I lived with my own ma.

And once I was almost a mother. I felt Lawrence's baby move and squirm inside me, until I lost them both. My little boy is buried in the corner of my heart now, a small mound of pain just left of my breastbone. I can't even take flowers to my mother or Mrs. Kelly's grave sites. Mama is buried far away in Deerfield, and my dear Sophie was put to rest in the family graveyard in Torrington.

Enough of this! What would Mrs. Kelly think of my feeling so sorry for myself! I don't need children. I don't need a mother. I need to go pick my own bouquet.

"To my little one's cradle in the night comes a little goat, snowy and white." I sing the old lullaby as I tromp across the meadow. *"The goat will trot to the market, while Mother her watch does keep, bringing back raisins and almonds . . ."* I continue the tune all the way down to the creek where the serviceberry bushes bloom.

The first night I heard that song was the night I saw my first birth . . .

* * *

"Steady the lamp," Mrs. Kelly orders. "Please!"

I'm shaking like a leaf in a windstorm. Even though I grip the lantern's wire handle with both hands, the shadows dance.

I would have preferred to stay outside in the dark, but Mrs. Kelly said she might need me. Anyway, where would I have waited? Alone in the alley?

The worn-thin mother, lying on the pallet in this one-room shack down by the river, lets out a deep groan. I try not to look, stare up at the cobwebs on the ceiling and at the newspapers pasted on the walls to keep out the wind, but the woman's white belly glows like the full moon.

I met the midwife just a few hours ago, and we were on our way to talk to a mother of twins, who might need me, when a boy raced up and begged the midwife to come.

Now the lad leans against the door frame in the shadows. His knickers are torn, and he has one deformed ear. He may have been born that way, or possibly somebody cuffed him.

"Buster," Mrs. Kelly commands, "make yourself useful."

The kid shuffles over. "Here, you hold the lantern. Elizabeth, kneel down and pull hard on the mother's hands; it will give her strength."

I'm like Buster, don't want any part of this, but Mrs. Kelly is hard to refuse. I crouch low, so close I'm in the pregnant woman's face.

"Next time you feel the pain, I want you to push *with all your heart*," the midwife instructs. (I now use the same words with my patients.) She glances at the pocket watch she wears on a ribbon around her neck. Before the next groan, the patient opens her legs, puts her chin on her chest, and I know she means business.

"What's your name?" I whisper, when she lets go of me.

"Magda." The tired woman blows her long hair out of her eyes, which spark green in the kerosene lamplight.

"I'm Elizabeth. You can call me Lizbeth, everyone does."

Buster is silent, just endures with his arm straight out, holding the metal lantern, steady as an oak branch when there's no wind, tears streaming down his face, making dirt streaks. He looks about nine.

Mrs. Kelly is at the woodstove, heating up water and getting out her clean cloths and scissors, when, with the next push, the patient shouts something that I think must be Polish, and the infant tumbles out. The midwife sees what's happening, steps over, and hands the new life to me. I have no choice but to take it, all wet and slimy, wiggling and crying with the cord still attached. It was the smell of the birth that made me gag. Now I actually like it, sweet and earthy.

I hand the newborn over to Magda, who has fallen back on the bed. "Here's your baby." Buster sets the lamp down and runs from the shack. The midwife kicks the door shut to keep out the cold, and I can hear the little boy sobbing.

In fifteen minutes, we have the place tidy. Buster, still hiccuping his sobs, shows me the way to the pump in the alley, and I bring in more water. "Everything's okay now," I tell him as we walk back toward the shack. "Your mother's fine. You have a pa?"

He tilts his head toward the railroad tracks. "Just started graveyard shift, throwing coal for Pittsburgh Steel." That's good, I think. They'll have someone to look after them.

When we leave, Magda is settled, with a worn blue-and-brown patchwork quilt covering her. Buster sits next to her on the bed and touches his tiny brother with the tip of one finger.

The mother lifts up her face, and I notice for the first time that she has a harelip, but not a bad one. She still looks like a print of the Madonna in Lawrence's art book.

"We'll pay you when Zarek gets his first wages," she says to Mrs. Kelly in a thick accent.

"No," Sophie responds. "You need the money more. Get Buster some new britches, and take care of that baby. Breast only. No cow's milk or gruel. I'll come see you next week." She runs her hand through the boy's thick brown hair and pats the mother on her cheek.

I help the midwife with her heavy coat, throw my blue cloak around my shoulders, and pick up her carpetbag. Then we go into the bitter night, back to the trolley stop. When I turn, pale lamplight shines through the one four-paned window in a golden path along the cobblestones, and I can hear Magda singing *"To my little one's cradle in the night comes a little goat, snowy and white . . ."*

25

Bolt from the Blue

On the way back across the meadow, with my sweet-smelling Mother's Day bouquet of white serviceberry blossoms and pink phlox, I'm startled to see a vehicle sputtering up Wild Rose Road. It can't be the vet; he left on the train yesterday. Not likely Katherine MacIntosh either, unless Bitsy's with her and she's on the run again. The sheriff?

I trot into the house, lock my diary, and shove it under a sofa cushion. I plunk my flowers into a quart mason jar and then hang my red kimono on its nail behind the kitchen door. Maybe it's Becky Myers, come to check on me after her excessive worries about the Klan, or perhaps a father, looking for the midwife.

I'm surprised when Mildred Miller and Mrs. Potts get out of the battered black open hack. The two are dressed in their church clothes, dark dresses with bright white lace collars and white hats that frame their faces. The old lady is using a cane, and her companion helps her up the steps.

"I'll get right to the point," Mrs. Potts starts out once she settles on the sofa.

"I love your house," Mrs. Miller interjects. "It's so nice and clean. Smells so good. It must be your flowers. Is Bitsy here?"

"Her room's upstairs, but she's gone into town to spend the day with her mother, Mary Proudfoot."

Mrs. Potts tries again. "My heart's been skipping around and causing me dizzy spells. The doc says it's weak. Thinks I ought to stop running around after babies."

"She had a fall last week, out in the

garden, and lay there for two hours until one of the Bowlin boys passed!" That's Mrs. Miller.

"I tripped on an old tomato stake! Could happen to anyone. The point is, Patience, I need your help. You're young and strong, and I could turn my mothers over to you. I'll still come to the births in the daytime, just to be companionable, if I'm feeling well and the roads aren't bad. The doctor says I have a few more years if I'm careful." She declares this last part so offhandedly: *a few more years.* I'm taken aback, shocked at the sound of it. Mildred stares at the floor.

"Would there be many?" I ask in an attempt to get practical. "Usually I do two births a month; since the hard times came, maybe three. People who used to think a home delivery too old-timey are now calling on me because they can't afford the hospital or they've heard bad stories from other new mothers."

"I do 'bout the same. Two or three a month, but more of my patients are black mothers and they aren't as much trouble as white girls. Got more grit." I smile at her comment. She's possibly right, with the exception of fourteen-year-old Twyla, who screamed her way through labor.

"Mrs. Potts, I'm honored, but I don't know how to say this . . . Bitsy and I have to make a living. We can't always do deliveries for free. Would people pay us? Would you and I split the fee?" I feel like a money-grubber even bringing this up. Mrs. Kelly believed that delivering babies was a sacred act, close to serving Communion, but midwives don't live on light alone. Even if we grow and preserve our own food, we also need coal, kerosene, cornmeal, and sugar.

The old lady chuckles. "Of course we'd divide everything, unless it's a chicken! And if I don't make it to the birthing, the chicken's all yours."

"Would the families accept me? They're used to you. Would they even *want* me? I'm white, and I'm new. Trust is important."

"That's why I'd come to the deliveries with you at the beginning, as much as I could . . . I've been a midwife in this community for over sixty years, delivered white and black babies all over the place, and if I say you're good, they'll know you're good."

I make the two ladies sassafras tea in my best blue-and-white cups while I think it over. If we got paid for the deliveries, it would make a big difference—and anyway, how can I say no?

"So do we have an agreement?" Mrs. Potts asks.

"I'm honored," I reply, wondering what I just got myself into.

Mildred Miller gazes at the painting on the wall behind the sofa. "Is that you at the ocean? I went there once to see my cousin in South Carolina. The water was cold and salty. I didn't like it."

"It's me when I was sixteen. My baby's father painted it, and that water is Lake Michigan near Chicago. It's not salty."

"I didn't know you had a child." Mrs. Potts picks up on the "my baby's father." "Is he grown?"

"No, he died. Died at birth. They both died within days of each other." Mildred sucks in her breath, and Mrs. Potts puts her veined hand over mine.

"That's what makes you a good midwife," the old lady says. "You know the value of life, and you know loss. My father used to say the two are one, like the bramble and the rose. Life and death . . . the bramble and the rose."

Discarded

Tears have a way of humanizing people, though I don't cry much myself.

What's making me think of such things is my trip to Liberty today. I had bicycled in to check on Twyla and the baby. Bitsy stayed home and took her bike down to the Hope to go fishing. Didn't want to come to town, she said. She'd had all of Twyla she could stand for one month.

When I got there, the mayor and Mrs. Hudson were in the parlor having tea with Mrs. Stenger, the pharmacist's wife, so I just said hello, checked on Twyla and little Mathew, who has already gained a pound, and then headed down the back stairs, intending to leave through the kitchen. I had my hand on the knob when Twyla's mother, Nancy Savage, stopped me.

"She doing pretty good, ain't she?"

"She is. Twyla's taken right to motherhood."

"That's why I hate to see it."

I'm adrift in this conversation. "See what?"

"The judge planning on giving our baby away. Says little Mathew got to go. Either he goes, or Twyla and I can leave with him. He says there's no place for a baby in his home. He means a black baby."

"What does Mrs. Hudson think? It doesn't seem right. It's not the judge's baby to give away."

"She disapprove, but she says he the boss."

"Nancy!" It's her mistress calling from the parlor. "Can you bring us some more tea, honey?" The cook bites her chapped lips. "Coming!" she calls and picks up the teapot.

"Pray for us, Miss Patience," she

whispers as she leaves, and there are tears in her eyes.

Before riding home, with a heavy heart, I decide to visit Becky at her clinic in the courthouse. I'm wondering what she thinks of the whole mess. She's mentioned this possibility before, but I didn't think the rumors could be true. We haven't spoken since our tiff about the Klan, and that was weeks ago.

"Hello," I call, entering the empty waiting room of the Women's and Children's Health Program. "Hello?"

The receptionist's wooden desk is unoccupied, but that doesn't surprise me. The clinic runs on a tight budget, and Mrs. Cooper, the secretary, works only part-time. I take a seat, prepared to wait a few minutes, figuring that Becky must be in the single exam room with a patient.

To kill time, I inspect the small space, which smells faintly of Lysol. This is where the home health nurse holds her classes. What interests me are the posters. The yellow announcement by the front door exhorts the benefits of

CORN: FOOD FOR THE NATION, SERVE SOME AT EVERY MEAL. An attractive dark-haired woman is baking corn bread. I didn't know corn was that healthy! I'd better plant more next year.

Over the desk is another sign, this one with an orange border and a man sneezing into a handkerchief: COUGHS AND SNEEZES SPREAD DISEASES. Finally there's one next to the restroom: STAMP OUT TUBERCULOSIS! Santa Claus holds a letter with the famous Christmas Seal on it, a fund-raiser for the National Tuberculosis Association. I let out a long sigh. My mother and grandmother both died of it, the Great White Plague.

There's a muffled sound inside the exam room and I straighten my skirt, ready for Becky and her patient to come out, but the door doesn't open. Then I hear moaning. A chair scrapes, and there's moaning again. "Becky?" No answer. "Becky?" a little louder.

I stand up and step closer. Becky and I are friends, but this is her place of work and I can't interrupt her; still, it does seem odd that she won't answer. Maybe she's ill . . . I move right up to the door and press my ear against it. "Nurse Becky? Are you okay?"

The woman clears her throat. "Just a minute . . . " I sit down again, but she doesn't come out. By Mrs. Kelly's gold pocket watch it's 3:10. Five minutes later she still hasn't shown. Finally I step over, tap twice, and crack the door open. "Becky?" I whisper. "It's Patience. Can I come in?"

"Oh, it's you, Patience . . . yes. You'd better. You'd better see this."

That wasn't the answer I expected. I open the door, step inside, and close it behind me. "Are you all right?" I can see that she isn't. Her face is mottled, her eyes are red from crying, and tears run down her pale cheeks. "What's wrong?"

She turns to her side and indicates the exam table. That's when I see it. Lying on a clean blanket is a tiny baby boy, smaller than a doll and clearly dead. Its skin is so thin that you can see the blood vessels, and its face is dark and bruised.

"When I came in this morning," starts out Becky in a small voice, "I found a box tied up with string at the door. The waiting room was full, so I didn't open the package until everyone left. Then I almost fainted. This is so sad! I never saw anything like it. Do you think the baby could have been alive when I got here? Do you think it died because I didn't look right away?" She starts to sob and touches the infant with one finger. I touch it too, but the baby is so cold and stiff, I pull my hand away.

"Oh, Becky. I don't think so. Really. Look at the body. He was so early. I doubt he ever took a breath. His lungs wouldn't have been formed yet. I've seen infants born prematurely before. This baby wasn't ready to come. It's nothing you did or didn't do . . . But whose baby is it, anyway? Do you think it's one of your patients or one of mine?"

"I don't know. I thought it might belong to one of the traveling families, someone passing through who heard about the clinic. Some of those people moving north, looking for work up in Pittsburgh." She folds her hands as if in prayer and starts to cry again. My arm around her, I cry too, but my tears are different.

I'm thinking of the little boy I lost. Would he have looked like this, so frail, so not ready to live on this earth? And his little body, would it have looked like this? I don't even know where they buried him.

There's a knock at the outside door. "Mailman!" a low voice calls out. Becky jumps up and uses her body to shield the baby, though there's no way the postman can see through the closed exam room door.

"Thank you, James," she yells out. "Just put it on the desk. I'm with a patient." Then to me, in a whisper, "What shall we do with him?"

We both collapse back into our chairs and I squint, not understanding. The nurse goes on, "Well, we can't just throw him away. He has to have a proper burial."

"We could let the sheriff take care of it."

"No! If we do, there will be a manhunt. He'll want to know whose baby it is and will search the vagrants' tents down by the riverbank. He might even put someone in jail."

Now I see what she means. This is not really my affair, I just came by to visit, but I know what to do. "Give me the baby."

"What?"

"I'll take him home. Bury him on the farm. *You* can't do it. You live in town, with neighbors on either side. Out in the country, no one will know." There's a long silence, and Becky wipes her tears again.

"You'd do that?"

"Come on. It will be simple. Just wrap him up in the blanket and put him back in his box. I have a basket on my bike."

Becky offers to drive me home, but I tell her no. Afterward I think it might have been smarter. I had to carry the baby in the carton past the sheriff as he strolled down the courthouse steps. I also passed Mrs. Stenger coming out of Judge Hudson's and had to stop on my bike to say hello, and then I had to get around Bitsy.

* * *

"I was wondering when you'd get back," Bitsy calls from the porch as I walk my bike through the gate. "What's in the package?"

I consider telling her outright, "a dead premature baby," but I don't know how she'd take it, so I lie.

"Produce scraps from the grocery store. Mr. Bittman was throwing them out and sent them home for the chickens. I'll take them out to the barn."

"Supper in fifteen," she responds, turning back inside. "I caught a mess of fish."

The hole behind the barn isn't big, but it has to be deep so that foxes and raccoons won't smell the baby and dig it up. It takes me five minutes. Then I kneel at the grave site, my hands folded up against my chest. Just a moment of silence for the mama who has lost this too-early-baby, a woman somewhere with her breasts filling up and a heart so heavy she would sink to the bottom of the Hope River if she jumped in.

I didn't have a grave site for my premature son. I don't even know if he was buried properly or just thrown away. I pull a flat rock over the exposed earth, tamp it down gently with my foot, and wipe my tears on the back of my sleeve. This will be my secret gravestone, for both tiny babies.

True Knot

With the dramatic and probably illegal burial of the unidentified premature newborn, I didn't get around to telling Bitsy about Twyla until this morning. We are standing out in the side yard, preparing to beat the dust out of the front room braided rug with two home-made wire rug beaters that we found in the basement. The heavy floor cover-ing hangs over the clothesline, and the sun comes in and out of big white and gray clouds.

"How was Twyla?" Bitsy asks me, taking a swat. *Whack! Whack!* Dust rises all around us, and I can see this cleaning is long overdue.

"She's fine. Looks like she was meant to be a mother the way she holds and cuddles that baby, but things are sticky with the judge."

"How so? I bet he can't stand it when the baby cries, but all newborns cry. No way around it. Ma says it's good for 'em."

"He wants to give the baby away." *Whack. Whack.* "It isn't right. I don't know if Twyla even knows, but Nancy told me. Judge Hudson says he doesn't want a baby in his house. Either the baby goes up for adoption, or he's putting them all out." *WHACK!* "It seems wrong. Steams me just thinking about it." *WHACK! WHACK!*

Bitsy just stands there. "He doesn't want a *black baby* under his roof. That's what he means."

"Well, he can't do it, can he?"

"It's his house."

A dark cloud now covers the sun. Bitsy throws down her rug beater and marches back into the house. Doesn't even say anything. Her shoulders are high, and I think she's crying.

"Bitsy? Bitsy!" But she doesn't answer. Even when I go back into the house with the rug, she won't talk. She's

curled at the end of the davenport staring at the open pages of *Up from Slavery.*

Not long afterward, as I'm out in the
barn cleaning Star and Moonlight's
stalls, there's a commotion. Dogs bark
and a cart approaches, moving fast up
the road. A kid not more than thirteen
trots up to the fence.

"Ma'am." The freckle-faced boy with
flaming red hair introduces himself.
"Name's Albert Mintz from Horse Shoe
Run. My papa sent me. He went to get
Mrs. Potts in the truck, but my ma's
paining real bad and he said I should
try for you too—just get someone fast.
Heard you was Mrs. Potts's helpers."

"Is it far? Do we have time to get
washed up?" I rub my dirty hands on
the back of my pants.

The boy's eyes get big, put on the
spot for an answer that could be critical. "Took a good while to get here,
and I was pushing hard. There will be
three of us in the cart on the way back.
Better come as you are. It's Ma's seventh."

Bitsy shakes herself out of her dark funk and runs for my satchel. We are still in our work clothes, so I grab two flowered aprons from the bottom kitchen drawer and a couple of wet rags to wash up with.

As we bounce down Wild Rose and around Salt Lick, we do our best to make ourselves presentable. This is *not* how I wanted our first birth as Mrs. Potts's backup to go. She is always so neat in her black dress, white apron, and white turban. No use fussing over it.

Before we get to Horse Shoe Run a hard rain begins. Bitsy pushes the satchel under the wooden bench, and I sit on the aprons to keep them dry. Not that the aprons will help much. Our hair is plastered, and water trickles down our necks. At least Albert is wearing a straw hat.

Not twenty minutes later we arrive at a run-down, unpainted, one-story farm-house at the mouth of a narrow hollow. The privy sits to the side. Three little boys, one with red hair like Albert's, watch from the porch as we ride into the yard.

Before we reach the door I know something is wrong. Bitsy and I look at each other and tighten our jaws. The boy's dirty faces are striped with tears and a woman's voice keens from inside. This is the sound I heard Katherine MacIntosh make when I first gave her the bad news about her baby, the wail that goes right to your heart. Despite my dread, I take the steps two at a time, pushing open the door. Bitsy follows at my heels.

"Mrs. Mintz!" I call out. "It's Patience, the midwife. Mr. Mintz? Mrs. Potts?" The high, repetitive cry starts up again, and I follow the sound down a dark hallway to a bedroom where a mother sits on the bare wood floor, holding what appears to be a lifeless baby. I step over and take the body in my arms, still attached to its limp umbilical cord. The newborn is covered in sticky, dark brown fluid, which I know to be baby poop. Meconium, DeLee calls it; not a good sign.

"Bitsy, tie and cut the cord, get the

mother back in bed, then start massaging her uterus," I order, grabbing the infant. I wipe the inside of its mouth with the corner of my work shirt and commence to breathe for it. *Come on, baby. Come on.* There's no response, and part of me knows there won't be. The baby is cold, and the mucus all over him is already dry. I keep trying anyway. Puff. Puff. Puff. I put my fingers to the chest. No pulse. Puff. Puff. Nothing, but I can't stop.

"Miss Patience?" That's Bitsy, standing beside me. She shakes her head to indicate that what I'm doing is useless. Even my young apprentice sees that. And I hope she sees more, sees that what we do for a living is like walking on a straight razor: life on one side, death on the other.

"My baby. My baby!" The mother starts up again. Outside there's commotion, and minutes later Mrs. Potts hobbles in with her cane, followed by a thin man dressed in coveralls who I presume is the father.

He looks at me sitting on the side of the bed with his dead baby. "What have you done?" He whirls to Mrs. Potts. "What has she done?"

Mrs. Mintz raises one pale hand. "Ernest," she says weakly. "Ernie . . ." He's not listening.

I try once more. Puff. Puff. Puff. *Come on!* I can't believe this is happening.

"It's okay, honey," the old midwife tells me. "That baby's long gone. Give it here." She wraps the limp female infant in a blanket and hands it to the mother. This is something I've never seen before, giving a dead baby to the mother.

"Gladys," she says, "hush your crying. That little girl has gone back to Jesus. Sing her a song."

Gladys looks at Mrs. Potts with big tear-filled eyes but does what she says. *"Swing low,"* she begins weakly, *"sweet chariot. Comin' for to carry me home."*

"Swing low, sweet chariot," Bitsy joins in as she delivers the afterbirth all by herself. It lies in a pool of red on a white towel, covered with more of the brown goo.

"Get me a bowl, Ernest, and a pot of warm water. We'll need some clean linens," Mrs. Potts orders. The man, his jaw rigid, stalks out of the room.

"The baby was already born when I got here, Mrs. Potts. I didn't do anything to it, I swear! When Bitsy and I came in the room, Mrs. Mintz was sitting on the floor, already holding the baby. I did my best. I did what I could." We all stare at the pool of water and blood in the middle of the floor.

"It's all right, honey. You can tell by the cord the baby was in trouble." She shows us the twisted rope of flesh with a true knot and three dark purple clots. Somehow I don't feel any better knowing the cause of the infant's death.

When Mr. Mintz comes back and sits next to his wife, the old midwife shows him the unusual cord. "See this, Ernest," she instructs. "It's a true knot. Your little girl was swimming around in the womb and made the loop-de-loop herself. I don't want you saying anything bad about this new midwife. These things happen, and it wasn't anyone's fault."

Mintz shoots me a hostile look, then turns his attention to his wife. "I'm so sorry. I'm so, so sorry," he says, pushing back her red hair and stroking her face. "If we'd only had the money, I would have carried you to the hospital."

Mrs. Potts interrupts, "Now, Ernest, don't you go blaming yourself, neither. I already told you. The baby's time had come. Some of us get ninety years on this good earth. Some get nine days. Your little one didn't get nine minutes. There's nothing those doctors at the hospital could have done. I can tell by looking this baby's been gone for two days. The good Lord *giveth,* and the good Lord *taketh away.* Your job is to take care of your woman. Make her life easy until her heart mends."

By the time we've cleaned up the blood and remade the bed, the shadows of the mountains lean into the room. Mrs. Potts, Bitsy, and I move into the kitchen to wash the limp infant and leave the couple alone. The old lady wraps the tiny girl in a clean blanket and carries it out to the children.

"Come here, boys." She sits down on the porch rocker. "I want you to see your dead sissy. She's just a little bitty thing, but Jesus took her home early. She's an angel now." The four boys, their faces white with sorrow, gather round the rocker.

"Mama was crying," one of the kids whispers. "We never heard her cry before."

"I should have gotten Miss Patience here sooner. I tried." That's Albert.

"Don't you go reproaching yourself either, son! You did what you could. That's all God asks of us." Albert wipes his eyes.

The youngest boy touches the dead baby's hand and then wipes his tears. "Look at her itty-bitty fingers!"

May 14, 1930. Three-quarters moon.

Stillborn female infant. Angel Mintz, child of Ernest and Gladys Mintz of Horse Shoe Run. Born dead with a true knot and three clots in the cord. Also, there were only two blood vessels. Mrs. Potts said there are usually three . . . The baby seemed

perfect in every other way, but she weighed only 5 pounds. She was covered all over with brown baby poop. I tried to get her to breathe, but it was too late. Probably died before labor, Mrs. Potts said.

Present: Bitsy, Mrs. Potts, and I. No payment. Didn't expect any. Bitsy felt very bad too and said she would go back to Hazel Patch with Mrs. Potts. Now I will have to go to the courthouse to fill out a death certificate. I hope I don't get blamed.

Summer

26

June 3, 1930. Sliver moon, thunder with lightning in the west.

Thomas came for us again in his cart, riding fast through the summer storm. He brought two heavy slickers, which he must have borrowed from some of the miners because they were so big that Bitsy and I drowned in them. There wasn't any time for talking. He carried us back around the mountain to the Wildcat Mine, where we delivered without fuss Gincey Huckabee, one of the women whose

husband was killed in the spring cave-in. The mine owners let her stay in her shack because she was a widow and pregnant. When the baby boy was born, Gincey cried and cried. It was so sad about her husband, Bitsy and I cried too. Male, 6 pounds, 4 ounces. Named for his father, Harold Huckabee, Jr.

Brook Trout

Spring turns to summer, and today Bitsy and I took Star down to the river to graze in the grass while we fished. I rode at the beginning while Bitsy walked, and then we switched. It was our first time out of the pasture, and Star did fine. You'd never know by watching her what a mess she was in a few months ago.

After we rested on the riverbank, we picked a mess of greens: dandelions and shepherd's purse, ramps and watercress. Bitsy says you can eat stinging nettles too, but you have to get them when they're young and tender and boil the heck out of them.

At this point I'll try anything edible because our larder is nearly empty and so is the root cellar. In addition to four jars of last year's canned green beans and a few carrots, there are a couple dozen seed potatoes that are starting to sprout, but we'll need them for planting, and though the peas are up, nothing in the garden is ready to pick.

Last week we had rabbit for two days, kind of stringy but not too bad in a soup. I'm amazed at how many critters I've eaten this year: rabbit . . . coon . . . possum . . . duck . . . deer . . . squirrel . . . wild turkey. Since Moonlight was bred and is no longer producing milk, our only supply of protein, other than the game, is two eggs on a good day.

This lack of meat and milk makes me feel nearly destitute, but I forget I still have Mrs. Vanderhoff's ruby ring and Katherine MacIntosh's golden moon pin, hidden on the top of the closet in an old red Calumet baking powder tin. I promised myself I wouldn't sell them unless I was truly desperate, and apparently I'm not there yet. Even if I wanted to, where would I go? Who would have cash money to pay me?

As we explore the riverbank, Bitsy and I are surprised to find three tents set up under the trees. From the looks of the first two, constructed with tarps tied over two well-used old pickup trucks, the occupants are on the road with all their household goods. The third, a lean-to, is set about a quarter mile downstream where an older man with a week-old salt-and-pepper beard tends his fire. We give him a wide berth and stop around the bend. Then, while Bitsy readies our fishing poles, I tie Star where she can walk in the shallows and graze in the grass.

"Here, Patience, watch me," Bitsy orders as, without flinching, she threads an earthworm onto the barbed metal hook. I follow her lead, but it takes something out of me. The worm is still alive, and it's writhing. I have fished before, but it was years and years ago, when I was a girl, and Papa always baited the hooks for me.

My companion gives me a few tips about casting and moving along the bank slowly in the shade. Then she hands me an old tobacco can with three more worms that she dug out of the garden and heads farther upstream in her high rubber boots.

"Meet me back here when the sun is straight up," Bitsy instructs. "Good luck."

I watch as she expertly flicks her line and realize how dependent I've become on her. Once I was her benefactor. Now she's mine.

For hours I wade without getting a bite. Finally I plunk myself down in the grass and just dangle the pole, let my bait drift along in the current. It's a sunny day with white puffy clouds drifting over me, and I play a game I used to play as a kid, looking for animals in the sky. There's a horse . . . there's a chicken . . . there's the face of a hog . . . Wild pink roses crawl along the edge of the woods, and their sweet scent fills the air.

My musings end abruptly when I feel a tug at my line. At first I think it's a snag, so I jerk the pole, but the line pulls back. Holy cow! I've got one! I stagger to my feet and walk backward into the brush.

"Bitsy!" I call, but she's a mile away. I whip the homemade willow pole back and forth, back and forth, until a flash of silver hits the air. Oh my gosh! It's still alive. For some reason this surprises me. The foot-long silver-and-brown-spotted fish lies on the bank, with its gills opening and closing, drowning in the air.

Now I must kill the fish to end its suffering. I pick up a rock and smash the trout in the head until it lies still; then, to keep the flies off, I dangle it back in the river, still on the line.

"Some people just throw them alive in a bucket of cold water. Keeps them fresh," a low voice comments from behind me. When I twist around, I find one of the men from the tents, a thin swarthy fellow standing in the brush with a string of his own fish over his shoulder.

It occurs to me that this might not be the safest place for a woman alone, but he seems harmless enough, so I smile. "It's my first catch, and I'm not very experienced . . . It looks like *you* did all right." He holds up about a dozen brown and rainbow trout.

"That's why we stopped here, to fish and rest for a few days, my wife and our two kids and my brother and his family. We're heading for Pittsburgh.

"Name's Earl Cook. Came up from Beckley. Heard Carnegie Steel is hiring." He sits down in the grass and starts to roll a cigarette. "It's been a long trip. We thought we'd rest a spell. Lost the farm to the bank last month. There's no work for us back home."

I'm surprised he's telling me all this, and I'm thinking there may be nothing for him in Pittsburgh either, but I keep that to myself. All he has left is his pickup, his family, and hope . . . but things could be worse.

It's high noon, with the sun at its zenith, so Mr. Cook and I part. He goes downstream, back to his campsite, and I look for Bitsy. She's already started a fire upstream and has gutted her fish on the river's edge. A quartet of rainbow trout is arranged on a flat rock waiting to be cooked, but my one fish is the biggest, almost a foot long, and I'm proud of it.

"Nice trout," Bitsy comments and then shows me how to clean the creature. I watch as my fish's innards are washed away in the current. This self-reliance is getting to be a bit much!

Next she demonstrates how to skewer the trout with a straight green willow limb and hold it over the coals. Everything for our feast is in her knapsack, even tin pie pans to use as plates, forks, and salt. We sit on the riverbank, the green life around us, enjoying our supper, and I think to myself, *Things could be worse.*

27

Waltz

It's a sticky night, and I'm sleeping downstairs on the davenport under one sheet in front of the open screen door when I hear an engine chugging up Wild Rose Road. I've just blown out the lamp, locked my diary, and tucked it under the sofa cushion.

The sound isn't welcome. Lately a visitor has meant trouble or another delivery, and I'm still disturbed about Mrs. Mintz's loss, as if it were my fault, though I know it wasn't.

"Miss Patience," a man's voice calls from out in the yard. I throw on Nora's red kimono and stand in the dark just inside the screen. "Yes?"

"I'm Pete Dyer, and my brother John says his wife, Hannah, is paining. He sent me to fetch you."

"Be right there."

Bitsy is already clomping down the stairs as I hurry upstairs to dress. "I'll leave food for the cow, the chickens, and the dogs," she tells me.

In ten minutes we're settled in the front seat of the Model T Ford truck, a battered affair that sits far off the ground, perfect for the rough dirt back roads that, with the depression, are now full of potholes. The county has no money to fix them.

At the Dyer home, a two-story stone farmhouse on a rise above the Hope River, we are surprised to find Hannah and her husband, John, both in their early twenties, dancing in the living room to a waltz on the gramophone. I recognize the tune, "The Blue Danube."

Bitsy and I look at each other, drop the birth satchel near the door, and plunk down on the high-backed leather sofa to watch. This doesn't seem right! Either the woman isn't in labor, or we were called way too early.

Hannah wears a white nightdress that rises around her ankles when the two of them spin. Her long straight black hair is loose, and her feet are bare and so are her husband's. It's clear that the two have taken ballroom dancing lessons, and I recall now that both went to Torrington State, he for agriculture, she for literature. John and his younger brother inherited their grandparents' expansive bottomland farm when their grandma died of heart failure a year ago.

The couple have eyes only for each other, so, though I'm miffed at being called so early when I could be home asleep on the sofa. I keep my peace and wait for the music to end. I don't have to wait long. The recording keeps playing, but Hannah stops in midtwirl and says two words: "My back."

The husband sits down in an easy chair, nods toward us as if he's just noticed our presence, and begins to massage his wife's sacrum. He kneads and caresses, not just her lower back but also her buttocks and thighs. Bitsy looks away, but I'm transfixed, watching something that most people think belongs in the bedroom. The music goes on, and when the pain is over the couple embrace and start dancing again.

"There's cider on the table and fresh-baked muffins," Hannah calls gaily, looking over her shoulder as she twirls across the room. Bitsy and I wander into the kitchen.

"What do you think? Is she in labor?"

Bitsy shrugs philosophically, biting into a muffin so golden it looks like pure butter. "I guess. Want to take a spin?"

"I don't think so!"

"I'm serious." My friend grabs my hand and drags me back to the living room. This is the first time since the day I told Bitsy about Twyla's baby being given away that I've heard her laugh. "One, two, three. One, two, three." She puts her arm around my waist and leads me across the room. "One, two, three."

"That's the beeswax!" Hannah encourages us. Her face is pink and moist and beautiful. After a few minutes, I'm feeling rather fine myself. "One, two, three. One, two, three."

I can't remember when I last danced. It might have been at our wedding at the Labor Union Hall, Ruben's and mine. We'd courted for only six months, but the drums of war were already roaring and people didn't waste time back then.

France, Germany, Russia, the United Kingdom, Hungary . . . the whole world was involved; it was only a matter of time until the United States jumped in. Ruben was an isolationist, like many in those days. "We'd just be sending our boys over there for cannon fodder," he objected. It's not that he was a pacifist, he just didn't see that the war in Europe was any of our business.

Looking back, my years as Ruben Gordesky's wife were the happiest of my life, like dancing, that's how I remember them. Six short years . . .

Hannah

Bitsy and I spin around until I'm dizzy, almost bumping into the other couple, who stop suddenly for another contraction, this one apparently harder.

"Whoops! Something just happened!" Hannah lifts her gown and stares at a wet spot on the worn pine floor. "It must be the baby's fluid. Let me get a pad," she tells her husband. "Then I want to try the Charleston. You put on the recording of 'Syncopatin' Sal.'" The young mother-to-be gathers her nightdress between her legs like a woman stomping grapes and heads awkwardly upstairs.

I follow and motion to Bitsy to bring the satchel. "If you wouldn't mind, Hannah, I'd like to check the baby's heartbeat, figure out its position. When did your pains start?"

Hannah doesn't answer; she's squatting at the top of the landing, holding on to the wooden post.

"Jiminy!" she exclaims. "That was a hard one. I'm gonna have to dance faster to keep up." Before she gets clean bloomers out of her dresser, she has another pain and then another. I consult Mrs. Kelly's gold watch. Three minutes apart. Things seem to be progressing faster than I had thought.

Bitsy pours water from the flowered pitcher into the porcelain basin on the stand, and I wash my hands. Then I have Hannah lie down so I can listen to the baby's heart sounds and make sure it's head down. When the next contraction comes on, before I can assess the strength, Hannah rolls away from me and struggles to get up.

"I can't do this lying down!" she wails, for the first time sounding a little out of control. John, the husband, bounds up the stairs, pulls his wife to her feet, and holds her against his chest. He's changed the recording to a slower tune, "Black Mountain Blues" by Bessie Smith.

I remember that tune from when Ruben and I won a dance contest at a speakeasy in McKeesport. In the early twenties no music was more threatening than jazz and blues. We were traveling in the fast lane, and jazz and blues were the background music for the revolution. I remember with fondness the clubs in Pittsburgh's Hill District where blacks and whites danced together. Now people can listen to the same songs on the Victrola in their own homes. What a world we live in!

I shake my head. There's no point getting nostalgic, and there's no point arguing with Hannah about staying in bed, either. She's not going to do it.

Bitsy carefully puts down our sterile newspaper under our cloth pads on top of the bed and clears the dresser for our supplies. She places Mrs. Potts's hemorrhage tincture and a bottle of olive oil on the side. "Don't forget a smaller bowl for the afterbirth," I remind her. My friend rolls her eyes, letting me know she doesn't need reminding.

All around the large room, on the white plastered walls, photographs of stern ancestors from the 1800s stare out at us from black oval frames. What would these old people think of all this? The father in the birthing room! The mother dancing! Blues rising sweetly from the talking machine downstairs!

Though the Dyers have electricity, there's as yet no water closet. But that doesn't bother Hannah. For an educated young lady, she's as earthy as a peasant woman and has no qualms about periodically squatting over the white enamel potty. There's nothing for me to do but wait, so I rest myself in a high-backed soft chair, close my eyes, and enjoy Bessie's song. I haven't heard much music lately, not since Christmas, when I sang with Mr. Hester. I'm almost asleep when I hear the noise I'm waiting for . . .

"Uggggggggh!" My eyes pop open, and I see Hannah squatting on the commode with her husband kneeling in front of her. "Oooo!" she exclaims. "I've got to pooh!"

"No, you don't, Hannah! That's your baby coming, time to get back in bed. Bitsy, get a wiggle on! We need the hot water!"

"But I don't *want* to lie down. I can't

lie down! It hurts when I lie down!" Hannah complains.

I could throw her down, but she'd just bounce up like a rubber ball. I let out my air in frustration. This wouldn't be the first time I've let a woman push when out of bed. I just don't want to make a habit of it. What would the community think if word got around? What would Mrs. Potts think of me, letting my patients deliver like aborigines?

"Well, what do you want to do, then? Are you going to have the baby standing up?" I remember the Amish girl, how it had almost come to that, but Granny had insisted she get back into bed.

"Uggggggggggggggh! Yes!"

John looks hopeful. "Could she? I'll hold her." Hannah's so hot she throws off her gown.

I pull my sterile gloves on, shaking my head. These young people, with ideas of their own!

When Bitsy returns with a steaming teakettle and a small bowl for the afterbirth, she laughs at the sight of Hannah standing naked, bearing down, in the middle of the bedroom.

"She won't get into bed," I explain. "Can you hand me the oil?" I grab a pillow and kneel on the floor behind and below the mother. Bitsy pours the warmed liquid on my fingers, and I'm surprised, when I check, to find the head almost crowning. "Slow it down, Hannah!" I yell. "Slow it down or you're going to tear. Get her attention, John!"

The man takes his wife's face in his hands and insists that she make eye contact with him. "Look at me, Hannah. Look at me!"

"Why?" she snaps. "I'm trying to have a baby here!"

"The midwife says to stop pushing. She says to slow down or you're going to rip."

"Oh, for Christ's sake! What am I supposed to do, then?"

Bitsy steps up and gives her the drill. "Push a little. Blow a little. Push a little. Blow a little."

In ten minutes, I'm sitting in a pool of warm amniotic fluid with a crying female infant in my lap.

"My baby!" Tears run down Hannah's face as she takes the beet red child away from me and wraps it in her discarded nightdress. The cord's still attached and dangles between us like a swinging bridge.

"My darling wife!" That's John.

"Will you lie down *now*?" That's me, and Hannah complies.

The recording downstairs has finished, and the scrape of the phonograph needle is getting on my nerves. "Can you please fix that, Bitsy?" I nod toward the sound.

Bitsy trots down and a few minutes later is back, boogieing through the door to "Oh, Gee! Oh, Gosh!," a ragtime favorite. I can't help but smile. John takes Bitsy's hand, and they do the Lindy Hop together while Hannah holds up the baby. "See, honey?" she asks the wobbly newborn. "Are you going to be a dancer like your poppy and Bitsy?"

Then she gets serious. "I think we'll call her Mary," the new mother announces. "Don't you think that's nice?

A plain name, but also the name of our savior's mother."

"Yes," I agree, thinking of Mary Proudfoot. "That's a beautiful name: brave, strong, and proud."

June 19, 1930. Quarter moon waning in a clear sky.

Birth of Mary Dyer to John and Hannah Dyer of Stony Creek. Six pounds, 11 ounces. Mother and father danced through labor. Even Bitsy and I joined in! Hannah stood up for the birth and I thought she would tear, but she was fine. Blood loss less than normal.

I was surprised as natural as she was in labor that Hannah had a little trouble with breast-feeding. The infant rooted vigorously, but Hannah has very flat nipples. If I had known, I would have had her do some tiddy-pulling the last month to get ready. You can't do it sooner because it causes contractions.

When women come to my house to arrange for my services, I must remember to ask to examine them and ask Becky to do it too, since she is seeing some of them in her clinic in town.

Present were Bitsy, yours truly, and John. Payment, a side of bacon and a promise of a cord of wood this fall, but the birth was so fun, I would have done it for free.

28

Ghost Town

At last we are getting produce from the garden, small peas that we eat without shelling, lettuce, and chard. We enjoyed Hannah's bacon and we fish in the river, but we are down to a cup of flour, the sugar is gone, and our money jar is empty except for a few last coins. I stare at them now, scattered on the table, as I pull on my town shoes.

"Man does not live on fish and berries alone, or woman either," I announced to Bitsy this morning. "I'm going into Liberty. Maybe I can find work. If we don't get paid for the deliveries, we have to get money somehow. I also have the last few birth certificates to turn in for a quarter apiece at the courthouse. That will be something."

I was surprised when Bitsy ran upstairs to find me something nice to wear and helped braid my hair, but then I realized that she's just as worried about our financial situation as I am and probably wanted to increase my chances by making me look like a lady.

It seems a long shot, but my thought, as I get my bike out of the barn, is that maybe Becky Myers or Mr. Stenger, the pharmacist, will know of someone sick or injured that Bitsy and I can take care of. As I fly on my bike past Maddock's farm, I'm surprised to see Mrs. Maddock sitting in a wicker rocker on the front porch. I wave but am speeding so fast down the steep hill that I almost tip over, and she doesn't wave back. An hour later, behind the Texaco station, I park and wipe the dust off my face with my wet cloth, then walk sedately down Main.

The first thing I notice is that the

streets are so desolate and the traffic
sparse. It's been weeks since I've been
to town, and Liberty is almost aban-
doned. A few autos pass, then a buggy
pulled by a swayback mare, but other
than that, there are just four out-of-work
miners smoking cigarettes on the
wooden benches in front of the courthouse, two blacks and two whites. One
white guy whistles, and the two blacks
get up and walk away. The last thing
they need is to be accused of hassling
a white woman.

I'm relieved when I get into and out
of the County Records Room without
hearing any more catcalls from the fellow outside. The only awkwardness is
asking for a death certificate for the
Mintz baby, but the clerk doesn't question me, so I guess word has already
gotten around. She hands me five quarters, one for each form.

Back on the street, the coins jiggling
in my pocket, I think briefly of buying
an ice cream cone. What would that
be, five cents? But the ice cream parlor
is closed. The Mountain Top Diner is
closed too. Bittman's Grocery is still

operating, so I stop in and get a sack of flour, a can of lard, and five pounds of sugar, an extravagance, I'll admit. That leaves me only two quarters in my pocketbook and it won't last long.

Fortunately the crooked tin sign in Stenger's Pharmacy's front window says OPEN. When I enter the almost empty establishment, I see Mrs. Blum, the physician's wife, asking question about Lydia E. Pinkham's Vegetable Compound. Her shiny blond hair frames her pale face and sets off her unusual green almond-shaped eyes. She nods as if I'm a stranger, though she's met me many times. No "Hello Patience" or "How you doing?" I guess I'm too far beneath her.

On the newspaper stand just inside the glass door, I pull out a copy of the *Torrington Times* and peruse the headlines. A sudden run on the Brotherhood Bank in Berkeley Springs forced it to shut down. It's the eighth bank in West Virginia to close in the last two weeks, and the state legislature is having a special session about the economy. This is all new to me. Without a radio or newspaper, my world has narrowed to the valley between Hope Ridge and the mountains on the other side of Hope River, and even there I don't really know what's going on. I don't even know my closest neighbors, the Maddocks.

The cash register rings and snaps closed, the pharmacist hands Priscilla Blum her package, and I step up to the counter.

"Hello, Patience. What can I do for you?" I'm sure Mr. Stenger's hoping I'll buy something expensive: rubber gloves, brown soap, or a new hairbrush.

"Oh, I don't need anything, Mr. Stenger. I was just wondering how your mother is doing and if she, or anyone else you might know, requires nursing." I hesitate. "I could trade for food. Times being hard and all . . ." My cheeks glow with embarrassment, like coals from the heater stove.

Stenger rubs his small auburn goatee, stippled with gray, and burrows his fists in his white lab coat pockets.

"I thought you knew. Mama passed away this January. Got pneumonia."

"I'm so sorry . . . I didn't hear . . . we

were snowed in most of the winter. She was a nice old lady . . . I hope she didn't suffer." I stare at the red sign on the wall behind him exhorting the benefits of Himrod's Asthma Powder and clear my throat. "Know anyone else with sick relatives?"

Stenger shakes his head slowly.

"Well, if you hear of anyone . . ."

I knew it was a long shot, but I still leave disappointed. I'm on my way over to Becky's when a Model T bounces up on the curb. Who should it be but Rebecca Myers herself.

Down by the Riverside

"Get in," the home health nurse orders.

"Well, hi to you too! What's up? I have my bike back at the Texaco station." I'm thinking maybe Becky will offer to carry me home, and this time I'll take her up on it. As we travel, I can ask her about possible employment.

"Forget your bike. I'll bring you back later. There's a situation down by the river. I just tried the hospital, but Dr.

Blum is in Delmont at a medical meeting. Thank God I saw you." I hop in and she makes a U-turn in the middle of Main and heads back toward the stone bridge over the Hope at the edge of town.

"What? What's the big emergency?" I'm holding on to the door frame as she careens through the nearly empty streets.

"You'll see." She pulls up in the dry grass, bouncing into the gravel. "You hear that?" There's no way to miss it, a high-pitched scream.

The vehicle sputters to a stop, we jump out, and she pulls me along through the grass heading under the bridge. The wail rises, then falls. Rises and falls.

"It's someone crying. A kid or a woman."

What we see next surprises me. Three men, two whites and a black, squat around a small open fire behind one of the bridge's stone pillar. Their lean-tos, canvas supported on poles with cardboard layered over them, are arranged close together on a rise above the riverbed. These are not campers just passing through: they plan to stay for a while. The fellows jump up when they see us.

"Is someone in trouble here?" I ask authoritatively.

"This is the midwife." Becky introduces me. Apparently she's already met them.

The oldest guy, a man of about fifty wearing a wool cap like a paperboy, steps forward and nods toward the smaller tent. "It's the Girlie," he says as if that's her name. "She's with child. My name's Will Carter."

"You the baby's pa?" I'm looking at Carter, but all the men shake their heads no. As the other fellows introduce themselves, I take in the scene. Not a pretty picture: tin cans litter the ground, a string of laundry is tied between two trees, and an old stovepipe sticks out of a metal barrel, making a cookstove.

"We ain't kin. None of us. Girlie just joined up with us in Cool Springs. The goons at the MacIntosh spur drove us off the rails, threatened us with our lives, so we been making it cross-country, heading for Torrington. She's on the run from her old man in Beckley. Nice little lady. Pretty damn good cook even with the hobo stove. Calls us her 'knights in shining armor.' Can you help her?"

"Is she alone in there?"

"We ain't got no womenfolk," the young colored man explains.

"No money either," the third guy mumbles.

The cry comes again, followed by a whimper. Becky pulls on my sleeve. "You better check her."

I pull the tent flap aside, and my eyes fly open. "Holy cow!"

The mother, a pale-skinned slip of a thing not more than sixteen, is lying on her side with a baby's head halfway out. The girl's not even trying to push, just lying there crying. The trouble is that the tissue all around the infant's head is beet red and distended, as if the head's been crowning for a long time.

"Her name's Docey," the home health nurse tells me.

"Lord, Docey, how long's this been

going on?" That's me. Becky is kneeling to one side, trying to bring some order to the dirty pallet. She picks up the wet, bloody rags with the tips of her fingers and throws them out the tent door.

"How long has the head been down here?" I ask again.

Docey opens her eyes, a startling blue-green, the color of the river in winter when the ice first opens. She shakes her head as if time has no meaning and she's too tired to talk but not too tired to cry.

"Eeeeeee. Owwwww!" she whimpers when a contraction hits her, making no effort to bear down. "It burns so bad, I think I'm going to split open."

"It's her first," Becky fills me in. "I got some of her medical history the first time I was here. It was Judge Hudson that called me. Apparently everyone who's crossed the bridge today has heard a woman scream. After the third complaint he wanted someone to go check. For some reason he thought of me, not the sheriff."

I am hardly listening. If I don't do

something soon, she really might split open, right to the rectum. She won't die from it, but she might be ruined for life.

"It's gonna be okay, Docey. You can do this . . . We're going to need warm compresses."

Outside, I throw orders around like Napoleon. "Where's the hot water? Did it boil yet? Get more wood. I need a clean bowl, some sterilized twine, and a sterilized knife. Who has one?"

The black man holds out his pocketknife and wipes it with the tail of his plaid flannel shirt. "Good enough, get it in some hot water . . . Now, do you have any lard?" All activity stops, and the men jerk up from their appointed tasks.

"Lard?"

"Yeah, I said lard. Do you have any? Bacon grease? *Anything?*"

The crying starts up in the shelter again. The older guy, Will, rustles around in a canvas knapsack and comes up with a tin decorated with a smiling pig.

"Patience!" That's Becky. "Patience!"

When I reenter the tent, the home health nurse is so anxious you'd think maybe she's never seen a birth before. "Don't leave me!" she says. What do they teach these people in nursing school?

"Make a low table for the water, the lard, and the sterilized knife just outside the tent!" I yell to the men.

Docey yells louder. "OW! OW! OW!" She still lies on her side, and the head hasn't moved. I consider listening for a heartbeat, but how do I know if the baby is even alive? Better concentrate on just getting it out. I indicate that Becky should hold the girl's upper leg, and she does so with shaking hands.

"Docey," I try, "you have to stop screaming. You're scaring the baby." I remember Bitsy's words with Twyla, and they seem to work. The girl doesn't shut up, but she turns down the volume.

"The baby's stuck right at the opening, but I'm going to ease it out. You have to push when I tell you. Even if it hurts, you have to push, but just a little at a time. Once we get ready, it will all be over in a few minutes."

It occurs to me that my optimism may be misplaced. What if the swollen tissue is not what's holding the baby back? What if the infant's shoulders are wedged up behind the pubic bone?

Outside the tent I hear rustling, and I look out to see the men making a platform with two rounds of wood. The oldest guy brings over a pot of hot water. The bearded fellow hands me the can of lard, and the youngest one proudly shows me his pocketknife, gleaming in a still steaming pork-and-beans tin.

Hope

Docey cries out again and again, throwing her head back and forth.

"It's okay. It's okay," I soothe.

"It's okay," Becky copies me, patting the girl's arm as if she were a dangerous animal about to bite.

"It's gonna be okay. You're gonna have a baby in your arms soon." That's me again.

With a twitch of my head, I tell Becky to get the warm compresses. She wrings one out, glad to have something useful to do.

"My theory is that the warmth will soften the tissue and help the mother relax," I explain. It seems to be working. Between pushes, I can now get two fingers in, indicating that there's a little more stretch, and with the next contraction we see some real progress.

"Look honey, the baby is coming." The hairy head peeks out just a little more.

The men can't help themselves. From outside, they shout their encouragement. "Atta girl!" "You're getting her now!" "That's our champ!"

All my attention is focused on that tight, swollen ring of fire. *This is the part where I'm fully awake.* I make a crown with my hands and just pray that the baby's still living.

"I can see ears. A few more pushes, and the widest part will be out. Push a little. Blow a little. Whoo. Whoo. Whoo."

With the next effort, progress happens fast, and my fears of the shoulders being too big prove unfounded. A wailing pink infant girl flops into my lap, followed by a gush of blood and then the placenta.

Docey's blue-green eyes fly open as she realizes it's really a baby and not just more searing pain. "My baby! My sweet!" It's the first words I've heard from her, other than about how bad it hurts.

"Hot damn!" a man utters behind me, peeking in. "Pardon."

The guys can't help themselves; they have to see. I block their view of the mother but let them get a glimpse of the baby.

Will wipes beads of sweat off his face with a crumpled blue bandanna. "Watcha gonna call her?"

Docey doesn't answer at first but inspects the jewel in her arms. "What's the name of this river?"

"The Hope," Becky and I answer together.

"That's her name then, Hope."

Twenty minutes later, I accept a hot cup of joe from the men around the fire. Becky stays in the tent to show the mother how to breastfeed, her hands no longer shaking. Birth is a messy, primitive event, and I've noticed before that it's not for everyone.

"How were you fellas going to care for Docey? Did you have a plan? She can't travel like this, and it's too cold for the baby to live in a tent." A chill wind has come up and ripples the river.

"We didn't know she was this close to term," Will explains. "We just figured we'd lay up here for a few days, let Girlie rest, and then get on to Torrington to a church or someplace, find someone who would take care of her. Then this morning she started paining."

I run over the options. They could stay here and try to keep warm. I could take the mother and babe up to our house . . . or . . .

Here Becky sticks her head out the flap and surprises me. "She can come home with me. I'll take care of her until she gets on her feet." She hands the lard and the unused rags out to the fathers. I know they aren't really the fathers, but the beams on their mugs make me think of them that way.

Will stubs out his hand-rolled fag,

saves the butt in a tobacco tin, and ties his knapsack closed.

"I'm going with her," he tells me. "The other fellows will stay with our stuff. We don't have much, but if we get robbed, we'll be as miserable as sin."

I look over at Becky. "No, you won't," she counters. "There's only room for Docey and the baby." The men are clearly disappointed. They hang their heads as if being told that their favorite grandmother has passed.

Becky shakes her head. "Sorry," she says. "Really I am, but there's just nowhere for you to stay. You can visit every day." At that the men cheer up, and within an hour we have Docey and Hope up the hill and situated in the Ford. Becky gives the fellows her address and directions, and by late afternoon I'm on my bike crossing the bridge for home.

Will and the others stand and salute as I pedal past. These are good working fellows, I reflect, unemployed, down on their luck, not vagrants or bums, as some people call them. In my mind,

Docey is Mary and they are the three Wise Men.

June 20, 1930. Moon obscured by the clouds.

Birth of baby Hope down by the riverside. The mother is Docey of Beckley, West Virginia. (Didn't get the last name.)
I was called to a tent set up under the bridge by Becky Myers, the home health nurse. The patient had been crowning for hours, and the tissue around the vagina was swollen, thick, and red. With warm-water compresses and lard I was able to ease the baby out without a tear. Mother and infant were taken to Becky's house. Present were myself, three traveling men that were camping with the girl, and Mrs. Myers. They told me that Docey, the mother, was escaping from an abusive husband and they had taken her under

their wing. I fear she will have a hard go of it.

Hester

On my way home, bicycling down Salt Lick, I decide at the last minute to go by the vet's. He gets around. Maybe he'll know of some work. Except for the birth of the baby, and my few supplies, the coins I received at the courthouse, the day didn't net much reward. While I'm at his house, I can also get a cold drink of water.

Noting his black Model T parked in the drive, I walk my bike across the wooden bridge. Under me, the north branch of Salt Lick gurgles over slate as smooth as a sidewalk. For a minute I think of removing my shoes and wading in the clear water. Skimmers float in the slow places. A minnow flashes, then disappears, but I remember I'm on a mission.

There's no sign of the vet in the yard or the barn, so I approach the front door of his stone farmhouse. "Anyone home?" I knock at the back door, expecting it to swing open. No answer. I know he must be here, because his Ford's in the drive . . . With my hand over my eyes, I scan the surrounding fenced meadows and then knock again, harder.

"Yeah?" comes a muffled voice from upstairs. Stepping off the back porch, I look up at an open window. "Mr. Hester?"

"Yeah."

"It's Patience Murphy."

"What do you want?" So curt. What's up? The voice softens. "You having trouble with Star or Moonlight?"

"No. They're okay. What's wrong with you, anyway? Why don't you come down?" A silence follows, filled with ringing cicadas.

"I've been injured."

"Can I come up?" More silence, as if he's trying to decide how much of his private life he wants to reveal. We aren't actually friends, though we've shared a few moments.

"Okay . . . the door's unlocked."

As I enter the kitchen, I note a sink full of dishes. There's an unwashed milk bucket on the counter, and past the wall telephone I locate steep wooden stairs that lead to the second level. Just outside the room that I surmise must be his bedroom, I find a white porcelain potty with the lid off, full to the brim with dark yellow liquid. The smell is not good.

Without thinking I reach down, replace the lid, then tap twice and push the door open. Daniel Hester lies in a rumpled four-poster double bed, a three-day beard covering his bruised face. His left arm is in a sling, and one very purple bare leg and foot is supported on a feather pillow.

"Wow! You look like you got in a fight with a bull and the bull won!" I make a joke of it, but in truth I'm shocked.

Hester waves at a nearby chair and indicates that I should sit down. "I was in a fight, and you're right, I did lose, but not with a bull." He notices me staring at an unlabeled bottle of clear booze . . . gin, or maybe vodka . . .

"Pain medicine," he excuses himself.

"What can I do?" I'd like to change his bedding, clean him up. Attend to his wounds. I was looking for a nursing job, but this isn't for pay. He just looks so pitiful.

"Nothing. I'm okay."

"Sure! You can't even empty your own pee pot. What are you doing about milking?"

"Not much. I've milked once a day, and it took me an hour to get to the barn and back." He coughs and holds his ribs on the side of his injured arm.

I shake my head. "What happened? You were kidding about the fight, right?"

Hester shakes his head no. "It was three fellows over near Burnt Town. You probably don't know them, the Bishop brothers."

I reach over to straighten Hester's pillows, wrinkling my nose. He smells like sweat and something else, manure . . .

"So how did you get in this state? It must have been quite a battle."

"I went over to attend their sick horse, and when I got there the three of them were two sheets to the wind. There are four brothers, really, all small farmers and moonshiners, but the one I usually deal with, the oldest, Aran"—he nods toward the bottle—"wasn't there.

"Anyway, as usual, they called me when it was almost too late. A lot of stockmen do, trying to save money, hoping whatever is wrong with their animal will miraculously disappear. They were in a surly mood. Drink does that to some men, and they were worried about their animal."

He struggles to turn on his side so he can see me better, but tears come to his eyes and he gives up, staring helplessly at the ceiling.

"When did this happen?"

"Two days ago. I was summoned because their favorite horse, Devil—"

"Devil? You're kidding, right? The *Bishop* brothers have a horse named Devil?" I think this is funny, but he doesn't laugh.

"Yeah. I was called because Devil had colic."

"Just a minute." I trot down the stairs, light his gas stove, pump some water into a big pan, and put it on to heat.

"What were you doing?" he asks when I get back. For the first time I notice the framed paintings and prints on the white plaster walls: race horses, farm horses, and hunting horses, some original, some reproductions. There's even a faded photograph of Hester as a young man in an army uniform, standing with a wagon and two horses. The horses are wearing gas masks. I flick my eyes away from the gallery.

"Warming water for a bath."

The vet smiles his first smile of the day, his half-crooked one. "I smell pretty bad, huh?"

I nod. "You reek."

The only time I smelled something similar was when Ruben came back in the spring of 1920 from organizing the miners at Matewan. He hadn't bathed for a week and had had only one set of clothes with him. He cried when he told me how things had fallen apart at Tug Fork.

"Three thousand men signed the union's roster at the community church, though they knew it could cost them," he told me after I'd washed his back and hair and made him put on a clean nightshirt. "If we failed in negotiating an agreement with the mine owners, they'd lose their jobs.

"And that's what happened. The Stone Mountain Coal Company fought back with mass firings. Women and children were actually thrown out of their company cabins into the rain. The mine boss brought in the Baldwin-Felts Detective Agency, those goons from down near Bluefield, to do the dirty work with machine guns, but the miners had rifles and pistols and were ready for them. We weren't even striking yet, just trying to get organized. A gunfight erupted on Main Street. It wasn't clear who fired the first shot, Sheriff Hatfield or one of the Felts brothers, but ten men died. It was senseless."

It's funny how just a smell can evoke such a strong recollection. I remember all that as I straighten the room. It was the first time Ruben had been involved in armed fighting, and it changed him. After that he carried a Colt revolver.

* * *

The vet groans again and goes on with his story. "Anyway, the horse, Devil, is already in bad shape when I get there. Bad. He's their favorite mount, the one that always leads the Fourth of July parade in Liberty with red, white, and blue ribbons in its tail . . . They'd been walking him around a pen in the yard. He was pretty far gone, covered in lather and foaming at the mouth, buckling at his knees, trying to lie down. A bad sign.

"You never want to let a horse with colic roll," he goes on. "It can cause torsion of the bowel and end in death. I knew Devil wasn't long for this world when I counted his respirations and saw how his eyes were white with fear . . . I was pissed as hell but tried not to show it.

" 'How many hours has this been going on?' I asked.

" 'Since this morning,' the youngest one, Beef, answered. He's a guy about five-six and two hundred pounds, all muscles, no brains, carrying a plank about four feet long, and now and then he whacked the horse on his backside to keep him moving. I was shocked.

"'We called you three times.' A gallon of moonshine sat by the barn door, and they all smelled like whiskey.

"I didn't believe them. I'd been home all day, in the house, reading the new issue of *The Breeder's Gazette*. I only got the one phone call and I went right away, but I just went on with my examination.

"The horse's temp was a hundred and four and the pulse was weak, never a good sign. Horses can't take as much stress as other big animals. I asked the usual questions about the progression of the illness, when it had started, and what they'd done. The brothers had tried castor oil, but the horse was still impacted. I had to be honest with them.

"'This horse has been blocked for longer than a day. Look at him, he's in dire pain. I can give him a sedative and try to pass a stomach tube, but I can't promise you anything. His bowel is already inflamed. He may not make it.'

"'So do we have to pay if he kicks

the bucket?' smirked Beef, the one with the plank."

The vet shakes his head. "I never even got to do anything. While the brothers were giving me grief about my fee, the horse started to go down. We all put our weight on him, but he's a big one, crashed to the barn floor, and that was the end. I pulled out a syringe and tried a shot of adrenaline . . . but the stallion's heart had already stopped beating.

"Then Beef started hitting the poor animal with the plank. That really got to me. I know he felt bad. Tears were streaming down his face, but he kept whacking the horse. 'Get up, you black beast!' he yelled over and over, 'Get up!,' spraying his words and swiping his eyes. 'Get up, I say!'

"One of the men was laughing, busting his sides open. No one made Beef stop—and I lost it. Just lost it. I grabbed the plank, threw it across the pen, and slipped in the castor oil. That's when I twisted my ankle."

He indicates his blue-and-purple foot and I wince, wondering what I would have done . . . I can't imagine watching a man beat his dead horse. It would make me furious too. The noble animal laying there . . . an animal that could have been saved.

"Well, things got ugly then . . . Beef came at me, and I pulled him down. We were wallowing around in the straw and castor oil, both upset, seeing the horse die right in front of us, and I started beating the man in the face with my fist, straddling his thick belly. That's when one of the others picked up the plank and hit me in the back . . . hit me over and over until Aran, the oldest brother, showed up. That's the old guy I've bought moonshine from. He's pretty normal.

"'What the hell!' he yelled, standing there in the barn door with a bucket of water he was bringing out for the stock. He took it all in, the dead horse, the grown men involved in a barnyard brawl, and threw the water all over us.

"That's when I jumped up and left. Just grabbed my hat, staggered out of the yard, and hobbled as fast as I could for my Ford. I could hear Aran hollering at them as I started my vehicle, but the brothers just laughed."

"Did you go see someone for your injuries?"

"No."

"Why not? Something could be broken!" I rise and move toward the kitchen, unable to stand the disorder.

Hester groans. "You know medical people never go to doctors. Nothing's broken but my spirit. The worse part, for me, is the horse . . . the unnecessary death of the beautiful horse." He wipes his wet eyes. "Assholes!"

In the next half hour, I dig through Hester's dresser to find a clean pair of skivvies and help him clean up. Though he seems a meticulous surgeon, his sense of personal order is no better than Ruben's was. The drawers are filled with a tangle of unfolded clothes. None of the socks are matched. I can hardly tell what's clean and what's dirty.

With difficulty we remove his sling, and Hester lets me wash his upper body, his neck, and his back. He can move his left arm, which is black and blue from the elbow to the shoulder, so I have to agree with him that it probably isn't broken.

While he bathes below his waist, I run downstairs, tidy the kitchen, and heat a can of Van Camp's Pork & Beans that I dig out of the pantry. Then, while he eats, sitting up in a chair, I change his linens. Finally he collapses back onto the bed like a steelworker at the end of the day.

"So what was your plan?" I ask with a smile when my nursing tasks are done; two quart jars of clean drinking water rest on the bedside table and his potty, now shiny white, is nearby.

"Plan?"

"Yeah. How were you going to get by in this state? Were you going to call someone? Dr. Blum or Becky Myers?"

"Hell, no. Anyway, Blum was in a bad auto wreck last week on his way home from a night call. His car went into the ravine along Bluff Creek. Reverend Miller was out on a call and found him, but his auto is beyond repair. He told me he's through. Doesn't want to live like this anymore, going out day and night in all kinds of weather, risking his life for almost no pay. As soon as he can, he's taking his wife and joining his brother's practice back in Charlottesville."

I let out my breath thinking about the pregnant women in Union County, especially the ones with problems, and how this will affect them. But I don't let myself get diverted.

"So what *was* your plan?" I ask a second time. "What were you going to do about your injuries and your stock? Just lie here and rot and let your animals starve? You could hardly get down the stairs to cook or get water unless you slid on your bottom."

His eyes are laughing. "I was waiting for an angel of mercy."

June 30, 1930. New moon rising.

Called to the Klopfenstein farm again, this time to deliver Elvira and Moses Klopfenstein's fourth baby (a boy named Daniel, 7 pounds, 2 ounces). She

was **Ruth Klopfenstein's aunt, the one with the limp at the first birth I attended at their compound. Granny Klopfenstein has decided to leave birthing to me.**

Again the women sat in a row at the bedside, wearing their black dresses, round eyeglasses, and scarves, only this time the golden-haired Molly was nursing her baby and everyone was happy because Elvira delivered quickly and in bed. I was glad Bitsy was there to see what they were like. No one seemed shocked that she is colored. I guess word gets around. Fast delivery. No tears. Moderate blood loss. Bitsy delivered the placenta.

29

Independence Day

Morning and evening, for the past week, Bitsy and I have been visiting the vet. We milk his cows, feed and water his horses and chickens, empty his pee pot, and try to keep the place decent. When I cook for him, he tells me I should take some of his supplies home, so I help myself to a sack of cornmeal, a bottle of milk, some sugar, and a half can of lard.

By the seventh evening he is much better, and I find him sitting at the table downstairs reading a veterinary text. He has on clean clothes, and a cane leans against his chair. He holds it up. "Found this in the closet when I moved here. I couldn't imagine ever needing it, but I never threw it away." There's a lull while he limps across the room, finds a newspaper, and spreads it out on the oilcloth.

"Next Saturday is the Fourth of July celebration in Liberty." He shows me the announcement. "You and Bitsy want a ride into town? We could make a day of it. See the parade and the fireworks."

I shrug, thinking about the last Fourth of July celebration I went to, in Washington, D.C. I've avoided such celebrations ever since. "We could. I guess." The vet's face gets red, and I guess that I've hurt his feelings.

"No, I'd like to go." I endeavor to whip up some enthusiasm. "It would be fun."

A few days later, we're standing in front of Stenger's Pharmacy waiting for the parade to begin. "Nice dress," the vet comments, taking in my white outfit and white stockings. He probably didn't know I had such frocks, having mostly seen me in trousers. Because it's Independence Day, I am wearing Mrs. Kelly's little red hat. He looks rather dashing himself in a pale blue shirt with the sleeves rolled up and a Panama straw hat with a black band.

"Want a soda?" The vet points to the red metal cooler with the famous white cola symbol on the front just outside Bittman's Grocery. I look at the sign: five cents a bottle.

"No, thank you." The money for just one Coke could purchase a nice loaf of bread. Hester grins, limps over to the store, and buys us two bottles anyway, then finds us a seat on the courthouse steps. His extravagance bothers me, but not enough to keep me from enjoying the icy cold beverage.

I gaze along Main, making note of the boys in patched overalls, the little girls in hand-me-down dresses, adults with worries etched into their faces. There are so many shuttered stores. Even Mullin's Hardware, where I once bought periwinkle blue paint for my front door, has a sign saying FOR SALE.

Far down the street and around the

corner we hear the *rat-a-tat-tat* of a drum, then music, and the crowd stirs and looks toward Sycamore. It's the Liberty High School band, playing "The Stars and Stripes Forever." They march proudly down Main and are followed by a color guard from the American Legion, then the Oneida High School Band and the snappy All Negro Drum Corps from Delmont. Trailing a good way behind them are the Civil War veterans.

We stand up along with everyone else for the ancient soldiers, who stroll past us in their tattered uniforms. Mrs. Kelly had explained that when West Virginia seceded from Virginia in 1863, the people of the region were deeply divided. These old soldiers would be about seventy. Four are dressed in blue, three in gray.

I swipe my eyes with the back of my hand when I see the little children, their bicycles and pets festooned in red, white, and blue trailing along behind them. One little girl is leading a dog dressed up as Uncle Sam. Hester looks over, but I don't care. Though I think of myself as a citizen of the world, there's something about simple patriotism that moves me. I inevitably get a lump in my throat, and I don't even know why. Maybe it's because in Deerfield when I was young, Independence Day was such a big event.

First thing on a hot July Fourth, Father and I would go to the park near the river, spread our blankets on the lawn to save our place for the picnic . . . the Hungarian Polka Band would play in the Gazebo . . .

"Here come the horses," the vet says, breaking me out of my reverie. Mares and stallions, ponies, and even burros prance along, their coats gleaming, their hooves washed, ribbons braided through their manes and tails.

"See that pinto?" He directs my attention to a beautiful white-and-brown horse. "See how she limps a little. Tore her back left leg on a barbed-wire fence last year, a hell of a repair. It took two hours, and I had to use chloroform." And a little later, "There's Mrs. Dresher riding sidesaddle on her new Morgan."

The last two horses, black stallions,

are ridden by men in long white gowns with white masks ending in a point, poor reproductions of KKK costumes. A hush runs through the crowd, then someone laughs and everyone joins in except for the vet and me. My jaw is so rigid I can barely speak. "Is this for real?"

"No, just some guys clowning around, trying to get attention by tagging behind. The parade committee wouldn't allow any reference to the Klan."

As the crowd disperses, he puts his arm through mine and guides me away toward a blue handcart where a vendor is spinning some kind of pink goo. The hot summer air smells of sugar. COTTON CANDY, the sign says. "Want to taste it?" Hester asks. He's trying to divert my attention.

"*No!* Twenty-five cents is too dear. You already bought me a Coke." The truth is, I'm still sick from the sight of the men in the Ku Klux Klan costumes. What if Bitsy saw them? She's in the crowd somewhere with Big Mary. What if Thomas and Mrs. Potts are nearby? I am gritting my teeth so hard I might break them.

"It's okay," my companion says, pulling a quarter out of his pocket and handing it to the vendor. "You can't take it with you." Before he can receive the pink sugar stuff on a stick, I feel his shoulders stiffen and his head jerk up. Three heavyset men in overalls, across the street, are heading toward us.

"Hey, vet! Kill any good horses lately?" the one with a white cloth hanging over his shoulder yells.

"The Bishop brothers," Hester mutters as he grabs my hand. "Let's go." He doesn't even ask for his money back.

Race Riots

The last time I left a Fourth of July parade in a hurry was in our nation's great capital.

It was 1919, and Ruben had to go to a meeting with Samuel Gompers of the AFL on July third, so he came up with a plan. "Why don't you come?" he asked with his usual enthusiasm. "We could make a holiday of it."

"I've seen fireworks and parades before."

"Yeah, but not in Washington! A person should experience the festivities there at least once in a lifetime. It will be an adventure. We can stay with Sam Gompers."

We both had money then. I was still working at Westinghouse and wrangled a day off with the section supervisor. Ruben was full-time with the union. We packed a bag and took the Capitol Limited out of Union Station on the second.

It was a bad time in the United States after the Great War. Patriotism had been whipped to a fury to overcome ordinary Americans' reluctance to join what many thought was a European conflict. When the soldiers were discharged and came back needing work, there weren't any jobs.

Meanwhile, in Russia, Lenin was riding the wave of the revolution and threatening to take over the world.

There were a few bombings by anarchists in the United States, and suddenly people imagined a Bolshevik in every closet. The feds even pounded on *our* door one night, looking for Ruben, but Nora charmed them, wearing her red silk kimono, while Mrs. Kelly and I hid him in the attic.

Then the lynching of blacks started again in the South, sixty in 1918 and more in riots all over the country in 1919, several men still in their army uniforms. Pittsburgh wasn't like that. Segregation was illegal, and there was a sense of peace regarding race relations, not that people of different races mixed freely, except radicals and jazz musicians.

Still, I should have known there would be trouble, but I was clueless until I saw the headlines of the *Washington Post* on Mrs. Gompers's dining room table: 13 SUSPECTS ARRESTED IN NEGRO HUNT; WHITE POSSE SEEKS BLACK RAPIST OF TWO WHITE WOMEN.

"What's this?" I ask the union leader's wife as she pours tea for me from a silver teapot and the men talk union business in the parlor.

"Don't pay any attention to that trash, dear."

"Why not?"

"It's a pack of lies by journalists competing with each other for the most sensational headlines. Race relations are already tense in Washington." She passes the sugar "And the newspapers are making it worse, just whipping up trouble." To illustrate, she shows me another stack of papers on the ornate oak buffet: the *Washington Times, Evening Star,* and the *Washington Herald.*

POSSES KEEP UP HUNT FOR NEGRO . . . WHITE POSSES AID POLICE IN HUNT FOR COLORED ASSAILANT . . . NEGRO FIEND SOUGHT ANEW!

"Have there really been that many rapes?"

The older lady shakes her head. "Not one that I know of, but the city's become a racial tinderbox. There's so few jobs that ex-doughboys are panhandling on Pennsylvania Avenue. The white soldiers bitterly resent the few black men who've been able to get work . . . even the lowest-paying jobs like messengers or elevator boys."

The next day at the parade there was a scuffle, and I saw what she meant. As the U.S. Navy Band, dressed to the nines, marched past us, three white guys grabbed a black man in an army uniform, dragged him into an alley, and beat the stuffing out of him. Ruben chased them off, and we carried the injured fellow to a side street, grabbed a cab, and took him to Walter Reed General Hospital, but after that the fireworks held no interest and we left on the train the next day.

Sitting in the coach, leaning into each other, staring out the window as we chugged through Virginia, Maryland, West Virginia, and Pennsylvania, we struggled to hold on to some dream we had of America.

A week later, we read in the *Washington Times* that a white mob had grabbed another black man near Howard University, hung him up like a cow for slaughter, and shot him. After that, all hell broke loose. Mrs. Gompers was right. There was rioting in D.C., black man against white. In the end four men died on the streets of the capital of the land of the free, the home of the brave . . . but that was over ten years ago.

As Daniel Hester and I hurry away down Main Street, away from the crowd and around the corner to his office, the three brothers watch us, hate in their eyes.

30

July 10, 1930. Full moon rising.
Like the one blind eye of
heaven.

Birth of Chipper Mayo, 8
pounds, 4 ounces, fourth son of
Phoebe and Delmar Mayo of
Panther Branch. When we got
to their farm, I thought for sure
that we'd come too early. Phoebe
was running around trying to
tidy their small house. Bitsy and
I pitched in. Bitsy even had the
little boys out beating rugs on
the clothesline. I finally had to
tell the mother to go upstairs
and lie down. She was exhaust-

ing herself, but she wasn't in bed more than twenty minutes when we heard a yell. By the time we got there, a baby was lying on the bed between her legs in a mess of blood and water, crying up a storm.

The placenta, with a short thick cord, was sitting on his little wet head like a cap. I could have died laughing. No rips or tears. Some extra bleeding, but penny-royal and massage quieted it down. The father, Mr. Mayo, came home a bit later and exclaimed, "Well, isn't he a chipper chap!" That's how the baby got his name, "Chipper." Present, only Bitsy and I, and we didn't do much. Paid one fat chicken and made it home by supper!

Storm

The garden is now producing plenty of good food. Our table is laden with peas, lettuce, kale, tomatoes, beans, yellow summer squash, new potatoes, and onions. The potatoes help to take the place of bread because we are again out of cornmeal and flour. We haven't been to town for three weeks, but we're tranquil, away from the news about the failing economy, the sights of the hungry men begging for work and the travelers hitching the roads with their scrawny kids and wives, all moving north and east, where they think they'll find jobs.

In the evening, since it stays light so long, Bitsy and I sit on the porch and laugh at the 1920s articles in the old *Ladies' Home Journal*s I found in the attic. Those were the boom times that everyone thought would last forever. Easy money. Easy women in their short flapper skirts. I wore those short skirts myself with silk stockings and garter belts when Ruben and I went to the jazz clubs in Pittsburgh. We danced all night in the loud smoky halls. I noticed in town that the hems have come down, along with the stock market and everything else.

Moonlight has not yet delivered, but
when Mr. Hester came over to check
on her, he calculated that she would
soon. Standing at the sink, washing his
hands, he gave us instructions on how
to tell when she goes into labor.

"The first thing to watch for," he lec-
tured, "is restlessness. Keep her in the
barn. If you let her out, she may wander into the woods. What she's looking
for is a safe place to calve." I was jot-
ting this all down on a piece of wrapping paper.

"Next, her vulva will spring. This may
happen a few days before the birth."

"Spring?"

"Yeah, become loose, kind of open.
Then her water bag will break. From
now on, you probably should check on
her a few times a day. Come for me if
you think it's time."

"You gonna be Moonlight's midwife?"
I joke. He doesn't laugh.

"I'll be her vet."

All day, every day, the sun beats down.
It's so hot that Emma and Sasha hide

under the porch and the chickens cover themselves with dust. A hundred and three degrees! That's what the tin man-in-the-moon thermometer on the side of the barn says. Usually in the mountains, even in July, it only gets up to eighty. Poor pregnant Moonlight! Her vulva hasn't *sprung* yet, but she's definitely restless.

We get up at six and weed the garden for a few hours before dawn, but by nine we just want to hide in the springhouse. By ten we're finished, and then, as a reward, we walk Star down to the stream, play in the dwindling cool clear water, and pick raspberries.

Today, around five, just as we're drying off, a hot wind comes up and black clouds boil over the mountaintops.

We both look up. Sniff the air like wild animals. "Bitsy, your hair! It's standing on end!" (This is not a good sign; the atmosphere must be supercharged with electricity.)

"Yours too!" she yells. I raise my hand and feel the loose strands springing out around my face. Then all hell breaks loose.

First comes the thunder, rattling across the sky from the west, deep rumbling so close it makes the earth shake. We make it to the barn just as the sky cracks open and push Star through the doors. By the time we get to the house our clothes are soaked and our hair hangs in strings.

From the front windows I watch the crooked bolts of lightning pierce the black clouds. One jagged bolt strikes a tree across the valley, and the crack echoes for miles. I glance over at my companion, who has pulled the flying goose–pattern quilt over her head.

"Criminy!"

Escape

A few hours later, when the storm slows to a steady drumbeat and Bitsy and I are making supper, the blue door bangs open against the wall.

"Help!" someone cries. Because of the rain, we'd missed the sound of the vehicle sliding up Wild Rose Road and the frantic knocks. Katherine steps in onto the braided rug, her short bob plastered down, her eyes red from tears, a crying child in one arm and a suitcase in the other. Outside, a dark sedan sits just beyond the picket fence.

"Oh, Patience, Bitsy, hide me!" She paces the room like a fox in a cage. "He'll come for me this time!" Bitsy takes the wailing baby and tries to soothe him. I pull Katherine's wet silk middy off and wrap her in my kimono. We make tea, while our meal of fried potatoes and collards turns cold, and try to get the frightened woman calmed down.

It isn't until I sit next to her on the sofa that I notice the fresh bruises on her throat, four finger marks on each side. Katherine sees me staring and touches her delicate neck. "He grabbed me from behind when I was packing. Mary ran upstairs and was screaming at him to get off. She finally had to snatch my silver mirror off the dresser and hit him three times. The glass broke in shards all over the floor." She starts to cry again.

"I ran to the Stengers' house just

down the street, but no one was there, so I snuck back, took the keys off the hook in the kitchen, and stole William's car, but there's something wrong with it, one wheel is wobbling. I almost ran into a ditch."

I want to ask what started the row. Had Mr. MacIntosh been drinking again? Has this been going on since the last incident? But it doesn't matter. She and baby Willie are here, and sometime tonight or tomorrow William will come to that conclusion.

"Did Mary knock him out or just stun him? Was he conscious when you left?" I'm trying to figure out how much time we have.

"He was just stunned but still drunk. Mary wouldn't come with me. I begged her, but she wouldn't. She just stood over him with what was left of the mirror . . . I need to get a train to Baltimore." She looks wildly around the room, as if expecting a locomotive and coach to pull up on the porch.

"I thought William would change . . . that his drinking and outbursts were the result of stress, but I'm beginning to think he has a mean streak and his troubles have just brought it out of him. I've seen him strike his men in the past; now he's turning on me. I'm going back to my family. This is it. I'm done trying."

The rain starts up again, slashing the house at an angle. It roars so loud we have to raise our voices. With the storm it's not likely that the angry husband, with or without the sheriff, will come to-night. We just need to get Katherine out by morning.

I take a deep breath. "Can you eat, Katherine? We have food on the stove. William won't come for you until the rain stops. The weather's too bad. By the morning, we'll get you somewhere safe." I say this authoritatively, but am I so sure? Who knows what the enraged man will do?

"We're getting ourselves in way too deep," Bitsy mumbles after moving the car into the barn, out of sight. We are sitting at the kitchen table eating our reheated fried potatoes. Katherine is upstairs exhausted, sleeping in my bed with little Willie.

"What?"

"Black folks don't need to get involved with the law."

"Well, we can't just send Katherine and the baby out in the storm."

Bitsy shrugs. "She should have stayed at the Stengers' or run to the sheriff. This isn't going to end good."

I'm surprised and a little miffed at this turn in my friend. "How about your mom? She didn't hesitate to help. Mary hit Mr. MacIntosh in the head to save Katherine."

"You think she'll have a job tomorrow? She'll be lucky not to be arrested for assault. A black woman beating on a white man?" Bitsy pushes her chair back, drops her plate into the sink, and stomps upstairs, each footstep a warning.

More Trouble

All night, I lie wide awake on the sofa, staring at the crack in the ceiling, trying to figure out what to do. We've got William's car, but Katherine says it's not running well and I'd be afraid to drive it to Torrington. What if we lose control and run into a ditch? There's that bad place along the river with the steep bank. Can I ask Hester for a favor again? Who else is there? Where will we hide Katherine if the law comes?

The rain fades, then stops. Lightning flashes far off to the east. Dawn. The sound of the dogs barking. The distant roar of a vehicle. Damn! MacIntosh didn't waste any time. I fumble for my glasses, wipe what little sleep I got out of my eyes, and step to the window. Far down Wild Rose, passing the Maddocks' place, a black sedan churns slowly uphill. It slides back and forth, rolls into a muddy ditch, and comes out again, relentlessly chugging on.

"Bitsy, Katherine! Wake up! We got company!" I take the stairs two at a time, throw open the bedroom doors. "Someone in a black auto is coming up Wild Rose Road." The injured woman rubs her face as if coming out of one nightmare into another.

"Come on! Come on!" I gently shake her arm. "Get moving." Bitsy has already pulled up her slacks and is throwing Katherine and the baby's things into the valise.

"Take Katherine and little Willie out the back door and hide in the barn," I order. "Watch through the cracks, and the three of you be prepared to head over the mountain on Star if someone comes out there. Ride fast, to Hazel Patch. Reverend Miller will protect you. Forget the car; whoever is coming will just chase you down."

Bitsy does what I tell her and has the mother and child through the back door and out of sight by the time the mud-spattered vehicle pulls up to the gate. It's not William MacIntosh but the sheriff and one of the city lawmen.

I straighten the quilt on the end of the sofa and scan for anything that belongs to Katherine. A baby blanket is on the floor, and I kick it under the piano. Then I open the blue door to meet the men as they step up on the porch.

"Patience Murphy?" the sheriff begins. He's a tall man with very blue eyes, the type who can eat as much as he wishes and never gain weight, clean-shaven with a scar straight across his chin.

"Yes, I'm Patience."

"Sheriff Hardman from Liberty." He opens his jacket and shows me a badge, though this is only a formality. We've seen each other in town. I turn to the other fellow, waiting for an introduction, but he's silent as Mount Rushmore.

"Is your colored girl here?" Hardman asks. This startles me. Why is he asking for Bitsy? Maybe she's right, just being black makes you a criminal.

"She lives here, yes." I hate the way he asks for *my colored girl,* but I don't make an issue of it. I have enough trouble without getting into that. "But she's not at home."

"Can you tell me where I can find her? Mary Proudfoot, her mother, had an accident and was rushed to the doctor."

"An accident?" Where would Bitsy be this early in the morning? What's my excuse? The sheriff doesn't ask for her whereabouts.

"Mrs. Proudfoot fell on the stairs at

her employer's home. Mr. MacIntosh found her unconscious this morning and brought her to the doctor. She appears to have collapsed during the night."

From the corner of my eye, I watch the other lawman step down from the porch, stroll around the edge of the house, and stare at the barn. Sasha and Emma start to growl. "Stand down," I order, wishing I could signal *Attack!* The fellow retreats back to the bottom step.

"An accident? Mary? Is she okay?"

"We don't know. The nurse just called and insisted I let her kin know she's injured and confused. There's a son too. Thomas Proudfoot."

"Bitsy went fishing early, down at Hope River," I fib, hoping it sounds a little plausible. "Thomas lives at the camp at the Wildcat Mine."

Sheriff Hardman clears his throat. "There's something else. Mr. MacIntosh's wife, Katherine, and his young son have disappeared. You wouldn't know anything about that, would you?

MacIntosh told us you and her were friends."

"Not really friends," I contradict. "I was her midwife . . . I haven't heard from Katherine lately." This is just a white lie. We have no phone, so we haven't *heard* from her. That doesn't mean she's not hiding out in the barn.

"Well, I have to get back. Tell the Proudfoot woman the doc said to come soon." The two move toward their police van. "Oh, and let me know if Mrs. MacIntosh shows up. William MacIntosh is awfully worried."

Before they climb in, the city lawman with the granite mug stops. "You aren't from Union County, are you?"

"No, not originally. Why do you ask?"

The man shrugs. "Your accent isn't local." I watch from the porch until the van disappears, a black stain in the mist by the river. Then I run—run for the barn.

Flight

Two hours later I am driving William's wobbly Olds back into Liberty with Daniel Hester following behind. Katherine, Bitsy, and the baby ride with him. It's still early and steam is rising off of the river when, behind the Texaco station, I tuck the keys under the seat of the mud-spattered vehicle and get in with them. Bitsy is going to see Mary, and the rest of us are on our way to Torrington, where Katherine can catch a train to Baltimore.

"Give Mary a hug from me," I tell Bitsy when, to save time, we drop her on Main. "We'll be back late tonight."

Katherine, who is scrunched low with the baby on the Model T's back floor, reaches into her brassiere and pulls out some folded green, part of her getaway cash. Without rising, she sticks her hand out the window and waves the money at Bitsy. "You'll need this for the doctor's bill," she whispers. "And maybe food . . . Thank your mother from the bottom of my heart. I just know she fell trying to keep William from following me. *I just know it."*

Then Hester and I, in front, with Katherine and the baby staying low in the back, speed north up 92 toward Torrington. Everywhere there are leaves on the road, torn from the trees during the thunderstorm. Twice we have to get out to pull big branches off the road.

"Thanks for helping us," I whisper to the vet.

He shrugs. "It's nothing."

"I didn't know where else to turn."

He repeats himself, flicking his gray eyes to my face and tightening his jaw as if he means business. "It's nothing."

I keep looking over my shoulder, expecting to see William MacIntosh, or maybe the sheriff, hot on our trail, but there's nothing back there except the empty two-lane blacktop.

By dark we're standing in the doorway of a one-room tourist cabin on the outskirts of Torrington, the last one available at the Riverview Travelers' Lodge. We have just learned that the next train for Baltimore doesn't leave until seven in the morning and are trying to make the best of it.

Exhausted, Katherine collapses on the single bed and falls asleep nursing Willie. I pull the covers over them. The poor battered woman is dead to the world. My idea was that she and I would sleep together in the double bed and Hester would lie down on the single, but I hate waking her and making her move, and apparently so does the vet.

"I guess I'll take this," he says quietly, indicating a battered upholstered easy chair next to the door.

I wince. It looks really uncomfortable. He won't sleep at all.

"No, I'll sleep there. I got you into this."

"I don't mind."

I let out my air. I'm dog tired and in no mood for arguing. "Okay, let's share the big bed." I turn down the stiff sheet and red-and-black-striped cotton Indian blanket. "We can keep our clothes on." The truth is, I'd feel guilty taking the bed while he sat up all night, and even if we traded halfway through, that would mean less than four hours of shut-eye for each of us.

Hester looks dubious but then raises his eyebrows and grins. "Whatever you say. We're already outlaws, helping Katherine sneak out of town with the coal baron's baby. Sleeping together won't sully our names any worse."

We remove our shoes but nothing else, and I use the tiny water closet to unfasten my brassiere. The vet reaches up and turns off the light. "Good night," he murmurs, turning away.

I swallow hard. It's the first time I've slept near a man, since . . . since Ruben died, and Hester's warmth comes clear through his clothes.

Outside the small window, the neon sign winks NO VACANCY. Red, then green. Red. Green. Red. Green. Hester stirs in his sleep.

Oh, Ruben! Why did we go to Blair Mountain? I wipe my face on the corner of the blanket and choke back my sobs, but the tears keep coming.

31

Lost

"Do you think she'll make it?" I ask Hester as we see the train off. Katherine is still waving through the Pullman car window, looking like any other mother and baby on a holiday. The sleep has done her good, and her color is better.

"Yeah, I explained the situation to the porter, a nice guy, who says he knows Thomas Proudfoot. He promised he'd look after them. If the law doesn't search the train at Cumberland, they'll be okay."

"I hope she writes. I asked her to. I just want to know she's safe."

The vet has been especially solicitous this morning, helping me on with my sweater, pulling out my chair at Minnie's Breakfast Diner, opening the door for me. I worry that he may have heard me crying in the night.

We're halfway back to Liberty on Route 92, each lost in our own thoughts, when he poses a question that surprises me. "Have you ever been hurt by a man?"

"Why do you ask?" He's probably thinking about my tears in the night.

"Some men think it's their right."

"Not the ones I know. My men friends believed in equality between the sexes." Except Mr. Vanderhoff, I think . . . but that was way back . . . and anyway, he wasn't a friend.

By the time we make it back to Liberty, it's half past three. "Where to?" Hester asks.

I shrug. "The hospital."

The two-story brick house, Dr. Blum's clinic, sits back from the street on a tree-lined lot, and a woman in a white uniform and a little white hat sits at a desk in the front hall. Apparently nurses no longer wear aprons.

"We're here to see Mrs. Proudfoot," the vet starts out. "I'm Dr. Hester, and this is Patience Murphy." The lady looks confused. She probably wonders who Dr. Hester is, and I try to hide a smile behind the back of my hand. I'd forgotten veterinarians called themselves doctors.

The nurse scans a clipboard in front of her. She runs her finger up and down a short list. "We don't have a patient named Proudfoot . . . There must be some mistake."

"Maybe she's been discharged already. Is Dr. Blum here?" Hester continues. "Can you check your discharge roster?"

"Dr. Blum's gone. Left for Virginia four days ago. The hospital's staffed by nurses and Dr. Holden from Delmont, when he can come." She runs her short nails down a separate clipboard. "There's no Proudfoot here." She shakes her head irritably.

"It was a fall, we were told. Maybe a concussion."

"Are you kin?" the nurse asks.

"Just friends," I interject. "I'm sure you'd remember her, a big colored woman. Maybe you could ask the matron."

A light goes on in the little nurse's eyes. "A Negro woman?" We nod. "Well, she wouldn't come here. We don't cater to Negroes." My stomach goes hollow.

"Come on," says Hester, grabbing my arm. I can see he's pissed off. It's the way she said "We don't *cater* to Negroes," as if this were an ice cream parlor or beauty salon.

Outside, standing next to the car, Hester looks down at me. "So . . . where is she?"

"I don't know. *I don't know.* I'd heard that Blum didn't deliver black women at his hospital, but I didn't think that meant he wouldn't take care of any colored people ever, even in an emergency."

"God damn Blum!"

"I was flustered, I'm sorry."

"Let's go. The son of a bitch!" We get back into his Ford, whip down the street, and pull up at his office.

Inside the white house with the sign on the front, DANIEL HESTER, DVM—DOCTOR OF ANIMALS, LARGE AND SMALL, I'm ushered to a seat in the waiting room.

"'Bout time you came in," says a large, pale, corseted female sitting at a desk. Her gray hair is pulled tight away from her face, and she looks like someone even Hester would be scared of. "Mr. Rhodes called three times, and he's really sour about it. His best milk cow won't stand up, has lost her feed, and he wants you there pronto. You have to remember to leave me messages so I know where to find you. I've been trying all morning."

"I need to use the phone, Mrs. Armstrong." Hester grabs the receiver. "Tell Rhodes, if he calls again, I'll be there in an hour." Before this, it hadn't occurred to me that the vet might be losing business by helping us. I've been so caught up in Katherine's troubles, I hadn't even thought of my own responsibilities, and in my mind I quickly run over the mothers who are close to term. They should be okay . . . I hope they are okay. I could have at least sent word to Mrs. Potts that I'd be gone. Even then, I didn't expect it to be all night.

Hester cranks the phone. "Stenger? It's Hester . . . William MacIntosh's cook, Mary Proudfoot, had a fall and was taken to a physician. We checked Blum's hospital, but she's not there . . . The colored physician, I guess, what's his name, Robinson?" He's talking to the pharmacist. "Okay," he says to the other end of the line. "Yeah, I know where it is."

Five minutes later we're back in the Model T motoring toward Mudtown. This is the part of Liberty where most of the blacks live, maybe a hundred of them, lowland that used to be a swamp, but I've never been here, not even to a birth. Crossing Main, I observe that William MacIntosh's sedan is still parked at the Texaco station, but it's been moved forward into the mechanics' bay.

We bump across the tracks, and I'm

surprised when we pull up at a handsome two-story white clapboard house with its own sign out front: HARPER ROBINSON, MD. I had no idea there was a black doctor in Liberty. Did Mrs. Kelly know? We were here only a year before she died and we were only delivering white babies then, so she wouldn't have needed him.

Here in West Virginia, until I became acquainted with Bitsy and Mrs. Potts, my life was completely involved with the whites. But "involved" is not the right word. I was never *involved* with either blacks or whites, only an observer. Once again I see how separate the two worlds are, like a left hand and a right hand that don't know what the other is doing.

We both jump out, but Hester warns me with a look that he wants to handle this. I collapse back onto the leather seat but leave the door open, watching a group of brown children play in the road.

The rest of the houses along the tracks are much smaller than Robinson's and are identical except for small changes that have been made since they were constructed: a picket fence here, a porch there, shutters on some. Twenty years ago, the dwellings all belonged to the railroad and were constructed for the workers who built the M and K line for the Baltimore and Ohio. That was back when West Virginia was logged in a flurry, from 1900 to 1920. Mrs. Kelly gave me the history. I only heard her get mad three times . . . That was one.

"The whole damned state was clear-cut," she said. "And the trees that weren't chopped went up in smoke with the forest fires that followed." Other than that, there was just that time when Mr. Finney beat up his pregnant wife and the other time when those street boys made fun of the crippled girl and Sophie chased them away.

The vet and a dark man of about seventy wearing a black suit, vest, and tie stand on the porch talking. They shake hands like two professionals after a consultation. The gentleman, who I take to be Dr. Robinson, adjusts his horn-rimmed glasses, looks down at the car and nods. Then Hester comes around and gets in beside me.

"What? Doesn't he know where Mary is either?"

Hester runs his hands through his short hair and clears his throat. "Mary's gone."

"Where, home? To the MacIntoshes'? Not back to the MacIntoshes'!"

"No, I mean . . . dead. She's at the Emmanuel Funeral Home. Died two hours after she was carried to Dr. Robinson, before Bitsy even got here. Traumatic cerebral hemorrhage, he thinks, but the county coroner will have to decide. She died on Robinson's operating table before he could do anything." He reaches over and takes my hand, which is lying on my lap like one of Bitsy's lifeless trout.

But she can't be dead. Not Mary Proudfoot! She was brave and strong. A little fall down the stairs couldn't kill her! She's supposed to be cooking corn fritters, chicken, and biscuits forever! Suddenly I'm very hot. I want to get out of the car, but Hester has already started the engine and Dr. Robinson's still standing on his porch, watching.

"Well, where's Bitsy, then?" I shout, as if the vet's hiding her. Really, I'm just angry with myself. How could I let this happen? Why did I think it was more important to get Katherine out of town and to the train station than to support Bitsy and her family? Was it because Katherine is white? If it is, I despise myself.

"Dr. Robinson thinks Bitsy's at Reverend Miller's out in Hazel Patch. The preacher and his wife came to get her when Robinson called. I can take you there later, but I have to go see that cow first . . . Mr. Rhodes will be madder than hell. I should have been there hours ago. If you come with me, I'll take you to Hazel Patch afterward." Though I desperately want to get to Bitsy, he doesn't leave me much choice.

"Just go!" I wave my hand, indicating he should move the car . . . *anywhere.*

Three hours later, after a painful interlude with an angry farmer during which the vet passed a stomach tube into the ailing Jersey and relieved her blocked intestine with castor oil, we're bumping past Hester's farm on the way to Hazel Patch. We haven't eaten all day and the sun has gone down, but he's too much of a gentleman to turn in at his place and make me walk the last two miles.

When I think of it, he's been involved in affairs that don't concern him, with people he barely knows, for forty-eight hours: first facilitating Katherine's escape, then searching for Mary and Bitsy, now carrying me to the pastor's house. My sadness drags behind me like a black cape, and I can't tell if my dark mood is sorrow at losing Mary Proudfoot, guilt over leaving Bitsy, or worry about how she must be hurting.

Thomas

We don't get to Hazel Patch until well after dark, but the lights are still on when we drive up to the front of the pastor's substantial log home. "Do you want to come in?" I ask Hester. I'm thinking the man must be exhausted and needs to get supper and care for his animals, but he surprises me by opening the driver's-side door and getting out.

"I'm into it this far. I met the Millers at the Wildcat Mine cave-in, remember?"

We tap softly, and Mrs. Miller greets us. She's wearing a long green chenille robe and has a hairnet over her head. Behind Mildred, on the fawn velvet sofa, sitting with Bitsy, are the preacher and a very tall black man who I remember from the flood at the Wildcat, the young fellow who went into the hole with Thomas and Mr. Cabrini. Only a table lamp, with a pale green silk shade, lights the room.

"Bitsy!" I rush in, fall on my knees, and take her hands to my cheeks, a supplicant begging forgiveness. "I'm so sorry, *so sorry.* Sorry about your mom and sorrier still for not being with you." Bitsy smooths my hair like I'm a child. She doesn't say anything, just wipes my wet face, then wipes her tears so that they mix together on her brown hand.

Mildred Miller pulls up two more

chairs as the pastor stands to greet Hester. "Can I get you some coffee?" she offers.

"Sure," the vet says. "Thank you."

"None for me." I just want to go home, take Bitsy with me, and tuck her into bed.

I look around the room. "Where's Thomas?"

No one answers. Eyes meet each other, but they don't meet mine.

Finally. "He's gone into Liberty." That's the tall fellow on the sofa. His voice is very low, and I can't help but notice that his Adam's apple goes up and down when he speaks.

Mildred bustles back into the room with a tray: coffee for anyone who wants it and a glass of water for me.

"Is he making burial arrangements?" I still don't get it, but I should have realized that no one goes to a funeral home at this time of night.

"He let out of here about nine on his burro," Bitsy tells me. "Went to see William MacIntosh. He knows about Katherine's escape, the bruises, and the fight. I told him I thought William must have pushed our mother down those stairs. I shouldn't have said that. Oh, I shouldn't have . . ."

"Child. Don't start again!" Mrs. Miller reprimands. "You are *not* responsible. Let's just pray your brother has some sense." I slump down on the floor, leaning my back against the davenport, held between Bitsy's knees.

"Do you want me to go back to town to look for him?" the vet asks.

"We already tried," the young man responds.

I finally turn to him. "I'm Patience Murphy. This is Dr. Hester, the local vet." I've never called him a doctor before, and I don't know why I do now. The men nod, and Hester stands up and shakes hands.

"Byrd Bowlin," the young fellow introduces himself. "I saw you at the Wildcat flood . . . Thomas is my friend, but he has no place going into Liberty looking for MacIntosh. It's a good way for a black man to get his head shot off." I know what he's thinking. Just last year a colored miner was gunned down in Mingo County for sassing the sheriff.

Nothing was even done to the lawman. They called it self-defense. But that was in the southern part of the state. Union County shares a border with Pennsylvania and is north of the Mason-Dixon Line. It's more civilized here.

Byrd Bowlin goes on, "The reverend and I already drove all around town but couldn't find him. We know he stopped at the colored speakeasy behind Gold's Dry Goods. The bartender told us he was making accusations and was pretty drunk, but after that we lost his trail." A colored speakeasy in Liberty? That must mean there's a white juice joint too! I'm so out of touch.

"We drove by MacIntosh's house three times," Byrd continues, "thinking maybe we would see his burro if he was there, but the place was dark and we never could find him. Figure he stopped somewhere on his way home along Salt Lick, crawled under a tree to sleep it off."

There's a shuffle on the porch steps, and we all look up. The men rise expectantly. We women stay seated, hoping to see Thomas, maybe drunk as a skunk but all in one piece. When the pastor opens the door, it isn't Thomas. With a shock, I recognize Sheriff Hardman.

"Evening." The sheriff nods. His blue eyes sweep the room as he removes his hat. "Can I speak to you, Reverend?" Miller doesn't invite him in but steps out on the porch. Daniel Hester goes too, and that strikes me as strange. Maybe he thinks he can help in some way. Byrd stays where he is, but Bitsy flashes him a look and motions toward the back door. There are dynamics in this house I don't understand.

I've associated with Commies and radicals, suffragettes and anarchists, but this is something new to me, the level of powerlessness blacks suffer in a white community. Even those under Reverend Miller's wings tremble, fearing they will be blamed for something . . . anything.

I'd like to go out on the porch to find out what's happening, but I'm rooted to the floor. Has Hardman come about Thomas? Is there trouble in town? Is the law still looking for Katherine? Are they looking for me?

Byrd wanders casually toward the kitchen. The hand pump squeaks, and water runs into the sink. There's the clink of a coffee cup on the counter. Now Bitsy unfolds herself, and when I turn she's at the back door, kissing him tenderly. He places both hands on her waist. At any other time, I would be happy to see that Bitsy has a sweetheart, but tonight I just fear for him and hurt for her.

Her mother is dead. Her brother is missing. Now she is sending her new beau away into the night, for his own sake.

"Here they come," Mrs. Miller whispers, dropping the corner of the lace curtain and turning quickly. I suppose it's poor form for a preacher's wife to be seen snooping.

A car engine cranks up, and the door swings open.

"Is Thomas okay?" Bitsy asks first thing.

Reverend Miller looks very old, and

Hester looks weary. "Yeah," the vet says. "As far as we know . . . but the cops are looking for him. They heard he was at the black speakeasy earlier tonight, mouthing off . . . then later a neighbor reported a Negro man yelling threats in front of the MacIntosh home."

"The cops went to the speakeasy?" I ask. "You'd think the law would shut it down." The vet rolls his eyes, indicating that I'm naive.

"His deputy drove by William and Katherine's house a few times earlier tonight, but the lights were off and no one was around. Hardman came here to order Thomas to stay out of town until he cools off."

After fear and great sadness comes exhaustion, and it's hitting us all at once. Mrs. Miller yawns. The pastor looks at his watch. The vet stands with one hand on the knob. I turn to Bitsy. "We'd better go home."

"Okay," she says sadly. She gives Reverend and Mrs. Miller a hug, then moves to the door.

"I'm so sorry," I tell her again and again, sitting with my arms around her in the backseat of Hester's car. "I'm so sorry."

It isn't until we are halfway up Wild Rose Road that I remember Moonlight. I left feed for her yesterday, but other than that she's had nothing to eat. Has she given birth? My thank-you to the vet is hurried and lame. "Thanks," I say. "Thanks for everything."

Upstairs, I tuck Bitsy into bed, then rush down to feed the dogs, who are jumping all over me. When I finally slam out of the back, I find Daniel Hester latching the barn door.

"Moonlight's okay," he informs me. "She had enough water and hasn't calved yet. I threw her some hay and tossed the chickens some feed. By the looks of her, she'll calf soon. Keep an eye on her . . ."

We stand together in the warm night, looking out across the moonlit pasture. It's so bright, the grass actually looks green. All around us are green growing things, and in the distance I can hear the Hope River. I lean into him, a silent thank-you, and he puts one arm around me. The smell of the animals is still on his shirt, and the almost full moon sails in and out of the clouds.

32

Comfort in the Night

The days since Mary's death have passed slowly. Is it three? Is it four? I count back. Katherine ran to us Tuesday night, the day of the big thunderstorm. Mary fell Tuesday night and died early Wednesday morning. We didn't learn of her death until that evening. Now it's . . . I consult Stenger's calendar . . . Friday or Saturday. It's all a blur. Death does that. Stops time.

The garden's full of weeds, and I have no heart to pull them. Twice Bitsy and I have ridden on Star to Wildcat, but no one has seen Thomas. Then

Bitsy went into Liberty with the Millers to make arrangements for the funeral, but they can't put Mary into the ground until Sunday because the Emmanuel Funeral Home has another burial in Delmont on Saturday. Thank goodness they are trained embalmers, or Mary would start to smell. Gray clouds hang over us like a shroud, but the rain doesn't come.

In the night, I wake to hear Bitsy crying on the other side of the wall. The sound slices through me, uncovers my own buried grief for my mother . . . for Lawrence . . . for Ruben . . . for Mrs. Kelly . . . for all those I've lost.

I light a lantern, put on the red silk kimono, and go down to the kitchen. When I come back, I don't even knock at the door to her bedroom. I don't ask if I can sleep with her, just nudge her over, fluff up her extra pillows, then hand over the last of Mrs. Kelly's blackberry wine. We finish the whole mason jar, lying up against the metal headboard, not saying anything, just sharing our sorrow.

"Thanks," Bitsy says as she rolls away from me onto her side. I curl around her, one arm around her waist, as I once did with Katherine, when we thought her baby was dead, our loose bodies folding into each other.

Bitsy kisses my hand, holds it to her cheek. I know what she's saying: we are more than two roommates who share a house, more than two women who share a vocation, more than friends, and this makes me cry, one sob from that deep alone pocket under my heart.

In the morning Bitsy gets up at dawn, as usual. Over tea and the homemade bread that Mrs. Miller pressed on us when we left Hazel Patch, we are silent about last night. I hold my pounding head in one hand, thinking about the blackberry wine, and Bitsy tells me that she still has Katherine's ten-dollar bill and the Hazel Patch folks are paying for the funeral. We've come out richer, but there's no joy. Mary Proudfoot is gone, Katherine is gone, and Thomas . . . we still don't know where he is.

When I trudge out to the barn with a headache the size of Lake Michigan, I'm surprised to find Moonlight licking a small miniature of herself. With the events of the last few days, her delivery was the last thing on my mind.

"Bitsy!" I scream. Moonlight looks over at me and then turns back to her calf. "Bitsy!" I yell. "Bitsy!"

My friend slips through the barn door and leans with me against the side of the wooden stall. It's another female and she's already nursing, butting her little black-and-white head into Moonlight's udder.

We name her Sunny.

Bad News

"Bitsy," I ask. "Do you know much about calves and mother cows? I mean, are we supposed to start milking right away or wait until Moonlight's supply is established? This is something I didn't think of." We are washing up the midday meal dishes, each of us in her own world.

"You could ask Mr. Hester. Maybe he would have an old veterinary book you could borrow. Why don't you ride Star over the mountain?" I take a big breath and let it out slowly. Maybe she just wants to get rid of me. Is she also hungover from the blackberry wine? Or is she just so weighted with grief that silence is the only dark place that soothes her?

At the top of the ridge, where the sandstone cliffs drop off, I stop to wonder at the checkered hills, rectangles of emerald green, moss, and gold; pastures, woodlots, and fields of grain. It's good to get away from the farm and the leaden weight of Bitsy's sadness. Moving anywhere brings me back to my body. It doesn't take away the grief, just puts it into perspective. Here and there black-and-white cattle, the same breed as Moonlight, graze, so small in the distance they look like toys. Far off, there's the faint whistle of a train.

Thirty years ago, this was virgin forest, thick with huge poplar and oak, maple and chestnut, spruce and fir, some over one hundred feet high. The industrialists scraped all that from the land with the coming of the railway. Now small farmers till the poor soil, eking a living out of the steep slopes and in the narrow hollows. Winding through the valley bottom in and out of the second-growth trees, the Hope River sparkles like beads of glass.

As Star and I come down the hill, I spy Hester shoveling manure out of a wagon, looking like a real farmer in blue denim overalls.

"Hi." I slide off Star's back and tie her to a tree. He glances over but doesn't smile. Probably thinks I'm trouble on the way. "Moonlight had her calf last night."

"Everything okay?" He stabs his pitchfork into the earth and wipes his face with a red bandanna. "You should have come for me."

"I would have, but it happened in the middle of the night." I don't tell him that it happened in the middle of the night when Bitsy and I were half drunk and I forgot to go out to the barn and check on her. "The calf's beautiful, black and white like Moonlight. A female! She's eating and nursing, but I realized I never asked you if I should start milking her now or wait? Do you have anything I could read, maybe an old textbook?"

"Let's go in. I have something to show you." He doesn't answer my question, so I figure he's going to give me a pamphlet or old text on animal husbandry.

Inside the shadowy kitchen, I pump water while he washes up. For a change, the counters are clean and there are no dirty dishes in the porcelain sink. When Hester returns from upstairs, sweat free, his hair combed down, wearing a short-sleeved blue work shirt under his overalls, he hands me yesterday's copy of the *Liberty Times.* I don't have to wonder what he wants me to read; the headlines scream everything: COAL BARON FOUND STRANGLED IN HIS OWN HOME.

"Shit!" I swear, then bite my tongue. I don't usually use such foul language.

I read the first paragraph aloud. "The

body of William MacIntosh, owner of MacIntosh Consolidated Mines, was discovered by a neighbor, Mrs. Dyke of 140 High St., Liberty, around nine Friday morning, a rope around his neck . . ."

I toss the newspaper on the table. "I can't finish this."

Hester fills me in. "The reporter says MacIntosh was found in the dining room with a rope around his neck. There was a chair turned over, but it's unclear if he took his own life or was murdered. There's no note. The death is under investigation."

"Shit," I say again, this time without cringing. "You think it was Thomas?"

Hester shrugs. "The night before he died, remember, there was that complaint to the sheriff's office that a black man was standing outside the MacIntosh home yelling for William to come out. And listen to this." He straightens the paper and reads aloud for my benefit, "Sheriff Hardman is also investigating a related missing-person case. Mrs. Katherine MacIntosh and the couple's young son were reported missing three days prior to her husband's death. Readers with any knowledge of either event are instructed to call the sheriff's office immediately. Withholding information in a capital murder case could be construed as collusion."

"Shit! Shit!" I don't seem to be able to control my expletives. "What the hell do we do now? Bitsy and I have been to the Wildcat Mine twice, asked around, but no one's seen Thomas, and it isn't like him to go away like this. If he isn't at Mary's funeral service tomorrow, we'll be really worried. Do you think he did it?"

Daniel Hester goes to the sink and pours each of us a glass of cold water. "Drink this."

I'm pulling at the roots of my hair. "*Could* Thomas have killed William?" I ask again.

"A man might lose control if he thought his mother was thrown down the stairs by her inebriated employer."

"But *Thomas* . . . he isn't like that. I don't think he is, anyway. And should we tell Hardman we know what happened to Katherine? She didn't just disappear, she went home to her mother in Baltimore to escape her drunken husband. If we withhold, we could be in trouble." My mind jumps from one thing to another like oil in a hot skillet.

"Take a deep breath," Hester orders. I try, but it's more like a gulp of air. "We should wait," he goes on, "until we talk to Thomas, get all the information, hear his story. In the military you get a feeling for men, which ones will go off like a loose cannon and which you can trust. If Thomas did kill MacIntosh, the asshole deserved it."

An hour later, I find Bitsy sitting on our front steps, stroking Emma's head and staring into some sorrowful space two feet in front of her. I hand her the copy of the *Liberty Times.* Her reaction surprises me.

"I'm glad!" Then slowly, as she reads the whole article, her brown face turns ashen.

"They'll think *Thomas* did it! He *never* would. He's a Christian. He might mouth off some, but he's told me before he doesn't believe in an eye for an eye." She reads the story for a second time, and I read over her shoulder.

Dust to Dust

"Here, let me fix you." I tie Star to a fence and straighten Bitsy's collar. I'm wearing my best dark dress, a navy blue flowered print, with my hair done up high. She wears her black one with white lace on the sleeves and collar and looks like a young Mrs. Potts. We both step out of our long pants and put on our good shoes, then dust off our faces with a cool rag Bitsy brought in a basket. I link my arm through hers to give her support, and we head for the front of the little white chapel.

"Wow, look how many people!" I whisper. I'm surprised by the number of buggies and vehicles parked along the road and on the wide lawn next to the cemetery. There's also a hearse with purple-fringed curtains and Sheriff

Hardman's black roadster with POLICE stenciled in white on the side.

We enter through the double oak doors and are escorted by an usher in a dark mourning coat to the first pew, directly in front of the wooden casket. I'm relieved to see Thomas already sitting there, wearing a simple white shirt open at the throat. He rises and hugs his younger sister tight, rivulets of tears running down his strong face. Bitsy sobs too. We are all crying while Mildred Miller, the organist, plays "Nearer, My God, to Thee" without even looking at the sheet music.

In between hymns I scan the chapel. Mrs. Potts is there, and a score of others I don't recognize. Some of them must be from the A.M.E. Church in Liberty. There are only three other white people in the chapel, and I'm shocked to see Katherine MacIntosh, sitting with a man in his sixties, probably her father. She must have made it to Baltimore, stayed a few days, and come right back when she heard about William's death. Daniel Hester is here too, sitting alone in the back pew.

Since I've never been to a Negro funeral service, I don't know what to expect, but other than the singing it's the same as any other funeral I've ever been to, and there have been several, all for women, I realize . . . my grandmother, my mother, and then Mrs. Kelly.

My father's body was lost in Lake Michigan. Lawrence's scorched body, after it was removed from the mangled train, was returned to his family in Iowa. Ruben, with the other unclaimed miners' bodies, was buried near Blair Mountain. I've always thought I'd go see his grave someday, but it's never happened. Probably because I've been afraid that if I went to southern West Virginia someone would recognize me, and also because I imagine I would see Ruben's blood on the ground, a brown stain, all that's left.

"Ashes to ashes, dust to dust," Reverend Miller intones. Today I cry for them all, Mary Proudfoot and those others, long dead. I do not cry for William MacIntosh, although maybe I should. Surely he was once a decent fellow. Katherine told me how carefully he had tended the roses, the azaleas, and the butterfly bushes in front of their home.

When the service is over and their mother's coffin is covered with earth, Thomas pulls Bitsy into the shade of a spreading black walnut tree and confers with her earnestly. Not wanting to intrude, I stroll over to speak to Katherine, Daniel Hester, and the other white man.

"This is my uncle, Reverend Martin . . . Patience Murphy, my midwife," Katherine introduces me. Her eyes are dull and dry, so I can't tell how she taking her husband's death. Does she believe it was suicide . . . or murder? Does she believe Thomas would have done it? Does she even care? I study her face, a mask I can't read.

No matter how difficult their relationship, William was her lover once, her friend. They made two babies together, and she knew his most intimate side. What she probably mourns is not the angry, violent, self-absorbed husband who felt himself a failure but the gentle man who loved flowers.

"Are you okay?" I whisper to Katherine as Hester and Martin gaze over the fields and comment on the crops and the drought. I pull on the sleeve of her soft gray linen dress and lead her to a bench at the side of the church. "Are you okay? It must be hard. Such a shock about William."

Katherine looks down at her carefully manicured, ladylike white hands and twists a ring that I notice is not her wedding ring. She surprises me when she answers. "I'm not shocked. He was a good man once, years ago when we courted . . ." She shakes her head slowly. "But it wasn't a happy marriage. You know that. He'd threatened suicide before, more than once . . . every time I tried to leave.

"I'd only been back in Baltimore for a few hours before he started calling. He was drunk, begging me to return. Nothing had changed. 'Come back,' he blubbered over the phone . . . over and over. 'You belong to me. I can't live without you.' It probably sounds terrible, but I'm not even sad . . . It's like a great weight is lifted off me." She looks me in the eye, waiting for a reaction, a woman compressed into steel.

I return her gaze, my mouth pressed tight. "You had to leave. You had to leave him for the baby's sake, and for your own. You can't let a man manipulate you that way . . . There was an article in the newspaper calling William's death suspicious. Did you see it?"

She waves it away as if batting flies. "Oh, that!"

"You don't think there could have been foul play?"

"Never. William had guns all over the house. He would have blasted any intruder."

When I glance up, Bitsy is sleepwalking across the churchyard. Far up the hill, behind the small chapel, moving through the green oak and maple, a white shirt disappears. Thomas, probably because of Sheriff Hardman's presence, is taking the back way home.

Katherine stands up and embraces

Bitsy. "I can't tell you how sorry I am. *So* sorry. Your mother was a saint. If it weren't for her, I might have been killed the night I left. There will never be anyone like her."

Bitsy blows her nose. You can tell she's running out of tears. "Thank you, Katherine. You and the baby meant a lot to Ma. She always worried after you . . ."

Out of the corner of my eye I see Mrs. Potts moving carefully across the lawn with her cane. "There's a reception at the Millers'," she announces. Her eyes sweep the whole group but end with me. I take a deep breath, knowing I should be supportive of Bitsy, but I'm exhausted and just want to go home. Bitsy lets me off easy.

"It's okay. Byrd Bowlin says he'll drive me home. You should probably check on Moonlight and the calf."

"I'm sorry, we have to go too." That's the Reverend Martin.

Hester offers to drive me, but I have Star, so I give Bitsy and Katherine a hug.

"Will we see you before you leave again for Baltimore?" I ask Katherine.

"I'll try," she says, "but I need to make arrangements about what's left of the estate, then get William back to Baltimore on the train for his funeral next Thursday. He has family coming down from Boston." I hug her again, holding on tight, trying to give her some strength. Then I turn toward the back of the church for my mount.

At the fork of Horse Shoe Run, I cringe when I spy the sheriff's car waiting at the intersection.

"Where's Bitsy and her brother?" the gruff fellow demands.

"Stayed for the reception at the preacher's house." I tell a white lie, knowing Thomas is halfway over the mountain, slipping through the spruce trees like the shadow of a gray fox.

"By the way, I talked to Mrs. MacIntosh before the funeral. Why didn't you report that she'd gone back to Baltimore after a domestic dispute?" Hardman gives me the squint eye.

"We were scared. We didn't want

William to try to find Katherine. We were scared."

July 30, 1930. Nearly full moon sailing through fast-moving clouds.

Birth of Daniel Withers, 6 pounds, 14 ounces, seventh child of Edith and Manley Withers of Hog Hollow. Bitsy and I delivered the baby together, my hands over hers. The Witherses are another family associated with Hazel Patch Baptist Chapel. Mrs. Potts was feeling poorly and didn't come.

Present, besides Bitsy and me, were the two oldest girls, Ida and Judith, 10 and 12. Bitsy showed them how to cut the baby's cord. Edith declared, when she put the baby to breast, that the afterbirth pains were worse than the actual labor, but I told her they were good because they'd keep her from bleeding. We were paid $2.00

and one home-cured ham. Seeing a new life come into the world after Mary's death did both Bitsy and me good.

33

Drought

Flat gray clouds press down like iron, and I scan the sky each morning for a change in the weather. The air is full of wetness, but it won't come down.

This morning Bitsy and I began to water the limp corn and beans by hand. The root crops, potatoes and carrots, are deep enough to find their own moisture. The tomatoes, Bitsy assures me, are more heat resistant. Back and forth we go, carrying two buckets each from the spring to the garden, giving a quart jar of liquid to each drooping plant.

"It's a drop in the bucket," I joke with my friend, but she doesn't laugh.

Bitsy sets down her pail and arches her back, her eyes closed. "No rain today."

"How can you tell?"

"No breeze. The wind will come before the rain."

"I think the rain god might just send down a flood to mock all this work we're doing," I make light. My companion shakes her head and goes back to her watering. Maybe my reference to a rain god offended her. Since her mother's funeral, she's been reading the Bible daily. Twice as I passed her bedroom door I saw her praying on her knees.

A few hundred buckets later, our arms aching, our backs groaning, Bitsy looks up at the late-afternoon sun just burning through the haze. "I think I'll take Star for a ride." A frown flashes between my eyes, but I keep my thoughts to myself. Over to the Wildcat again. Is she checking on Thomas or going to see her sweetheart, Byrd Bowlin?

* * *

Thirty minutes later, I'm dragging my aching body up the porch steps with my basket of green beans when I catch the sound of a horse and buggy barreling up the lane. The dust is so thick I can't see who's coming. There goes my bath in the cool creek water! I'm so sweaty, I can hardly stand myself.

"Need you in Black Springs!" the young driver yells before he even pulls back on the reins.

"What's up?"

"Mr. Hart says come quick, his woman's bleeding."

"I don't know Mrs. Hart. Is she having a child?"

"She's carrying, if that's what you mean. It's still in there."

"Okay," I mutter, "I'll be right with you."

Great, I think, as I run upstairs and pull my everyday gray-blue flowered housedress off the hook. Just when Bitsy leaves, I have an emergency. Luckily, Star, Moonlight, and the calf are out in the pasture, where they can graze and get water from the stream, and the chickens are locked in their pen. I grab the birth satchel and, as an afterthought, tie a bandanna over my head.

"Please hurry, ma'am. Mr. Hart was in an awful state."

It's going to be a rough ride.

Kitty

An hour later we pull up, in a cloud of dust, to an unpainted dogtrot farmhouse with two sections, a kitchen on one side and the living quarters on the other, separated by a central outdoor breezeway. Two white women wave frantically from the long shady porch. One is short and round, wearing a stained red-checked apron. The smaller of the two is crying and looks to be an albino: white hair, white skin, and pink eyes crying.

"Come in. Come. Hurry!" the round lady cries. "Lord help us!"

The scene in the bedroom is more terrible than I could have imagined. Blood is everywhere. It's on the floor, on the bed, and all over the mother, who's barely alive. There are actually bloody handprints on the poor woman's swollen belly where someone has been trying to push the baby out. "Damnation," I say under my breath and instantly regret it. Would Mrs. Kelly or Mrs. Potts talk like that? The two ladies who greeted me hover uselessly at the bedside. A third, gray-haired woman in a bloodstained green dress kneels next to the patient. Mr. Hart is nowhere to be seen.

"You the midwife?" the senior of the three asks. I nod. "The baby is stuck, and it's killing her. We tried, but we can't get it out."

"Stuck. Stuck. Stuck," the albino girl says, waving her hands in front of her face.

I study the patient. Something is very wrong here. Her limp legs are two sizes too large and full of water under the skin. A small, hairy head is visible between her thighs, and she's hemorrhaging. I could take time to check the fetal heartbeat, but what would that prove? The baby may already be dead, and if I don't do something fast, the mother will die too.

"Hold her legs back and open," I command. The women all have tears running down their cheeks, but they do what I tell them. I rip open the birth bag and grab some gloves and the sterilized scissors. I've never before had to use them before, but this may be the time.

"How long has she been paining?" I ask as I begin my examination, trying to figure out why the baby won't come.

"Three days," the ladies answer in chorus. It's like the vet told me: when times are hard, families don't call him for their sick animals unless they're on the verge of collapse . . . only this is someone's wife, sister, or daughter.

"Has she had children before?" I continue to take her history as I oil my gloved hand and slip it around the infant's skull. There's an ear just under the pubic bone. Now I understand. The small head is trying to come out turned sideways instead of facing the sacrum. With a tiny baby this sometimes happens. I try to turn it, but it's wedged in tight.

The round woman answers, "This is her first."

"Is it before her term?" I unwrap the scissors and make one quick snip. The patient's green eyes snap open.

"We think maybe a month early. She was due in the fall."

"How long's she been pushing?"

The trio look at one another, and the older woman guesses, "About four hours." No wonder the patient is as limp as a wet noodle.

"Okay, now, Mother." I touch the patient's face with the back of my bloody glove to get her attention, but she doesn't react. "You must push. I've made more room for the baby. It's stuck, but I think I can turn it if you push hard."

"What's her name?" I ask the three attendants, indicating the woman in bed.

"Kitty," the albino offers.

"Kitty, I'm Patience, the midwife. I know you're tired, but if you give this your all, the delivery can be over in few minutes." There's no reaction. "Kitty!" I pinch her arm. The girl's eyes fly open again. She's not dead yet.

"We *need* you to push. Here, we're going to get you up in a squat. Just do what I tell you. It will help spread your pelvis." With great effort the three assistants hoist Kitty upright. Then, with one hand on top of the uterus and one hand below, I push down and a small head pops out. It is about the size of a large apple, one of those commercial kinds at Bittman's Grocery.

My helpers ease the mother back on the bed, and the whole baby slides forth. I blow on the little girl's belly, but there's no reaction. I blow again. No grimace, no stretching of arms or gasp. Nothing. I try a few puffs into her nose and mouth, as I did with little William, but still no response. No heartbeat either under the frail chest. The limp body just hangs there between my hands.

Now everyone is crying. Everyone but the mother, whose eyes roll back in her head as her body goes rigid. She stiffens her arms and screams.

Maynard

"Get the husband. Get Mr. Hart!" I command. The short round lady in the gingham apron runs for him. I lay the dead baby in the wooden cradle and try to get Kitty's womb to ball up, but she's shaking so hard I can't keep my hands around it, and there's no way I can get her to drink Mrs. Potts's tincture.

It isn't until Kitty's body grows limp that I'm able to check her pulse. By Mrs. Kelly's watch, it's 140 beats per minute, way too fast, weak, and trembly. When I pull the patient's eye open and inspect the tissue in the crevice below, it's almost white. Mrs. Potts told me to do this when I need to judge a woman's stamina: dark red, her blood is rich; pale pink, the patient is weak. Kitty is way past weak.

The grim lady in green begins to pull away the bloody sheets and swab them on the wet floor.

"The baby's dead, isn't it?" the albino girl asks.

"Yes, honey. I'm afraid she is. She's

gone to Heaven now." I'm starting to sound like Grace Potts.

"Here, Kitty." I try again to get the exhausted mother to swallow some water mixed with the tincture, but she's in some kind of coma and the green liquid dribbles down her chin.

From the front of the house I hear the screen door slam open, heavy boots in the hall, and Mr. Hart runs in. "What? What's happened? Is my wife dead?" I can see why he thinks this, but I know for a fact that her heart is still beating. Just to be sure, I take my wooden horned fetoscope and put it to her breast.

"She's not dead yet, sir. Kitty had a fit and then fell into a slumber. She'd already lost all this blood before I got here." I don't know how to say it nice, so I just say it. "The baby died. It was stuck in the birth canal too long."

Tears are streaming down the man's lean, high-cheekboned face clear down to his whiskers. He kneels in the blood and shakes Kitty's shoulder. "Wife! Wake up!"

"She can't wake up, Mr. Hart. She's

had a fit. She's in a coma. We need to get her to a hospital."

"You know I don't have any money! I would have taken her to the hospital two days ago if I had." So you called me, I'm thinking. Called me too late, so that I could take the blame and the heartache.

"Well, if we don't get going, *you won't have a wife.* Forget about the money."

"Dr. Blum's gone," the green dress reminds us. "Moved back to Virginia."

"*Someone* will help us if we show up at the hospital. That other doctor from Delmont or maybe a nurse. Does anyone have a vehicle, a truck? Maybe we should go right to Dr. Robinson, the colored doctor."

"No black sawbones is touching my woman!" Hart slashes out and swipes his wet face, wiping blood across his eyes.

I bite my tongue, almost cutting it. What difference does the hue of the physician's skin make? The mind has no color. Robinson would know what to do.

"Dr. Robinson could give her medicine or put in an IV. Mr. Hart, your baby is dead because you didn't go to the hospital before or call me sooner. Didn't you notice your wife was swelling? Didn't you know the baby was too early? Do you understand, if we get in an auto right now, your wife might still make it?" I repeat myself, but I'm getting nowhere.

Hart stomps out of the room, followed by the woman in green. I know he's distressed, but he has to listen!

"Mr. Hart, please!" I run after him and pull on the sleeve of his neatly patched work shirt. "There must be *some way* to get to town. I'm telling you, your wife is very weak and ill. If she has another seizure, she may not make it."

Hart steps out on the porch, slams his fist into a porch pole, and groans.

"Maynard, listen to her," the older lady says. "Kitty needs help."

"Miss Patience!" someone in the house calls. I run back inside.

The albino girl is holding her sister's head, and the shakes and rigors have started again. We women gather round, holding Kitty's limbs. The bed blossoms red under her buttocks like a begonia opening, and now she's bleeding from her nose too.

What is this? It's like she's shaking the life fluid out of her, and she's not breathing either. If she doesn't stop seizing, she'll expire right now.

For two, maybe three minutes, we hold Kitty while Mr. Hart stands expressionless at the bedroom door. I know he must have feelings, but he's gone somewhere else, far from this horror, fishing down on the Hope River, maybe.

In the end Kitty takes a big breath and swoons again. I feel for her pulse, but it's too fast to count. She opens her eyes one last time, sees her husband in the doorway, reaches out to him, and dies. Her poor heart has stopped beating. All our hearts stop.

Women's Work

"We need to clean this mess up before it brings in the flies," I say out loud as a big one buzzes around my head. The birth smell is sweet and heavy, but this is something else. The blood smell is overwhelming. I almost gag but swallow hard and try not to think about it.

"What's your name, honey?" I ask the albino.

"Birdy," she answers. "Kitty is my sissie. She's dead now, isn't she? And the baby?" The girl blows her nose on the hem of her skirt. Birdy and Kitty, I think. The parents must have had a sense of humor.

"I'm sorry. Yes, they're both gone to Heaven now. Why don't you sit and hold your sister's head while we clean her up." Birdy does what I say, lifts Kitty's head into her lap and strokes her long hair, which I notice now is yellow-blond and straight like a Norwegian's. She hums a little song under her breath and presses the dead woman's eyes shut. One comes back open, but she closes it again.

Where is Bitsy when I need her? I wonder again. How will I describe this scene to her? Maybe I shouldn't. She might not want to come to births with me anymore.

The lady in green, I learn, is Mr. Hart's

sister, Edna, who scrubs on her hands and knees without speaking. While she wrings out her rag in the galvanized bucket again and again, her tears drip into the crimson water. The short round woman, Charity Moon, is the wife of the neighbor who drove me to this hell-hole.

The other women cry while they work, but not me. My sobs are tamped down like clay at the bottom of a fence post hole. I've thought this before. Life is too hard. You are born, and you die . . . that's the sum of it. In between you love someone or you don't, and if you are lucky you leave behind some-one who loves you.

By the time we are done mopping up and sitting at the kitchen table with strong coffee in chipped cups, the sun is going down and Maynard comes back to the house with red eyes. He takes off his shirt at the sink and washes his face and his arms.

"Will there be a service?" I ask.

"Just something with neighbors and kin," explains the aunt. "Kitty wouldn't have wanted a big to-do, and we can't afford to have her embalmed. We'll have the reverend bury her here, the fellow from Clover Bottom. You're welcome to come."

"I'll try," I say, knowing I probably won't.

"Thank you for coming." Maynard turns to me. "I don't have money to pay you."

"I know . . . it's okay. I'm sorry I couldn't do more."

"The neighbor man, Moon, will drive you home." He goes back out the screened door, and I watch as he crosses to the barn, then leaves with a shovel over his shoulder. Is he going back to the fields? No, he's starting Kitty's grave. He needs to bend and sweat and curse. Dig a hole. Where will Mr. Hart sleep tonight? I wonder. Will he lie down beside his dead wife, take the lifeless baby that's wrapped in a pink blanket and place it over his heart?

Edna, his sister, watches him too. "There's a family graveyard yonder, all our relations. This is Maynard's second wife. The first is already up there, died of pneumonia three years ago. He's not a bad man," she explains. "He loved Kitty, just had too much pride to ask for charity care."

Before I leave, I go back to the bed-room one last time to say good-bye to the dead woman, who lies now on a faded rose quilt in a white nightdress. The floorboards are still stained red and always will be.

34

Thunder

The ride home in the dark with Mr. Moon is cheerless. There's still no rain, and the air is so thick, I can taste it. Twice I think I hear thunder, and once I see lightning out of the corner of my eye, but neither of us speaks or makes note of it.

Clip-clopping along in the faint moonlight, the goldenrod and tall joe-pye weed in the roadside ditches look covered with frost, but it's only thick dust laid down by the buggies and Model Ts. As we turn up Salt Lick, I break the silence.

"Drop me at Daniel Hester's, the vet. You know where that is? Another mile up ahead. He'll drive me the rest of the way home." I say this with sureness, but I'm only hoping. For all I know, Hester could be out casting the leg of a damaged hound or ministering to a sick mare.

Bitsy won't be home yet, if she comes in at all, and I can't go to sleep twisted around the nightmare of this terrible delivery. Mr. Moon follows my instructions and leaves me at the vet's mailbox, turning his cart around in the drive. We raise our hands in silent, sad salute.

On the wooden bridge, the soft trickle of the creek below startles me. Considering the drought, I'm surprised it's still running. From the barn, I hear metal grinding. Hester stands in the lantern light pedaling the grindstone, sharpening his garden tools. Suddenly I'm apprehensive. What am I doing here? What will I say?

"A woman died today because I didn't know how to save her"? "A mother and her baby died needlessly because her impoverished and prideful husband didn't call me earlier"? "The world is a terrible and tragic place, too hard, too hard for Patience Murphy"?

Thunder rolls over the mountains, and a breeze hisses through the dry willow leaves; then lighting flashes—for real this time. Though I should be grateful for any rain, it's not a good time. If it starts to storm, I can't change my mind and hike home over the mountain.

The vet pauses in his work, and his silhouette steps into the amber light pouring like honey out of the barn's double doors. "Hello!" he calls out, seeing my shadow advance across the yard. "Who's there?"

Tears are already running down my face, the first tears I've shed, now that the ordeal is over. I guess it's over. It suddenly occurs to me, with a cold feeling right in my middle, that I could be charged for the mother's and infant's deaths and lose my midwifery certificate.

"Patience, what's wrong?" Hester's wearing just his trousers and a white undershirt, the kind with no sleeves, and his arms shine with sweat. "Is it Moonlight? Is it Star? Is it Bitsy?" Even as the tears fall, this strikes me as typical, that he should ask about the animals first.

"A patient died today. Kitty Hart," I whisper. "It was bad. Bad. Blood all over, even coming out her nose, and then she seized up and died." I know I must sound incoherent. He takes me in his arms, and the smell of him almost overwhelms me: earth, pine, vanilla.

"Come in. Come in." He leads me into the barn and makes me sit on a wooden bench.

"Here." From his back pocket he pulls out a silver flask. I'm not much of a drinker, but I take a big swig, almost choke, and then whip my head back and forth to shake out the fire. It's strong stuff and not nearly as pleasant as a rum toddy or blackberry wine.

Hester smiles at my reaction, but the smile drops away. Outside, the thunder rumbles closer and the branches of the weeping willows sweep back and forth.

"Maynard Hart's place?" he asks.

"Broken-down farm over by Burnt Town?"

I nod, taking a big breath, trying to get my emotions under control. He holds out the flat silver container again. This time the liquid goes down easier, just burns at the back of my throat.

"I'd never met him or his wife before," I explain. "A young woman, Kitty. The neighbor, a Mr. Moon, came riding fast up Wild Rose Road. Bitsy had just left for the mining camp, and I was alone." I start to cry again, leaning over, holding my face in my hands, and he sits down beside me. Thunder again and then lighting. Wind slams the side of the sturdy wooden building.

Remembering the terrible scene, I cry and cry, as if my tears could float Kitty Hart out of her deathbed, up and away down to the Hope River, where she'd be found alive lying in the damp grass nursing her newborn. Hester pats my back as though I'm a baby, humming a little tune under his breath, but I can't stop blubbering and the sobs get louder, more out of control. He puts his arm around me again. It's a cloudburst of emotion. I'm crying again not just for Kitty and her baby but for myself and *my* baby, for Lawrence and Ruben and my mother and Mrs. Kelly and all the times I've been alone and afraid with no one to help me.

"So you arrived . . . ?" Hester asks, trying to get me to talk about what happened . . . anything to quiet the weeping. "I went there once to stitch up a mare. Beautiful horse. Got her leg tangled in some barbed wire. So you arrived and then?"

I reach for the flask and swallow two more mouthfuls, then take a big breath. "It was the worst thing I've ever seen. When we pulled into the yard, two women were hollering from the dogtrot porch. 'Hurry! Hurry!' all hysterical. I ran into the bedroom, and there was blood all over the floor. All over the bed. A young lady lay there almost unconscious and hemorrhaging with the baby still trapped in the birth canal, a premature baby with dark hair, wedged sideways." I describe how I got the baby out but it was stillborn and about the continuous bleeding that I couldn't stop. I tell how Mr. Hart refused to go to the colored doctor and how the seizures came and then Kitty died.

The vet frowns, trying to picture the events, takes a swig from the silver flask, then hands it back to me. "I don't know much about women, but cows get seizures related to milk fever when they lack the ability to quickly move calcium into their milk and end up depleting their own blood levels. And there's a condition in cats and dogs called disseminated intravascular coagulation that's related to the depletion of clotting factors. Basically they use up all their platelets and protein and start hemorrhaging from everywhere . . . There's also eclampsia. Maybe that was it."

He may be attempting to comfort me by providing clinical information, and at some other time I might be attentive, but right now I'm overcome, not interested in a possible explanation. I put my hand to his mouth to silence him, and he takes it and kisses my palm, a strange gesture—an agreement, perhaps, that he should shut up. The rains have started for real now, first a pitter-patter, then a hiss.

"You have blood on your face." He touches my cheek. "And your neck . . . here . . . and your dress." He takes his bandanna, steps over to the door to wet the cloth in the downpour, and wipes my face, then my neck. He's so close I can smell his sweet breath, and I close my eyes and turn my cheek to feel his hand better.

Lightning flashes, then thunder a few seconds later, so close and so loud that it shakes the barn walls. He unbuttons the two top buttons of my dress and I let him, my heart pounding so hard that I think if it wasn't for the sound of the now-continuous claps and booms, he might hear it. When we stand, the moonshine has affected me more than I realize, and I almost fall into him.

The rain roars on the tin roof now, roars all around us, and we step to the barn door to watch the sheet lightning. He holds out his bandanna to wet it again and wipes my hands and nails, still grimy with blood, then leads me out into the downpour, where we stand with our arms around each other. My face against his wet undershirt, his face looking into the sky, flashing white, then yellow, then white again, we sway like dancers in an all-night dance marathon.

Hester unbuttons a few more buttons and then washes my neck almost down to my nipples. Shivering, I watch his fingers work. He kneels in the mud and wipes my legs, then wipes me between my legs, over and over with his soft bandanna, washes me like a baby, and I begin to cry again. No one has bathed me since my mother died. I have bathed others, patients in labor, newborn babies, old people who were ill, even just today I washed a dead woman, but no one has washed me.

When I unbutton the rest of my dress and step out of it, there's nothing underneath. No brassiere, no corset, just my drawers. I'd changed out of my work clothes in such a hurry when Mr. Moon came for me that I hadn't bothered with the other things. I'm shocked at myself but don't pull away. I'm a woman in a dream removing her silver armor. Hester doesn't seem surprised by my lack of modesty and tosses the shift into the dry barn.

Again and again thunder fills the air like boulders colliding across the mountains. The vet just continues to hold me, naked, while the holy water washes us clean.

River

Morning. Blinding sun through a dusty windowpane in a room that at first I don't recognize. I'm lying naked in a four-poster bed like the one at the MacIntoshes' home, but the room is nowhere near as fancy. My eyes roam the white plaster walls with high windows framed in wide dark oak molding, the bare wood floors. There are paintings of horses in gold and black frames, landscapes with hunting horses and workhorses and racehorses and a photo of a young soldier standing with his horses. I know this place now. This is where, weeks ago, I bandaged the vet's leg and brought him soup while he healed from his fistfight with the Bishop brothers.

I run my hand over the twisted sheets and the empty space where Hester had slept. I guess he slept. Sometime in the night we left the hayloft and ran through the mud, into the house, and up the stairs; then, before dawn, the telephone rang and he left me. I heard his car start up and move away down Salt Lick, but I was too undone to care. It was the alcohol, I remind myself, that brought me to this man, not exactly a stranger, not exactly a friend.

I run my hands over my body and, finding myself still the same person, dress quickly, ignoring Kitty's old blood on my damp dress, which I find laid out neatly over the back of a chair. It's too soon to tell how the events of last night will change my relationship with Hester . . . or if they will. I pull on my shoes and realize with a wave of guilt that unless Bitsy came home, our animals were out in the rain all night.

At the crest, I look down toward the Hope River and am surprised to see the valley looking no different after the storm. The dust has been washed off the tired plants, but even hours of hard rain can't turn the grass green. Nothing has been altered, except inside me. I am laid open.

When I get to the house, I am surprised to see smoke coming out of the kitchen chimney; Bitsy is home. The doors to the barn are open, and I can hear her singing to Moonlight while she milks. *"Oh, sister, let's go down. Let's go down. Don't you want to go down? Oh, sister, let's go down. Down to the river to pray . . ."* It's the first time she's sung since her mother died.

"Morning," she says as she strides into the house ten minutes later, swinging a pail full of warm white liquid. I've only had time to brush the straw out of my hair. She eyes the birth satchel as I replace our supplies.

"You were up all night at a birth? I'm sorry, I should have been with you. Who delivered? Everything go okay?"

"No . . . no, it didn't go well." I sit down at the table. "It was Kitty Hart.

Someone we never met. She died. Her baby died too."

Shocked at my words, Bitsy drops her bucket into the sink, and the milk splashes over the side. She plunks down in the chair next to me, puts her hand on my arm. "Oh, Patience, baby. I'm so sorry. I should have been there. I should have been there to help you . . ." She waits for me to explain, but I'm too exhausted to even talk.

"I have to change." I indicate my bloodstained dress.

"Can I heat water? Bring in the tub?"

"No, I'll go to the river. I'll tell you about the birth later."

This surprises me. Why do I want to go to the river?

When Star and I arrive on the banks of the Hope River, now rushing brown from the great storm, I'm greatly relieved to see no trailers or tents. The vet has already washed the blood off my skin; it's my soul that needs cleansing. I pull off my dress and bloomers. *"Oh, sister,"* I remember Bitsy's song,

"Let's go down. Down to the river to pray."

I step into the water, deliciously cold, float on my back, and stare up at the white scarves of clouds. I haven't prayed in so long. Who would I pray to?

August 14, 1930. Full moon already waning.

(It's been three days. I couldn't write about this before.) Still-born baby girl born to Maynard and Kitty Hart of Burnt Town. Arrived at the home after mother was in labor for three or four days and had been pushing for four hours. Baby was a month early and wedged in the birth canal with its head turned sideways. After I got there, birth was accomplished in less than ten minutes, but it was too late for the baby. Mother was swollen and began to have seizures. Bitsy and I looked this up later in DeLee's text; it's called eclamp-

sia. There was nothing I knew how to do, no herbs or anything. Sometimes women live through these fits, but Kitty had already lost so much blood I believe her heart stopped.

Others at the birth were her sister, Birdy (surname unknown); Edna Hart, the husband's sister; and Mrs. Moon, the neighbor lady. Bitsy was in Hazel Patch. A very sad day.

Autumn Returns

35

Fall from Grace

Dark shadows over the mountains. Slate clouds like dirty sheets that won't come clean. They blot out the sunshine during the day, blot out the stars at night. There are no jobs in Union County. One out of four men stands idle, and that doesn't include the farmers who can't sell their crops or the women who used to work before the men came back from the war.

It's been weeks since the big rain, and the heat all over the South is fierce, one of the hottest Septembers the locals can remember. When they cut hay, cattlemen are averaging two bales instead of four. Scores of houses and farms are listed for auction or foreclosure in the *Liberty Times,* and people are moving east and north in droves like flocks of migrating birds.

This afternoon, while Bitsy and I trudged around the garden inspecting the parched dry brown tassels of our corn, a vehicle bounced up the road with a cloud of dust rising behind it.

What's this now? Another delivery.

We watch from the fence as Reverend Miller gets out of the truck and moves around to the passenger side to open the door for his wife. He's wearing a white straw fedora. Mildred is waving a large church fan with a picture of Jesus on it. The two advance toward the house without smiling, the dry yellow grass crunching under their feet.

I figure they've come to see how my friend is faring after her mother's death or maybe to bring news of Thomas. He hasn't been seen for weeks. Bitsy runs for the house to wash up and bring out some cold sweet tea.

"Howdy," I call out, wiping my forehead with my blue-and-white bandanna. The reverend nods formally.

Mildred Miller calls out, "How you doin', honey?"

We settle on the wooden benches in the shade on the porch. I offer Mildred the one rocking chair, and she insists that her husband take it. Then Bitsy comes out with a wooden tray and four glasses of tea. The spring water is so cold we don't need ice. Not that we have any.

"Have you heard from Thomas?" Bitsy starts out. I know she's been worried, but with Sheriff Hardman looking for him, it's better that he's disappeared. We just need to know that he's safe.

"No," the pastor answers. "No word yet. We've come about something else. This is hard, so I'm going to tell it to you plain . . . Mrs. Potts went to meet her maker last night. She died in her sleep, a good Christian woman. Hemorrhaged from the cancer, that's what Doc Robinson says."

"Cancer? I didn't know. She seemed so vigorous for her age. What kind of cancer was it? Did anyone know?" I'm so shocked, I keep babbling. Bitsy doesn't say anything, but Mrs. Miller reaches for her and holds her tight.

"What this means," Mildred goes on, passing her Jesus fan slowly back and forth in front of her face, "is that we now have only one midwife in Union County; that's you. Dr. Blum's gone too, you probably heard."

"What about the other physician, Dr. Robinson?"

"He doesn't do deliveries, and he doesn't go to people's homes anymore. If you're sick, you have to go to him."

"There's Becky Myers, the health nurse," I suggest.

"Yes, Becky . . . but she won't go out after dark and she's no great shakes about birthing. Too nervous." This, I must say, I agree with after seeing her at Docey's birth down under the bridge; she's a real nervous Nellie.

"Anyway," the pastor continues, "we thought you'd want to know that people will be calling on you." He takes Bitsy and me in with his eyes. "Not just for births, women's things. Infant things."

Great, I think, and what will we tell them if they ask about hot flashes, strange rashes, and monthlies? I'm not a doctor, and I've never had female troubles . . . except my periods, which come when they want to, but that never bothered me.

I take a big breath. "Thank you for letting us know."

"When are they putting Mrs. Potts in the ground?" Bitsy asks. It's the first thing she's said.

"Sunday. The whole church service will be dedicated to her. Samantha and Emma, you remember them from Cassie's birth, will be singing the solos."

Bitsy escorts the couple to their car, standing for a few minutes at the passenger door while I take the tray of empty glasses into the house. When I come out, the green truck is sputtering back down Wild Rose Road in the dust.

"They say anything more about Thomas?"

"No." She looks away, and I know she doesn't want to talk about it.

I collapse on the wooden bench in the shade and flop my head back against the white clapboard wall. What will come next? So many deaths. I count back. Six this year. The Mintz family's little girl, Angel. Mary Proudfoot. William MacIntosh. Kitty Hart and her baby. And now Grace Potts. The world will be smaller without her.

Across the valley, on the other side of the Hope River, a shard of lightning pierces the clouds. No thunder. No rain.

Circle

The Sunday service devoted to Grace Potts is more spectacle than funeral. I imagined something simple like Mary Proudfoot's, but this is more of a celebration.

Again Bitsy and I dress in our best dark dresses with knickers under them and mount our horse. This time we leave early and take the long way around Raccoon Lick to Hope Ridge and up the south fork to Horse Shoe Run. It's cooler in the shade where the hemlocks and maple trees hang over the creek.

As we come out of the woods and trot up Horse Shoe Road, the dust is so thick we almost choke on it. Autos and buggies stream along in the same direction, heading toward the freshly whitewashed chapel where the wooden doors, decorated with wildflowers, open like arms. Again we tie our horse with the other horses in back. Bitsy heads directly across the yellowed grass to talk to Byrd Bowlin, and I, feeling conspicuously alone, wander toward the church. I thought maybe Thomas would be here, but he's nowhere around.

I'd expected to be the only white person in the crowd, but I am surprised to see others. Mr. Stenger, the pharmacist, and his wife are sitting at a picnic table with Becky Myers, Mr. Bittman the grocer, and Daniel Hester. The vet lifts his hand but doesn't come over. Mrs. Wade, the fruit fly who was such a pest at Prudy Ott's birth, is talking to Sheriff Hardman.

What's Hardman doing here, anyway? Snooping around for the whereabouts of Thomas? That pisses me off,
and I decide to confront him. I never
particularly liked Mrs. Wade either.

"Nice to see you," I say to the woman
with a smile as sweet as sweet potato
pie. She's dressed in a navy blue suit
with white buttons the size of silver dollars and a wide white straw hat. Perspi-
ration shows on her upper lip, which is
covered in bright red lipstick. "Sheriff . . ." I nod and bare my teeth in a
smile. "I didn't know you were acquainted with Mrs. Potts."

"She *delivered* us. Bill is my brother!"
That's Red Mouth cutting in. The fact
that the two are related surprises me,
and I look at them in a new light. Not
much family resemblance except for
the way they hold themselves, their
backs straight and their chins tilted
high.

The lady goes on, "Our mother died
a few years ago, but Mrs. Potts was
her midwife and they always stayed
friends. Many is the time we would

come in the kitchen and find the two of them laughing over sassafras tea."

Then Sheriff Hardman takes up the story. "Mrs. Potts was only a young woman when she starting delivering babies in the 1800s, and she didn't call herself a midwife then. She'd been to a few births over in Maryland. Ma and she were just girls, really, eighteen and nineteen. There were no doctors in Union County then. Grace Potts was it."

The church bell chimes, and the crowd files into the little white chapel, men, women, and children. I follow the sheriff and his sister but squeeze in with Bitsy, who is sitting with Bowlin in the third row. I guess Thomas isn't going to show. Probably feels it's too hot for him here after MacIntosh's death.

The reverend begins with a prayer and then leads us in the old spiritual "Will the Circle Be Unbroken?" He follows with another prayer and then an account of Mrs. Potts's life, how she had come from Maryland through Front Royal and over the mountains into West Virginia in 1870, a former slave, released along with her mother by her master when she was a child before the end of the Civil War. Her husband, Alfred Potts, was born free in New York State, a trained blacksmith and farrier, and they settled along Horse Shoe Run, a creek Mrs. Potts actually named.

I had never thought of Grace Potts as a slave. How could that be? Such a dignified, well-educated community leader? We all have our histories, but this is a revelation to me.

The pastor goes on, telling us that the couple had four children, all of whom died in an outbreak of yellow fever in 1878. I think again what a woman she must have been. All of your children dying in one year? What would that do to you? Four little graves . . .

"Grace Potts was truly a saint," Reverend Miller intones.

"Amen," the congregation responds, and then we sing another spiritual. *"Oh, when the saints go marching in, Oh, when the saints go marching in."* The harmony raises the roof of the little church and sunlight streams through the windows. I wonder why I didn't visit the old midwife more, why I didn't try to learn from her while I had the opportunity. Once we had Star to ride, it would have been easy. She was always so open with me. I guess I thought she would be here forever, but I should have known better.

Next the pastor asks everyone who was delivered by Mrs. Potts to come forward. Two-thirds of the congregation rise, from babies to men and women Hardman's age. I'm surprised to see Mr. Maddock, my neighbor, push his wife up the center aisle in a squeaky wicker wheelchair; the woman I'd thought so stern and disapproving, the woman who never came to the door or asked me in. Now, as I glance at her withered legs under the green-and-white crocheted blanket, I understand why. There's another surprise.

"Is that Twyla? With the baby?" I whisper to Bitsy.

Bitsy whispers back, "Well, she was delivered by Mrs. Potts, and her baby too, with our assistance." I can tell she's proud of the role she played that very wild day. The infant begins to fuss, and

Samantha goes over and picks him up, carrying him over her shoulder like a little sack of potatoes.

"This is Mrs. Potts's legacy . . . her gift to the world," the reverend explains. "She called all her babies her *angels*."

Emma begins to sing in her low contralto, *"Nearer, my God, to thee, nearer to thee."* Bitsy squeezes my hand. Mrs. Potts's angels move slowly back to their seats, many crying, the children and older people too.

I sink into myself, pull down my mind's purple curtain, hardly listening to the rest of the prayers, thinking about death, thinking about birth and all the beautiful mess in the middle. I don't come out of it until Bitsy elbows me.

Mrs. Miller is standing by the piano. " . . . and there are two other people that we'd like to introduce today," she's saying. "Patience Murphy and Bitsy Proudfoot, please rise." I frown. What's going on? Bitsy pulls me up.

"These are the midwives for Union County now." All heads turn to look. "If there was anything you ever planned to do for Grace Potts *someday*, then do it for them. If you owed anything to her, you can pay back the girls. I'm sure Mrs. Potts would approve." I almost laugh at the reference to us as "girls." My companion may be young, but I'll be thirty-seven by the end of the year. Bitsy pulls me back down, and I plunk into my seat, feeling my face beet red. Still, it's a generous and unexpected thing for the Millers to do.

When the service is over and Mrs. Potts is laid to rest, the church ladies arrange food on wooden picnic tables under the trees. I prepare my plate of greens, fried chicken, potato salad, and baked beans and plan to sit next to Bitsy or maybe at the table with Becky Myers and the Stengers, but when I look around Bitsy is sitting with Byrd Bowlin on a blanket under the trees and the table with Becky and the others is full. I'm wondering where to go when Mr. Maddock beckons me over to a green wooden table where he's already served both himself and his wife. I sit down on the bench across from him, expecting one of them to say hello, but they're mum. Maybe I'm supposed to start the conversation.

"I'm Patience Murphy," I announce, turning to Mrs. Maddock.

"I know." She smiles. She has a nice voice like a motion picture star. "I'm Sarah Rose Maddock. You should come for tea someday."

"I'd love to."

"And your friend." That surprises me. Bitsy has slowly been accepted in the bedrooms of white women, as my birth assistant, but no one has ever asked us for tea.

"We'd be delighted," I accept formally.

Maddock is already standing. Enough of the pleasantries, his rangy body says. He adjusts his suspenders and pushes his Sunday farmer's hat down firmly over his thinning dark hair, then takes both their plates and places them in their woven picnic basket. "I have to get home to milk," he announces, though we both know it's way too early. "Do you need a ride?"

"No, thank you. I have my horse."

Mrs. Maddock nods good-bye as he

bumps her wheelchair across the grass and out to their truck on the dirt road. I look around again for Bitsy. She's still sitting with Byrd, their thighs touching, her hand on her cheek, listening carefully to something he's saying.

I'm contemplating getting on my mare and leaving without her when Samantha, the church soloist, comes over, still carrying Twyla's baby, Mathew, and pushing two shy pregnant girls in front of her, one coffee-colored and one ebony. She stops and introduces them as Harriet and Sojourner Perry, her nieces. Harriet, the smaller of the two, is sucking her thumb. Twyla stands with them, arm in arm.

"I know where you got your names," I tell the girls. They look up from their white Sunday shoes. "I do. I bet Harriet is for Harriet Tubman, the ex-slave who risked her life to lead over three hundred others to freedom, and Sojourner for Sojourner Truth, the famous black orator who stood for women's and Negroes' rights."

Harriet takes her thumb out of her

mouth and grins. "How'd you know that?"

"Our grandma named us," Sojourner, the older, adds. Her pink-and-yellow flour-sack dress stretches tight over her belly, which I calculate may be eight months along.

"Where I lived before, we had a book on famous Negroes," I explain.

"These young ladies are some of Mrs. Potts's patients," Samantha explains. "I thought they should meet you. They're from Smoke Valley, Kentucky, and are staying with us . . . my brother's girls. We wanted Mrs. Potts to deliver them, but now we have you."

I feel like a leftover, lopsided red velvet cake at a cakewalk, but I don't think she means it that way.

"When their time comes, will you and Bitsy be there?"

"We'll plan on it," I say, picking up where Mrs. Potts left off.

"It wasn't so bad," says Twyla, now an expert on childbirth. "It hurt, but you'll do better if you relax. Try not to tighten up, that's the secret. And don't scream. It just scares the baby."

36

Third Degree

On Saturday afternoon, I ride my bike down Wild Rose Road and around Salt Lick into Liberty to turn in my birth certificates at the courthouse and pick up supplies, again washing up behind the Texaco station. MacIntosh's vehicle is nowhere to be seen.

When I have to ask the crimped gray-haired woman behind the elbow-high wooden desk for another death certificate, I cringe, but she doesn't say anything. The coroner must fill out one for Kitty, there's nothing about that in the midwifery code. As I leave, I spy Sheriff

Hardman standing in the hall and make myself small, trying to slide past him.

"Miss Murphy?"

"Sheriff." I nod and keep moving, but he reaches out and touches my arm.

"Can we have a word?"

"Uh, I'm sort of in a hurry . . . I need to get downstairs to consult with Mrs. Myers about a pregnant patient." This is a total lie, but I think it sounds possible.

My excuse doesn't work. He crooks his index finger and motions me into his office. "I just have a few questions. It won't take long." He sits behind his big wooden desk and motions for me to take the other chair. "Katherine Mac-Intosh came to me a few days before she returned to Baltimore. She feels certain her husband killed himself. Said he had threatened to do it before. I know you were close to the family. Do you have anything to add? Come clean this time. No more lies."

I'm staring at a cluster of wanted posters arranged on the wall behind his desk half expecting to see my own mug, but there's no one I recognize.

Though the Battle at Blair Mountain seems like yesterday to me, it's nine years ago, probably old news to the rest of the world.

"What did you want to know?"

"Everything you know."

I take a big breath. "Well, I wasn't really acquainted with them at first. I attended Mrs. MacIntosh in labor. You probably heard." Hardman nods without expression. Just as I thought . . . probably everyone knows about the dead baby that came alive.

"Mr. MacIntosh was having a hard time financially. Katherine said he was burdened by debt. I didn't learn that until later. The baby was born the day after the stock market crashed." The lawman nods again.

"Later, after Bitsy got fired and moved in with me, Katherine ran to us twice with bruises all over her upper body. The first time, William said he was sorry, but then it happened again. The second time she came in the middle of a rainstorm, and Mr. Hester, the vet, was kind enough to drive us to Torrington to the train station. She was in the barn the morning you came up Wild Rose Road. I didn't tell you because I thought you might try and take her home. They weren't a happy couple. That's all I know, except . . . well, Katherine said he'd beaten her, many times . . . and like I said, he'd done it before."

"And Thomas Proudfoot? What do you know about him?"

I tilt my chin up. "Just that he is brave and kind and helps whoever he can and wouldn't kill anyone. I don't think he would, anyway. Kill someone." Hardman picks up a pencil and taps it thoughtfully on the desk, looking at me for a long time. Outside on the street I hear a woman laugh.

"Can I go?" I consult my pocket watch on a ribbon.

"For now."

I couldn't get out of there faster!

Annabelle

Still sweating, only this time not from the heat and humidity, I trot down the steps, grab my bike, and head around the corner to find the grocery still open. The young Mr. Bittman greets me, takes the four quarters I've just received for filling out the birth certificates, and wraps up my few supplies (a bag of cornmeal, some flour, and a small box of sugar) which I secure in the basket of the bike in a feed sack. Then I head through town. Two miles past the bridge, still shaky after my encounter with the sheriff, I spot a rough truck pulled off in the grass. At first I think it might be Reverend Miller, but a white man waves wildly.

"Lady!" the guy yells. "Hey, lady!"

I stop in the dust.

"My missus. She's carrying a child, and she's paining bad. Is there some woman who could help us? We aren't from around here and must have made a wrong turn."

"I'm a midwife."

"Oh, praise the Lord."

"I don't have my supplies with me, but I just live another mile and a half up the road. Is your woman far along?" He leads me to the front of the truck, where I see three towheaded children under seven sitting in the grass throwing rocks in the creek and a thin blond lady slumped in the front of the cab with her feet pressed to the dash.

The woman whips her yellow bob back and forth and growls.

I know that sound well, and I have no gloves, no soap, no scissors to cut the cord! Nothing.

"Ma'am?" I inquire, opening the passenger-side door and wondering how the hell they'd packed all the kids in. "I'm Patience Murphy, a midwife." I turn to the husband, who grasps his dark hair in handfuls until it stands on end. "What's your wife's name?"

"Annabelle."

"Annabelle, I can see you're very uncomfortable, but can you please stop pushing?" This seems ridiculous, phrased so politely. Holding back a baby when it's down in the birth canal is like holding back an avalanche with your bare hands. "My house is just a few minutes away, and if we could get you there, I have everything we need. Can you blow, like this? Hooo! Hooo!

Hooo!" I demonstrate. The mother looks at me wildly.

"It's coming!"

"You're probably right, but I'm serious. I have a nice little house down the road. If we can just get you there . . ."

She growls low and pushes again.

"Mister!" I change my approach and turn to the wild-eyed fellow. "Get the kids. We can make it if we hurry. I'll leave my bike and show you the way. Children, come now!" The father tosses the youngsters in and cranks up the engine. I jump on the running board. "Straight ahead! Hooo! Hooo! Hooo! Annabelle! Listen to me. Do like me. Hooo! Hooo! Hooo!"

"Ugghhhh!"

"No, you don't! Blow!"

The lady wails, and I think that the head must be close to crowning. We bump up Wild Rose, and I catch sight of Mrs. Maddock sitting on the porch. Mr. Maddock stands out in the field up on a hay wagon, where a hired man holds the horses. They stare as we speed by in a cloud of dust, me still on the running board holding on for dear life.

"Hooo. Hooo. Good girl." The truck lurches to a halt at the gate. *"Bitsy!"* My friend runs out the blue door. "Birth satchel." I don't need to explain further; she leaps back inside.

"Okay, now, Annabelle. Just take little steps. It's not much farther. Children, sit under the tree!" The father lifts them down one at a time and points to the old oak. I have my hand on Annabelle's bottom, and through her worn wet cotton dress I can already feel the top of the head.

"Up you go." The father and I almost lift Annabelle up the steps, and as she goes into a squat, Bitsy throws my green patchwork quilt down under her.

"Ugggggggh!" Annabelle collapses onto her side. Two pushes later, a rosy pink infant is crying in my arms. The mother is strangely silent. The children, unable to help themselves, peek through the porch rails. The father brushes his wife's hair off her damp forehead, then takes the kids back to the tree, where they all sit down in the shade.

* * *

"Well, I thank you ladies kindly. Ain't no way we can repay you, but when we get settled up north I can mail you a few dollars." That's Rolly, the father of the family, dark-eyed, dark-haired, and handsome in his worn denim pants and work shirt. Usually people who are down and out want to tell me their story, want to show me that they weren't always so destitute, but this fellow is mum about his history.

I figure he's another miner out of work or maybe a storekeeper who's lost his store, another guy fallen on hard times. We're at the kitchen table, sharing our meager supper of greens and rabbit stew. The children lick their bowls as if it's the best meal they've had in weeks. He doesn't ask our mailing address and I never expect to get a penny, but I know he means well.

By dusk Rolly has retrieved my bike and cloth bag of groceries from the roadside ditch; we've installed the mother on the sofa and set up pallets for the rest of them in the barn. Bitsy and I sit on the porch, watching the clouds turn pink and then red, taking turns holding the baby while the exhausted mother sleeps. They named her Norma.

September 8, 1930. Full moon waning.

Norma, daughter of Annabelle and Rolly Doe (I realize I don't yet know their last name), travelers I met on Salt Lick. Female infant, 6 pounds, 6 ounces. The family has three other children and no home. They were on their way north to look for work when they got lost on the back roads and she went into hard labor.

Delivery went fine, out on our front porch. No vaginal tears and only about two cups of blood. I made Annabelle drink a sip of Mrs. Potts's potion, just in case. She was so pale and thin. No offer of payment, but the mister split up a mess of wood. Didn't expect any pay.

Foundling

Twice during the night, the baby cries and I tiptoe downstairs, take her out of the basket Bitsy has fixed up and let her suck on my finger. The exhausted mother shifts a little but doesn't turn over. When I try to wake her to breast-feed, she moans and brushes me away. I know from my wet nurse experience that it's better to put the baby to the breast right away, but Annabelle's milk won't come in for a day or two, so I let her be. Mrs. Kelly told me that in the Orient, they don't start nursing until two days after birth and their babies survive.

At dawn the rooster crows, but I put my pillow over my head and hope for another hour of shut-eye. Bitsy wakes me a few minutes later.

"They're gone," she says, standing next to my bed fully dressed.

"Gone?" I wrench myself out of dreamland (something about flying over Lake Michigan with my arms outstretched). "What do you mean, gone?"

"I mean twenty-three skidoo! No note or anything." For the first time I notice that she has the baby in her arms.

"Holy cow! They forgot their baby!"

"I don't think they forgot."

The travelers abandoning their new-born flabbergasts me. Over breakfast we discuss what to do.

"Maybe you could take the baby to the sheriff," Bitsy offers.

"I'd hate to do that." I take her in my arms. "Isn't there an orphanage in Union County or somewhere?" The baby starts crying again, rooting at the front of my red silk kimono, and with-out even thinking I open the front and offer her my breast. She finds the nip-ple as if she's done it before and draws it in.

Bitsy bugs her eyes and then looks away. "Miss Patience!" she says, her teacup halfway to her mouth. "Is that proper? To nurse someone else's baby?"

"It's okay, Bitsy. I don't have milk, but sucking will give the baby some com-fort while we figure out what to do. I was a wet nurse once, you know." Reflecting, I realize that I've never talked to Bitsy about that part of my past. Never told her much of anything really, fearing once I got started the dike would break and everything would spill out: my days at the orphanage, my life at the Majestic, my teenage pregnancy, the death of Lawrence and the baby, the theft of the ruby ring, my radical days in Pittsburgh . . . and the worst part, the march on Blair Mountain.

Bitsy pushes her chair back. "There's no orphanage. Usually, around here, kin just take care of kin. What about the home health nurse, Mrs. Myers, wouldn't she have some connections?" She stands and puts her teacup in the sink. "I hate to leave you right now, but I've got to go to Hazel Patch. It's about Thomas."

"Is he okay? The sheriff isn't still watching for him, is he? Katherine was so sure William had committed suicide, I thought the manhunt was over."

"He's fine. Just laying low, farther up in the mountains." I watch through the open back door as she heads for the barn, gets her bicycle out, and walks it through the dry grass out to the road. Part of me is relieved to have her gone for a while. Breastfeeding an infant when I don't have milk is causing my uterus to contract, and I'm about to swoon.

"What are we going to do with you, Norma?" I release her little mouth from my nipple, insert my pinkie, and jiggle her up and down. "Your parents are on their way north to find a better life. They just don't have enough money, and there are three other children." Norma, as if she understands and is really mad about it, stops sucking, spits out my finger, and begins to wail again. What the heck, I guess I can stand it. I put the baby back on my breast and pace back and forth to distract myself. Surely no woman has ever had an orgasm while nursing a foundling. It just can't happen!

Angel

As the sun reaches over the trees, Norma finally falls asleep again and I place her in her basket, tucking the blanket around her. She keeps sucking the way infants do when they dream, and I stand looking down at her. Times are hard, but there must be some childless couple who would like to raise this beautiful baby.

I consider the folks at Hazel Patch, a good-hearted community if there ever was one, but this child is white. Would adopting a white infant be possible for black people? There might even be Jim Crow laws.

I contemplate keeping the baby myself . . . but how would I manage? What would we do with Norma when Bitsy and I had to go to a birth in bad weather? Take her out in the cold? I look down at the sleeping newborn again, touch her cheek with one finger.

"How about Gladys and Ernie Mintz?" I wonder out loud. It's only been four months since the loss of their baby. Maybe the woman could reestablish her milk supply.

The Mintzes don't have money, but they have their own farm and a cow. Unless one of the parents gets ill or injured, their family will survive. It may seem outrageous, but it could be just what Mrs. Mintz needs . . . I run upstairs to put on my second dress and white apron, wanting to impress them this time, look more like Mrs. Potts, a respectable midwife.

At the last minute I take down my red Calumet baking soda can. The weight of the stocking tucked inside is reassuring, and Katherine's gold-and-pearl pin plops out, along with Mrs. Vanderhoff's ruby ring. I thread a blue hair ribbon through the ring and tie it around the baby's neck. Maybe the Mintz family will have a way to get to Torrington to trade it for cash, or maybe they will consider it a good-luck charm. In a way, I am glad to get rid of it.

An hour later, with the baby swaddled in a white sheet against my chest, I trot into the Mintzes' yard and awkwardly slide off Star. The three little boys are playing with bits of wood in the dirt next to the porch, and they stop to look up at me. I straighten my dress and pat the baby. Albert, the oldest, comes around the side with a bucket of feed for the chickens.

"Here goes nothing," I say under my breath as I approach the house. "Don't take it personally, little one, if they don't want you. I'm an orphan myself, you know. We'll figure out something."

"Miss Murphy," Albert says, tipping his straw hat and eyeing the bundle attached to my front.

"Your ma home?"

"Inside . . . She's poorly."

I frown, ashamed of myself for not ever making a visit. By the time Bitsy and I left their home after the stillbirth, Mr. Mintz had stopped verbally berating me, but I still felt he blamed us for his baby's death and I'd never returned, not in all this time.

"In the back," Albert directs, opening the screen door.

I pass through the dark hall and hesitate at the closed bedroom door. "Gladys. It's Patience, the midwife. Can I come in?" There's no answer, but I hear movement on the other side of the wall. "Gladys?"

A woman clears her throat. "Come

in." This is uttered without enthusiasm. As the door swings back, I discover the mother sitting up in bed in her night-dress, her long lank hair drooping over her shoulders, a plate of untouched beans, dandelion greens, and corn bread next to her on the bedside table.

"Good morning, Gladys. Are you do-ing okay?" I can see that she isn't.

"Can't seem to get my strength back," Gladys answers with hardly enough air to get out the words. "The mister cooks for us, says I need to make new blood, to eat lots of collard greens and organ meats. He even killed three chickens and cooked up the liver and giblets, but losing our Angel has knocked something out of me. I don't think I can get it back."

She stares out the window, her face a wall of grief, doesn't notice the bun-dle on my chest until it begins to mew. "What's that?" she asks. "It sounds like a kitten."

"A newborn infant that was left to me." I ease myself into the rocker and undo the sheet. "Her name is Angel too." This is a fib, but it comes out like the truth. Now that I think of it, there is some resemblance to their baby. Same dark hair and little bowed mouth. I plunk the child into the grieving mother's lap, and Gladys raises her hands as if she's seen a ghost.

"Where'd you get that?"

"Another woman birthed her yesterday and left her with me. She needs a ma and a family."

Mrs. Mintz tentatively touches the baby's hand. She picks her up, cups the infant's head, and looks at her face, then opens the blanket and inspects her body.

"Who's the mother?" she asks.

"A stranger named Annabelle. She and her husband were passing through Union County on their way north to look for work. They had three other children and got lost on the back roads. I found them near Bucks Run over by my place, where she was about to give birth in their truck, and they spent one night with us on the farm, then left before dawn without saying good-bye. Didn't get their family name. They weren't from around here."

The baby whimpers, then begins to cry, and I notice, with interest, breast milk leaking through the woman's night-dress. Gladys swings her feet around and sets them on the floor. She holds the infant against her shoulder and pats it, the way all mothers do.

"You could feed her," I encourage.

"There's some grits in the kitchen. Can newborn babies eat grits mixed with cow's milk? I've always breastfed before."

"Why don't you try it?" I nod toward her front.

"Suckle the baby? I'm mostly dried up." She glances down at her rather flat chest and sees the wet spot, a sure sign of letdown.

"Milk will sometimes come back if you have a baby to nurse. It hasn't been that long. I'm sure she knows what to do." (I am definitely sure Angel knows what to do!)

"I'm so weak . . ."

"Not that weak. When there's a baby, a mother finds her strength. You know what you would do for your other children."

With hesitation the woman fumbles to open her gown, and I watch as the baby roots back and forth. Mrs. Mintz grins when the tiny girl latches on. For me, it's like meeting the real Gladys for the first time. The other one was a husk of herself.

Suddenly there's a commotion in the hall, the sound of hard boots, and the door swings open. Mr. Mintz stands there, his hands on his skinny hips, his worn patched overalls hanging from one strap. Albert, with the three little boys, follows. The youngest one worms up to the bed.

"What the hell's going on?" That's Ernest. He darts his eyes back and forth. "Haven't you caused enough pain?"

"Where'd you get the baby, Mama?" "Can I see?" "What's her name?" That's the kids.

I move back out of the circle. Ernest glares, then turns to his woman. A few seconds ago, he was prepared to throw me out, the meddlesome midwife wandering into the shadow of his family's tragedy, but his Gladys is breastfeeding with a Mona Lisa look on her face, pensive and sweet.

He reaches over and touches the gemstone on the ribbon around Angel's neck. "What's this?"

"A gift," I answer.

"We ain't beholden—"

"You won't be. Someone gave the ring to me. It's a real ruby, and I'm passing it on."

"What's her name, Ma?" That's Albert.

"She's called Angel," Gladys whispers. "And she's ours."

September 12, 1930. Waning moon in a clear violet sky.

Another birth. Feast or famine. Julie Twiss, 8 pounds, second daughter of Ferris and Mina Twiss of Lick Fork. Born after eight hours of labor. Mina's sister, who had come up from Charleston and had three babies with twilight sleep, was amazed to see a baby born so

simply and easily. Mina did her-self proud. She stayed out of bed for the whole labor, and then she lay down on her side and pushed her big baby out with no fuss.

I remarked to Bitsy that Mina sang the perfect birth song. Mrs. Kelly had taught me about that. If you listen, you will hear the laboring woman's voice change. Normal and chatty at first, the pitch goes up as the womb opens. When the baby comes down, the voice drops. It's universal. Italian, Polish, Ger-man, Negro, Irish, all sing the same song.

Present were Mrs. Bessie Rich-ards, the sister from Charleston, Bitsy, and I. Paid five bucks and two whole chickens.

37

Harvest

A busy time for us, the last two weeks, as we pick and can beans, tomatoes, yellow squash and make applesauce, sunup to sundown. On frames of wood covered with cheesecloth, we also dry apples, rose hips, and corn. We've even picked and hung, under the porch, huge bunches of pennyroyal, mint, shepherd's purse, tansy, comfrey, valerian, blue cohosh, and lavender.

The potatoes are the easiest to preserve and will keep in the root cellar, along with the carrots, beets, and onions that we'll dig in a fortnight. The winter squash, acorn and butternut, will be stored in the attic along with onions and strings of red pepper, which need to be kept cool but dry.

It is my greatest pleasure to see our stores grow. Well, maybe not my *greatest* pleasure; there was that night with Hester, but the vet and I have not talked since the thunderstorm. The only times I've even seen him since were at Mrs. Potts's funeral, though we didn't talk then, and weeks later, when Bitsy and I went to Union County Fair.

We decided that we should enter some of our winter squash and rode Star, carrying our produce in gunnysacks over her sides. The trip was the longest we've taken, a break from our daily hard labor, and our butternut squash won a blue ribbon and a two-dollar bill donated by the Ladies Home Society. I told Bitsy she should enter her new batch of blackberry wine, but she said they don't have a category for wine since Prohibition.

Hester was in the animal tent when we passed him, judging woolly lambs and half-grown goats. He nodded but didn't come over. I don't know what I wanted him to do: leave the group of men, gather me in his arms, and press his body against me? What was I thinking when I stood naked with him in the rain?

The trouble is, I wasn't thinking! The whiskey and his kindness, after Kitty Hart's horrible death, swept me away. "It is what it is." That's what Mrs. Kelly would say. "It is what it is."

"Bitsy! Miss Patience!" I look all around. "Up here!"

Bitsy laughs and points up toward the Ferris wheel. Swinging precariously in a yellow gondola are Twyla with Sojourner and Harriet, the two pregnant girls from Hazel Patch. "What in the Sam Hill are they doing up there?" I ask my friend.

"Having fun."

"But they are mothers, or almost mothers."

"They can still have fun."

"But where's baby Mathew? The

judge . . . the judge didn't give him away, did he?"

Bitsy slips her arm through mine, and her warmth flows through me. She has never done that in public before. When I think of it, she's never done it anywhere before, not even at home.

"Twyla and Mathew live with the Millers now. It was my idea. She cleans the church and works on the farm for her keep. Then Samantha takes care of Mathew in the mornings so Twyla can go to school. They visit Nancy every Saturday."

My mouth is still open. Bitsy pushes my chin up and laughs. "It was my idea, and I took care of it," she says and laughs again.

Horse Power

No breeze today. No rain at all for two weeks, and the already brown locust leaves rattle in the dry wind. When we were at the fair, we learned that farmers are already using this year's hay, which is meant for winter, to feed their livestock. That news reminded me that I must get in a supply of feed for our own cows and Star. With the local shortage we can't afford to buy it; the price will be too high. Of course, I still have Katherine's golden moon pin, but it's the old story, there's no way to pawn it.

Bitsy says I worry too much. "The Lord will provide," she says. "Like with Twyla and Mathew. They needed a home, and the Lord provided." And maybe she's right. Yesterday we received a gift I could never have imagined.

"Do you know how to make a sweet persimmon pie?" Bitsy asks me. "A little sugar, a few eggs, and a nice crust with lard . . ." We are planning our supper of pie, pie, and more pie, along with some cold milk, as we wind our way home from the river, where we've picked a basket of the soft orange fruit.

Rounding the corner of the barn, riding double on Star, the first thing we see is a shiny black sedan just outside the picket fence. My thought is, it must be the law again, but Bitsy doesn't think so.

"Company," she comments, sliding off the horse and leading her to the water trough by the spring. "It must be Miss Katherine. I thought she was in Baltimore."

"Or William back to haunt us," I quip, recognizing the Oldsmobile I once drove when Hester and I took Katherine to the B&O station, only it looks a lot better than last time. The black metal gleams, and the chrome has been polished.

I run up the porch and throw open the door, expecting to see Katherine and the baby waiting for us on the sofa, but there's no one there. "Katherine?" No response. "Katherine?"

Funny. Maybe they went for a walk.

Bitsy joins me on the steps, setting the basket of persimmons down. "Where'd they go?"

"Beats me." I pick up a small box with a ribbon sitting on the rail. "What's this?" We both raise our eyebrows, staring down at the gift, and I call one last time, not wanting to spoil our friend's surprise. "Katherine?!" There's still no answer, so I tear the package open.

A gold key on a gold key chain with the Masons' symbol on it and a note in a fine woman's hand falls out. Carefully, I unfold the linen stationery and read aloud while Bitsy picks up the key.

Dear Patience and Bitsy,

I didn't get a chance at Mary's service to thank you properly for all you have done for me and little Willie. I truly believe I owe my life to you and to Mary too. That may seem dramatic, but William's drinking and outbursts were escalating, and if I hadn't gotten away, I have no doubt that someday I'd have been beaten to death.

I told you, Patience, that he'd threatened to commit suicide before. I shouldn't speak ill of the dead, but he threatened and pleaded right up to the end. The last time we talked by phone, a

few days before his suicide, he said we were married forever and if I didn't come home I'd regret it.

I told him firmly that his life was his own. My life was mine, and I would never come back. That's why he killed himself, I'm sure of it. Before I left Liberty, I told all this to Sheriff Hardman, and I think he accepts it. The last thing I want is for Thomas to be blamed.

Enclosed in this box are the keys to William's car. I want you to have it. Mr. Linkous, the lawyer handling what's left of our estate, said he would find a driver and bring it to you when he got it fixed.

Thank you again with all my heart, Katherine and Bitsy and Thomas too. I will never forget you. You gave me hope. You gave me my life back.

Love,
Katherine

I fold the letter, put it back into the envelope, and let out a sigh. "You never know, do you?" My companion isn't so reflective. She leaps off the porch and heads for the auto.

"Let's take her out for a spin!" She cranks up the engine and revs it to life.

An auto of our own! I run my hand along the black metal. It's not new, maybe ten years old, but never would I have expected such a gift. Like royalty, with the windows open, we drive down Wild Rose Road, around Salt Lick, into Liberty, and home again, a big circle.

Looking back, our hour-long excursion in our wonderful wheels wasn't the greatest idea. We sputtered home on an almost empty tank and ended up having to push the Olds into the barn.

If we had been watching the multiple brass gauges and dials, we would have noticed the E for empty. Obviously, Bitsy and I will have to bone up on our motoring skills before we take the auto out again, and that may not be for a while. Katherine, in her expression of gratitude, had forgotten that we have no money for gasoline. At ten cents a gallon, it is out of our reach.

September 17, 1930. Moon behind clouds and I have lost track.

Frost on the garden. Baby boy, Morgan, 7 pounds 4 ounces, to Sojourner Perry, aged 18. No vaginal tears, No problems. She will go back to Kentucky when her lying-in is over. Baby took to the breast right away. The family gave us $3.00 for coal or for hay.

September 24, 1930. Harvest moon, not one week later, another baby.

Sojourner's little sister, Harriet Perry, delivered a baby girl, Dilly, only 5 pounds. Looked about a month early but breathed and cried vigorously. Mrs. Miller got right in there with warmed

blankets, and I'm sure the baby
will be fine.

Harriet didn't want to breastfeed, but with such a tiny baby I
told her she had to or Dilly might
die. After she tried it, she was
okay. Mrs. Miller, the reverend's
wife, gave us another $2.00 and
a cord of wood.

38

High Tea

This afternoon when I went to the mailbox, I was surprised to find a plain square envelope addressed to Patience Murphy in tiny handwriting. We get so little mail, I tore it open right in the yard.

"Look at this." I hold the pale pink note card, decorated with a border of roses, up to Bitsy, who sits at the table shelling the last of the dried beans. It's an invitation from our neighbor Mrs. Maddock. Kind of a surprise; she never seemed to like me until I had lunch with her and Mr. Maddock at the church. I put on a high-toned accent and read the note out loud: "Mrs. Sarah Rose Maddock requests the company of Patience and Bitsy for tea on September 29, 1930, at two P.M."

"I can't go." That's Bitsy.

"Why not? We can take a few hours off the farm."

My friend looks down. "I have a quilting bee that day at the Hazel Patch Chapel."

"Quilting bee! How come you didn't mention it? I like to quilt."

"I stopped telling you about things at the church a long time ago because you never want to go. And anyway, afterwards I'm going to meet Byrd." She says this with a shy smile.

Though I was younger than my friend when I first got pregnant, I've been concerned about Bitsy . . . I clear my throat. It's not like I'm Saint Patience, but this has to be said.

"Bitsy, is Byrd Bowlin courting you proper? I don't want you getting in trouble. Sometimes this happens when people are grieving. They feel alone and seek comfort. They can forget themselves."

"Miss Patience, how can you say that?"

When she reverts to "Miss Patience," I know she's mad.

"Byrd loves me and we've kissed, but it hasn't gone further. The Reverend Miller's wife gave me the same sort of talk . . . What kind of a person do you think I am? What kind of man would Bowlin be if he expected that?"

"Well, you know, all those young girls, like Twyla and Harriet and her sister Sojourner, aren't just tramps. Love has a way of undoing buttons. I just don't want you getting in trouble." I think of my own thunderstorm night. After the loss of my first baby, I was never able to get pregnant again, but being sterile has an advantage. No worries about getting knocked up. Not that (with the exception of Hester) there's been any chance since Ruben died.

"I wish everyone would just leave me alone!" Bitsy jerks up to get another bucket of beans, then bangs down in her chair in a huff. "After the quilting bee we're going to his parents' for dinner, and then he'll bring me home in his father's truck."

I'm tempted to say something like "Don't come in late," but I let it go. I've said my piece. Instead, I croon with a grin, *"By the light of the silvery moon"* and throw Mrs. Maddock's invitation across the table at her. *By the light—of the silvery moon—to my honey I'll croon . . .*

Tuesday morning we cut hay from the back pasture with the rusty scythe I found in the barn and sharpened with a file until the blade was razor thin. I swing the wooden-handled implement like a peasant woman in a painting, and Bitsy rakes the long sweet grass into piles and then drags it in an old blanket to a fenced-in area behind the barn. The stack is as high as our heads, but we'll need a lot more with a horse, cow, and calf to feed.

At noon we quit and, behind the springhouse, strip down to our waists and scream as we pour buckets of cold water over each other. Then Bitsy puts on her second-best dress and rides her bicycle to Hazel Patch, and I put on my second-best dress and wander down the dusty road to Sarah Maddock's for tea.

I knock on the three-paneled oak door with a leaded glass window. I hadn't noticed the ornate pattern before because the screen was across it, but the glass is edged with a delicate border of flowers and leaves. No one answers, so I knock again. There are lace curtains hanging, and I can't see inside. I hope Mrs. Maddock didn't forget about me.

"Hello!" I yell. "Anyone home?"

"Come in," a woman answers from deep in the house.

I turn the knob.

"Patience?"

The call seems to come from way in the back, so I pass through the living room and enter the empty kitchen. On the way, I admire the cast-iron Phoenix woodstove with the ornate silver-plated top, the carved oak fold-down desk, and the floor lamp with the fringed blue silk shade, but there's no time to linger.

"Here."

"Mrs. Maddock?"

"On the back porch."

I'm expecting something like my own back porch, a small room where we keep buckets, our washtub, old rubber boots, winter coats, things that need fixing, and wet dogs, but I'm surprised to find a screened-in room that runs the length of the house with high-backed white wicker furniture and ferns in hanging baskets.

A round pedestal table is set with white cups and plates bordered with tiny pink flowers and cutlery that looks like real silver. There's also a silver tea set and a vase of deep purple asters. Mrs. Maddock rolls herself over in her wheelchair and takes my rough red hands in both of her thin, cool ivory ones.

"Call me Sarah Rose, honey. I'm so glad you came. Is Bitsy here too?" The table, I notice, is set for three.

"No, I'm sorry. I probably should have come down to tell you. She has a quilting bee at the church and then dinner with her beau. She's courting." I say this with a smile and a slight shrug.

"Those were the days!" When Mrs. Maddock laughs, it's like silver bells tinkling. I sit down in the closest chair. I'm not used to the ritual of formal tea and am unsure what comes next. Is this high tea, like I've read about, the kind they have in England, almost a meal—or low tea? Looks like high tea to me, but what would I know? My women friends in Pittsburgh drank black coffee in mugs around a kitchen table where we talked world politics.

The wheelchair-bound woman pours me a cup and hands me a tiny embossed silver pitcher. "Cream?" Then she lifts a glass cover off a rose-glass plate and reveals white sugar cookies with white frosting. In another bowl are canned peaches.

"This is quite a spread. I'll be honest, I didn't know what to expect. I feel I should have worn white gloves and a bonnet."

"I'll be honest too. I haven't had anyone to tea for fifteen years. Not since I got infantile paralysis. I was twenty-four."

I glance at her legs and then at her face. If she was twenty-four fifteen years ago, she's close to my age now.

Sarah Rose

"Polio?"

"It was 1916, and I was pregnant and so happy and at first we didn't know what it was. I just had a fever, a bad headache, and stiffness of the back and neck. I thought I had some kind of flu, but I soon lost the strength in both legs and couldn't even get to the commode. That's when we called in the doctor and they took me to the hospital."

"The polio epidemic was awful, wasn't it?" I respond, not knowing what else to say. "I heard seven thousand people died in 1916 in the U.S. alone. You were lucky you made it."

"I guess." She runs her hands down her withered thighs. "Four times that many people were left paralyzed. At the time, I *wanted* to die."

"I've felt that way too."

She looks at me with interest. "When was that? When you felt you wanted to die?" she asks gently.

That's why I don't socialize. There are so many things I don't want to divulge; it's like trying to dance with your legs tied together. Sarah Rose is still waiting. I'll tell just a little . . .

"I was pregnant and engaged to be married when I was sixteen and my fiancé, my lover, was killed in a train wreck. Seven days later I hemorrhaged and lost our baby. I almost died too. That's when . . ." I take a big breath. ". . . That's when I wished I would die."

Mrs. Maddock reaches over the plate of cookies, now half gone, and rests her hand over mine. Her skin is so translucent you can see the blue veins.

I could tell her the other times I wanted to die. When my mama passed away . . . when I left Chicago on the run without a friend in the world . . . I could tell her about Blair Mountain, how I killed my best friend, my lover, my

husband, but how could she understand, a sheltered person like Sarah
Rose? The tears come then, just hanging there. I wipe my eyes and stand up
to look out the screens toward the hills,
but she scoots around the table in her
wicker wheelchair and pulls me back.

"That's okay," she whispers, thinking
I'm weeping for my baby. "It's good to
cry. I lost my little one too . . . when I
had polio. The paralysis was moving
up, and if it got to my chest I would
stop breathing. The doctors thought
there was no way I would make it. They
talked Mr. Maddock into letting them
do an emergency cesarean section,
and he gave our little girl to my cousin
who couldn't get pregnant. No one
imagined I would recover, and then,
when I did, I couldn't ask for the baby
back.

"In a way, it doesn't matter. Both my
cousin and little Sue Ann passed away
a few years later, during the Spanish flu
epidemic. I never even got to hold her.
I have a picture, though, when she was
two, a tiny blond girl. I'll show you

sometime." She holds out the plate of cookies again.

I shake my head no, but she insists, so I eat three. "Did you make these?"

She laughs. "Yes; just because my legs don't work doesn't mean my hands can't. Didn't you notice when you came through the kitchen that Mr. Maddock has made everything low so I can use my wheelchair? He made this screened room for me too, because I don't get out much."

I take in the view, the mowed meadow down to a brook, a pen filled with white sheep, the Hope River in the distance.

"So what do you do out here?" I look around for an embroidery hoop or maybe some knitting, but on the shelves is only an assortment of books and papers. "You like to read?"

"I do," she says. "I write too."

That interests me. "You write? I started a diary. It seems so much has happened in my life . . . like I've lived three or four lives, really."

Sarah puts her elbow on the table and rests her chin in her hand. "Like what? Tell me one of your lives." Her clear blue eyes wait, not leaving my face. "I like stories."

Slow down, Patience, be careful. Some secrets you just need to keep to yourself.

Sarah waits while I stare at the ceiling. "Well . . . I grew up in a little town in Illinois," I begin slowly. "My mother was a schoolteacher and my father was a mate on a big freighter on Lake Michigan."

I go on to describe my innocent childhood, as if it were a Louisa May Alcott story, to the point where my grandma dies of consumption, my father dies in a Lake Michigan shipwreck, and we find out he's gambled away all our money. I stop my tale where I run away from the orphanage and get a job at the Majestic. It makes a good yarn, if I say so myself. "That's lives one and two."

Sarah hasn't said anything except "How sad" and "That must have been horrible!" until I get to the part where I become a chorus girl.

"Oh!" she shouts, clapping her hands

like a five-year-old girl. "I was in the chorus line too! At a dance hall in Charleston." *This* is a new image of Mrs. Maddock!

She laughs. "I was in my twenties. My sister, a waitress, got me the job. My mother didn't approve, of course, and neither did Mr. Maddock once we were engaged. That's where I met him. He could really cut a rug at the time.

"In those days we were encouraged to be friendly with the patrons after our show, get them to buy drinks, though the real money was in the gambling." As she talks, Mrs. Maddock gets prettier and prettier in the golden slanting light. The low sun drops behind the mountains, and the scattered clouds turn first orange, then pink, and finally lavender.

"Milton and I were so in love. We married, and I got pregnant right away. He's never forgiven himself for giving away our child. But you see, he thought I would die from the polio. So many did. Widowed men didn't take care of children in those days." I reach for her hand, cool and soft.

She looks around the beautiful porch room. "During the war, because he worked in the chemical plant in Charleston, he was given a deferment, and then when my grandmother died and we inherited this farm, we moved back here. That was ten years ago. I was born in this very house, you know . . . with Granny Potts."

"I remember. You came up to the front of the church at her service, one of her angels." I smile, but she doesn't smile back. She's on another thought.

"Sometimes I think he protects me too much, Mr. Maddock. His love is like a cocoon, but I don't argue. I have a good life." We are still holding hands, and suddenly it's too much for me.

"You know, I had better get back. I need to milk. Thank you for asking me to tea. Is there anything you want me to get you before I leave? Can I clear the table and wash up?"

"You're as bad as he is! A fussy mother hen. I'm quite self-sufficient, so long as he brings the supplies." She rolls herself into the kitchen, and I notice now that the doorways are a little wider than in my house and there's a long pantry on one side. I run my hand over the smooth low maple counters and the low sink.

"Milton did all the woodwork himself," she explains. "He'll be home soon. He went into Delmont to the stock auction. Not to buy anything, just to listen and watch. The vet will be there too." She says this as if she thinks I'd be interested, and I am, just a little.

39

Forgiveness

Hiking home up Wild Rose Road, I reflect on what I learned at our tea. Mrs. Maddock, who I thought was aloof and judgmental, is curious and graceful and gay. Mr. Maddock, who I thought was hard and unfeeling, is in fact passionately in love with his wife. The Patience I thought had to maintain her secrets . . . was today open and honest . . . up to a point.

I've had a difficult life, or I think I have, an orphan widowed twice before she was thirty, but how do you measure suffering? Sarah Maddock almost died of polio, lost the use of her legs, and had her baby given away. All four of Mrs. Potts's children died of yellow fever within one week. Mrs. Kelly suffered the loss of her husband and their only child and then, after a ten-year relationship, lost Nora to another woman.

The vet in the Great War saw pain and horror I can't even imagine. Bitsy lost her mom and then Thomas, who's gone into hiding. Life, it seems to me, is all about loss, just a series of losses. I kick a stone and kick it again.

I was not just a widow the second time; with Ruben, I widowed myself . . . I lash out at the stone a third time and end up twisting my ankle and falling into the ditch. When I pull myself up, my leg hurts badly but not as badly as my heart.

Sometimes I've felt I was dreaming; this evening I'm awake and would like to crawl into dreams again. The first star rests on the top of the mountain. A whippoorwill sings. The bare trees are black against the lavender sky. It's funny how beauty rides the back of pain . . .

It starts with a few tears, then comes the flood again, muddy water raging over rock, hard sobs, and hiccups. Fearing Mr. Maddock will come home and see me sitting in the ditch crying my eyes out, I crawl over his rail fence and limp through the pasture until I come to a creek. Here, in the woods, I fall backward into the dry grass, arms at my sides, a shell of myself. Behind my tear-filled eyes, a flickering black-and-white picture show begins.

"I *have* to go, Lizbeth!" Ruben barked, pacing around the living room we shared with Mrs. Kelly and Nora. "There's trouble in the West Virginia coalfields, and John Lewis wants me and a few of the others to go down there and settle things down. It's for the workers. It's what I do, you know that!" (Lewis, Ruben's old friend, was now the president of the UMWA, the United Mine Workers of America.)

This was in 1921, a week or two after Sheriff Sid Hatfield, who'd stood up for the Matewan miners and their families, was murdered along with his good friend Ed Chambers. They'd traveled to McDowell County to stand trial for charges of dynamiting a coal tipple, but were executed in front of their wives by a group of Baldwin-Felts agents standing at the top of the courthouse stairs. Hatfield was killed instantly, and Chambers was slaughtered with a shot to the back of his head.

Word spread from mountaintop to dark hollow that Hatfield, the miners' hero, had been murdered in cold blood, and armed union men were already congregating along the Little Coal River, talking about revenge, about marching on Mingo County to free other radicals, end martial law, and organize the non-unionized miners. The plan didn't make sense, but that's the way of a mob. Nothing has to make sense.

"Please, Ruben. I have a bad feeling about this! Don't go!" I pleaded. Mrs. Kelly was in the kitchen with Nora, trying not to listen. "West Virginia is so violent, all you have to do is sneeze to be beaten and tossed in the tank!" But

Ruben could never say no to John Lewis.

Then Nora got involved and said the three of us could go with Ruben, make an adventure of it. Mrs. Kelly had no mothers due for two weeks, so we all began to collect medical supplies and food for the camps. The next day, I went down to Union Station for train tickets.

It's the dog days of August, muggy and hot, when our little Pittsburgh coalition climbs out of the passenger coach in Marmet, a village on the banks of the Kanawha River. Right away we can see there's big trouble. Close to ten thousand miners have already gathered, and the men are armed with rifles and revolvers. I've never been in such a crowd and the mood of the men is ugly.

Ruben and the other men from our coalition rush off to try to talk to the leaders, but no one will listen. Urging them on is Bill Blizzard, the fiery southern West Virginia organizer. He pushes Ruben aside. Deep in the crowd, our friend Mother Jones stands on a dynamite box, but her back is turned and she doesn't see us.

"Tell your husbands and fathers . . . tell them there's no need for bloodshed!" she cries, seeing how things are going and where they may end. "Bring them to their senses!" The women, mothers and sisters, daughters and lovers, try, but it's no good; the union men's anger has already been ignited. They begin marching like soldiers, wearing red bandannas around their necks, toward Logan and Mingo, the last of the nonunionized counties. They're going for the mine owners, the bosses, anyone who opposes them. They don't give a damn!

Like an army of ants the mass moves south, thirteen thousand of them now, some say, over mountains and through valleys, high on their own rage and moonshine. We should have just gone home when Ruben saw how it was, but he still thinks he can do some good. For one brief moment my husband and I hold each other. He wears a red bandanna, like all the others, and I kiss it for luck. "Love you," I say with my hand on his cheek. He picks me up laughing and swings me around; then Nora, Mrs. Kelly, and I lose track of him and travel along with the medics.

It's on the third day, at the edge of Logan County, that all hell breaks loose. The coal company forces, wearing white armbands, have built fortified positions at the top of Blair Mountain; their weapons, machine guns and carbines, point straight downhill. Within minutes we're surrounded by men in hand-to-hand combat, guns going off and the smell of liquid courage on half the fellows' breath.

Through the crowd I catch sight of two men down on my lover. One has his hands around Ruben's throat.

It wasn't a bullet that killed my husband. The truth is much worse. I held the murder weapon, a rifle still wet with blood, that I'd lifted from a dead miner's hands. One slashing blow, from the butt of the gun, used as a club and meant for the man straddling Ruben's chest with his hands around Ruben's neck, crushed my lover's skull. Rage is

contagious, and I meant to kill someone, just not my husband.

Ruben's brown eyes go wide and snap
shut as his life's blood flows out of him,
down around his red bandanna, onto
the ground, and I collapse as if the blow
had hit me.

"Lizbeth!" Nora yells and whips into
action. She crawls forward, dodging
bullets, grabs the rifle, and throws it like
a red-hot poker; it skitters on the road
among the men's feet, and she drags
me, screaming, back into the crowd.

Within hours we were hidden in the
back of a Baptist preacher's wagon,
heading north toward Pittsburgh. Two
hundred men died that day. Some say
three hundred. I never saw Ruben again,
and no one else knows what really happened but Mrs. Kelly, who's under the
ground, and Nora, four thousand miles
away.

I untie my shoes and sink my feet into
the cold creek water. For years I have
carried that rusted tin box of guilt with

me. Even if I trusted someone and explained that it had been an accident, who would I tell? If they'd never been in a riot or on a battlefield, experienced the chaos, the fear, and the guilt, how would they understand?

Oh, Ruben . . . I take a deep breath, blow away the sorrow. Above me a small bird in the naked branches preens in the last of the golden slanting light. Bitsy and I call her the "water bird" because of her song, like water in a brook running over the stones.

"Water bird," I whisper, wiping my tears and pulling myself up on my knees, "these hands have killed and these hands have brought life into the world. If I were a religious woman, I would call upon God to ease my soul."

I try to think what my prayer would be. *Light of the World, take this sorry heart and cleanse it. Take my sorry self and make me new. Forgive me . . . forgive me for everything . . .*

I hold my work-worn mitts up into the fading sunlight, then bend over and wash them in the clear, cold creek water, wash away the guilt and sorrow. I cup the cold water and wash my face, wash away the tears, all those tears. *I once was lost, but now I'm found* . . . I sing the words we sang at the Wildcat Mine cave-in, then I lean back and stare up at the evening star.

A few years ago, I would have been afraid to lie in the leaves alone in the darkening woods. Now I find peace.

40

October 5, 1930. Rainbow
around the almost full moon.

Another delivery, Carlin Hummingbird, 10 pounds! The third
son of Addie and Norton Hummingbird, the Indian family of
Dark Hollow. The baby was born
without fuss in their log cabin
along the creek. Mr. Hummingbird stayed in the kitchen, and
Addie was very self-sufficient. I
just rocked in a chair and Bitsy
tended to everything, then we
did the delivery together. Very
little bleeding. No tears. Mrs.
Hummingbird gave me a beaded

basket that will be very nice for my knitting.

Target Practice

It's been a few cold rainy days, but around two, when the sun comes out, I see Bitsy, through the front window, lead Star out of the gate, heading, I imagine, toward the Hope River. She's been strange lately, running over to the Wildcat Mine and to Hazel Patch nearly every day. Twice I saw her sneaking food from the cupboard wrapped in a white dishcloth. If she wants to take food to Thomas, she doesn't need to tiptoe around. The fact is, though I haven't really admitted this to her, I miss her company, her puttering around the house, the sound of her voice.

"Bitsy!" I lock my journal and stuff it under the cushions, then throw open the blue door. "Bitsy! Can I come?"

She shrugs. "Okay," she says, surprised, and pulls me up on the horse behind her.

* * *

Cloudless blue sky, smell of fallen leaves, the sound of the Hope roaring over its banks in the distance . . .

We clop along Wild Rose Road, riding double, and I wave to Mrs. Maddock, who sits in her wheelchair on her front porch. She's wearing her blank public face today, but she nods. If I hadn't had tea with her a few weeks ago, I would never have guessed the warmth that's inside her.

"Are you going to hunt?" I ask my companion, making reference to the gun balanced in its case over Star's neck. "What for? Ducks? Geese? Turkey?"

"Just target practice. I don't like to do it around the house. The sound of the rifle might irritate you." She's probably right. I have been a little snappy lately.

I surprise myself when I ask her, "Will you show me how?"

Since Blair Mountain, I haven't touched a firearm and before that never, not even Ruben's Colt revolver.

I can't see my companion's face because she is sitting in front of me, but her back softens, like a smile, against my chest. "Sure. I didn't know you were interested."

"I don't know if I am. I just want to feel what *you* feel when you shoot. I know you like it, and who knows, someday I might need to hunt for myself." Bitsy shrugs as if she can't imagine such a thing, and that's the end of it until we get to the dirt path that winds down to the raging water.

"I have targets set up along the bank." We slide off Star's back, lead her through the brush, and tie her to a small sycamore. On a rise where the willows thin out, my friend has nailed three old rusted signs to the trees: a red Coca-Cola sign with a soda jerk peeking out from behind the bottle, a green Case Tractor sign, and a Days Work Chewing Tobacco sign, all riddled with bullet holes. Scattered along the trunk of a fallen tree are tin cans, which we begin to set up.

"Where do you get these cans?" I break the silence. "We haven't had any store-bought food since that Heinz soup Hester gave us when he was injured."

"Mildred saves them for me."

"Mildred Miller? She knows you shoot?"

"Sure, I bring them a rabbit now and then. She makes a stew almost like Mama's." This surprises me, as if Bitsy has another life, one I don't know about.

"Okay," I say, banishing my dark reflections and adjusting my wire-rimmed specs. "Let's get going. What do I do?"

Bitsy is a patient teacher. She shows me how to load the rifle. She demonstrates how to stand sideways and aim through the sight. She shoots off a few rounds, perfectly knocking the cans off the logs.

"Now you try. Tuck the stock into your right shoulder where it fits."

I experiment with a few places, but nothing seems right.

"Here," she says and places the gun where she thinks it should be. "You'll have to get used to it. Put your other hand under the body of the rifle, aim down the barrel, then pull the trigger."

I squint, dreading the loud noise.

"Hold it tight against your shoulder! Don't let it slip, or it will kick you in the arm."

I swallow. Why is this so hard? It's supposed to be fun.

Boom! The Favorite Sweet Corn can flips off the log!

"I hit it!" I'm dancing around.

"Hey, watch the gun!"

That clears my head. "Pretty good, huh?"

Bitsy smiles at my enthusiasm. "A born cracker shot."

"Can I do it again?"

All afternoon, we take turns back and forth. My first shot, it turns out, was beginner's luck. It takes eleven more before I hit another can. "We better not waste any more bullets," I say, cutting short the practice. "You might need them for hunting."

"It's okay. Byrd will give me some more." Byrd Bowlin again! I plunk down on the log, and Bitsy sits next to me, putting the rifle back into its case.

"It's serious with him, isn't it?"

She shrugs and gets a faraway look in her eyes. "He's my family now." That hurts a little. I thought I was Bitsy's family. "Thomas isn't coming back, and Ma has gone to the other side."

"Thomas is gone? I thought he was still hiding out in the mountains. Gone where?"

"Philadelphia. Last week Reverend Miller and I drove him to Torrington, where he hopped a freight train. He had a little cash set away and has already sent word through the reverend that he got a job driving electric streetcars.

"I told him the sheriff was probably going to drop the investigation after Katherine talked to him, but Thomas doesn't want to come back. Says it's too dangerous for any black man who wants to be something and mining's no life for him anymore."

Black men and white, I reflect as I pick burrs off my trousers, work side by side in the mines, but a black can never supervise a white or use the heavy machinery. Negroes get the same pay but worse work. If he stayed, he would be handpicking coal forever.

"Thomas wants Byrd and me to come

east," Bitsy goes on. "Says he can get Byrd a job like his with the Atlantic Railway."

My heart sinks. Truly that hurts me, that I wasn't included as one of the trusted few when Thomas left and that they are thinking of leaving, but I keep it to myself. "Do you and Byrd want to live in Philadelphia?"

"Maybe." She stares toward the roaring Hope as a pair of mallards rise. "You could come too . . ."

For a minute I contemplate the idea. I used to think I'd do anything to go back to the city, but now I'm not sure . . . the noise, the crowded streets, the stench of the smoke from the factories.

"No, I lived in Pittsburgh and before that Chicago. I like it here now . . . the sound of the river, seeing the new leaves in spring, watching them turn colors and fly away in the fall." This surprises me, that my exile is no longer a punishment. "So are you going? Going to Philly to live with Bowlin?"

"I'm thinking about it. I miss Thomas . . . And I have dreams."

Dreams . . . I let out my air. She has dreams. Of course. Bitsy is young and smart, why would she want to live at the end of Wild Rose in someone else's house forever? But what are my dreams? I've never had any. Just lived from one high or low, one triumph or catastrophe to the next.

Bitsy stands, collects her rifle, and unties Star as if ready to leave. "And it would be better work for Bowlin, driving a streetcar. I can't help remembering the cave-in at the Wildcat. How the emergency siren went on and on, ripping the sky. I was so scared . . . I'm seriously thinking about it." She turns for the road, expecting me to follow, and leads the horse back through the brush.

I just sit there. One of the bullets has gone through my heart.

41

Quarrel

Thursday, returning at noon from cutting hay all by myself in the back pasture (Bitsy is off to Hazel Patch again), I'm surprised to find, on the front porch, a cardboard carton with an envelope attached.

Thinking it must be something from one of the families we've helped or maybe another gift from Katherine, I tear the box open. What I find is a collection of medical equipment, a blood pressure cuff, some medicines whose names don't look familiar, and a packet of gauze. There are also two medical books: *Health Knowledge,* which includes everything from care of infants to care of old people, and *Pediatrics, the Hygienic and Medical Treatment of Children,* volume 1. This must be something from Dr. Blum. I go back to the note, folded in quarters on lined paper and taped to the top. It's from Becky Myers.

"Dear Patience, I waited as long as I could, but I thought you might have gone to a birth and I have to leave this afternoon. I'm on my way to Charlottesville to be Dr. Blum's nurse. He wrote me a few weeks ago asking me to come, and I agreed to go because the state is out of money and has cut my funding. Apparently a public health nurse, in these hard times, isn't considered essential. Anyway, it will be an adventure.

"I still worry about you. Please be careful!" She underlines "careful." Always the worrywart, I think. "The mood in town is ugly. So many of the unemployed are just hanging around. You know what they say: idle hands do the devil's work. I'll send my address when

I find out where I'm to live. Wish me luck driving over the mountains.

"All my best. Becky Myers."

I kick the carton across the porch. What good is this stuff if I lose another friend? Katherine's in Baltimore. Bitsy is thinking of moving to Philadelphia. Now Becky's on her way to Charlottesville.

By evening Bitsy is still not home, so, in a glum mood, I milk Moonlight early and heat up leftover potato soup, all the while getting more aggravated. Around nine, I hear an engine whining up the road and look out the kitchen window to see Bitsy jump out of Byrd's father's truck. She kisses her lover, long and sweet, then trots into the house, just a little too bouncy.

"Have a good time?" I ask sarcastically, but she doesn't get it. I'm itching for a fight; I just need a topic.

"You bet! I delivered a baby, and Byrd showed me how to drive a tractor! We were helping the Millers bring in the last of their hay." She pulls out a two-dollar bill and proudly lays it on the table.

"What baby? Whose baby?"

"Oh, this lady from Cold Springs. You don't know her, Fiona Lincoln. She was visiting Hazel Patch and this was her fourth . . . her third or her fourth . . . She's Mildred's cousin, not due for another few weeks, but the baby was fine and breathed right away. When her water bag broke, they called me in from the fields."

"Bitsy, you can't just go around catching babies whenever you feel like it! You aren't even certified. What if something happened?" In my irritation, I ignore the fact that I'm no great expert. I was only certified a few years ago.

"And besides, you didn't have any supplies. What if the cord was tangled around the neck? What if the feet came first? What if the mother hemorrhaged? You think this birthing business is a lark, but it's truly life and death!"

"Mrs. Miller was there. She's been to four deliveries, and I've read DeLee's text on obstetrics cover to cover. Mildred boiled water and scissors and twine for the cord . . . What was I supposed to do? The baby was coming . . ."

There are tears in her eyes, and even though my attitude is unreasonable, I don't care. I stand and throw my soup bowl into the sink, watching with satisfaction as it breaks and the potato gruel splashes up on the wall, then grab my work jacket and slam out the back door. "You were way out of line!"

Drunk with righteous indignation, I enjoy the hot rush at first, but the cool night air sobers me.

"Miss Patience," I hear Bitsy calling into the black. "Patience?"

Maybe I should get on Star and ride somewhere . . . but where? To the vet's? I don't think so . . . instead, I head down across the pasture to the creek and sit on a flat rock, listening to the water. There's the smell of the fallen leaves on the ground and frost coming. When my butt gets too cold, I wander back to the barn.

It's not just that Bitsy did a delivery without me. She's right, the woman needed her, and who am I to be so sanctimonious? It's everything else . . . Shivering, I quietly pull open the barn door and seek the warmth of the hay.

"Miss Patience!" Bitsy calls out the back again. "Patience?" She sounds like she's crying.

Prepared to sleep curled in the loft, I grab Star's horse blanket and climb up the ladder. The real issue isn't Bitsy doing a solo delivery; it's that each day I feel her slipping further away. And why shouldn't she leave? She has a community with the Hazel Patch folk. She has her brother Thomas in Philly. She has her lover, Byrd Bowlin!

I squirm and turn over to get comfortable. That's when I feel it, not a kick or a thump, more of a tickle. It's been over twenty years, but the feeling's unmistakable. I place my hands on my lower abdomen. There's something moving inside me, something alive.

Quickening

How could I have not noticed? But then I haven't been stomach sick or any more tired than usual. And my periods, always irregular, when did I have my last one? The flutter inside happens again! No need to figure it out. There was only one night I could have gotten pregnant . . . Through the cracks in the barn walls, I see the lights in the house go off.

"Moonlight," I whisper to the cow downstairs. "We're going to have a baby!" For a few minutes, I lie in the dark, overjoyed, but that doesn't last.

Fears swiftly besiege me like wasps dropping out of their paper nest. How can I tell the vet he's going to be a father? But how can I not tell him? On the other hand, how can I raise a child alone? Despair follows fear. The shame of it! The gossip . . . I'll be an outcast. My short-lived career as a midwife will be over.

Though it's chilly in the barn, I wait a few hours, until Bitsy must be asleep,

then sneak into the house, crawl between the warm covers, and lie staring
out the window. Maybe Bitsy will help
me. She likes kids . . . no, she wants to
be with Bowlin. How about Becky Myers? No, she's too proper, and anyway
she's far away in Virginia by now. Mrs.
Maddock? Ridiculous! I've had one intimate talk with her. That makes us best
friends?

In the morning, while Bitsy's out in the
barn milking Moonlight, I pore through
my obstetrical textbook looking for a
way out. I try to remember what Mrs.
Kelly told me about tansy and pennyroyal, two herbs that might cause my
period to start.

My recollection is that she once ad-
vised Molly Doyle, who already had
nine children, to make a strong brew of
both herbs and then drink it three times
daily. "The tincture will sometimes re-
store regularity," she told the frightened
woman. "God will decide if you are to
have another child."

At the time I was shocked; they were

both good Catholics. I asked Mrs. Kelly, in the self-righteous way that the young will do, "How could you, a midwife, a bringer of life into the world, make such a suggestion? You're basically telling her how to have an abortion."

"You could look at it that way," Sophie responded, "or you could think of the mother as a *person*. Can the poor woman survive another baby? Catholic, Baptist, or Hindu, every woman has her limits. And can the family manage to absorb and nourish another child without becoming paupers? The herbs aren't that strong. Sometimes they work, sometimes they don't. It's up to the Lord who lives and who doesn't."

Now here I am considering the concoction myself. I press my hand just above my pubic bone. How many months has it been since I was with Hester during the thunderstorm? Early August, late July, and it's now mid-October. Around fourteen weeks! According to DeLee, too early to feel movement. Too late for a miscarriage. But Dr. DeLee doesn't know everything.

October 13, 1930. Waning moon still high in the pink sky at dawn.

I might as well record it. Day before yesterday, Bitsy delivered her first baby alone. The mother is Mildred Miller's cousin Fiona Lincoln from Cold Springs. Very short labor, less than one hour. No time for me to come. No problems. Present were Mildred Miller and Bitsy. Male infant. Weight unknown.

Liberty

Air crisp as an apple right off the tree. The smell of frost on the fallen leaves. It's almost dark, and over the mountain, the three-quarters moon rises, big as a goose egg.

"Is that Maddock?" Bitsy asks as we ride up Wild Rose Road on the way back from the grove where we have been gathering hazelnuts. We never talked about our fight, just got up the next morning and went on with our work. Then we got so busy cutting wood, it seemed as though it never happened. Bitsy still doesn't know my condition. A gunnysack, half full of the small soft-shelled sweet nuts, rattles over my lap. "Is that Maddock? There by the fence."

The man stands at his mailbox wearing a dark coat and hat; all I can see in the dim light is his white, deadpan face. He puts out his hand like a traffic cop.

"Sheriff Hardman's looking for you," he announces, and the peace of the evening drains out of me. This is the last thing I was expecting. With my worries about my pregnancy, our other troubles have taken a backseat. The lawman's visit could be anything: more questions about Thomas, questions about the baby I buried behind the barn, or even the long-feared arrest for what happened on Blair Mountain.

"Do you know what he wanted?" I act as though it's no big concern, as though Hardman is likely to visit any old time, but inside I grow cold.

"The grocer's wife is in labor, the blind woman. Her husband, Mr. Bittman, asked Hardman to get the midwife right away. My Sarah told him I would drive you." He looks away, embarrassed to seem neighborly. My stomach is still in knots, but maybe the copper was only trying to be helpful.

Forty-five minutes later, after rushing home to clean up, get our birth kit, and take care of the animals, we bump into Liberty in Mr. Maddock's Ford pickup. The entrance to the Bittman apartment, located above the grocery, is up the back stairs.

Standing on the wooden porch, I knock twice as Maddock pulls away in his truck and am surprised when Mrs. Wade answers. Not her again, Hardman's sister, the woman who drove me crazy at Prudy Ott's birth!

"What took you so long?" she begins by way of a greeting. "We've been worried sick." Behind her, five people sit at a round oak table, just finishing supper. Lilly, the young pregnant woman, a tall redhead, stares blankly at a space over the stove, but her face is turned our way.

"Oh, Patience," she says with a laugh. "We're so glad you're here. Mother's been fretting all day, but I'm fine. These are my parents, Mr. and Mrs. Wade, my uncle Billy Hardman, and of course B.K. Is Bitsy here too?"

"Right behind you." My friend has already moved into the room. She puts down the birth satchel and touches Lilly on the shoulder as Lilly reaches up and hugs her. If Mrs. Wade is still offended by the color of my partner's skin, she knows not to say it. To the blind girl we all look the same, just as it should be.

"You smell good," Lilly says when Bitsy hugs her.

"It must be Patience's homemade soap. She puts lavender in it."

"Oh, we must get some for the store, then! Could we, B.K.? Wouldn't that be lovely? If it wasn't too expensive, the women would snatch it up."

"Yes, honey," says B.K., standing and placing his dish in the sink.

The beautiful redhead stops her chatter and begins to swing her head slowly from side to side. It's a new gesture to me, but I recognize a contraction when I see one. The room goes quiet, and B.K. steps up behind his wife to rub her shoulders. When she's done, she rests her head on his stomach. "Thanks, hon."

"Lordy, how long must this go on?" Mrs. Wade wonders.

"Bertha," Mr. Wade warns, "it's the midwife's job to figure that out. You can take a break now, go back to the spare bedroom, and read." Bertha slashes him a look but does what he says, clears the table, and stalks out. "I'm going over to my office," Lilly's father tells us. "Call if you need anything."

"I better get a move on too." That's Hardman, *Uncle Billy.* "I came by your place on Wild Rose and waited for a while, but had to get back to town. Maddock bring you? He's an odd duck . . ." The sheriff doesn't wait for my opinion but shrugs into his police-man's jacket. "Give 'em hell, honey!" he encourages his niece.

"I have something of yours, Miss

Murphy," he says to me, then moves out the door.

This can't be good. "Something for me?"

He nods his scarred chin and tips his head toward the porch. Outside a fog has moved in and silenced the street. Hardman pulls out a yellow sheet of paper folded in quarters. "It's been in my top desk drawer for a long time."

My hands shake as I take the document and hold it up to the porch light. I'm thinking that this is something I've feared seeing someday, a wanted poster with my photo on it.

I'm surprised, when I unfold the parchment, to discover a drawing of a woman who only vaguely resembles me. The hair is dark, they got that right, and there are wire-rimmed glasses, but the face is too long and the almond eyes look almost Asian. An artist has sketched a composite from a vague description.

"Two Hundred Dollar Reward," the announcement reads, "for the arrest of Elizabeth Snyder, approximately 30 years of age, known radical and union organizer from Pittsburgh. Miss Snyder, an associate of agitator Mother Jones, is suspected of the murder of coal miner Ruben Gordesky of Matewan. Information about the whereabouts of the suspect can be given to any local law enforcement officer."

"Almost everything about the notice is wrong." I look up.

"I know," Hardman agrees. "Picture doesn't look much like you, either. That's why it took me so long to figure it out."

"I wasn't an organizer, just a sympathizer. My husband was the organizer, Ruben Gordesky. He was a wonderful man but never a miner. We lived in Pittsburgh, where he worked for the UMWA, and he just came to southern West Virginia to see if he could settle the miners down, avoid a riot. I'm proud of him." It isn't until I say Ruben's name that the tears come. "So what now? What are you going to do? Arrest me?"

"This." He looks straight at me, rips up the paper, and stuffs it into his shirt pocket.

"And those other lawmen involved? The outsiders. Do they know?"

"They were here on another matter. Revenuers from Pittsburgh. Someone in Union County has been running moonshine into the city. They aren't interested in Blair Mountain or what happened there. No one else is either. There haven't been any prosecutions for years."

I let out my breath and stare down at the gas streetlights. In the fog, they look like they have rainbows around them. "It was the worst day of my life. They were shooting at us. Ruben was down. One of the goons was on him. I was only trying to keep him from choking Ruben . . . and I bashed in my husband's head instead . . . an accident."

"I've watched you for a year. You're no killer. Too soft."

Though I should keep my mouth shut, I can't let that go by. "Midwives aren't soft. We are warriors."

He smiles. "Okay. But you still wouldn't hurt a fly unless you had to. I can see that. Not on purpose." He places his hand on my shoulder, a stiff gesture but one of acceptance, and I would like to hug him, but just then Bitsy yells from the bedroom. "Patience?"

"Got to go." I pull open the screen.

"Give 'em hell, honey." He uses the same words he used with his niece Lilly. "And tell Bitsy to say hello to Thomas for me. Proudfoot is a good man. After Katherine MacIntosh told me about her husband's previous suicide threats, I dropped the investigation. Finally closed the case as a self-inflicted death yesterday."

In the empty kitchen I lean back on the door. By his words, everything in the room has been altered; the light is brighter, the colors more vivid, the shadows less dark.

"Patience?" my partner calls again. I want to tell Bitsy that a great weight has been lifted. I want to tell her that her brother is safe, that the cops are officially done with it, but there's no time.

"Patience, *where are you?*"

"Coming!"

* * *

In the Bittmans' small bedroom, I'm surprised to see the lights dimmed. There's not much space to move around, but our patient is making the most of it. She stands in the candlelight in a blue checked nightdress in the center of a blue braided rug, swaying back and forth during a contraction and making little noises in a high-pitched voice, almost as though she's singing. "Mmmm. Mmmm. Mmmm." Bitsy wrinkles her brow at me, wondering where I've been, but even if there was time, I wouldn't try to explain.

"Hi, Lilly, it's Patience." I touch the girl on her arm. "Are the pains coming regularly now?"

"Every five minutes, right on," answers B.K., consulting his pocket watch.

"Well, if you're ready, I can check you and your baby. Bitsy and I are here for the duration."

I watch as Lilly easily feels her way back to the bed and, without hesitation, flops down and pulls up her shift. Her underpants are still dry.

"No leaking fluid yet?"

"I don't think so." Lilly's palest blue

eyes are open and she stares at the ceiling, seeing only blackness . . . or perhaps red or blue . . . maybe it's like when you lie in the sun with your eyes closed and see colored lights.

I place my hands on her belly, feeling for the baby's position abdominally. Then I have Bitsy check and listen to the fetal heartbeat.

"Around a hundred and thirty beats per minute, and the head's down," she reports with a grin.

I double-check and nod. One hundred thirty.

"Is she close?" B.K. asks, standing at the door with his back turned.

If the vet wants to know the status of a horse in labor, he just sticks his hand into the horse's vagina, but the men who wrote the West Virginia Midwifery Code think we midwives wouldn't have enough sense to limit our internal examinations or use sterile gloves, so I break the law only when I have to, and right now there's no need.

"Best guess, the baby will come after midnight," I hedge. (That could mean two A.M. or six.) "In an hour or so, we'll have a better idea. If Lilly could rest, that would be good."

"Horsefeathers! That's not going to happen," the redhead interrupts. "It hurts less when I'm sitting or walking. Are you done now, Miss Patience?" The "Miss Patience" gives me the shivers, but I let it slide. "Whoooo, here comes one now!" The woman jumps up and sways her whole body, her long red curls moving with her. "Mmmm. Mmmm. Mmmm." B.K. steps back into the bedroom, wanting to help but unsure how.

"Hold her like this," says Bitsy. She has him step forward and put his arms around his wife so she can lean into him.

"That was a doozy!" Lilly informs us.

"Good. The strong ones will bring the baby. I'm going to make sure all of our supplies are in order. Did you sterilize your sheets?"

"I went to Nurse Becky's baby class before she left for Charlottesville. Ma and I ironed everything and wrapped it in paper."

"That's great. I know she gives good instructions." I slip out of the room. The apartment is small, and I can hear the patient's birth song through the walls. My plan, since Bitsy has decided she's a big midwife, is to let her take the lead and see how she does.

Bertha

When I return to the kitchen to make tea and check to be sure everything is ready, I'm disappointed to discover Mrs. Wade back at the table.

"Hello. I thought you were napping." There's no way I want this busybody around Lilly, making her nervous, distracting her from her job, even if she is the girl's mother.

"I tried to, but I couldn't. She's our only child, you know. We adopted because we couldn't have our own, and then when she went blind . . . I know I'm overprotective."

"Lilly wasn't born blind?"

"No. She lost her sight the year all the children got measles. A half dozen went blind in the county, and a few were struck deaf too. Thank the Lord, no one got both. She went to the School for the Blind in Charleston for a few years, but we missed her so, we brought her home. She can read Braille and do housework, even sew."

"All the children?"

"Yes, it was that bad winter. Sickness swept through Delmont and Liberty, Torrington and Oneida. Lilly was four. Many didn't survive." I realize she's talking about an epidemic of German measles, the three-day kind, a wicked strain that causes high fever.

There's a groan and then B. K. Bittman's voice singing, low. *"Will the circle be unbroken . . ."* Mrs. Wade sweeps me a big-eyed look, and I put my hand over hers. It's an unexpected gesture. I was horrified to discover the intrusive woman here an hour ago, but now I find myself sympathetic. That's the way it is, Nora once told me. No matter who they are or what they've done, when you hear someone's story you see him or her differently.

"By and by, Lord, by and by," B.K. goes on. He has a strong voice and accompanies himself on the guitar.

"There's a better home awaiting."
Bitsy joins in and then Lilly.

Bertha smiles. "They've been married five years. We'd given up on grandchildren. I thought maybe Lilly would be barren like me, but God heard our prayers."

Barren, I think . . . I assumed I was barren too, and look what happened!

For the next hour, as the contractions roll on, I double-check the contents of the birth bag that we so hastily packed while Mr. Maddock waited in his truck. With the excitement, I'd even forgotten to eat. I've had no food since breakfast and am feeling a little sick, so I ask Mrs. Wade for a cold glass of milk. I still have no clue what I am going to do about my *nonbarren* state. For a moment sadness overcomes me, but I shoo it away, as if it were a pesky housefly. No time for self-indulgence.

When I peek into the birth room the first time, Lilly is slow dancing with her husband, wiggling her hips erotically in a way I might find embarrassing if it weren't part of the birth dance. The second time, she's leaning over a chair while Bitsy rubs her back. Sweat now beads on her brow, a good sign. I catch Bitsy's eye and lift up my thumb.

Bitsy gives me a thumbs-up too and says out loud, "She's the cat's meow!"

Lilly laughs.

"For sure!" B.K. adds.

Lilly

The third time I tiptoe down the hall, Mrs. Wade follows. "Can I peek too?" I nod reluctantly. At least she's getting the idea that we want to disturb them as little as possible. When a laboring woman has found a successful routine, you don't want to break it.

In the dim room, lighted only by a gas lamp, Lilly now swings her hair and moans, then closes her sightless eyes and takes a deep breath.

"They're getting stronger, Mama, but don't worry."

"Okay, sweetheart. I'm so proud of you."

"How did she know you were standing with me?" I ask when we're back in the kitchen.

"Smell," the patient's mother answers. "She says my distinct smell is like bread baking. Will she need a birth bath?"

That takes me aback. Then I remember Prudy's wild labor and how I invented the "birth bath" just to get Mrs. Wade, Priscilla Blum, and my nervous friend Becky out of the way. Apparently, she now thinks a bath is the latest thing for women before they deliver.

"Do they have a tub?"

"Just a little one. Nothing like the Ott home."

"Well, we'll see. It couldn't hurt, but she might not need it. Prudy was awfully tense. Lilly is loose as a goose, which is what you want . . . until pushing. Then you hope the woman can bear down like she means it."

By the sounds in the bedroom, I can tell that the contractions are coming one after the other. "Can you boil the water? It might be soon." Mrs. Wade stands up and bustles around, glad to be put into action, and I slide back into the bedroom.

"Oh, Patience, I don't know if I can do this!" Lilly complains when she hears me approach. "It hurts like the dickens!"

"It won't be much longer. If it helps, you can lean on the baby a little, nothing too forceful. No holding your breath." I picture just a rim of the cervix left, and I've found that at this stage, between letting go and bearing down, it helps to give the patient something to do. Any time now, I expect her voice will drop and we will know that the baby is coming.

Bitsy stands back and puts one arm around my waist. We both find pleasure in watching a woman who's comfortable with her body. Each time a contraction comes, Lilly's blind eyes get big and she takes a few breaths, then holds on to her husband and rocks back and forth.

"Should I get out of the way soon?" B.K. asks nervously. "There's a shipment of canned goods down in the store that need shelving—"

"No, sir, Mr. Bittman!" This is Lilly. "I want you *here.* You helped make this baby, you can damn well help me get him out!" That seems to settle the matter. B.K. shrugs. Bitsy catches my eye. Now we know for sure that birth is imminent. When a well-bred woman begins to curse, she's nearly ready.

"It's fine either way, B.K.," I reassure him. "I've had several fathers stay for the delivery, and they were very helpful. That's one thing about giving birth at home. In the hospital, the papa would never be allowed in the delivery room, they'd be afraid he'd faint, but here we can do what we want. If your being in the room will help Lilly, we don't mind."

B.K. stares at the bottles of tincture and olive oil, the sterile packs of scissors and cord, the packages of rags we've laid out on the bureau and turns, overwhelmed, but before he can slip away another contraction comes on and he's called into action as Lilly's leaning post.

The beginning of the pushing stage isn't clear; no dramatic "Uggggh!" But after our patient has been bearing down in earnest for an hour, I call Mrs. Wade to bring the hot water. It isn't Mrs. Wade but Mr. Wade, eyes averted, who carries in the steaming cast-iron kettle.

"How you doin', honey babe?"

"Want to stay, Daddy?" Lilly asks, surprising us.

"No, ma'am!" he says good-naturedly, backing out of the room. "I'll be in the parlor with my head under a pillow."

"Lilly knows Pa by the smell of his tobacco and the sound of his size-thirteen shoes," Mrs. Wade explains, slipping past him from the hall.

"I can hear you, Mama!"

The soon-to-be grandmother puts her hand in the shock of red curls and pulls gently. "We are never going to get the knots out of your hair."

Just to be dramatic, Lilly thrashes her hair around like a cabaret singer. Then a contraction hits, and she goes back to work.

Caulbearer

Bitsy smooths the covers, giving me the signal that she thinks it's time to get the patient into bed, but I shake my head no. Lilly hasn't complained of burning at the opening, so I think the baby's not there yet.

"Oh, honey, oh, honey," Mrs. Wade fusses, watching her daughter's face turn beet red and the veins bulge out on her neck. "I'm so sorry you have to go through this."

"It's okay, Ma. How do you think babies get born?" Lilly says with a laugh between contractions. B.K. rolls his eyes sympathetically toward his mother-in-law.

Finally I intervene. "Would you want to lie down for a minute, Lilly? See if it's time?"

"Do you think it could be?"

"Soon, yes. I think so."

The patient waddles over to the bed. B.K. lowers her down in front of him and is wedged against the headboard with his wife almost in his lap. When she spreads her legs, my mouth falls open and Bitsy and Mrs. Wade gasp. It is not a hairy little head sitting at the vaginal opening but a strange smooth wet orb, unearthly, the intact water bag. I've never seen a baby born in the caul before. The new mama reaches down to feel it.

"Is this the head? Is everything all right? It's so squishy." Lilly's fingers are her eyes, and she keeps tapping the bag, confused. B.K. turns away, afraid to look.

"It's the baby's sac. Your water still hasn't broken. The old midwives say it's a lucky sign, to be born in the caul. Keep pushing!"

Lilly does what I tell her, and I step back to give Bitsy an opportunity to catch the baby. She's done most of the labor coaching, and it's clear from the birth at Hazel Patch a few days ago that I won't always be at her side.

My partner moves in with her sterile gloves on, and I pull on mine too. The head, or the head inside the water bag, emerges slowly, and the bag gets bigger and bigger but doesn't pop. The slippery sac gradually dilates everything until the baby, water bag and all, slips into Bitsy's hands. She looks at me as if to ask "What now?"

I reach over with a placenta pan, pinch the sac, and let the water flow out. Bitsy peels the sac off the infant's face the way, long ago, I pulled the sac off the filly's face when I went with Hester to the delivery of the foal.

"Is it okay?" Lilly whispers. "I don't hear a cry!"

I pull the baby into my lap and give it a rub. "It's a girl, and she's fine."

"The eyes are open." B.K. is seeing for his wife. "Now she's moving around. Here, feel." He takes his wife's hand and places it on the baby's stomach.

"Now she's turning pink," the husband continues. The baby lets out a reassuring wail.

That's when Lilly grabs her up, still wet with the cord dangling. "Oh, my baby!" she croons. "My baby." The end of the birth song.

Ten minutes later, I'm sitting in the rocking chair while Bitsy cleans up efficiently. What am I going to do without her if she and Byrd Bowlin move away? Behind me, I can hear Mrs. Wade sobbing. "Thank the Lord. Thank you, Lord Jesus."

I feel like crying myself, and I'm not sure if it's from the wonder of birth or just plain exhaustion. Then there's my situation. Even in the best of circumstances pregnant women are emotional.

I wipe my eyes and watch as Lilly and B.K. explore their newborn. The husband paints pictures for his wife. Having a baby with such a husband would be a different matter. But I have no husband, no man to share a child with.

"I think her hair is going to be red, no surprise," observes the father. The new mother pinches the chubby little arms. She sniffs the infant all over, holds the baby up to her face, and licks it. That surprises me, but then I think of Moonlight. She licked her baby too.

Mrs. Wade edges up to the bed. She can't help herself.

"Oh, Ma! Look. Isn't she wonderful?"

"She's a beauty," Mrs. Wade says as she pulls Lilly's hair back and kisses her cheek. "Just like her mother."

"I'm going to call her Velvet," the new mother tells us, "because she's so soft. Oh, look at her little mouth, like a rosebud, and her tiny ears, like shells." Lilly's laughing and reading her baby with soft quick happy fingers as if she's reading Braille, and it comes to me . . .

We are only on this earth, as far as we know, one time, and we deserve to be happy. It's our job to be happy. In my mind I raise my hand, and another hand, my wiser hand, reaches out to me.

Let it be . . .

October 24, 1930. Sliver moon rising.

Birth of another female. This one to Lilly Bittman and her husband, B.K., of Liberty. Lilly is blind from German measles as a child, but you'd hardly know it. Her labor went well, and she

insisted that her husband stay with her.

I don't know why I got the impression from Mrs. Kelly that men couldn't be counted on at a delivery. All my experiences this year, with the exception of William MacIntosh, who fainted, have been good. The healthy female infant was born in the caul. The first time I've ever seen that. Bitsy delivered and did as well as I could myself. 7 pounds, 3 ounces. No tears, little bleeding. They named her Velvet.

Paid $10.00 credit at their grocery store, which is the best we've received in a long time.

42

Peril

In the dark hours of night, I hear Emma and Sasha barking, then the sound of a vehicle coming up Wild Rose Road. Sam Hill! I'm so tired . . . Mr. Wade missed the turn onto Salt Lick when he brought us home, and we didn't get in until midnight. Then I stayed up to write my notes and drink valerian tea.

Headlights flicker on the pitched bedroom ceiling. What now? Another baby? When I pad to the window to look out, I'm surprised to see three vehicles winding up the hill. This doesn't seem right.

"Bitsy!" I yell through the wall, "get your clothes on!" No one comes for the midwife with three autos. "We got trouble!"

As I hustle into my work pants and an old brown sweater, I hear Bitsy's feet hit the floor. Downstairs, I pull on my boots, grab the dogs, order them to stand down, then peek through the curtains. A truck and two dark sedans stop at the gate.

My companion crawls across the floor and holds on to my knee. "Who is it?" she whispers, crouching low.

"I can't tell. I can't see."

A man snickers in a high falsetto, and the car doors slam.

"Shuddup!" someone orders in a lower tone.

"Make me," the guy with a nasal voice counters. Laughter.

"There must be more than ten." I swallow hard, thinking of Becky Myers's warnings and watch as the gang pulls on white hoods, not the full Klan regalia, more like pillowcases. Bitsy knows what this means. Becky Myers did too.

"I'll get my guns." That's Bitsy.

"No, there's too many of them. If they have weapons and there's a firefight, we'll lose. We don't want shooting." I strain behind the curtain to see what's happening. No one has entered the yard yet, but two of the fellows move along the picket fence in either direction and another three are tying something to the gate.

We have no phone to call for help and, though we have an auto, sadly no gas. We could try to run for it on Star, but we'd be exposed in the meadow and the men might shoot or get to us before we could mount. There's a roar, and the fence under the old oak tree bursts into flames.

"How do you like that, nigger lover?"

"Nigger lover with her chocolate drop girlfriend!" the nasal guy yells, passing a glass container that shines in the firelight.

I put my hands over Bitsy's ears, but she shakes them off and I can feel tears on the side of her face.

"Yeah, ya nigger-loving slut . . . hey, hand me the jug."

Both sides of the picket fence are blazing now, circling us in a ring of fire, and the men stand back while someone pours gasoline on the handmade crooked cross tied to the gate. It bursts into flame.

"I'm so sorry, Patience," Bitsy whimpers, as though it's her fault. She slides down further on the floor and leans against the wall.

"Shhhh!" I rest my hand on my friend's head. No way are they going to get to her. No way are they going to put their rough white hands on her beautiful brown body. I'll go down trying to stop them.

Emma begins to growl again, and I tap her muzzle. I don't know what advantage silence gives, but I want it. The fire is dangerous, but perhaps the men only mean to frighten us, to intimidate. (If that's their plan, it's working.)

More swearing. More taunts. "Come on out, you sluts! Let's party!"

"Yeah, we want some pussy!"

"You take the white one. I'll take the brown."

"Hell, I'll do them both!"

That goes on for a while. The men in hoods have no faces. They could be anyone. I remember what Becky told me: when times are hard and people are suffering, there will be those who want to hurt someone.

Bitsy is sobbing now. I'd like to cry too, but what good would it do? I'll cry later. If there is a later . . . "Get a grip, Bitsy, and if it will make you feel better, go get the guns."

My friend scoots across the floor toward the pantry where she keeps her rifle and shotgun. She crawls back and sits with her back to the door, loading the ammunition. My mouth is as dry as a bale of hay, and I wonder, if she gives me a gun, will I remember how to use it?

Dancing shadows in the flames, the smell of kerosene and burning wood. A short, thick man pulls a half-burning picket off the fence and waves it like a torch. Three others follow. Then someone gets the bright idea of throwing his flaming brand at the house.

"Watch it, you almost hit me!" the low voice yells.

"Aw, shit, Aran! We're just having fun."

There's a scuffle, and the big man busts the smaller one in the chops. "I said no *names!*"

Aran, I think. That's one of the Bishop brothers, the moonshiners who gave Hester a hard time. What did we ever do to them? And the short loudmouth, that's probably Beef, the guy who kept whacking his horse when it died.

The Klansmen, or pretend Klansmen, whoever they are, continue to throw burning sticks at the house. *"Buffalo Girls, won't you come out tonight, come out tonight, come out tonight?"* someone sings.

"Yeah, I'll make mine *come.*" More laughter. More throwing of torches. One flaming brand hits the porch roof but skitters off into the leaves. The ground is too damp for the fire to spread, but if one should ignite the shingles, our roof will go up like a tender box.

"Bitsy, we gotta get out of here. We'll head for the barn, free the animals in case they try to set it on fire, and maybe in the confusion we can get on Star and ride away. If we stay here, we could be burned alive or captured, and there's no way I want those men to lay their dirty paws on us." What I'm thinking is, I'd rather go up in a blaze, but that might be an exaggeration.

We grab our jackets and crawl toward the kitchen. But what about the dogs? If I free them, they will attack the intruders and maybe get shot. If leave them in the house and it catches on fire, they'll be burned alive. I don't have a plan, except to save ourselves, so while the shouting goes on, I kiss them each on the nose and creep out the back. Sasha whines.

"Shhhhh!" I command, shutting the door and feeling terrible.

Buffalo Girls

Sheltered by the shadow of the house, we stay low and dash straight for the barn door. Inside, Star whinnies, but I lay my hands on her and she quiets down. First we push Moonlight and her calf out into the yard. Moonlight looks at the fire with bulging white eyes and trots around back with the calf right behind her. Then we grab the chickens, which refuse to get out of their boxes until we pick them up and throw them out the double doors. I can't blame them. How would we like to be yanked out of bed and hurled into the night?

For a moment I stare at our idle Oldsmobile. If only we could rev it up and roar out in it, past our attackers and down the mountain, but I know all that's left in the gas tank is fumes, and anyway, their vehicles are blocking the road. Finally I climb up the slatted side of Star's stall and mount her. Bitsy hands me her shotgun and slides on behind.

"Wait." I point down at two white feed sacks hanging over the hayrack. I don't yet know my intention, but I pull one over my head and hand one to Bitsy. "Put this on."

"What?" I can imagine her shocked expression. "I can't see."

"Shhhhhh!" I yank them off, lean over toward the scythe hanging on the barn wall, and slash two eyeholes in each of them. Feed sacks back over our heads, we look at each other. I'd laugh out loud if our situation weren't so terrifying.

Outside, Star trembles and shies when she first sees the fire, but I guide her away around the side of the barn. Apparently the men, still singing out front, don't know we're gone.

We have two choices. We can continue our course, trot around the rail fence, and escape up the back, or . . . something bothers me about running, leaving our little house, barn, and dogs for the fools to burn up. I've been running my whole life.

The Buffalo Soldiers were the brave black U.S. Cavalry men who fought in the West in the Civil War. The intruders call us the "Buffalo Girls," and that settles it!

"Hold your gun up where they can see it, Bitsy. Change of tactics. Those guys tick me off!"

"Oh, Miss Patience!" Bitsy squeaks, but she shifts her position and does what I say.

"Buffalo Girls, won't you come out

tonight?" the guys warble drunkenly. The wild laughter crescendos, the fire flares, and two more flaming pickets twirl toward our roof.

I nudge my horse into a canter. "Hold on," I growl, more for myself than for Bitsy. I have no idea what I'm doing. I just don't feel like sneaking away, coming back in the morning to find our sweet little home a pile of coals.

"You fucking pillow heads!" I yell the worst words I know as we gallop into the light, right up to the knot of men. The anger and fear in me come out like a roar. If Sheriff Hardman could see me now, he wouldn't think me so soft. I'm more pissed than these men could ever be. A pregnant woman protecting her nest!

"You fucking pillow heads!" my friend echoes and fires once into the air.

The singing comes to an abrupt halt. In the flickering firelight, the men are confused. Who are these new masked riders? Bitsy and I, on top of the wild-eyed beast, tower over them. "You have business here?" I growl in the lowest voice I can work up, nudging Star farther into the crowd. Bitsy reaches down and strips off one man's mask. He's too startled to speak, covers his face, and jumps into his truck.

"Coward!" I yell through my dusty feed sack. Bitsy gets into the spirit of things and fires into the air twice more.

I dance Star around as we pull off three more head covers. The other men duck down where I can't reach them and bump into one another as they scuttle like crabs. I'm sure they don't realize that the aggressors on the horse are Bitsy and me, in control now—the Buffalo Girls!

Flames, I am sure, are shooting out of the top of my head, and I'm reckless with fury. I haven't felt like this since the day on Blair Mountain. All the pain and the worry of the last few months, all the sadness and fear gushes out of me like Fourth of July fireworks. It's a good thing Bitsy is holding the gun, because I would be dangerous!

I work my way further into the throng, causing Star to be more anxious than needed by swinging her head back and forth and making her snort and whinny. The short man with the nasal voice falls on his knees almost under us, and I'd be happy if he was trampled, but one of his brothers pulls him away and shoves him into the Model T.

"That's right, Beef. *Run!* You too, Aran Bishop!" I feel like shaking the spit out of them! "Take your friends. Put your sweating coward tails between your legs and hit the road!" The first two vehicles have already turned and are hurtling down Wild Rose. Men are fumbling to crank up the third.

Bitsy nudges me and nods down the hill. In the distance another line of lights moves toward us. Our situation has just gone from bad to worse.

Remember Me

The fence is a circle of fire with the crooked cross still burning as the new caravan of Klansmen gets closer. We should get going while we have the chance, but my righteous indignation is out of control. If more pillow heads are on their way, I'm ready for them!

There are three vehicles speeding down Wild Rose Road while three more labor up, but they don't pause when they meet each other. The new autos stop just outside our burning fence.

"Do Lord, oh do, Lord . . ." It's Reverend Miller, Mrs. Miller, Byrd Bowlin, and Twyla from the Hazel Patch Baptist Chapel, singing at the top of their lungs. Behind them are a pickup and a Model T Ford. *"When I am in trouble, do remember me."*

Bitsy slides off the side of the horse and slumps on the ground. I slip down next to her, and we both pull off our feed sacks, feeling foolish.

"Everyone okay?" The Hazel Patch folks pile out of their hack. Daniel Hester gets out of his Ford, and in the pickup truck, I'm surprised to see Mr. Maddock and his wife, Sarah Rose. Maddock doesn't say anything, just jumps down and starts kicking the flaming cross with a viciousness that surprises me. Byrd Bowlin enfolds the sobbing Bitsy.

"Everyone okay?" the reverend asks again, stepping over a flaming board and pulling me to my feet. Daniel Hester in his long veterinarian coat comes up behind him.

"Yeah, we're all right." My legs are shaking and I want to throw up, but for some silly reason, I have to act strong.

"It was a close one," I say, making light of it. "The sight of us on our big horse took the men by surprise. Then Bitsy started pulling their masks off . . . did you see them? They were trying to act like the Ku Klux Klan." I pick up a discarded mask to illustrate. The vet takes one look at Star's trembling body, grabs the reins, and takes her away from the fire. I watch as he runs his big hands down her neck, whispers in her ear, and ties her in the shadows, where she can calm down.

"How did you know? How did you know we were in trouble?" I ask Reverend Miller.

"Dr. Hester was on his way back from a call, coming along Salt Lick through the valley, when he saw the vehicle lights in the distance surrounding your house and your fence in flames. He drove to my place and called the sheriff, and then we headed back." The vet is now letting the howling dogs out of the house. They bound down the steps but find no threat or danger, nothing but friends who reach out to pet them.

"We're just glad you're okay," the pastor summarizes, patting me on the back and moving on to Bitsy. I wander over to the Maddocks' truck. "Sarah," I say. There's a rifle resting across her lap, and I believe she was prepared to use it.

"I was so scared," she explains. "When I first saw the fire from my bedroom window, I thought it was your house ablaze, but Mr. Maddock heard the mob and could tell it was the fence burning. About that time we saw Hester's Ford and the Hazel Patch folks coming up Wild Rose. I'm so sorry this happened." She reaches out the truck window and hugs me with one arm, and I'm startled at the strength of it.

As I go over to thank Mrs. Miller and Twyla, it begins to snow. Too early, I think, but I laugh and raise my hands anyway. Small hard flakes drop straight down to the ground.

"Most people around here aren't like those men, you know that, don't you?" Mildred Miller asks me, putting her hands on my shoulders and looking into my eyes. Twyla stands next to her with her baby wrapped tight in a wool shawl. "Most people appreciate what you and Bitsy do." The young mother nods, and I realize they're right. Most people do appreciate us. Most, if they'd known what was happening, would have come to our rescue too. The reverend's wife looks up into the falling flakes. "You could come home with us, honey."

"No, that's okay. We'll be fine. They won't be back. We let our stock out at the height of the fracas so if they tried to burn the barn down, the animals would get away. Now we have to round them up and get them in."

"Are you sure?" I nod my head yes. "Well, then." She takes my hands. "We better get back before the roads get too slick."

As if by command, Mr. Maddock tips

his hat and climbs into his truck. The Millers and Twyla turn to their hack while Bowlin cranks her up. I tighten my mouth when I see Bitsy get in next to him in the front. She lifts one hand and waves good-bye.

From far away, around by the stone bridge over the Hope, I hear the wail of a siren. A little late, Sheriff Hardman is on his way, but the reverend will meet him and have him turn back. It's all over in minutes. Hester is the last to leave.

"I'll help you with the animals."

"Thanks," I say feebly, suddenly very tired, all the fury drained out of me. Bitsy is gone, and I am alone again.

Within a half hour, we locate Moonlight and her calf down by the creek and get the horse in. There are only the chickens left, but it's too dark to find them and I just pray they make it back in the morning.

"Nice auto." Hester motions to the Olds parked in the back of the dark barn.

"It was William MacIntosh's," I explain. "Katherine gave it to us, but we can't afford gas." He shrugs as if he understands, gives the stock some hay, then secures the doors.

"Maybe I should stay." I know he's just being neighborly.

"No, I'm fine. Really. I don't need looking after, but thanks, thanks for everything." I mean more than thanks for coming to the rescue. The baby kicks hard, and I step away.

A few minutes later, he starts up his Ford and pulls out of the drive.

Around me, quiet. No wind. No animals barking, just the soft snow.

Mrs. Potts is gone. Thomas Proudfoot is gone. Becky Myers is gone. William and Katherine MacIntosh are gone and now Bitsy, but I am still here and a new life is coming. The snow sizzles when the flakes hit the still flickering remains of the picket fence, and it smells like we've been having a campfire.

From the front porch, I watch as the vet's taillights get smaller and smaller, then almost wink out. Then I watch as he stops at the intersection of Salt Lick and Wild Rose Road and turns the

Model T around. He must have forgotten something. The Ford creeps reluctantly back up the mountain.

"I can't leave," Hester says, slamming the roadster's door.

"Why? I told you I don't need looking after."

He lifts his eyes from the ground. "You don't?" And gives me his half smile.

"Okay, maybe a little." For me this is a big admission.

The snow falls harder, dampening the ring of fire. I take Daniel's palm and lay it over my abdomen. There's no need for words. He looks at me a long time, not surprised about the pregnancy. He's an animal doctor . . .

Shelter

"Sasha! Emma!" We call the dogs in. They've had a great time chasing the departing cars, and they shake their wet smell over everything. Hester throws more logs on the fire and opens the damper. Then, without talking about it, we go up to bed and strip off our damp clothes . . . all of them, even our socks. We lift our cold feet and pull up Mrs. Kelly's feather quilt. Unlike the last time we lay together, I am shy, unsure what will happen.

"Close your eyes, Patience," Hester says. "I'll be here in the morning."

"My name is Lizbeth . . . and I need to tell you my story."

He turns on his back with his hands under his head and says softly once more, "Close your eyes, Lizbeth. I'll be here in the morning." Then he takes a deep breath, and I can tell he's asleep.

Most of my life I've felt I was dreaming. Now and then I wake up, sometimes for months, sometimes for minutes. Tonight I'm awake, and I lie thinking about the recent events and the people whose lives have crossed mine like veins in an old woman's hands. Their faces float past . . . the twisted and the lame . . . the strong . . . the loving . . . for we are all twisted and lame, strong and loving.

There they go, moving down the Hope River. Mrs. Kelly and Mrs. Potts, who never knew each other, holding hands, their wet gray hair plastered over their heads, then Bitsy, Mary, and Thomas Proudfoot, wading tall in the shallows, and William MacIntosh too, floating facedown.

Ruben and Lawrence are there, and they race each other as they dive into the water. Katherine sits on the green grassy bank, keeping her golden bob dry and playing with baby Willie. There are rocks in the river that are unavoidable. Some of us will be bruised; some will be torn. Some will be sucked under, but some will be freed.

I rest my cheek over Daniel's heart and take shelter in the sound of its beating.

About the author

Meet Patricia Harman

Patricia Harman has spent more than thirty years caring for women as a midwife, first as a lay midwife, delivering babies in cabins and on communal farms in West Virginia, and later as a nurse-midwife in teaching hospitals and in a community hospital birthing center.

© Callie Lindsey Photography

She spent more than a decade in the sixties and seventies in her wild youth living in rural communes in Washington (Tolstoy Farm), Connecticut (The Committee for Non-Violent Action), and Minnesota (Free Folk). During the Vietnam War years, she and her husband, Tom Harman, traveled the country, often hitchhiking, as they looked for a place to settle. In 1974, they purchased a farm with a group of like-minded friends on top of a ridge in Roane County, West Virginia. There on the commune, they built log houses, dug a pond, grew and preserved their own food, and started the Growing Tree Natural Foods Cooperative.

It was during that time that Patsy attended her first home birth, more or less by accident. Some people are destined," she has written. "I was staying at a woman friend's commune when she went into labor and I ended up delivering my first baby." Soon after, Harman traveled to Austin, Texas, to train with a collective of home-birth midwives. When she returned, she became one of the founding members of the

West Virginia Cooperative of Midwives. Her passion for caring for women and babies led her to become an RN as the first step in getting licensed as a certified nurse-midwife. In 1985, with her children, a yowling cat, and her husband she traveled north, pulling a broken-down trailer, to begin her training at the University of Minnesota, where she received her MSN in nurse-midwifery.

For the past twenty years, Ms. Harman has been a nurse-midwife on the faculty of the Ohio State University, Case Western Reserve University, and most recently West Virginia University. In 1998 she went into private practice with her husband, Tom, now an ob-gyn, in Morgantown, West Virginia. There they devoted their lives to caring for women and bringing babies into the world in a gentle way.

When, in 2003, the cost of liability insurance for obstetricians skyrocketed from $70,000 a year to $140,000, the Harmans decided to give up deliveries. Though many loyal patients grieved the loss of their favorite midwife/physician team, the change in lifestyle gave the author time to begin writing her first book, *The Blue Cotton Gown: A Midwife's Memoir.*

Patricia Harman still lives and works with her husband, ob-gyn Thomas Harman, in Morgantown, West Virginia, at their clinic, Partners in Women's Health Care. Though she no longer attends births, she provides care for women in early pregnancy and throughout the life span. She brings to this work the same dedication and compassion she brought to obstetrics.

About the book

A Q&A with Patricia Harman

What motivated you to write this book?

After I finished my first two books, *The Blue Cotton Gown: A Midwife's Memoir* (2008) and *Arms Wide Open: A Midwife's Journey* (2011), I got so much positive feedback that I wanted to start another book right away.

I decided it would be interesting to try fiction, take some of my home-birth experiences and write a novel. Because our country and indeed the world is going through the biggest economic crisis since the Great Depression, it seemed timely to begin the tale the day after Wall Street crashed.

What inspired the story?

The courage of people has always moved me, so I wanted to write about someone who had been faced with many difficulties and whose life took some extraordinary twists and turns.

What kind of research did you have to do to make the past come alive?

The details of Patience's life were meticulously researched, mostly online. It's great what you can find out by doing a Google search: the price of bread in 1930; the name of streets in Pittsburgh then; herbal treatments for postpartum hemorrhage: the percentage of blacks and Italians in West Virginia coal mines.

It's also possible to find photographs of people and places from the past. I printed out images of faces I thought looked like my main characters and referred to them frequently. I also read a number of books about the Great Depression and several novels written in the 1920s and 1930s. One of the most helpful sources of information about the times was a copy of the 1927 Sears, Roebuck catalogue.

I didn't have to research what it would be like to live without electricity, running water, or a vehicle. I lived that way for fifteen years in log cabins on homesteads and rural communes.

I also spent many of my younger years as a peace activist and political radical. Though the issues of my time are different from those of Patience's time, I know what it feels like to live for the cause.

How realistic are the home births you describe? What kind of research did you do for them?

Over the years, as a midwife, I've delivered thousands of babies at home and in the hospital. I kept logs for most of those births and can remember the details even now. I found old medical books and articles to help me understand what Patience would have known about the physiology of birth.

Though some of the birth scenes depict rare situations, they are all very possible. Listening for a baby's heartbeat with a wooden fetoscope, for example, is quite difficult. If the pregnant woman didn't feel her baby move for a few days and the midwife couldn't hear that subtle tick-tick, it would be reasonable to think the baby was dead. There were no ultrasound machines or fetal monitors then.

The joyous parts of childbirth are also portrayed realistically. Birth when a woman is allowed to move or dance or even get into water is especially wonderful.

As a birth attendant, direct-entry midwife, and nurse-midwife for more than thirty years, I've seen almost everything. Thankfully I've never had a mother die, but I've delivered stillborn babies. I've seen hemorrhages. I've seen malpresentations. I have also been privileged, over and over, to witness the power, great courage, and ecstasy of women in labor.

How do you come up with your characters and story line?

A writer has to have a good imagination. I start with the protagonist, imagine what she looks like, what her personality is like, what her background is. Then I put her into an extreme situation. After that, it's as though I can see a film unrolling in my head.

A character walks into a room. I imagine the light, the furnishings, sometimes the smells and sounds. What happens next can be a complete surprise, something unplanned. Another person enters. Words fly back and forth. Words I didn't even think of! The story begins to have a life of its own.

Do you still work as a midwife?

I still work part-time in the women's health practice I share with my ob-gyn husband, doing prenatal care and gynecology. Because of the high cost of medical liability insurance for obstetrics in the United States, we no longer deliver babies. This was a great loss for us and for the community.

On the other hand, since I am not getting up at all hours of the night, I now have more energy to write! Though I haven't delivered a baby for years, it seems like yesterday and I still think of myself as a midwife, only now I empower, support, and educate women with my books.

Discussion Questions

1. The opening scene in *The Midwife of Hope River* presents a dark and scary view of birth. Do you think most women (and men) see birth that way, or do they look forward to childbirth as a peak experience? How do you feel about childbirth?

2. Have you ever lost a baby or known anyone who has?

3. Living without electricity was an ordinary part of rural life in the 1930s. We are so used to all our conveniences now. How would you feel about living without them?

4. Unions played a big part in Patience's life and an important part in U.S. history. What is your experience with unions? Have you ever

been a union member, or has anyone in your family? What place do
unions have in modern times?

5. Most people think of inhabitants of
Appalachia as Caucasian. Did it
surprise you to read about African-
American miners?

6. What did you think about the de-
veloping friendship between Bitsy
and Patience? Realistic? A stretch
of the imagination?

7. Have you ever had a servant in
your home? What was your relationship to them?

8. The author writes of Patience's
loneliness, living out on the farm
without Mrs. Kelly or her Pittsburgh
community of radical friends. Do
you think you could make it alone
like that?

9. What do you think the book says
about the human capacity to en-
dure hardship, loneliness, and fear?

10. Patience tells us of her grief and guilt over having killed her husband accidentally while trying to get the goon off him at the Battle of Blair Mountain. The experience defined her life for many years, yet she couldn't talk about it. How can a person let go of something like that? How important is it for a person to find someone to talk to?

Interesting Facts About Midwives and Childbirth

Worldwide, 80 percent of babies are born into the hands of midwives. In the United States, midwives attend only 10 percent of deliveries, but that number is growing. Ten years ago, it was only 3 percent.

Since 2002, certified nurse-midwives have delivered more than three million mothers in the United States. More families are choosing to deliver at home. In 2011, there were more than 26,000 home births in the United States.

During the period between 1900 and 1930, in this country, maternal deaths during or soon after childbirth were 7 per 1,000 women. One out of ten infants did not survive the first year of life.

Currently in the United States, there are more than 13,000 certified nurse-midwives. CNMs are trained in universities as RNs and usually have master's degrees. They can do gynecological care and some primary care and write prescriptions for medication as well as deliver babies in the home, a birthing center, or a hospital. There are also more than 400 certified professional midwives. A CPM is usually not an RN but a direct-entry midwife who specializes in natural deliveries in birthing centers and at home. The author has had two babies at home with midwives and believes it's a safe alternative for low-risk women if the provider is experienced, well trained, and has a backup plan in case of problems.

For more information or to find a midwife in your community, go to:

American College of Nurse-Midwives: www.midwife.org
Midwives Alliance of North America: www.mana.org